NEVER EVER
GETTING BACK
TOGETHER

NEVER EVER GETTING BACK TOGETHER

SOPHIE GONZALES

WEDNESDAY BOOKS
NEW YORK

Published in the United States by Wednesday Books, an imprint of St. Martin's Publishing Group

NEVER EVER GETTING BACK TOGETHER. Copyright © 2022 by Sophie Gonzales. All rights reserved. Printed in the United States of America. For information, address St. Martin's Publishing Group, 120 Broadway, New York, NY 10271.

Excerpt from *The Perfect Guy Doesn't Exist* © 2024 by Sophie Gonzales

Designed by Jen Edwards

www.wednesdaybooks.com

The Library of Congress has cataloged the hardcover edition as follows:

Names: Gonzales, Sophie, 1992–author.
Title: Never ever getting back together : a novel / Sophie Gonzales.
Description: First edition. | New York : Wednesday Books, 2022. |
    Audience: Ages 14–18.
Identifiers: LCCN 2022026555 | ISBN 9781250819161 (hardcover) |
    ISBN 9781250819178 (ebook)
Subjects: CYAC: Dating—Fiction. | Reality television programs—
    Fiction. | Contests—Fiction. | Bisexuality—Fiction. | LCGFT: Novels.
Classification: LCC PZ7.1.G6522 Ne 2022 | DDC [Fic]—dc23
LC record available at https://lccn.loc.gov/2022026555

ISBN 978-1-250-32378-1 (trade paperback)

Our books may be purchased in bulk for promotional, educational, or business use. Please contact your local bookseller or the Macmillan Corporate and Premium Sales Department at 1-800-221-7945, extension 5442, or by email at MacmillanSpecialMarkets@macmillan.com.

First Wednesday Books Trade Paperback Edition: 2024

10 9 8 7 6 5 4 3 2 1

To Sarah

NEVER EVER GETTING BACK TOGETHER

ONE

Maya

The guy next to me at the bar is grinning at me intimately, as though he knows all my secrets but likes me anyway. It's a little unsettling, mostly because I'm damn sure I've never seen him before in my life, and I'm good with faces. It *is* the sort of grin that'd instantly win over anyone with the ability to trust a man with a charismatic smile, though. I'll give him that.

It's a pity I'm not one of those people.

But as it happens, I want something from him, so I shamelessly mirror his silken smile, and wait. "I'm trying to figure something out," he says as an icebreaker after a few seconds, raising his voice over the music. It's a bass-heavy remix of a pop song, played about a dozen decibels too loud.

"What might that be?" I glance at the bartender as I speak, but he's just started serving someone else. We're gonna be here awhile.

Good.

"Why is it, do you think, that someone decided all the best-tasting cocktails on a menu were girl-drinks? What even makes a drink a girl-drink or a guy-drink? It's a *drink*."

When movies and TV shows told me to brace myself for guys to ask me a flirty question at the bar, this wasn't exactly what

I expected. Although, that might be because those bars are usually at an exclusive club or obscenely expensive restaurant. Maybe when you're standing at a bar inside a quirky bowling alley where the balls are neon, the tables are decorated with newspaper clippings of various dogs, and the signature drink is served in a soup bowl, you have to expect things to veer off the beaten track. Pickup lines and all.

"Sexism, I guess?" I say with a shrug.

"Well, yeah, that's a given. But you know it wasn't a girl who made that rule, so, why'd guys screw ourselves over like this? Guys can drink coffee without weird looks, but I bet you *anything* that if I brought an espresso martini back to my table I'd get endless shit from my friends. *Endless*," he repeats emphatically, slamming his fist on the bar. The bartender shoots him an annoyed glance, and he removes his hand abruptly.

A group of guys being dicks to one another about stupid shit is not exactly surprising. But I am a *little* lost as to why he's randomly decided to share this fact with me. "Who cares if you do? Is your masculinity that fragile?"

There's that dazzling grin again. "I know how bad this is gonna make me sound, but, yes. It is, unfortunately, and I'm working on that, but today isn't that day."

And, finally, it clicks. "Well, as it happens, I'm here with a whole table of girls who would be delighted for you to join them to drink an espresso martini in peace. No judgment included."

"Now *that*," the guy says, "is an interesting proposition."

He says it like I've come up with some sort of genius idea out of the blue, and he *totally, definitely* didn't bring this up to try to steer us toward him buying me a drink. Seems like a shit-ton of trouble to go to when I would've said yes if he'd just, you know, asked me if I wanted a drink, but here we are. Talk about taking the scenic route. "Okay, how about this," he goes on. "I get an espresso martini, and whatever you'd like to drink as a thank-you for your kind offer, then you introduce me to your table of nonjudgmental friends?"

I pretend to think about it while the bartender wraps up serving the other customer. Then, finally, I nod. "Sure, I'm down. Make it an espresso martini and a pink passion crush. Thanks."

Shortly after, both drinks in hand, the guy (who introduces himself as Andre) follows me back to my table. "Here, you can take yours now, if you want," he offers.

"Oh, it's not my drink," I say.

He slows his step as he steers around tables full of bowlers sipping pink liquid from soup bowls. "Who'd I just buy a drink for, then?"

"*You*," I say, "just bought my sister a drink for her twentieth birthday. Very chivalrous of you. We're at that table over there."

We reach my sister, Rosie's, table—well, specifically, it's two tables pushed together to fit all nine of us—and Rosie gives me a look of impressed approval. *Piece of cake,* I mouth.

She's the one who spotted Andre sitting with his own friends a few lanes over from us while we were bowling. She was very dramatic about it, too, declaring to everyone within earshot that she'd commit a federal crime to get his number. After we'd finished our game, we'd come to the dining area for the *real* draw of the alley for Rosie—Instagrammable mocktails and flower-covered walls set up specifically for photo opportunities—and Andre and his friends had done the same, only they'd sat on the other side of the area.

So, obviously, when we noticed Andre head to the bar alone, the table decided someone needed to wing-woman, and, also obviously, I had to volunteer. I'm pretty sure it might be illegal in some states to refuse your sister a favor on her birthday. Or maybe that's a Mafia thing. Anyway, I figured as long as he was single and into girls, I'd surely be able to convince him to wish my beautiful, single sister a happy birthday. Mission accomplished. Sort of.

"Rosie." I slide into my seat beside her. "This is Andre. He bought you a birthday drink."

"That is *so nice,* thank you," Rosie says as the other girls at the table give him innocent, pleasant smiles of their own, like we totally didn't plan this.

My best friend, Olivia, beckons for him to sit. "Well, she can't drink alone on her birthday, can she?"

Andre looks between Rosie and me, before grabbing a chair from an empty table nearby and setting up next to Rosie. If he's surprised about sitting with Rosie instead of me, he definitely doesn't seem upset about it. And so he shouldn't be. As far as I'm concerned, he's won the lottery with Rosie.

"How do you *do* that?" Olivia asks quietly. "I could never."

I shrug. "I dunno. Can't be my stunning good looks, because you've got those in spades."

"*True.*"

I return to my mango-lychee mocktail—which, thankfully, comes in a tall glass, and not a bowl. "I just talk to them. They're just guys, they're not intimidating."

"Only women intimidate you?" Olivia quips.

"Okay, you're joking, but literally. I could never just up and introduce myself to a beautiful girl. I'd die first."

"See, that's exactly how I feel with men."

Her smile fades at the end of her sentence, and her brow

knits as she looks at something above my head. I follow her gaze to the TV mounted on the wall behind me, above a pastel arch of crepe paper flowers.

The headline along the bottom reads: *Brother of Princess Samantha of Chalonne, Jordy Miller, Reads to Orphans; Provides Candy and Hope.* On the screen is Jordy Miller himself in front of an orphanage in Chalonne, receiving an enormous thank-you card from one of said orphans, his hand plastered over his chest like his heart's about to burst.

That goddamn motherfucker.

Some of the others look over as well, including Rosie and Andre. Andre is the first to react to our staring, happily swirling his martini. "I was friends with him when he lived here, you know," he says. His tone is more than a bit braggy. "I was one of his best friends."

"Really?" I ask, confused. "Did we ever meet?"

Like I said, I am *sure* I've never seen his face before, so I'm actually taken aback to hear this.

Now it's his turn to look puzzled. "Why would we have?"

"Um." Rosie laughs. "Because Maya dated him for, like, a year?"

Andre scans my face, like he's trying to place me. I'm pretty confident I know what's coming next.

Three, two . . .

"*Wait.* Wait, wait, wait. You're not the one who went all crazy when he moved, are you?"

One.

A few girls at the table boo him.

"Please, do not," Rosie says in a warning tone.

"We let you *sit with us*," Olivia adds with a glower.

Andre looks between us all in confusion. "Okay, okay. Sounds like there's more to the story?"

I stare into my drink, counting the ice cubes and *really* fucking wishing all of a sudden I hadn't offered to wing-woman.

"He's a cheating asshole," Olivia says. "And if you call Maya crazy again, that martini's ending up on your head and you won't have time to stop me."

"*Jordy?*" Andre asks skeptically, holding his hands up. "Like, our Jordy Miller? Reads to children, gives to charity, invented feminism Jordy?"

Lots of ice cubes in this glass.

Olivia doesn't back down. "He was Maya's boyfriend, he moved to Canada, cheated on Maya for two *months,* then when Maya found out he broke up with her. Not sure what part of that is feminist. Or maybe you need to read up on the definition."

"No, that's fair. I mean, the story I heard was a little different. But I hear you. Sometimes this stuff gets twisted."

The thing is, he's saying the right things, but I can tell by his tone he doesn't believe it. See, I've noticed something about people over the last year or two. Even when they consider themselves rational, and fair, they usually believe the story they hear first. Ever heard the phrase "the best defense is a good offense"? This is a prime example. The person who gets their version of events out first is the one who gets to author the history books. Writing history is easy. Rewriting it is the tough job.

Unfortunately for me, Jordy made sure to get his version of events out before I even knew there was a race. In his version, Jordy tearfully broke up with me when he had to move countries, and told me he'd never forget me. Then, I somehow took that to mean we were still together, despite Jordy's *very clear* breakup speech. Shortly after, I sent my friend in Canada to stalk him, and then flew into a jealous rage when she reported back that he'd moved on, accusing him of cheating on me for no reason.

It's a great story for Jordy. Sure does paint him in the world's most positive light. Da Vinci himself couldn't make a prettier picture.

Pity it's all bullshit.

Andre's friends must be wondering where he's gone off to by now, but he doesn't seem all that bothered about ditching them. Another pity.

Rosie, who doesn't look super thrilled to have him at the table anymore, notices my expression and takes it upon herself to change the subject. God fucking bless the girl. "So, did you go to Sigmund High, then?" she asks Andre.

As Andre replies, Olivia leans in to me. "Hey. You okay?"

I straighten and plaster a smile onto my face. "Mhm. I'm used to it."

Jordy's not on the TV anymore, but I can still see his face as he posed in front of the orphanage. Smiling at the presenter the way he used to smile at me. Like she's the most interesting person in the world.

God, that look used to make my heart feel like it was gonna burst clean out of my chest.

I wonder how many others feel like that when they see Jordy Miller smile at them from the TV. Or magazines. Or the posters on their walls.

How many of them see his shell and believe they know what's under those layers of charm? And what would they say if they found out?

Olivia gives me a skeptical look, and I'm about to insist I'm *really* okay in the kind of shrill tone that *totally* convinces people you're definitely not being defensive, when my phone rings. Saved by the bell. "Hold on, sorry," I say, bringing the phone to my ear. "Hello?"

"Hi, is this Maya Bailey?"

"Speaking."

"This eezgwendbushmeeford zhombareemaday—"

I get up. "Hold on, sorry, I can't hear you. Just let me go outside. Just . . . gonna . . . okay." I close the glass door behind me and flop on a bench in the parking lot. "Sorry, hi, who is this?"

"Gwendolyn Bushman, calling from Bushman and Siegal Productions. I'm reaching out because we have an exciting opportunity for you we think you'd love to be involved in."

I've never heard of this production company in my life, and I'm pretty sure this is a scam call. Any second now they're gonna ask for my credit card details, right?

"Sorry, where did you get my number?" I ask, hovering my finger over the "end call" button.

"From Jordy Miller."

If I weren't sitting down already, I would've dropped from shock. "*Jordy?*"

"Yes. Our team has produced some of the top-rated reality shows from the past few years. Are you familiar with *Nerds in the Jungle, Dating Without Caffeine,* and *Extreme Bathroom Makeovers?*"

"Who isn't?"

"All ours. We have an exciting new project coming up this year; a show called *Second-Chance Romance.* Each season will follow a leading suitor and their exes, as they re-date each other to see if any of that spark that made them fall hard the first time around is still there now that both parties have grown and matured. This year, we're thrilled to have Jordy signed on as our first-ever suitor!"

I take a second to process this. "Jordy Miller's gonna be on a reality show?" I ask finally.

"Yes. And, we hope, so will you?"

I look instinctively inside, where I can see the table full of my friends. I have a sudden, wild urge to sprint to them and demand they pile on top of me to bury me under their collective body weight and press out the *sheer rage* that's bubbling within me. "You want me to date Jordy Miller again? On TV?"

"Yes. The series will be filmed in Loreux, Chalonne, and you'll be accommodated in a *gorgeous* lakeside mansion, it's really something. All meals will, of course, be provided, and you'll receive a small amount of compensation for your participation—"

"Look, I don't know why Jordy put me forward," I interrupt her. "But I'm not interested, and he would know that."

"I know it can feel that way when a relationship doesn't work out. But the thing is, *something* drew the two of you together in the first place. When people grow, they usually change for the better. Chances are, he'll have retained that special something, but perhaps some of those differences that separated you will—"

"Let me be clear, Gwendolyn. I would rather be swallowed up into the bowels of hell and enter an arrangement with the fallen angel Lucifer than date Jordy Miller again."

Gwendolyn's pause of surprise stretches on long enough I almost laugh into the silence. "The fallen angel Lucifer is the devil," she says finally, like she thinks I made a small mistake there.

"Yes, Gwendolyn."

"You're telling me you would rather date Satan than Jordy?"

"I am telling you I would sooner go on a reality show with the prince of darkness himself, Gwendolyn, yes."

"That's a heck of a strong opinion."

"*Hell* of a strong opinion seems more accurate here."

I'm enjoying our banter, but Gwendolyn doesn't laugh. "How about I let you think on it?"

"I'd rather not."

"Can I have your email? I could send you through an information packet. It's quite wonderful, we made a little PowerPoint—"

"*Satan himself,* Gwendolyn."

"I'll put you down as a 'maybe.'"

"Please don't."

"It was wonderful to talk to you, Maya! I look forward to hopefully seeing a lot of you in beautiful Chalonne. Filming starts in two months, by the way."

"I literally could not care less, Gwendolyn."

She gives a trill of laughter. "Okay, take care."

"You, too, Gwendolyn."

I hang up, then spend the better part of five minutes staring into space, head empty.

Finally, a thought breaks through and screams bloody murder in the center of my brain.

I never wanted to have anything to do with him again.

It's a desperate thought, aching and furious and exhausted all at once. But I shove those emotions down because I am noping the hell out of this before it even gets started and therefore, I don't have to feel a thing.

Like hell I'm doing this. Absolutely not. Under no circumstances. Not if they pay me a million dollars.

Well, honestly, maybe for a million dollars. But Gwendolyn didn't say anything about a million dollars, and she would've probably brought that up if it'd been relevant, because god knows money would be a much more persuasive selling point than the promise of being romanced, screwed over, and gaslit by Jordy Miller.

Again.

So, calm and unaffected and totally casual, I head back inside, nonchalantly sit down next to Olivia, and smile like I don't have a care in the world. Because I don't. I'm fine. I'm goddamn *fine*.

She takes one look at me and furrows her brow. "Babe? What's the matter?" she asks. "You look like you've seen a ghost."

TWO

Maya

Rosie and I stare in shock at my phone as it vibrates on the kitchen table in the middle of breakfast.

Mom, oblivious, starts making her second coffee of the morning. "Anyone want anything while I'm up?" she asks.

She doesn't get a response, though. Because someone named DON'T YOU DARE TEXT HIM YOU GODDAMN MASOCHIST is calling me, and Rosie and I both know exactly who the hell that is, and therefore this is no time for coffee.

The name choice is a leftover from a lifetime ago, when I was feeling weak in the aftermath of the breakup, and Olivia helpfully changed Jordy's contact name as a reminder.

And it fucking sucks, because now I feel like I'm in trouble with my phone.

It's so not even fair, because this is *Jordy* contacting *me*, not the other way around. But still, the flashing name feels more like an accusation than a notification.

Failure!

Failure!

Failure who deserves to get her heart broken again because she's a weak-willed goddamn

Failure!

"Let it ring," Rosie says.

"Who's calling?" Mom asks. Oh, good, she's finally noticed our looks of unimaginable horror.

"Jordy," I say through gritted teeth.

"*Jordy?*" Mom repeats. "Pick up and put it on loudspeaker. I'll scare him off for good."

I bite my lip and reach for the phone, then pull my hand back at the last second. "I don't owe him a no."

"Definitely not," Rosie agrees.

"Honestly, I can't believe he thinks I'd even consider this," I say.

"He's a narcissist," Rosie says. "He probably doesn't think he did anything wrong. Probably thinks he's doing you a favor by letting you *bask in his brilliance.*"

"Maya, let me *talk to him,*" Mom insists.

I glance back at the phone, hesitating. Then the screen darkens, and the decision is made for me.

"Good," I say briskly. "Hopefully that's the last time he tries."

"Your loss," Mom says. "I have a *real* good speech. I've been working on it for two years now."

Rosie studies my face, frowning. "Are you okay, Maya? If you need someone to step in and tell him to back off . . ."

I wave a hand. "Nah, I'm fine. Really. They'll all give up eventually."

"Tell them half the truth," Mom says, pouring some milk into her coffee. "You've got college coming up."

Hmm. I *would* like to brag about that to Jordy, if just to see his reaction.

"Uh, actually," I say around a mouthful of oatmeal, "filming would wrap up before college."

As Gwendolyn reminded me by email no less than three times this week as she begged me to reconsider.

"But it's not just filming, is it?" Mom asks as she stirs. "You'll have interviews, and photoshoots, and people would recognize you, and . . . and you'd have all these job opportunities."

"Not job opportunities!" Rosie deadpans.

"I've seen those reality girls," Mom says. "Always hosting their little radio shows. You are too young to know if you're ready to commit to your own radio show, Maya."

"It doesn't matter anyway, because I'm not doing it," I say.

"Good. You can't afford the distraction in your first year. The best revenge you can get on that boy is to succeed, you know."

Rosie leans onto the table. "I'd argue first year is when you can most afford a distraction. Pretty sure most of the people in my class spent more time at parties than studying last year."

"But that's different," Mom says. "Maya's going to the University of Connecticut."

Her eyes widen and flash toward Rosie as soon as the words are out of her mouth. I duck my head to stare at my oatmeal and brace. Three, two . . .

"As opposed to me?" Rosie asks icily.

"No, Rosebud—"

"You can't lay off about my school for one second, can you? Mine is hard, too, okay?"

"Well, you're the one who said your classmates are all drunks, not me," Mom says, holding her hands up.

"Mom, we're college students. College students party. And I can assure you they party just as much at UConn."

"Okay, okay."

"No, not okay, because I didn't miss the radio show comment."

I stand up and hastily bring my bowl to the dishwasher,

eyes down. If I don't look at them they can't see me and if they can't see me they can't drag me into this.

"What, now I can't talk about radio without you somehow finding an insult in there?"

"Your point was that some careers aren't as *good* as others, wasn't it?"

"Honey," Mom says through gritted teeth, "I'm very proud of you, whatever you do. But I worked two jobs to get you girls into college so you could earn a decent wage and you'd never have to do that for your own kids! Maya understands that."

Oh, there I am. I pull out my phone and head back to the table, where I focus on scrolling through it. I don't exactly relish hanging around listening to them fight, but I know how these two get, and they need a witness to intervene if it starts to get too personal. For both of their sakes.

"Well, maybe I want to go into radio!" Rosie says.

Mom thumps her hands on the island countertop. "Since when?"

"Since right now, you make it sound so appealing."

My phone buzzes, and the sudden sound makes both of them turn their heads my way. At least it's not Jordy this time. Just another email from Gwendolyn. I wave my hand: *Nothing to see here. As you were.*

"I will get a job after college, Mom," Rosie sighs. "It might not make me a millionaire, but I'll survive with that, somehow. Don't worry about me, okay?"

I open the email to find a slideshow attached. Jesus our lord and savior, this woman just does not give up, does she? I tap to open it.

"I do worry. I worry about both my girls. I will not stop worrying until I'm old and gray on my deathbed. It's my job."

The slideshow is kind of hard to see on my phone—the bottom's cropped off. This is a laptop job. I get up to leave, and neither Mom nor Rosie seems to notice me moving.

"I'm great. Maya's great. You've gotta trust us to make our own choices."

I'm too far away to hear Mom's reply. In my bedroom, I set up at my desk, and pull the slideshow up.

The presentation starts on a title page covered in flowers, animated sparkles, and the words *Second-Chance Romance: The Ex's Handbook.*

I click.

Congratulations! You have been invited to appear on the PN channel's most exciting new show: *SECOND-CHANCE ROMANCE.* If you have received this invitation, one of your exes has been chosen as this season's Explorer. And he's hoping to re-explore every inch of you!

What in the unholy fuck is this?

Seconds later, Rosie bursts through my door without knocking and throws herself headfirst onto my bed to scream into my pillow. I watch her patiently until she tires herself out and peeks up at me with one eye. "I'm never visiting home again," she declares. "It's too dangerous for everyone involved. I am going to strangle her one day, and *then* we'll see what my employment prospects are like." She rolls over and notices my laptop. "What's that?"

I join her on the bed, and she scans the screen with a disbelieving look. I click onto the next slide.

So, what is this show all about? the title asks.

Glad you asked! it answers itself on the next slide.

Oh, that's helpful.

SECOND-CHANCE ROMANCE follows a chosen Explorer, who re-dates a select group of their exes, in order to re-explore their connection and discover which of them might be the one that got away. At *SECOND-CHANCE ROMANCE,* we believe that everyone falls in love for a reason. Statistics show that the things that cause couples to break up—disagreements, incompatibilities, location changes—usually resolve themselves with space and time, as we grow and change as individuals. But those wonderful parts of us that made someone fall for us to begin with? Those never change!

"Citation needed," I say, and Rosie snorts.

Sounds incredible! Who is this season's Explorer?

The next slide is a portrait of Jordy. A recent one, I'm pretty sure, because his once-longish, wavy brown hair is short and neat, and the minor chip in his bottom tooth is gone. He's smiling at the camera all crinkly eyed, like someone who's just told the world's most hilarious joke.

He looks like a fairy-tale prince.

Now *there's* a joke.

This season's Explorer is Jordy Miller! Twenty years old, handsome and charismatic, Jordy is best known for being the younger brother of Princess Samantha of Chalonne. Jordy first stole the hearts of the people of Chalonne—and the rest of the world—during his sister's wedding to

Crown Prince Florian of Loreux, and he's held those hearts ever since. Although he rose to fame due to his ties to royalty, Jordy is quickly making a name for himself as a humanitarian and a heartthrob in his own right. Last year, he received the King's Honor for Exceptional Service to Humanity after single-handedly raising enough funds to overhaul Chalonne's children's literacy program across all public schools. And, more notably still, last month he was named *Opulent Condition* magazine's eighth sexiest man in the world!

But despite being inarguably one of Europe's most eligible bachelors, Jordy has discovered that fame, wealth, and privilege are not all they're cracked up to be. Although he devotes his time to improving the lives of needy children, he, like the children he selflessly rescues from the clutches of homelessness and illiteracy, is no stranger to suffering. He laments that, although he has the pick of the litter when it comes to beautiful women desperate to marry him—

"Oh, *screw* this," Rosie says, shaking her head. I shush her.

—it's all but impossible to know when a connection is genuine, or when he is the victim of somebody ruthlessly seeking fame and wealth at his expense. But unlike the needy children of Chalonne, Jordy has had no savior to ease his pain. Until *SECOND-CHANCE ROMANCE* stepped in. By re-exploring his connections with his ex-girlfriends (this includes you!), this eligible bachelor is able to take his pick from the women who loved him before the world did.

And as for you? You can get to know Jordy in your own time, isolated from the millions of beautiful, talented, appealing women out there who would otherwise have been your competition. In *SECOND-CHANCE ROMANCE,* your only competition is the other women Jordy has dated in the past! Now those are good odds!

I take a horrified second to press my hands against my lips before I click on.

How do I win the Explorer's heart?

The way you go about this is up to you! It's none of our business. Outside of group challenge prizes, you will see Jordy during the weekly group challenge, and during the *Notte Infinita* event, where you will have an opportunity to attend a party with Jordy and the other remaining exes.

Where will the show be filmed?

Just outside Chalonne's picturesque capital, Loreux. You will be staying at our lakeside mansion with the other exes. Here is a picture of what to expect (Please note: actual mansion may vary).

Below the words is a pixelated photo of what looks like a Beverly Hills mansion, all lit up in orange lights at night. I'm about 99 percent sure they googled *mansion* and chose the first photo.

Actually, now I want to check. Seconds later, I find out I'm wrong.

It's the sixth photo. My mistake.

Do I need to pay a contribution?

All your food, bills, and rent will be covered during your stay in Chalonne. Don't worry about flights; we'll get you to Loreux, and send you right back to where you came from when you're done!

"That seems unnecessarily aggressive," Rosie says, drawing her knees to her chest.

Will I receive compensation for my time on the show?

Yes! All of our contestants are paid in memories, laughter, and, if they're lucky, a healthy dose of romance! How can you put a price on the chance to find true love? It's worthless!

"I think they mean priceless," Rosie stage-whispers.

"That, or they've gotten to know Jordy," I say lightly.

How long will I be on the show?

It's at our Explorer's discretion how long you spend in our mansion. Each week you will attend a *Notte Infinita* party, where you will have your final shot to satisfy the Explorer—

I'm sorry, to *what?*

—before he makes his call. You can be asked
to vacate the premises during any *Notte Infinita*
party. At the end of the sixth week, the Explorer
will make his final choice from those remaining.
Any loser contestants still residing in the mansion at this point will be required to remain in
pre-organized accommodation in Loreux after
the final choice and until the live Full Circle episode in the seventh week, where they will appear in the finale episode to cheer on the happy
couple!

"Oh no," I murmur. "This is the worst. This is . . . I mean,
it's just the worst thing I've ever seen. Is this the worst thing—"

"'*Loser contestants*,'" Rosie forces out in a high-pitched
voice through helpless peals of laughter. "'Sorry Jordy didn't
pick you, you *fucking loser.* Time to quarantine in the hotel
of shame with the other *losers* and drink each other's tears of
sorrow for sustenance while Jordy runs off with the girl who
satisfied him.'"

"Thank god for college, right?" I ask through helpless
giggles.

Rosie tries to calm her laughter with deep breathing. When
she composes herself, she shakes her head. "Maya, who's going to protect those poor girls if you don't go?"

I'm not laughing anymore, even though I'm not totally
sure if she's still joking or not. "What, like an undercover
thing? Go in and thwart Jordy from the inside?"

Rosie nods, slowly, then rapidly, like a bumped bobble-
head. "Well, you *could?*" My eyebrows shoot up, but that only
encourages her from the look of it. "You could change the
narrative. No more orphans, no more . . . goddamn puppies
and candy and six-packs. You'll be the one on camera for

once. You can expose him, Maya. Show the world who he actually is."

Maybe I'm delirious from all the laughing, but she's sort of making sense. "Like, tell the cameras my side of the story? Set the record straight once and for all?"

"Yeah! Or get the other girls to compare notes and confront him. You can't be the only one he treated like that. I'd bet you anything."

"Or," I say slowly, an idea forming. "I could satisfy him."

"Gross, Maya."

"Rosie, oh my god, shut up. I meant I can beat him at his own game. Make him fall for me again. Make it to the end . . ."

Rosie shoots onto her knees as it clicks. "And reject his ass on TV."

"Exactly."

"You could give a speech," Rosie says. "Like, list everything he ever did to you. And any other stuff you find out along the way. Because there *will* be stuff. Plenty of it."

"I'd be giving Gwendolyn the show of her life," I say. "It'd be the most dramatic finale anyone's ever seen."

That settles it. Leaping off the bed, I grab my phone from the desk. "I'm calling him back."

"You're actually gonna do this?" Rosie asks, eyes shining.

"I'm actually gonna do this."

"You're gonna call Jordy, tell him you're going on his show, and then march downstairs and tell Mom how it is?"

"I'm gonna call Jordy, tell him I'm going on his show, and then tell Mom how it is some other time when I'm feeling brave and she's in a better mood."

"Close enough!"

I pull up my call history, but before I can leap in, Rosie scrunches up her face. I know that look. "Uh, just . . . be careful, okay?"

I snort. "What's he gonna do, break my heart again? Like he could."

"Careful of—all sorts. This is gonna involve TV. Everything that happens will be public."

"Uh, yeah, isn't that the point?"

Rosie gives a one-shouldered shrug. "I'm just saying. Whatever you do or say on there, everyone will know. And people *love* Jordy. They might not like someone going on TV to trash him."

"So, maybe I don't trash him, then? Maybe I just make sure they see the real him? Light the match, and let him set himself on fire."

"Fire spreads fast."

I drop my phone to my side. She's kind of taking the wind out of my sails, here. "Weren't you just trying to talk me into this a second ago?"

"Yes, but it's just occurred to me that you could get hurt, and I want you to promise to be careful. Oh, no, I sound like Mom."

"I'll be careful. Wherever possible."

"That's not *super* reassuring, though. You know that, right?"

Smirking, I call DON'T YOU DARE TEXT HIM YOU GOD-DAMN MASOCHIST before she can come up with any more reasons why she's suddenly against the idea.

He picks up on the second ring.

"Maya Bailey. You called me back."

As soon as I hear his voice, I'm sixteen years old again, crazy in love and broken from the inside out.

Rosie glares at the phone with a curled lip. I try to breathe through the flurry of emotions and focus. I'm semi-successful-ish. "Of course," I say, forcing a smile. "Why wouldn't I?"

Jordy's laugh is all easy and warm and familiar. The *worst*. "Ahh, good point, good point. I guess I was just freaking myself out over nothing. It's been so long, I'd sort of convinced myself maybe you hate me now, or . . . I don't know. I'm stupid, ignore me."

Something important to know about Jordy is that he has an accent. It's supposed to be an English accent, but I'm pretty sure it's closer to how Americans think English people sound than an actual English accent. His dad is legit English and Jordy's always insisted he picked up the accent naturally by being around his dad and paternal cousins. Amazingly, though, his sister, Samantha, talks normally. What a strange and completely unexplainable mystery that one is.

Oh wait, never mind, I can totally explain it. Jordy Miller is—as his English relatives would say—a fucking wanker.

"Hate you?" I ask in feigned shock, while Rosie stifles laughter. "Why would I hate you?"

"I know, I know," Jordy says. "It's just my anxiety. I've . . . wow. You know, it's really great to hear your voice, Maya."

"To what do I owe the pleasure?"

"*Maya.* Are you playing coy with me? We know each other better than that."

God, he's really laying it on thick, huh? "I'm assuming you've called to ask me something. So, go ahead. Ask me."

Another golden laugh. "Okay, okay, stop stalling, Jordy. Got it. So, Gwendolyn told me she spoke to you a few days ago about the show, and that you said you might be too busy to fit it in."

I feel like Gwendolyn might have taken the paraphrasing a bit too far with that one, but, sure. "Something like that."

"Okay. Look, I get that, and I don't want you thinking I'm trying to push you into something you don't want to do here. But the thing is, I don't know if I even wanna do this if you don't come, Maya."

I roll my eyes and tip my head back. Rosie copies me. "Come on, Jordy." I can't even try to hide my skepticism at this one.

"No, Maya, seriously. It's . . . okay, it's embarrassing, but screw it. When I agreed to come on the show, it was mostly because I thought maybe it was my chance to fix what went down between us."

He's a great actor. Oscar-worthy, honestly. But like hell I'm buying that. "Really?"

"Yes. Is that the worst thing you've ever heard, or what? How mortified should I be?"

Rosie mimes strangling someone, and I try to keep a straight face. "I dunno, Jordy. It's a long way to go."

"It is. But it's not going to be a short trip."

I raise my eyebrows at Rosie. "I don't think you're allowed to promise me that."

"No. I'm not. Don't tell Gwendolyn."

"I wouldn't dream of it."

"I'd really, really love to see you again, Maya. Please?"

"I thought you weren't going to force me?"

"No. But I'm not above begging."

"Okay. Maybe try begging a little harder."

"You haven't changed a bit, have you?"

I wait.

"Please, Maya. I am *begging* you. Please don't make me do this without you. I promise I'll make it worth your while. I'll be ensuring VIP treatment for you. Anything I can give you, I will. Just, please. *Please* tell me I haven't just signed up for this for nothing."

He's convincing.

He always has been.

The weird thing about this call is it's reminding me why

I fell for him to begin with. I've spent so long being mad at myself for not seeing who he was, and for taking him at his word. But you know what? It wasn't fair to blame myself for that. There weren't signs. Not really.

That's what makes him so dangerous.

"I guess," I say finally, "I could take a look at my schedule and shuffle some things around."

"Wait, really?"

"Since you asked so nicely."

"You have just made my day," he says. "Oh my god. Awesome."

"I'm actually sort of busy right now, though. So, if you could just tell Gwendolyn . . ."

"Yeah, yeah, I'll let her know. So, you're in? It's a definite yes?"

"Yeah. I'll do it. Why not?" Okay. This is happening. No backing out now.

Cool. Cool, cool.

H e l p.

"Awesome. This is so awesome. Well, I am very much looking forward to this now."

"I'm glad. Sorry I can't chat. I've got important stuff to . . . stuff."

"No, please, go ahead. I'll, ah, talk to you soon, okay?"

"Okay. Bye, Jordy."

"Bye, Maya. It was really good to talk to you. Really good."

Rosie looks like she's about to combust. I hastily hang up the phone, just in time, as she lets out a squawk of disgust. "Is he for *real?*"

"All bullshit, all of it," I say. "He can't *breathe* without a lie in the exhale."

She nods, then bites her lip. "Hey, Maya? I thought of something while you were on the phone."

Oh, good, *that's* a promising tone. "Yes?"

"Do you think Skye will be there?"

My smile of victory fades into a horrified frown.

Shit. I forgot about Skye.

TWO
MONTHS
LATER

THREE

Skye

My dad has always said that I was born concerned.

He likes to paint the picture of a red, pruny little new-born who slipped into the world with a permanently furrowed brow and a suspicious frown, who would only smile for the lucky few I decided had earned my trust. According to him, I grew out of that when I went to school. The guardedness. Personally, I believe I got better at pretending I'm not suspicious of everyone.

People like you better if they can't see your walls.

Only a few people reside within mine. My dad is one, and my best friend is another. Someone else got close, once. Close, but not quite. But then, like people so often do, he left my orbit as quickly as he entered it.

I hadn't honestly expected to hear from him again.

I *certainly* hadn't expected to find myself in the Loreux International Airport, waiting to be whisked to a lakeside mansion, where I will be filming a reality show with the one that got away. No, that was most definitely not in my initial travel plans, and detouring from plans is highly uncharacteristic of me.

Then again, Jordy Miller has a habit of bringing out unexpected sides of me.

As I follow the crowd along a carpeted gray floor to baggage claim, I text my dad and my best friend, Chloe, to let them know I'm about to disappear. My phone begins to vibrate only seconds later.

"Hey," I say to Chloe, staking my claim on a spot with a good view of the carousel. "What are you doing up? It's, like, three a.m., isn't it?"

A middle-aged man stands directly in front of me to wait for his luggage. I step around and reposition myself next to him, but he conveniently doesn't seem to notice me.

"Yeah, but I couldn't go to sleep without saying goodbye. It's been bad enough not being able to hang out for the last six weeks, and now we can't even message. I'm going to miss you."

"Aww. I'll miss you, too." Suitcases are spilling onto the belt now, and I scan it for my backpack, despite knowing full well I have terrible luck with baggage claims and mine will be the last out, if it made it to the country at all. "But please tell me you aren't calling to try to talk me out of it again."

"Why not? It's not too late."

"*Chloe.*"

"I just don't get why *Jordy Miller* is the one you choose to break your one-strike rule for." Her voice goes from calm to shrill in the span of a sentence. She's been ruminating on this for at least the last hour, if I had to guess.

"I don't know." I breathe out sharply through my nostrils in a huff. "He was almost-special."

"Wow, can you tone the passion down there, Skye? You're in a public place."

"Is it really that shocking for me to want to see what could've been?" I ask.

"For you? Yeah. Hence, the ongoing shock. I'm glad you're catching on."

"He didn't really do anything wrong, though. You could argue that, technically, he has no strikes."

"Are we ignoring the part where he left you, then?"

"Moving countries doesn't count as voluntary abandonment, if you think about it."

"Maybe not, but he voluntarily stopped talking to you."

"True, but I did stop reaching out, so he thought I must have moved on. It was practically mutual."

"Funny. I remember it a little differently."

"Are we really going to spend our last phone call arguing about Jordy Miller?" I ask, slightly exasperated. The man beside me glances at me and raises his eyebrows. I lift my shoulders at him, and he returns to pretending not to notice me.

"*Fine*. Will you take lots of pictures for me?"

"I absolutely will not, they're confiscating my phone."

"Crap, right. Will you have the best time for me?"

"That I can do." I smile.

"Will you steal me a souvenir?"

"On it."

"Something expensive?"

"Probably not."

"Make me proud."

"Of the souvenir?"

"*No,* of you. And tell Jordy if he earns himself a strike, he's answering to me after filming."

"I'm sure he'll be terrified."

"Oh, he should be."

My backpack—a sixty-five-liter monstrosity with lime green straps—rolls into view. I dart forward to collect it, and my neighbor—who still hasn't received his—shoots me a bitter glance. With a sweet smile, I say goodbye to Chloe for the last time in a long time, and head off to meet the person assigned to collect me.

My flight from Zurich, Switzerland, to Loreux, Chalonne, took off at 11:05 this morning and landed at 11:58. This, according to the producer organizing my trip, is not at all an exorbitant waste of money that could be better spent in a hundred other ways.

At least they didn't send a helicopter to collect me, like the producer initially suggested when he found out how close I was, I suppose. Although it *is* possible he was being sarcastic. It's quite hard to tell by email.

Leaving the ugly carpet of the luggage collection behind, I cross onto glossy black tiles among a crowd of suit-clad business commuters and head toward the escalator. Just as I reach it, however, my phone begins to buzz in my pocket, so I pull over to one side to answer the call.

"Hey, you." Jordy's voice is warm and bright, and I can't resist the smile that touches my lips when I hear it. "Welcome to Chalonne. You've landed, right?"

"All of twenty minutes ago," I say, leaning my backpack against the barrier to relieve myself of its weight for a few moments. "I'm just about to leave the airport."

"I can't believe you're really here." Jordy lets out a breathless, exhilarated chuckle. "It's starting to feel real."

"Isn't it, though? Are you nervous?"

"Uhh. More excited than nervous. I'm excited to see you."

A fluttering in the pit of my stomach reminds me that, unlike Jordy, I am *quite* nervous. A feeling that's increased exponentially at the idea of him sitting in a hotel room, counting down the minutes until we see each other again.

"But, uhh, there's a reason I'm calling," Jordy says. "Other than to hear your voice, I mean."

I frown and shift my backpack higher. "And what might that be?"

"Actually, I wanted to give you a heads-up about something. A warning, I guess."

"You want to warn me about something the second I step off the plane in a foreign country?" I ask. If my voice is somewhat shrill, I suppose it's because I feel somewhat shrill.

"Do you remember my ex-girlfriend Maya?"

"I guess. I remember her name?"

"Cool, well, she's going to be there."

"As it happens, this doesn't come as a shock to me, Jordy. I do know the show I signed up for."

"*Right* . . . but I'm not sure you signed up for Maya Bailey."

"Could I have some specifics, please?"

"Honestly, I didn't think she'd come on the show. I really didn't want her here, but the producers insisted, because the show needs drama. And Maya is big on drama. That, and I'm worried she's going to have it out for you."

"Me?" I echo. "I've never even met her."

"Yup. It's . . . argh, hard to explain. There's history. Actually, there's a lot of stuff I didn't tell you at the time, because I didn't want to freak you out when I didn't need to. But when you and I started dating, she practically stalked me for a while."

"What? What happened?"

Jordy's tone is wry. "Have you ever had someone say no when you broke up with them?"

"Can't say I have. I didn't know it was an option."

"It's not an option for people like you and me. For people like Maya, though . . ."

"She didn't take the breakup well," I fill in.

"The breakup itself she took surprisingly well, but in

hindsight, I think it's because she was in some serious denial about it. It was when she found out you and I were dating that things got ugly. I don't want to worry you, but she actually got a bit threatening. She brought you up a few times. And, you know me, I'd never . . . do anything to hurt a girl, you know? But I got pretty defensive when she brought you up, and I made it pretty clear that she and I would not be on good terms if she contacted you. So, instead, she took it out on me. Spread rumors about me, called me a cheater, called me emotionally abusive, all kinds of stuff. It was a lot."

"And I'm only hearing about this now?"

Jordy sighs. "I know. I *know.* But you and I were so new at the time. I didn't want to worry you, but I also didn't want you to decide I was too much trouble. I hoped it'd go away, and eventually, it did. She never reached out to you, did she?"

"No . . ."

"Exactly. But now you *do* need to know. And, Skye, honestly, I'm probably being paranoid. I haven't seen Maya for two years. I can't imagine she'd still be after us. But on the off chance she is, and she starts shit for the cameras, I want you to be prepared."

"Yeah, thank you so much for the one-hour warning, Jordy."

"Like I said, I didn't think she'd come. I swear, Skye. I only just found out she's confirmed. I think the producers kept it from me because they knew I wasn't comfortable with her coming. For your sake, more than mine. I can handle anything she throws at me. But I don't know what I'll do if she comes for you. And now I'm saying that out loud, I'm realizing maybe that's what the producers want. Drama. But . . . yeah, you're my sore spot. Can't change that, can I?"

I don't let myself dwell in the happy buzz his words give

me. "What would she even do, though?" I ask. "There will be cameras on us all the time."

"That's exactly what I'm worried she'll use. She's angry, and she's manipulative. She can make the most far-fetched story sound like the truth. Sometimes she even made me question myself, when I *knew* what happened. You can't let her mess with your version of reality, okay? You know what you are, and who you are. Don't let her convince you otherwise. If you stand your ground, she won't be able to twist things for the cameras."

I draw my brows together. "You're scaring me a little."

"No, no, Skye, don't worry. You and I won't let any bullshit go down. *I* won't let it. If she starts anything with you, you come right to me. They can't do a show without me, so they have to play by my rules, and my number one rule is, Skye is off-limits."

The knot forming in my gut loosens a little. "You're probably right," I say. "About her moving on. Who holds a grudge like that for two years?"

"Exactly. I'm sure you'll get there and wonder what I was talking about. She's probably matured a ton."

Surely. Surely that's the case. The only thing is, Jordy doesn't sound entirely convinced.

What on earth did this Maya girl do to him?

After we say our goodbyes, I scoop up my bag again and finally step onto the escalator, my head swirling with Jordy's warning.

A short man with warm brown skin and black hair tied in a bun is standing at the bottom holding a white sign with SKYE KAPLAN written on it in all-capitals. He catches my eye, and his bored expression lights up.

This is really happening, isn't it? I've gone from sleeping in hostel rooms of eight and sprinting for buses and trains loaded up like a packhorse to being a Very Important Person in one fell swoop. It's a good thing I'm not easy to buy, or it might occur to me to try to win this show, if only for the upgrade in living standards.

As it is, I'm becoming more and more grateful by the second to past-Skye for signing up for this, because I've just remembered I'll be sleeping in my own room tonight. No snoring, no one barging in drunk at three a.m., no changing clothes in a tiny bathroom stall.

And all I had to do was sell my soul to reality television. It's the best deal with the devil I've ever made.

Okay, I say to myself. *Remember.* Hal *for hello,* aurenein *for goodbye,* sa *for yes,* nie *for no . . .*

"*Hal,*" I say, concentrating on the words as I hitch up my backpack. "*Unt Frechten* Skye. *Je tristois tu—*"

He shakes his head quickly and holds out a hand. "Uh, hey, Skye. Isaac Kassab. I'm one of the producers at *Second-Chance Romance.* How was your flight?"

Isaac—that means he's the producer I've been emailing over the past few weeks. For some reason, I'd imagined him a lot older, and with a Chalonian accent, instead of the American one he has, which, now that I think about it, doesn't make a lot of sense. Bushman and Siegal Productions is an American-based production company, after all.

What an excellent start. It's a good thing this person's entire job description doesn't revolve around highlighting my flaws and humiliating moments on TV for views, or I'd worry I'd just given him some material.

"Great, thanks."

"Cool, cool . . ." He trails off and looks above my head as though he's deciding whether to speak or not. Then, the trace of a smile appears, and he drags his gaze back down to me. "So, do you speak Chalonian, or . . ."

"Uh, no, I do not. I learned a couple of words."

"That was more than a couple of words. What did you say?"

I hesitate. "If you're asking so I can say it on camera, I might as well tell you now, I have no intention of doing that. I'd never live it down, and we both know it. If you want me to trust you, you won't—"

He holds up his hands. "Whoa, whoa, Skye, I'm just curious. Seriously."

I scan his face, but can't see any obvious signs that he's lying. "I was trying to say, 'Hi, I'm Skye. Are you the person I've been talking to?'"

"I *am* the person you've been talking to. But, notably, we've been talking in English this whole time."

"Yeah, but you don't barge into someone's country and start talking English at them," I say. "That's very rude."

"Oh my god, you're so Canadian," Isaac mutters. "And what would you have done if I'd burst into Chalonian in response?"

"Unt nie thierre."

"Which is?"

"I don't understand you."

Isaac gives me a long, searching look. Then, he seems to shake another thought off, this time choosing not to pursue it. "Cool. So, wanna get your backpack on a cart?"

I glance down at the straps buckled around my waist and chest. "I think I'm okay. I'm strapped in now. Getting it on and off is the hard bit."

We start walking to the exit. "You packed light. You know you were allowed two suitcases?"

"I did know, but I've been—"

"Traveling, that's right," he says, snapping his fingers.

"I have some more stuff in my London flat," I say. "Even

though I haven't officially moved in yet or anything. But I didn't get a chance to go and collect it before flying here."

"Wait, question," Isaac says. "Partly for me, partly so we can explain it right on the show. How can you live in London even though you don't work there?"

"I've got an ancestry visa. My mom was Scottish. I can live there for five years, if I want." My backpack straps are digging uncomfortably into my middle, and I slow my pace to loosen them slightly.

Isaac eyes my backpack in what can only be described as disbelief as I do. "You've really spent the last five weeks living out of that thing?"

"I don't need a lot of stuff." I shrug. "And you can squeeze in a surprising amount if you roll your clothes up."

He goes as far as to scrunch up his nose at this. I suppose the backpacking lifestyle isn't for him, then. "So, I guess you don't have a lot of dresses in there, huh?"

"I bought a couple in Italy," I say. "Just for this. And I brought some from home. They're somewhere at the bottom of the backpack, though. Is there a laundry room at the mansion, by any chance? And, uh, an iron?"

He nods and pulls up an organization app on his iPad. "We'll sort you out."

We leave the airport with the midday sun beaming right into our eyes. I blink into focus, and I'm greeted by blue. Royal blue, robin's egg blue, powder blue, baby blue, almost every architectural accent shares the same color story, from roofs to windowpanes to the flowers planted along the road where the taxis pull up by the sidewalk. The walls of the buildings themselves are neutral-colored, at least, so the effect is more interesting than garish. Very Chalonian.

I take a photo as we walk and send it to Chloe. Okay, you get one photo.

"That reminds me," Isaac says, glancing at my phone. "Send your final messages to everyone now. I'll need that before we get to the mansion."

Even though Gwendolyn claimed in the emails they confiscate our phones so we don't conspire with viewers at home to make a game plan to cunningly force Jordy to fall for us, I'm not sure I believe that excuse. I think it's more likely so we don't leak information to our friends—or worse—before the next episode goes to air, but I suppose they don't want to tell us that because that would sound like they don't trust us. Personally, I wouldn't be offended if they simply admitted it. Why *should* they trust a group of strangers they know nothing about? I wouldn't trust us in their shoes. And in my own shoes, *I* don't trust *them*.

So, I send a second message to Dad—I would prefer a call, but I don't want to wake him—telling him I love him. I hold tightly to my phone for as long as I can in case he replies, but Dad's the kind of person who begins yawning by nine. There's no chance of him burning the midnight oil to see me off, no matter how much he loves me back. So, eventually, I hand it over to Isaac, who's started to shoot me pointed looks. Dad and I did speak last night, so it's not as though we had no chance to say our goodbyes.

Still, though.

I gaze out the window as we drive. Stately blue-roofed buildings that have probably stood there for hundreds of years—some housing quaint local businesses, some housing Starbucks and McDonald's restaurants—line the busy main road. As we grow closer to the outskirts of the city, the businesses become quainter and quainter, and, just when the scenery is starting to resemble an animated movie more than real life, the businesses become cottages, then farmland and countryside. We travel through a thick forest and up a towering mountainside. Down below, through the trees, I can make out patches of a brilliant blue. Kool-Aid blue.

I've never seen a lake look like that. It's as though someone put a filter over real life. But there it is, a lake that looks as though it *must* taste like blue raspberry. If I knew a little less about parasites, I might be tempted to risk a drink, just to make sure.

But alas, the only thing I can think of that would be worse than contracting brain-eating bacteria is contracting brain-eating bacteria while bloodthirsty reality show producers air every moment of it for ratings.

Beyond the almost-certainly-undrinkable lake, at the foot of a hill and surrounded by a sea of flowers, is a mansion straight from a storybook. Its cream walls are dotted with flower-covered windows, and pointed turrets jut out of the blue roof.

I recognize it from the photos Gwendolyn emailed. It's leagues more beautiful in real life, however.

"And this," Isaac says, catching my eye in the rearview mirror, "is gonna be your home for a while. Pretty all right, huh?"

"It's amazing," I agree, staring at it in awe.

I couldn't explain it if you asked me to, but somehow, it feels as though we're driving toward a place where significant things are going to happen. It's warm, and electric, and *vivid,* somehow. As though I'm taking my first look at a building I'm going to think about regularly for the rest of my life.

As naive as it might sound, something inside me trusts that feeling. And I start to wonder if maybe this feeling is trying to tell me that things with Jordy weren't over after all. Maybe this guy I left in the past actually plays a big role in my future. Perhaps, as impossible as it might be for me to believe, people who leave you don't always stay lost to you forever.

Either way, looking at this mansion, I have the strangest sureness that I'm going to be here for quite a while.

FOUR

Skye

After the car pulls to a crunching stop in a gravel parking lot, I step out, haul my backpack from the trunk, and stare up at the towering mansion with a slow smile. The stone walls are covered in a blanket of intertwining vines and honeysuckle. Standing this close, the perfume from a thousand flowers forms a bouquet cocktail that stops just short of cloying.

"You're the last one here," Isaac says as we walk up the entrance steps. "So they'll probably wanna jump straight into things. Sorry if you were hoping for a break."

"No, I'm fine. It wasn't exactly a long trip." I try to limit the level of irony in my voice.

"That's the attitude I like to hear."

Isaac leads me through a marble-floored entryway with the highest ceilings I've ever seen, straight between the two grand staircases that stand on the far sides of the room, and over to a door at the back. When we enter the room, a bunch of heads whirl around at once. The other five girls, some familiar, some not, are already sitting in the center of the room on a bunch of folding chairs. I spot Maya, sitting at the end of her row, immediately. We lock eyes, and her expression remains carefully unreadable. Is she secretly seething at the sight of me? Or is Jordy being far too overprotective?

I drag my eyes away from Maya to a blond woman in her forties, who's standing in front of the girls at the head of the room.

She's one of those tall people who enjoys capitalizing on the fact, pairing a perfectly upright carriage and sky-high heels to tower over everyone else in the room. She wears a plum-colored blazer and black pants with gold jewelry, and overall looks so polished I'm suddenly aware of how *un*polished I must look in my airport outfit of an oversized corduroy jacket and my comfiest jeans.

Her face brightens when she sees me. "Skye! So good to see you. Grab yourself some *reux ferdeau* and join us, we're about to get started."

I recognize her voice as soon as she speaks. So *this* is Gwendolyn.

I head over to the buffet table where she gestured and help myself to a paper plate piled with *reux ferdeau*, a small Chalonian pastry filled with chicken, bacon, and raisins in a mushroom and garlic sauce. It's been on my list to sample one of these—I already ticked off street pizza in Rome, escargot in Paris, and fondue in Switzerland—so I'm *highly* pleased to be offered it for my very first meal in Chalonne. A travel achievement unlocked on day one. This place is just getting better and better.

"Hello, everyone," Gwendolyn says as I take the last remaining seat next to a girl with long blond curls. "We could not be happier to have you all here. I'm Gwendolyn Bushman, head producer of *Second-Chance Romance,* and on behalf of the whole team, I'm thrilled to warmly welcome you all to the inaugural season of the show. Now, I know you're all tired, and some of you have traveled quite a long way to get here, so I'm going to keep things brief. Soon, you'll be taken to your rooms, where you'll have a chance to settle in and get to know one another.

"At four on the dot we'll meet back in here to prepare for our welcoming party. You'll all be responsible for your own hair and makeup beforehand, and then we'll get you fitted in your dresses for tonight. You'll want to look your best when you see Jordy, who will be joining us at the party. Food and drinks will be available, but if anybody needs a snack before then, anything in the kitchen is a free-for-all. Any questions?"

Maya Bailey puts her hand up. "Are we allowed to use the pool?" she asks.

So that's what her voice sounds like. It's higher pitched than I'd imagined, and smooth. *Honeyed,* a voice at the back of my mind suggests. I didn't realize until now that I'd assigned a voice to a person I've seen dozens of photos of but never met, but apparently I did.

Gwendolyn trills a carefree laugh that doesn't quite match her judgmentally raised eyebrow. "Yes, any activities within the property walls are fair game from here on out. Just make sure not to leave the mansion. And, of course, make sure to leave yourself enough time to wash your hair before the party."

Maya's fingers go unconsciously to her shoulder-length, auburn hair. It catches the sunlight as it moves, causing it to shimmer with a golden highlight.

A girl I don't recognize, who's wearing her own glossy black hair in a long ponytail, raises her hand. "How long do these parties last for?" She speaks with a British accent. I suppose she's someone Jordy met after he left Canada. After he left me.

"That's at our discretion," Gwendolyn says. "But if you're

asking if you'll have a chance to speak to Jordy—yes. Everyone will have their chance to spend ample time with Jordy."

No one else has any questions after that, so Gwendolyn promptly moves on to room assignments. I'm directed to follow Isaac, along with Maya, and he steers us out of the room and up the sprawling staircases.

This is going to be interesting.

"You two belong to me," Isaac explains as we walk. "Anything you need, I'm your first call. If I'm not around, feel free to ask whoever you find, but if they can't help you, they can always get ahold of me. We're staying nearby, so I can be here in ten minutes."

"We belong to you, huh?" I ask drily, trying to catch Maya's eye with a smile. She meets my gaze, but remains expressionless. In fact, her face borders right on the edges of cold.

It seems entirely possible Jordy wasn't simply being overprotective. "My job over the next seven weeks is tied to you," Isaac says. "You do well, I do well, so you can *believe* I'll be looking out for both of you."

"Let me guess: You get a bonus if one of us wins?" I ask.

"If one of you wins, you'll be sending me and my boyfriend to Phuket for Christmas."

We grin at each other.

Maya glances between us, stares me down with a look so icy it makes my heart skip a beat, then turns her head to send a brilliant smile in Isaac's direction. "I'd say those are good odds for you," she says to him.

Isaac stops in front of a door. "You know? I've got a good feeling."

Behind the door is a dorm-style room. The ceiling towers above us, giving the illusion the room is much more spacious than it is, but on closer inspection there's only room for a rug, a desk and chair, and a set of bunk beds against the wall.

Maya and I look at him, waiting to be told whose room this is.

"Well," he says after an awkward pause. "Here you go."

"Who?" Maya asks, shifting in place.

"You. You two."

Oh. Oh no. It never occurred to me, given we're spending the show's duration in a mansion, that we might be required to share rooms. If it were anyone but Maya, this wouldn't be so bad. One roommate is *leagues* better than the eight-to-a-room dorms I've been staying in over the last couple of months. But it is Maya. And she's looking at me with an expression that can only be described as aghast. As though she's found out she's sharing a room with Jack the Ripper. Is it at all possible this is still a misunderstanding? Maybe there's an entirely innocent reason for Maya's reaction. After all, caution is good, right? You can't ever *really* be certain the person you've just met isn't a serial killer. Ted Bundy didn't seem the type, after all, and he turned out to be just dreadful. Maybe Maya simply has a healthy sense of stranger danger, and she'll warm up to me after an icebreaker.

Okay, fine, I'm not convincing myself for a second.

"I wasn't told we'd be sharing rooms," Maya says thinly.

Isaac shrugs. "There's not that many usable rooms in the mansion. Most are conference halls and ballrooms."

I fold my arms. "*Really?*"

"No, that's just the party line, honestly. Cramming you together forces you all to talk, and that gives us more content. You can shuffle around later, once girls start going home, if you want."

"Can we shuffle around now?" Maya asks.

Isaac grins and pokes her arm. "You're funny. I like you."

"No, really, what's your price?"

"Full of jokes. Okay, well, it's time for my lunch break, so

I'll leave you two to get settled in. Bathroom's down the hall, kitchen's downstairs, wander around long enough and you'll find everything sooner or later. If a door's closed, knock first, because our team takes no responsibility for anyone walking in on anything they wish was kept private, otherwise, go nuts. Anything you need before I go?"

We shake our heads, and he leaves us to get set up.

Maya grits her teeth and turns to face me so deliberately I almost call Isaac back, just so I can have a witness nearby when she removes one of those stiletto boots and drives the heel through my heart.

I stand by what I said: you can't tell who is a serial killer just by glancing at them.

Sometimes, however, you can take an educated guess.

FIVE

Maya

"I've got to say, I'm surprised. I've never heard of a mansion with bunk beds," Skye says, shattering the silence.

Cool. Cool, cool, I think I might scream the mansion down.

I'd thought Isaac was playing some sort of sick joke when he showed us the shared room. Like, I don't know, maybe they had hidden cameras ready to catch our reaction or something. The better to make the first episode super hilarious with, ha-fucking-ha. But no, he was deadly serious.

I am going to be in here, *with Skye,* until one of us leaves the show.

And I'll tell you something right now. That one of us is *not* going to be me.

She has the audacity to smile at me. That kind of awkward, brief flash of a smile you might give to someone who reaches for the same item as you in a supermarket. An "oops, well, isn't this a funny coincidence" sort of vibe.

My face almost betrays me by smiling back on autopilot, but I force my features to freeze. I am impenetrable. Ruthless. I am not going to be won over by a weak display of friendliness, not from Jordy, or Skye, or anyone. I am under no obligation to forgive anyone for anything they did to me, goddamn it. Especially without an apology.

"Which bunk do you want?" I ask, but, no, Skye has no right to pick what bunk she gets. She doesn't just get to waltz into my orbit and take my boyfriend, and my pride, *and* the bottom bunk. There is a *line*. "Because I want the bottom," I add the moment she opens her mouth.

Skye gives me a funny look, then tosses her bag onto the top bunk. "Okay then."

I raise my eyebrows, then start pulling out my clothes to hang them up, my back to her.

Cold. Ruthless.

"It's weird to not have phones, right?" she asks, apparently not noticing that I have no inclination to talk to her. "I keep going to pull it out and then, duh."

I purse my lips and hang up a shirt.

The silence thickens the air. Skye, who's either not the best at reading the room or the irritatingly persistent type, sucks in a loud breath through her nose. "Well, guess we just have to talk to people in real life, instead. What is this, the nineties?"

"If you want to talk to someone, maybe you should go see what the others are up to?" I say through gritted teeth.

If she hadn't caught on before, she sure as heck has now. While I turn to grab another shirt I catch sight of her, standing by the bed and staring at me with a half-wounded, half-indignant expression. The soft side of me feels a pang of shame, but the louder, angrier part drowns it out.

You don't get to do something like that to someone then barrel past it like it never happened and expect them to follow suit. Life doesn't work like that.

"I really hoped you'd let it go," she says finally. "But sure. Nice to meet you, too."

I keep my back to her as she leaves the room, so she can't see the look of shock that crosses my face at the goddamn *audacity*. She closes the door behind her—not exactly a slam, but not exactly *not* one—and then I finally breathe easily.

The universe has to hate me. It *has* to.

Of all the roommates.

My heart is racing from the outrage, and I give myself a few seconds to collect myself before returning to my task. Pick up. On the hanger. In the wardrobe. *Let it go?* Let it fucking *go*?

Pick up. On the hanger.

Did she really just say that to me? Did those words come out of her mouth? Can a real person actually be that shitty, that . . . that *callous*?

Pick up. On the hanger.

Repeat, repeat, repeat. I zone out until, finally, the emotions fade, and the colors in the room seem crisp again. I've got this. I am chill.

Then, I grab my iPad from its hiding spot inside my jeans, grin down at it triumphantly, and scan the room for a good place to hide it.

Seriously, who *am* I? Is this who I've become? Someone who gleefully smuggles contraband electronics, and isn't automatically nice to bad people just because they're nice to me, and who plans and executes an international revenge plot?

If I'm left to snowball, who knows where I might end up? It's a slippery slope from rule-fudger to world domination, and, baby, I'm already enjoying the ride a little too much.

Eventually, I decide that inside my jeans is still the safest spot for it, so it goes into my drawer, with as many other pants and shirts piled on top of it as I can manage.

Once I'm satisfied, I figure I should probably get out before Skye comes back, so I dart outside. As I close the door, a frustrated groan rings down the hall. It seems like it came from within a nearby room, and the door's open, so I peek inside to make sure everyone's okay.

One of the girls—Perrie, I'm pretty sure her name was—is sitting on the shag rug in the middle of the floor, with long legs stretched out in front of her, and a steaming mug of coffee on the floor beside her. On her lap is the binder of instructions Gwendolyn gave us, and she's flipping through it quickly. Her suitcases are empty already, and from the looks of the room, at least 60 percent of her luggage was made up of sneakers. There are at least fifteen pairs, lined neatly up against the wall.

"Hi," she says when she notices me in the doorway. "Come in. I'm just checking the cell phone rules."

"That's easy," I say wryly. "We can't have them."

"Okay, obviously. But I figured it was because they don't want us to contact anyone, right? So, I took the SIM card out of mine and brought it, but my producer confiscated it anyway! I'm checking to see if I can use the rules to argue my case."

I think of my iPad and wince. "What do you want a phone without a SIM card for?"

"Photos and videos." She turns the last page of the binder, then throws it off her knees in disgust. "I'm in a literal mansion, next to a glacier lake in Chalonne, and I'm not gonna have a single thing to show for it!"

"We get promo photos this afternoon, don't we?" I ask.

Perrie shoots me a disbelieving look. "Yeah—a photographer who's gonna make us all look identical. I'm talking proper content, for my profiles. I had a whole posting schedule planned out for when I leave the show, and now it's totally wrecked."

"Oh." I sit down next to her and flick through the binder. I don't really expect to find anything she didn't, but, you know, it makes me feel like I'm helping. "Have you asked your producer if you can borrow a camera or something?"

"Honestly, I haven't really had a chance. She sort of dumped us here then left."

I get onto my knees and put the binder on the ground. "Well, my producer seems pretty nice, and he's just downstairs. Wanna ask him?"

She considers this, then grabs her coffee. "Sure. The worst he can do is say no, right?"

"Exactly."

A few minutes later, we find Isaac in the cobblestone courtyard, giving directions to a man in an apron. All around us, staff and producers are weaving around, carrying string lights, glasses, flower arrangements, clipboards, chairs, and camera equipment. We watch them set up for tonight with interest as we wait for Isaac to finish talking, then Perrie approaches him with her request.

Isaac shrugs. "I don't see why you can't borrow one. We have a ton of equipment. Just make sure you don't take it home with you, or they'll bill you, and they'll charge you about three times more than it's worth, okay? Trust me, I've seen them do it."

"Yes, totally, I promise," Perrie says with a squeal as Isaac leads us to the equipment caravan.

Half an hour later we're both in bikinis, posing by the pool. Perrie is obviously a bit of an expert at this, because she jumps straight into creative mode, directing me to stand in specific spots and take the pictures at certain angles while she poses by the pool, in front of the fence, on a lounger.

"I need to get as many light neutrals and blues in the frame as I can," she explains, which makes me respect the hell out of her. The most thought I ever put into my photo aesthetic is whether my hair looks flat. Then again, I've got about four hundred followers, and I'm related to an embarrassing percentage of them, so effort equals output I guess.

It's not exactly hard to get the color palette she's looking for; the sky is a rich blue, and there's not a cloud in sight. It casts a warm glow over us, like we're at a tropical resort somewhere, and not a short drive away from the snowcapped Alps. The pool is practically glittering as the sunbeams hit it, too—in a way that the camera really can't capture. Or more likely, let's be real here, the problem isn't the camera, so much as the photographer. I've never taken photos with anything fancier than an iPhone before, so sue me.

"One last pose, one last one," Perrie says, fluffing her dark brown, natural hair, which is sitting on her shoulders in an explosion of thick curls, before turning to lean on the fence and stare out at the view; a skyline of snowcapped mountains. Blues as far as the eye can see. "Like this. Candid."

"Oh, *super* candid," I joke, snapping a bunch. "Okay, so, out of the thirty thousand options, you have about fifty shots that are better than anything I've ever posted in my life." I pass her the camera to flick through and return to recline on a lounger.

"Yes," she agrees, joining me. "Yes, yes, *yes*. Thank you. Now we can take fun photos."

"Those weren't fun?" I ask, and she turns the camera

around to face us for a selfie. I lean in and pose with her while she clicks it about twenty times.

"Delete the bad ones before giving the camera back to them," I warn, lying down as she flicks through them again. "Otherwise they'll probably go online as, like, exclusive behind-the-scenes content."

"I will. Hey." She sits up. "We should find the others and get some group photos."

I hesitate for only a *second* before I nod, I swear, but Perrie catches it anyway. "Or not?" she asks, squinting.

It's possible I have some acting training to do before I achieve world domination. Note to self: practice saying "Jordy and Skye are the best" in front of the mirror a hundred times before I have to go on camera and say it with a straight face for the world to see.

Cool. Cool, cool.

"No, we should," I say. "Just . . . don't be surprised if it's a little awkward with Skye. We butted heads a bit, right before I came into your room."

"Already?" Her mouth stretches into a wide smile, displaying perfect teeth straight from a filter. Definitely an influencer's smile. "Isn't it a bit early for drama? I thought we'd last until at *least* a few drinks in tonight."

"Sorry to disappoint," I say. "I'm a disaster bi."

"Literally or figuratively?"

"Literally. In every sense of the word. Where I go, drama follows. It's a curse."

She settles back into a lounging position. "That explains it."

"Seriously, though, Skye and I have history. Not, like, romantic. The other kind. I was hoping I might be able to avoid her, but, *of course,* she's my roommate."

"Oh, of course. What's the history, if you don't mind me asking?"

I hesitate. "I mean, I don't mind you asking, but it's not fair for me to drag you into drama in the first, like . . . *hour.*"

"Well, how about you give me some credit, tell me the facts, and I'll make my own mind up about if I want to be involved with drama. No offense, but I'm not automatically gonna take your side just because I met you first." She shrugs casually, but her eyes are glinting. "I could be neutral. You could even be in the wrong."

"Anything's possible," I say drily. It's not like she'd be the first die-hard Jordy fan to come to that conclusion. "All right. Well. Long story short, Jordy and I were in a long-distance relationship, Skye knew about it, and he cheated on me with her for two months before I found out. And I've yet to receive an apology or anything from her, so, I'm not interested in faking nice to her face. I'm not that sort of person."

Perrie considers this long and hard. "Okay," she says. "It's pretty clear I have to be on your side here."

"Yeah," I say, but I can't hide the tinge of surprise in my voice. Acting lessons, *stat.*

"I don't fuck with cheaters."

"Jordy's the cheater," I remind her. "He's worse than Skye. *She* was single, at least."

Perrie shrugs. "Yeah, well. I'm on an all-expenses-paid holiday in Chalonne with my rent covered back home right now. *And* I'm going on TV, which has *got* to help me get some followers. I don't mind fucking with him for a little while. My morals will allow it."

So Perrie's not a member of the Jordy Miller cult? *That's* why she believes me. "That's one way of saying you came on for the exposure."

Perrie clears her throat. "And you came here to start a dazzling romance with the guy who cheated on you while making besties with the other woman? Spare me. You have your reasons for being here, I have mine. Let's just have a good time while we're here."

I wish I had a glass of something to raise in a toast to that, but I have to settle for a fist pump. "Amen, Perrie. A! Men!"

SIX

Skye

I leave the room in a fog.

Everyone I mentioned the show to over the last two months warned me about this. *Don't expect to make friends,* they all said. *Reality show contestants are terrible to begin with, and you're competing over a guy you're all invested in already.* Every time, I'd shrugged and said that maybe it would be different, because we weren't handpicked in an audition based on our propensity for drama like many shows. We're simply a group of average girls, who happen to have one thing in common.

But they didn't pair me with an average girl. They paired me with Maya. Maya, who's exactly like Jordy warned she would be. Maya, who appears to be an elite athlete in grudge-holding. Maya, who's going to speak to me like that, and look at me like that, for who knows how long. Until Jordy sends her home, I suppose.

Coming here was a mistake.

My airway feels constricted, and I press against the wall and force myself to take several deep breaths until my throat relaxes and I can get enough air in once again. Okay. So.

Isaac said we could change rooms soon. All I have to do

is hold out until then, avoid Maya as much as possible, and I'll be free to seek shelter with one of the other girls. None of whom Jordy felt it necessary to warn me about, so, presumably, they're all perfectly lovely. Come to think of it, Jordy *warned* me about Maya, which means he knows just what she's like, which means he's highly unlikely to keep her around once he discovers she hasn't changed. For all I know, I'll have the room to myself any day now.

The realization calms me.

Steeling myself, I set off in search of others, hoping for a warmer introduction this time.

Halfway down the hall, I discover a room with an open door. Three girls are inside, one lying on the bottom bunk, the other two lounging on the rug with their backs against the desk and the bed frame.

I maintain that it's impossible to know for sure, but, at a glance, these three seem to be far less likely serial killer candidates than Maya does. For example, none of them are scowling, and I'm almost certain there's a correlation between scowling and murder. At least, logic suggests there would be.

The girl on the bed notices me first, and she rolls onto her side to get a better look at me. I recognize her immediately as the girl I sat next to during Gwendolyn's welcome. She has long, fluffy blond hair and eyes spaced widely enough apart to give her the type of ethereal look that a casting agent might describe as "alien, but in a good way." She's dressed like she's just finished a shift at an elite law firm, in a pencil dress with a high neckline, low hemline, and, I'm startled to note, the exact same floral pattern as my childhood bathroom's shower curtain.

"Hi, come on in," she says, beckoning, and the other two shuffle around to make space on the floor. "We were just talking about the party later."

"I heard he might be sending home half of us tonight," the

girl with the English accent, who's sitting crossed-legged on the floor, says in a high-pitched, panicky tone. She's twirling her straight black hair around a finger so tightly I'm a little worried for her circulation, and her thick-lashed brown eyes are darting around nervously. "Have you heard anything about that?"

The last part is directed to me. The Mediterranean-looking girl between us, who has an aquiline nose and curls long enough to brush against the top of her waist, looks to the ceiling until her eyes are whites-only. Apparently, this isn't the first time this question's come up.

I slump on the floor and grimace. "Uh, I haven't had a chance. We just . . . got here?"

"Well, Kim apparently overheard a couple of the producers earlier, because she was the first to arrive," the blonde on the bed explains.

"But I couldn't eavesdrop as well as I wanted to, because people kept talking to me," the British-accent girl—Kim, apparently—says, in an even higher voice than before.

"Kim, I promise you," the long-haired girl says in an Irish accent, resting a hand on her arm. "If there is a surprise elimination tonight, it's not going to be half of us, or they've got practically no show for the next two months. And if he is sending someone home tonight, panicking about it isn't going to increase your chances of staying. Just relax, and whatever happens, happens." She removes her hand, and turns to me. "Also, hi. I'm Francesca."

"That's Skye," Kim tells Francesca before I get a chance to introduce myself back.

I raise a questioning eyebrow. "Yes, it is."

"Sorry." Kim grins. "I knew who all of you were before we got here. I can't be the only one who stalked everyone else a little bit, can I?"

"I didn't stalk anyone," Francesca says flatly.

Kim sniffs and shoots her a resentful glance. "Well, I want to win. So."

The blonde gives me a little wave. "I knew who you were, too," she admits. "But I haven't stalked you. Well, not recently."

"Glad to hear it," I say, mildly alarmed.

I'm just beginning to wonder if it's too late to back out and get out of this lion's den of possible murderers and confirmed stalkers when she explains. "I was Jordy's girlfriend before Maya. You were all over his socials for a while, so I know your face. I'm Lauren. You're rooming with Maya, right? Wanna invite her over? We have some time to kill."

I don't mean to grimace. The grimace simply takes over my body, obvious enough that none of the others could miss it. Their expressions turn questioning as one. "I think she wants some space right now," I say, trying my best to balance not feeding my roommate to the other lions, and not lying. "That's why I came to see what everyone else was up to."

"Is she okay?" Lauren asks.

"Is she one of those possessive girls?" Kim asks.

I shift in place. "What do you mean?"

"You know. The kind of girl who sees everyone else as competition?"

Francesca double-takes. "Kim, you just spent the last ten bloody minutes freaking out that you might not win this thing, did you not?"

There's an impressive air of dignity to Kim as she nods her concession. "I want to win. I assume we all do. But that doesn't mean I'm gonna be awful to everyone."

"Ah, so you intend to crush us into dust, but you'll be nice about it?" Francesca says.

"Yes, exactly."

Lauren props herself up on one arm and locks eyes with me. "What they're asking is, do we need to be cautious around Maya?"

"I . . . think her problem's mostly with me," I say carefully. "I dated Jordy not long after she did."

"Maybe she thinks you stole him," Kim suggests.

"Oh, fuck off," Francesca says. "Who has the energy to get that worked up about a guy?"

Kim bristles. "I would've thought you did. You flew across countries for one."

Francesca rolls her head to the side. "I came here because it sounded like good craic. It's not that deep."

Kim takes a deep breath, twisting her hair into a pretzel. "Well, *some* of us are here because we really care about Jordy. *Some* of us take this seriously."

"We're here for the 'right' reasons, you mean?" Lauren teases.

"You never know," Francesca says. "I might fall desperately in love with him tonight. Don't count me out yet."

Kim looks distinctly ill at the thought.

"So, you're not invested either way?" Lauren asks Francesca.

"I mean, Jordy and I didn't exactly date or anything. We hooked up when he was on holiday and, like, a month later they asked me to come on this show. Honestly I think they were scraping the barrel with me a little."

Kim's smile is so tight it looks as though it might snap at any moment. Even Lauren appears alarmed at the news. "Wait, so you were his most recent . . . huh."

"Just his most recent hookup," Francesca clarifies. "Honestly, we've barely even talked."

"So you don't have feelings for him?" Kim asks.

"I mean," Francesca says, "no? But he was a good lay?"

Lauren chokes. "Oh, wow."

"Are you guys all into him, then?" Francesca asks.

The rest of us exchange uncomfortable glances. Actually, I wouldn't mind knowing the answer to that myself. We all had different relationships with Jordy, and some of those relationships would have been briefer, or longer ago, than others. It stands to reason that there would be a whole spectrum of emotions in this room.

Kim is the first to break the silence. "I was Jordy's girlfriend last year, while his family was in Liverpool. He was friends with my best friend, Vivaan. It didn't work out because of him moving around, but I don't think we would've broken up if he hadn't moved. I've got to be honest here, I don't love the thought of people coming on the show when they don't even like him."

Francesca frowns. "I don't really know him. But I'd like to. And he asked me here himself, so, obviously he feels the same. I'm not here to screw anyone over."

"No one thinks you are," Lauren says quickly, shooting Kim a warning look as she opens her mouth. Kim shuts it reluctantly as Lauren continues. "And Jordy was my first boyfriend. It was pretty short, but we were really young, so, who knows? I actually think this is fate. I've always kept track of the royal family. Even Jordy said it when he called me. He said they're gonna film an episode at the palace, and he was excited for me to feel like royalty for a day." She smiles dreamily and bounces back on the bed. "It's a little like a fairy tale, isn't it?"

"I'm sure Hans Christian Andersen was just about to start on the tale of the six princesses who battled to the death for the prince who'd already dumped their asses once," Francesca says drily. "That's some real magical shit, there."

I cover my laugh behind my hand and turn it into a cough.

Kim focuses on me as I train my expression back to blank.

"What about you, Skye?" she asks. "Do you still have feelings for him?"

All eyes in the room are on me, suddenly, like my answer is a make-or-break. I don't know what, exactly, it's making or breaking, but it feels significant. "Jordy meant a lot to me once," I say, choosing my words with care. "It's hard to say if anything's still there. But that's why we're here, right? To find out?"

Francesca gives a nod of approval. "See, at least that's rational."

"Who's being irrational?" Kim asks sharply.

"No one's being irrational," Lauren says. "Francesca, you're a wonderful person, but knock it off."

It occurs to me that's the most diplomatic way I've ever heard someone tell someone else they're acting like an asshat. I take notes.

"I just had a thought," Lauren says, before rolling off the bed. "I'll be back in one minute."

With that, she dashes out of the room, and the rest of us are thrown into an awkward silence. I make accidental eye contact with Kim, then Francesca, and tear my eyes away immediately before they pull me into small talk. Once again, I have the urge to pull out my phone to scroll through while we wait for her to return. How long is it going to take for *that* habit to fade?

Luckily, it doesn't take long after her footsteps fade away for them to thump against the staircase again, and moments later she bursts into the room bearing bottles of alcohol and a stack of plastic cups.

"We're all over eighteen, right?" she says.

I look around, then nod. "Yeah."

"The drinking age in Chalonne is eighteen. The kitchen's got a whole cabinet full."

The others perk up and grab cups.

"I forgot you lot can't drink until you're twenty-one," Kim says. "This must be weird for you."

"I'm Canadian," I correct her. "It's eighteen for us. Where I live, anyway. The culture shock was definitely a little odd when I got to Europe two months ago, though."

"I heard you've been backpacking," Francesca says. "That would've gotten you used to drinking fast."

"That's one way of putting it." I grin. To say the drinking culture is different here would be a slight understatement. It's not as though teens back home never drink. But here, many eighteen-year-olds drink often and hard. Sometimes, I wonder if my dad knew how things are here when I announced my travel plans.

I scan the selection, then have an idea. "Hold on," I say, hopping to my feet.

I rush back to my room, and pause in front of the door. Will Maya be inside? Will she be annoyed with me for bursting in? Or could she be napping the nastiness away?

I give a gentle knock, and when no one says anything, I peek in. Empty.

Well, good. The less time I spend in her orbit, the better. With any luck, she makes herself scarce and stays that way for the rest of the night.

I dig through my suitcase and grab what I was looking for: my dad's old iPod and portable speakers. He gave them to me when I complained about the ban on phones, and, therefore, music. It's filled with songs from the eighties and nineties, mostly, but old music is better than no music.

I return victorious with my prize. "Ambiance!" I declare, setting up the speakers. Moments later, Billy Joel's voice bursts through at top volume, and I hastily turn it down.

"Was Maya in your room?" Lauren asks. "You can invite her to come join, if you want. Only if you want."

"Nah, she wasn't."

"Good," Francesca says, ignoring Lauren's reproachful look. "We don't want a mood-ruiner right now. Speaking of, what did she say to you, exactly, Skye?"

"Yeah," Kim says, her eyes glinting with curiosity.

Well, I *would* like a second opinion as to how wary I should be of Maya tonight. So, keeping my tone as measured as I can, I pour myself a glass and tell them.

When I finish, Kim and Francesca look outraged. Finally, something they can agree on.

"You know," says Kim, "I knew there would be some weirdos here who wanted to make enemies because we dated the same guy."

"I think," Lauren says primly, "we should give her a chance to explain herself."

I nod. "Right. It could be anything. Maybe she gets crabby when she travels."

Francesca scowls. "Doesn't sound like *that's* what it was."

Frankly, I agree with her, but I'm happy to keep that opinion to myself for now.

"We don't know, because we don't know her," Lauren says.

"Jordy knows her, though," Kim points out.

"Look, I'll just see what she's like tonight," I say. "If she's normal, I'll pretend it never happened."

"What, and be all buddy-buddy with her after she was awful to you?" Francesca asks.

"We probably aren't going to be best friends now, sure. But I'm not exactly looking for opportunities to make enemies," I say.

Francesca thinks about it, then gets to her feet. "Nope. I'm gonna ask her to explain herself."

"Whoa, what?" I ask, scrambling after her. Lauren and Kim grab their drinks and follow suit. "No, come on. We're having fun. Why ruin it?"

"Because I have experience with bullies," Francesca says, marching down the hall. "If you don't call it out at the start, it escalates until it's too big to squash. She'll probably start slagging you on camera if you give her an inch."

I look at Lauren, the great pacifist, pleadingly.

Come on. Where are those de-escalation skills we've all come to know and love over the last thirty minutes?

Anything?

She frowns and tips her head from side to side like she's weighing up the options. "I don't think *that's* necessarily fair. But, you know, Francesca's probably right. Getting it out in the open will give us all a chance to start fresh on the right foot."

We reach the foot of the stairs and hesitate, looking to Francesca for direction.

"She said she wanted to try out the pool, didn't she?" Kim asks.

"Yes, the pool!" Francesca cries, making a beeline for the door.

"I don't want her to think I was bitching about her," I protest as we burst into the glare of the afternoon sun.

"You weren't bitching about her," Francesca says. "You were just factually telling us some factual things that factually happened."

"We'll tell her it wasn't bitching," Lauren assures me.

Somehow, I'm not comforted.

We find Maya on the pool loungers, lying next to Perrie.

They're giggling about something, apparently already the closest of friends.

Even though Jordy had warned me Maya's rage would be directed at me, personally, seeing this still stings. "Hi, Maya," Francesca says, storming straight up to her. I'm honestly glad Francesca's on my side, if only because I wouldn't want to be on the receiving end of that tone on the first day. It makes Maya's attitude seem positively tame. "How are you? What's up with you and Skye? She said you were a massive bitch to her."

"But she wasn't bitching about you," Lauren jumps in.

Wow, ten out of ten, everybody, wonderful work. I have the sudden, overwhelming urge to fling myself in the pool and refuse to resurface.

"Uh, hi," Maya says, her eyes darting to me. They narrow as they lock onto mine, and my heart skips a beat. "You're just jumping straight into it."

"I don't like small talk," Kim says.

"Right, right." Maya and Perrie exchange a meaningful glance. Why do I have a sinking feeling that Maya has already turned Perrie against me? What did Jordy say? Something about her being extremely convincing and manipulative?

Maya gives us a weak smile, and I notice she's steadfastly avoiding my gaze. "I don't think Skye wants to have this conversation in front of everyone."

As far as threats go, it's so thinly veiled it might as well be naked.

"Oh, right," Francesca says, smiling. It's rather terrifying. Like the sickly sweet smile of an assassin before they strike the killing shot. "You're so thoughtful. But Skye's here, so I think we're good to go?"

"Actually," Perrie says to Maya, "I wanted to go show you

that, um, thing I was telling you about inside, Maya. Maybe we can revisit this later?"

"I'm sure it can wait thirty seconds," Francesca says firmly.

"Skye knows what she did," Maya says. "I haven't gotten an apology from her, yet. So, unless she's ready to give me one, I don't see anything for the group to discuss."

"Apologize?" I repeat, incredulous. "Apologize for *what*? You're the one who should be apologizing here."

"She's not apologizing to you," Perrie jumps in before Maya can stop spluttering. "You stole her boyfriend from her. She has every right to be mad."

"It's the bloody joint-ex-boyfriend drama," Kim says. "I knew it. Didn't I tell you?"

Francesca waves her off.

"I'm sure there's just been some miscommunication," Lauren tries.

"Oh, you're sure, huh?" Maya asks. "And you know this because you were . . . there?"

"I didn't 'steal' anyone," I snap. "You can't be serious. Grow up."

Maya locks eyes with me and the others fall silent. This is a one-on-one battle now. The back of my neck prickles.

"Well, I mean, you did," she says. "It was basically the definition of it, actually."

I roll my eyes. "He moved away, he met me, he dated me. People move on, Maya. You can't blame me for that."

"Oh, is that what you call it? Moving on?" She sneers.

"Yes. He didn't have feelings for you anymore. He didn't even live anywhere near you! I don't know how you thought—"

"Skye, he didn't just have *feelings* for me. He was *with* me. He was my *boyfriend*."

My cheeks are heating with anger, but I keep my voice even. We can work through this like rational adults, as long as I keep my temper. I'm certain of it. "You weren't together. You *wanted* to be with him, but he wanted to be with me. It sucks, but that's just how it happens sometimes, and it was years ago, anyway. Who cares?"

Maya's voice goes up several decibels. "Uh, no, the person who did the wrong thing doesn't get to decide when it's been long enough to move past it. That's *my* call. And we *were* together."

I flounder, not quite sure how to respond to this. If Jordy says they weren't together, and Maya says they were, it all comes down to who I believe. Jordy isn't a liar, though. I've known him much longer than I've known Maya. And, so far, she's acted exactly as Jordy said she would. Which makes me wonder what she did to him that he won't even go into detail over.

Which makes me furious on his behalf. My skin prickles, and my heart rate starts to pick up.

"Exactly," Maya says into the silence. "So, can you please fuck off now?"

"Okay, it's clear Jordy was right about you," I say. Maya goes pale, which is quite a feat, as she's pretty pale to start with. She has the kind of creamy, freckle-adorned skin that has no business being out in the sun on a day like today.

"What's that supposed to mean?" she asks.

"He warned us," Francesca says.

"'Us'?" Lauren echoes, raising an eyebrow.

Francesca ignores her. "Jordy said you would try to slag him off. And that you'd come after Skye. He said you've been doing it for years."

"He said you lost it when he tried to break up with you," Kim says. "And that you wouldn't let him."

"Well, let's all believe Jordy, then," Perrie says, her voice dripping with sarcasm like syrup on bread. "No man's ever lied about something like that."

"If you feel that way about Jordy, why are you here?" Kim asks, fuming. "He'd love to hear you think he's a liar."

"No, don't tell him, please," Perrie deadpans, examining her nails.

"I don't think Jordy's a liar, though," Lauren says quietly. "Or a cheater. I'm sorry, Maya, but isn't it possible you both thought it was something different?"

"No," Maya says coldly.

"I don't think Jordy's a cheater," Kim says firmly.

"I don't really know Jordy." Francesca shrugs. Kim shoots her an annoyed glance, and she quickly adds, "But he seems like one of the good ones."

"He's not a cheater," I confirm. "And neither am I."

"Whatever helps you sleep at night, babe," Maya says, locking her eyes with mine. I hold her gaze, and we stare each other down, neither of us willing to be the first to break it.

"And if you're on the show to defame me," I say coolly, "you should think carefully about what you can prove. My lawyer's already advised me about my rights. We had a meeting before I left."

This, of course, is a bald-faced lie. I don't have a lawyer, and if Dad does, I've never been informed. Do people *have* lawyers when they aren't criminals yet? Regardless, it sounds intimidating, and I need intimidating right now. Without it, I run the risk of Maya turning me into the world's punching bag on the very first night. Jordy *did* say she knows how to spin a story. I was warned. And now I know what I'm dealing with, I have to admit, I'm a little worried. More than a little worried, in truth.

"Oh, good," Maya spits. "I love being threatened into silence. This *really* convinces me you didn't know what he did."

"I'm not threatening you, Maya," I say. "I'm just saying,

let's keep the drama away from the cameras. For both of our sakes."

"You're lucky," Francesca mutters. "If it was me you were accusing, I'd just sock you and be done with it."

"Me too," Kim says. "But figuratively."

"I meant figuratively."

"Did you?"

"I'm not going to actually sock someone, am I? Not when there's cameras."

"You'd probably have to borrow Skye's fake lawyer if you did," Perrie says.

I look at her sharply, and she gives me a sweet smile.

"Whatever," Maya says, leaning an elbow on the lounger armrest. It's as though she's trying to look nonchalant, but the expression on her face implies she's anything but. "Don't bother me and I won't bother you, okay?"

"Sounds wonderful to me," I say, as the girls tug me to go back inside.

Perrie calls out after us, "Just because there's more of you, it doesn't make you right!"

Francesca throws her middle finger up as we leave.

"Bloody Americans," Kim mutters.

"I'm American," Lauren says, wounded.

I glance over my shoulder before we reach the door.

Maya's staring at me with an intensity that makes my stomach drop.

I'm not entirely sure I believe her promise.

SEVEN

Maya

The ballroom is buzzing with frantic energy and activity when Perrie and I get there after dinner. The folding chairs that were set up earlier have been swept aside, and in their place are racks and racks of floor-length dresses, heels, and jewelry. Seriously, they could stock half a department store with this collection.

As soon as Isaac spots me, he tears me away from Perrie, who is sunshine and goodness, and brings me over to Skye, who is Satan's mistress. If Isaac wants to have a good working relationship with me, he's not off to a great start.

Skye's being fitted into a floor-length black gown that makes her look at least two inches taller. When she sees me, her eyes flash and she raises her chin like she's looking down on me. I'm still half a head taller than her, so that's pretty fucking rich.

"Hi," I say in a clipped voice.

She just stares me down, then looks right past me like I don't exist. If it weren't for the tiny, cocky smile touching the corner of her mouth, you'd think she hadn't heard me at all.

Keep your cool, I remind myself. *There will be cameras*

around all night. It'll be almost impossible to plead innocent if you're filmed lunging at her.

Ignore her.

But how the hell am I supposed to ignore her when she's always *there*, reminding me of what happened? Smirking at me?

Luckily, a distraction comes in the form of a short red-haired woman who'd been helping one of the other girls into a dress. She steers a clothing rack full of outrageously expensive-looking gowns over to me. "Maya, hi," she says in a Chalonian accent. "I'm Saskia, lovely to meet you, lovely. These, we believe, will be your size. Try them on, see which ones fit, and when I come back you can model them for me and we will choose together, *sa?*"

"*Sa.*" I smile. I pointedly turn my back to Skye so I can focus on the task without her stupid face distracting me, and scan the choices. My stomach flips as I do. I've never seen so many beautiful things in my life. I get to try them all on? And *wear* one on camera? Immortalizing the night I get to look like a legit fairy princess?

Things are looking up.

I turn to Isaac, who's beaming at me. "You don't need my permission," he says. "Go on. You can jump in one of the empty rooms if you want privacy."

A couple of the other girls are changing where they stand, while their producers fuss over the dresses with them. Hmm, brave, but I'm gonna go with option B: privacy. To be fair, I didn't raid the liquor cabinet all afternoon like some people, so.

I find a mostly empty ballroom a few doors down and lay down the dresses on the long table in the middle, then set about performing a fashion show for Isaac. And Skye, I guess,

Skye's there, too, but I totally don't see her because she is nothing to me and I'm ignoring her.

There's a slinky, sequined Jessica Rabbit gown in a shade of red that I think looks like trash—elegant trash, but trash—against my hair, but that Isaac insists makes me look just like the character. Skye might screw up her nose at this one, but I wouldn't know, because I don't see her at all.

Next is a sky-blue ball gown complete with a hoop skirt that Isaac had his heart set on—apparently it'd make me the center of attention at the party—but doesn't fit quite right in the bust. That one I *very* firmly reject, because I was not born yesterday, and I know for a fact that if the worst happens and I accidentally flash everyone, it'll end up as a blurred-out promo shot for the first episode.

"You could try stuffing your bra?" Skye asks in a syrupy sweet voice, but I don't hear her, and therefore I do not respond. Besides, even if I *did* hear her, I don't engage with terrorists.

Following that is a champagne-colored, slinky silk dress that Isaac describes as classic, and I describe as "if the raunchiest lingerie you ever saw was turned into an Oscars gown." It's possible Skye double-takes when I emerge in this one, but, who knows? Not me.

Then, a forest-green empire-waist dress that I initially call as the front-runner just because it's my favorite color to wear, but honestly, once I have it on it's a little plain. I figure if you've got one shot to wear a glorious princess gown, you don't choose the dress that you could wear to attend someone else's wedding without showing them up. Nope, if I'm going to do this, I'm going to sparkle, goddamn it.

Finally, there's the gown that caught my eye at the start. It's made of all these elegant, floaty layers of lavender-gray tulle, with adorned off-the-shoulder sleeves and detailed flowers covering the bodice. I wasn't sure the color would suit my hair, but now that it's on, it actually looks . . . beautiful.

Huh.

I linger for a little too long in front of the mirror, just staring at myself, but, honestly, it's not a feeling I'm used to. We never had a whole lot of money for things like fancy clothes, growing up. Mom had to support all three of us on her own, after all. It's not something that ever bothered me. It was just life, the only life I knew, and we were happy. But then I met Jordy, and his endless designer labels. Jordy, whose eyebrows raised in surprise when he saw my house for the first time. Jordy, who made two things very clear: one, that having money, and lots of it, made a person worth more in every sense of the word; two, that he didn't think I was smart enough to earn a whole lot of it myself. He made a comment once about how he couldn't see me going to college, because I used the wrong "they're," and I was like, dude, there're three versions of that word, who can keep them all straight?

Anyway, he was wrong. And in a few years . . . or, like, a decade or so . . . I'll be able to afford dresses like this all by myself. When I'm a doctor, no one's ever going to call me dumb, or trashy, again. And I can't fucking wait for it.

Even if it means I have to go to med school to become a doctor.

Content, I swoosh myself—all three tons of me, if you include this monstrosity—back to Isaac, who's fiddling with the strap on Skye's dress. They both look up as I approach. "Yes, definitely, love it," Isaac says.

Hard to say what Skye's reaction is, but it's possible she scans me slowly—achingly slowly—from head to toe, then turns away in annoyance. And if I hypothetically did see her do that, I'd feel victorious, because that's a sure sign I actually look great.

Across the room, Saskia glances our way, and double-takes with a smile touching her lips. I grin at her and twirl my skirt, and she gives me a thumbs-up.

The next half hour is a blur of being checked over for fit, with Saskia and her assistant rushing around making temporary alterations to straps and sticking necklines in place with tape. Shoes and accessories are easier—apparently this dress has a pair assigned: strappy, creamy heels that I can just *tell* are going to take off a chunk of skin around my toes—and a simple Tiffany swan pendant that's still fancier than anything I've worn in my life. Then we're herded into the front grounds for our first real taste of being in front of the camera.

We start with a portrait photoshoot for them to use in promo. They whisk Skye away first and pose her in front of a fountain surrounded by softboxes to capture the perfect light. Her smile is charismatic and a little cocky. The way she stands, you can just *tell* she considers herself the main character of everyone's story, and has never been given a reason to doubt it. In this lighting, her deep brown eyes are more of a toffee color, and her tanned skin looks bright and blurred. Like if you were to run a finger over her cheek, it'd glide across like velvet.

No wonder Jordy left me for her. She's actually stunning.

That bitch.

Before I can follow that thought train down into a tunnel of existential despair and self-pity, Perrie sidles up beside me. She's wearing a champagne gown with a slit up the leg, but where the dress I'd tried on in that color had washed me out, on her it's gorgeous against her dark brown skin. Even in the afternoon sun, she looks moonlit. "*Love* this," she says, gesturing to my dress. "It's a crime that I can't take the camera here tonight. It's the best we've looked."

"They're professionals, at least?" I say.

Perrie scoffs. "That guy? He's about as artistic as the people in the post office taking passport photos. I want, like, a moody close-up in those bushes over there, or a rooftop shot in the wind. All these options, and they really went for 'stand and smile in front of the fountain.'"

"You're right, and you should say it."

"Someone has to."

Skye finishes up, and Isaac beckons me to go up and take her spot. She can't resist staring me down as we swap, and for a second I think she's going to elbow me on her way past. But, no. Not with this many cameras on us, anyway.

So, the cold war continues.

Unlike Skye and Perrie, I'm not the kind of person who really "gets" the camera. To put it lightly. To put it more accurately, I tend to pose like a startled ghoul in anything that's not a selfie, but not on *purpose*. It's just my face. I can't help my face.

I'm pretty sure it stems from my childhood. My mom always used to direct me in family photos, begging me to smile bigger, no, *bigger,* bigger, Maya! A proper smile! Until I was smiling so wide my jaw ached and you could count my full set of teeth. In hindsight, I'm pretty sure that when Mom said "smile bigger" she actually meant "smile prettier," which, counterintuitively, was less of a "laughing at a comedy show" smile and more of a calculated, precise facial pose. Long story short, she pretty much messed me up for life and doomed me to a fate of always second-guessing whether my smile looks just a little bit possessed whenever I can't see the face I'm making in real time.

And, right on cue: "That's great, Maya, just a little more natural. Think of something really nice. Think of someone you love. Okay, like that, but halve it. You girls have been drinking all afternoon, huh? Wha—not you? Oh . . ."

Finally, they apparently get a usable shot—one that they

refuse to let me take a look at, which is a hell of a bad sign if you ask me—and I escape to chill with Perrie on a bench she's found near the mansion's entrance. The assistants start handing out glasses of wine and champagne, which feels super illegal and scandalous, even though I know legally it's not a problem for me to drink here.

It's not the first time I've ever had a drink, but it is the first time I've been offered one in public, with adults around. Suddenly, I feel way less experienced than everyone else. The other girls raise their glasses to their lips without pausing. For most of them, it's normal. The non-Americans have been legal adults for years. Lauren was a year above Jordy in school, from memory, which would make her twenty-one. At least Perrie, who's Jordy's age, looks as surprised as I am by all the alcohol.

I take a tiny sip of wine, then elegantly dribble it straight back into the glass. Wine, as it turns out, tastes a whole lot like sour swamp water.

People drink this on purpose? For what *reason*?

Only minutes later, we're herded again—this time to stand in a circle with our wine glasses by the fountain. Mine's been demoted to a prop as far as I'm concerned, although the other girls seem to have no problem downing theirs. Are they tasting the same thing I'm tasting? Surely not. Maybe my tongue's just broken.

"Okay, ladies, I just want you to clink those glasses in the center of your circle," Gwendolyn instructs from her place by one of the camera operators.

We do.

"Perfect," Gwendolyn says. "Now, again, but this time don't be afraid to react to it. You're *excited*, you're *cheering*, this is a *celebratory glass-clink*."

We try it again, this time with vocals, and even some fake laughter thrown in for pizzazz. I accidentally slam my glass a little too hard against someone else's, and I follow the arm up to see whose it is. Of course, it's Skye's. She raises her eyebrows at me, and I can't help but roll my eyes at the implied accusation in her look. I mean, Jesus, I'm not out here planning revenge-by-glass-clink. If I wanted to be passive-aggressive, I'd do it with my words, like a goddamn adult.

"Beautiful," says Gwendolyn. "Now, just one more time, so we can get it at another angle?"

We do it eleven more times. By the time Gwendolyn has her shot, I'm genuinely worried one of these glasses is going to shatter into elegant shards any second now.

Now that the photos and promo shots are done, it's time for them to ruin our beautiful evening wear looks by attaching mic-packs to our backs. Isaac, for obvious reasons, isn't able to help Skye and me get ours on, so Perrie's producer, Violet, takes us into a spare room to fix them under our dresses. "Rule is, these stay on at all times until after filming," she says. "If you get caught turning them off, there's a fine."

"What about in the bathroom?" Skye asks, before I can.

"I can promise you, we aren't going to use anything recorded in the bathroom on the show. Astoundingly, it doesn't make for good television." Violet zips up her dress and gives her a pat. "There. You're done."

Skye now has a lump the size of an angry fist sticking out of her lower back.

Stunning. She's a vision.

"Now you, Maya," Violet says, and I cut off mid-snicker.

Back outside, at the edge of the grounds, a man in a tuxedo stands talking to Saskia. He's blandly beautiful, in an "I guess you're symmetrical, but you also somehow look like the less famous, less charismatic brother of half the white men in Hollywood?" sort of way. Gwendolyn greets him and leads him over to us, where we're standing in a semicircle. "Everyone," she says, "meet Grayson Gains. I'm sure you're all familiar with him from his work on shows like *Velveeta or Volcano, Marrying the Enemy,* and *Cooking Under Constant Criticism.* For the next seven weeks, he will be your host for *Second-Chance Romance.* Please make him feel welcome. He has a few words to say before we get the party started!"

I have never seen this man in my life. We give Grayson a smattering of applause, and the cameras swing around to him. "Welcome, ladies, to *Second-Chance Romance,*" he says, in a slow, slightly exaggerated way that probably sounds great on TV, but comes across as a little alarming in real life. "I'm your host, Grayson Gains, and I am delighted to stand by your side as you re-explore what you once had with our Explorer, Jordy Miller."

"Cut, perfect," Gwendolyn says. "And again."

Grayson doesn't hesitate. "Welcome, ladies, to *Second-Chance Romance.* I'm your host, Grayson Gains, and I am *just thrilled* to stand by your side as you all re-explore what you once had with our Explorer . . . Jordy Miller."

"Beautiful, Grayson, beautiful. Just one more time for me?"

He does it seven more times before moving on to the next part of his spiel.

"Tonight, you will have the opportunity to spend some time with Jordy, and get to know him again. I urge all of you to use this time wisely, and to treat this as though you are meeting Jordy for the first time. All relationships have baggage. If you can leave that baggage on the platform, and look to what is standing before you right now, you might find yourself falling in love all over again."

I lose count of how many times he repeats that.

"Now. Are you ready to see Jordy?"

My stomach plunges. We chorus "yes," and again, and again, until the word seems to lose all meaning.

Now the cameras leave us as their operators hurry to the parking area. Perrie steps closer to me and sucks in a long breath. It sounds shaky. I can relate.

It's been a long, long time since I've seen him.

"Oh," Skye says softly, and I give her a questioning look. Then I see what she sees: a figure approaching in the distance.

He's tall and well-muscled, dressed to the nines in a black suit and tie, with his brown hair styled neatly. The broad shoulders and sturdy neck of someone who either spends a lot of time in the gym or does manual labor for a living (and you can bet your ass it's not the latter in this case). A square jaw, sparkling green eyes that crinkle in the corners, and up-settingly flawless skin that is probably the result of *extensive* pricey treatments, because it was nowhere near that glowy when I knew him.

Jordy fucking Miller.

Now there's a face I would've been happy to never see again.

EIGHT

Maya

"Jordy!" Grayson cries as he gets closer. The cameras swing past us like we aren't here. "How are you?"

Jordy's smile is blinding as he saunters up the path to give Grayson a handshake. "I'm good, Grayson."

I didn't notice on the phone, but Jordy's fake accent has, somehow, gotten even more obnoxious since I knew him. There's no way, there is just *no* way I'm the only one who notices how forced and inconsistent it is. The emperor has no clothes, goddammit!

Grayson steps back from Jordy and stands with one foot pointed toward the cameras, the other at Jordy. "Are you ready to re-explore your past relationships to find the one that got away?"

"I'm so ready." Jordy gives a small laugh that can only be described as *trained*. It's like an actor who's been instructed to play a character who's self-conscious, charismatic, and approachable. And as much as I hate to admit it, he's pretty good at the role.

"Then let's go to the party," Grayson says, sweeping his hands to the side.

Gwendolyn rushes forward to speak to Jordy and Grayson.

The other producers steer us all in a group around the back of the mansion to the grounds, which are glittering and twinkling with a Christmas Wonderland warehouse worth of fairy lights and candles.

"It's quiet," Skye says.

"My producer told me it's a copyright thing," Kim says. "If they use a song in an episode, they have to pay for it.

"Oh, great," I say to Perrie as we break away from the group. "A party with my ex, a bunch of girls who hate me, and no music. That's exactly what I hoped tonight would be like."

"Hey, you have me," she says. "And . . . food, thank god."

I follow her gaze to an open pair of double sliding doors that lead to a well-lit room full of tables of small snacks. We investigate and find a spread of what Kim calls mini sausage rolls—a meat-and-vegetable mixture covered in pastry—mini quiches, potato chips, carrot and celery sticks, and a huge, crusty bread bowl full of what looks like beetroot dip and melted cheese. I *think* it's a Chalonian dish, but have no idea what it's called. Next to the food is a tray of filled wine and champagne glasses.

Wine, my nemesis. We meet again. And so soon.

"Hi, girls!" A voice chirps about six inches from my ear, causing me to shriek and drop the quiche I'm holding.

"Gwendolyn," Perrie says in a strained voice, turning around. "Hi."

Gwendolyn grabs a wineglass and a flute from the table and hands them to us. "I just wanted to drop by and let you know that everything you see here is a free-for-all! Don't be shy, help yourself to some food and drink. There's *no limit*. If you run out, we'll just bring you more. We want you to have fun tonight!"

"You want us to get drunk tonight," I correct.

"Is there a difference?" Gwendolyn beams.

"Between having a nice night with great people and getting wasted and blacking out?" I ask. "No, I can't think of one. Perrie?"

"Toe-may-toe, toe-mah-toe," she deadpans.

"Wonderful!" Gwendolyn squeezes my shoulder before hurrying off while we stare after her.

"Real important to her that we get drunk on camera, huh?" I ask.

"*Real* important."

"Well, I'd love to give it a shot, but this isn't drinkable." I hold up my wine, and glance at Perrie's flute. "Is champagne any better?"

"Worse."

"How can it be *worse*?" I ask as we head back outside. "Are adults all playing a mass game of chicken to see who's the first to crack and admit wine sucks?"

Across the lawn, Jordy and Grayson are filming something in front of the rosebushes, and the other girls are sitting on a pair of love seats on the back porch. Two wicker chairs are still empty.

Perrie and I look at each other.

"We don't need to sit with them," she says quickly.

"But we should. What happens if I'm the first to leave? You can't *only* be friends with me."

"I could say the same to you."

"No, because it's me they're mad at. You just got caught in the middle."

She tosses her head. "If I have no friends, I have no friends. I'd rather be alone than pretend to like people who suck." Then she thinks on it some more, and frowns. "But we should probably try to be a little friendlier to them."

"Why *us*? We didn't do anything wrong."

"How about because, if we don't, all four of them can say we're awful people on camera, and the folks watching along at home will believe it because there's more of them than us?"

I stare at her in horror as I process this. "Motherfucker."

The girls whisper frantically as we walk up, and fall dead silent as soon as we're close enough. Like that's gonna stop us from knowing exactly what they were saying.

"You guys look gorgeous," I say calmly, sitting next to Kim, who shuffles away to put more space between us. "I think this is the fanciest dress I've ever worn. How cool is this?"

Skye folds one leg over the other—which is kind of impressive in that slinky dress—and rests her chin on her fingers. Her mouth doesn't move, but her eyes crinkle slightly in a way that's sort of half-annoyed, half-amused. I reply with an innocent smile, which tips her firmly into "annoyed" territory.

"They're nice," Lauren says, looking down at her own royal blue gown. "But I'm more excited for the ones we get to wear when we go to the palace."

"I didn't know we were going to the palace," Perrie says.

"Yes! Couldn't you just pass out?" Lauren says.

"That sounds cool," I say.

Kim gives me an annoyed look. "It's a few episodes away. We don't know who will actually be going."

"I guess not," I say coolly.

Perrie grimaces at me. Tough crowd.

"So, where are you all from?" I ask, persisting with a little desperation at the edge of my voice.

"Dublin," says Francesca.

"Liverpool," Kim says. "That's in England."

"Yeah, I know," I say.

"And I was born in Goa," she goes on. "That's in India."

Lauren jumps in hurriedly. "And I'm from Columbus."

She pauses, then gives Kim a sly smile, like she's holding back laughter. "That's in Ohio."

"She's American, she'd *know that*," Kim says defensively. "I just assume you lot don't know anything about anywhere else."

"You're not wrong, exactly," Perrie says in a soft voice, and Lauren giggles as the tension lessens a little.

"The cameras are coming over," I say, as I notice one of the operators head in our direction.

"Oh, so *that's* why you're being nice to us," Skye says.

"No." I bristle. "I just figured we're going to be around each other for the next few weeks, and it'll be more enjoyable if we can be nice to each other."

"Oh, *now* you think you might try that? What's changed in the last"—Skye pretends to check her watch—"five hours?"

"Maya, the cameras," Perrie whispers.

They're close, but not close enough to hear us yet. "I didn't really mean you," I say to Skye. "I meant the others. *They* haven't done anything."

Except listen to her lies about me, but that's not the point right now.

"Sorry to tell you," Skye says calmly, "but they don't want your fake friendship any more than I do. I'll be professional, but not—"

Francesca gives Skye a hard kick. The cameras are well and truly close enough now.

We all fall silent and look anywhere but at the camera. The operator sighs. "Don't be shy, girls, you're gonna have to get used to this. Just act like I'm not here."

No one speaks.

"Anyone?" the operator pleads.

Eventually, Lauren plasters on a fake smile. "So, Perrie," she says, a little stiffly, "what do you do?"

Perrie startles. "Um . . . well, I'm a receptionist, and I'm also studying marketing."

"Cool! Which college?"

I take in my surroundings as they talk. Skye is watching me like a hawk, so intensely it sends shivering prickles down my neck. Francesca is looking between Perrie and Lauren. Kim's craning her neck, staring at something behind me. I turn around to see Jordy striding across the lawn, followed by another camera.

Amazingly, I am honest-to-god glad to see him.

The conversation drops off as everyone notices Jordy approach. They were probably tipped off by the cloying smell of his cologne. It's so thick I'm surprised we can't see it hanging in the air like a cloud of poison.

"Hey, how's everyone doing?" he asks. "Maya, what do you think about going for a quick walk to catch up? It's been ages."

"Thank god," I murmur, jumping up.

The girls break into giggles, and Jordy makes a show of raising a single eyebrow. "I'm glad to see you, too."

With cameras and producers trailing us, Jordy steers me through the garden to an area closed off by hedges, where a gazebo decked out in flowers and lights stands in the center. The camera crew follows me closely as I sit beside him, and settles in only feet from us. My, how romantic.

Okay. I have to win him over. Focus. Be charming. I plaster on my most charismatic smile. "Hey, you," I say.

"Maya. Wow. It's good to see you. You look great. Look at you!"

"Look at me? Look at you. You're uh . . ." Compliment, compliment, compliment . . . *You look like you're trying really hard to convince the world you're a catch?* No . . . *You look like you've started using all that sponsorship money for some expensive skincare?* Also no . . . "Tall as ever."

"Thank you, I haven't lost a single inch in all this time. So glad you've noticed."

Oh no. He's giving me a familiar look. His eyes are glittering with the challenge of banter. And it's the worst thing ever, because suddenly I'm sixteen again, and we're swapping words like a Ping-Pong ball, picking up speed as we go. And he smells like he used to. Not his cologne—that's choking the air like a noxious gas, still—but his . . . *skin,* I guess. My heart speeds up against my will as it recognizes the smell, and the feel, of all of this.

But we aren't sixteen. And I don't want to banter. I don't want to relax into this.

So, I stick to the bland and safe. "Are you having fun?" I ask, and Jordy tips his head back to let out a sudden, stark laugh. Like I said the wittiest thing he's ever heard.

"I'm at a mansion, at a party that's all about me, with some of the greatest chicks I know," he says. "I've been worse."

"Mm, they're such great girls," I lie through my teeth. "It must be wild to see everyone again after this long."

"Yeah well." He tips his head to the side. "You especially. You've grown up."

I've gained an inch, so glad you've noticed, my brain wants to say. Wait, no, no banter, nope. "Thank you," I say instead. "It's been a while, I guess."

"It has. Too long. I've been wanting to reach out before this, you know. I just didn't know what to say."

A good icebreaker would've been to apologize for cheating on me. But no, that won't do, either. God, how am I supposed to have a conversation with him without lowering my defenses or attacking him? "Well, we're here now," I say instead. Oh my god, this is the most boring conversation I've ever had in my life.

"We are," he agrees. He gives me a funny look, but I can only give him a weak shrug in return. This is awkward, but I don't know how to make it *not* awkward.

I search desperately for a topic that feels safe. "How is everyone? How's *Sam*?"

"Oh." Something in his demeanor changes, but I can't pinpoint what it means. "They're good. Sam's good. Obviously, ha. She's never been better."

"I bet. How is it being a step away from royalty?"

"It's good. I'm a lucky guy." He shifts, and I become aware of the cameras on us again. "But, you know what? I talk about myself in interviews all the time. I'm sick of talking about myself. Tell me about you. How are your parents? How're Rosie and Olivia?"

Sick of talking about yourself, huh? You have *changed.*

Nope. Not gonna say that. "They're good. Rosie's got a boyfriend now. I sort of introduced them, so there's that. And Olivia's going to college with me this year."

There he goes again. Raising those eyebrows. "College, huh? Community?"

"The University of Connecticut," I say delicately. "The plan is to study medicine."

No abbreviations here. Nope, I'm a college student now, and I use whole words, and I can spell every version of "they're."

His eyebrows shoot into the atmosphere. "*Med* school, huh?"

Oh, it's all right when *he* does it.

"Yes. I actually aced my SATs, you know."

His laugh is more startled than I appreciate. "Well. You *have* changed a lot."

I am going to tear every strand of hair from his skull.

"Well," I say, pretending I'm not vividly imagining an act of violence against him, "I guess you made a good impression on me."

"Makes sense to me."

"It's too bad. Imagine if we never broke up. I might be curing cancer by now."

He lets out a delighted laugh, and I lean into it. "It's too bad we did," I whisper.

Jordy's smile freezes. Maybe he has stage fright? Can't think of anything else to say?

"It feels like no time has passed," I say encouragingly. "Do you get that? Or is that just me? I guess your life's been busier than mine over the last two years, so . . ."

I'd thought I was doing such a good job. Flirting, making him sound like the perfect guy for the cameras, refraining from ripping his throat out with my very fingers, et cetera. But he's gone cold. It's not something I can see on his face, but it's like the air changes. I recognize the feeling acutely. It feels like at the end of our relationship, when nothing I ever said seemed to be what he wanted to hear.

When he'd started seeing Skye.

"Well, I have to make sure I get to everyone tonight," Jordy says, standing abruptly. "But I might talk to you more later? See how we go."

I press my lips together, stunned, and my cheeks start to roast with heat.

God, what am I doing here? It was ridiculous for me to think I could pull this off. How did I not realize how difficult it would be to make Jordy fall for me now, when I couldn't even keep him interested the first time around? How can I possibly hold a normal, intimate conversation with Jordy when half of me is terrified he might worm his way in and make me forget what I know about him, and the other half of me wants to claw him? It was an impossible goal from the start. I should've seen it.

But I see it perfectly now.

"I'd like that," I say.

"I think tonight's going to go fast, though," he says. "We might not get a chance."

Message received.

"That's fine," I say crisply.

"Could you send Perrie over here?" he asks, and that pushes my patience one step too far.

"Sure, Jordy," I snap. "You could probably have gone to ask her yourself, but I guess you're used to being waited on these days, huh?"

The camera blinks one red eye in my direction. Watching closely.

Jordy frowns. "Wait, Maya, are you okay? You seem upset."

I storm off without replying, the camera operator hot on my trail. The group lounging on the love seats turns to look at me as one as I reemerge from the hedges. Skye and I lock eyes, and I scowl at her, before turning to Perrie. "Your turn, sweetie," I say.

Perrie gets up, but she seems concerned. "Are you okay? What happened?"

"Nothing," I say. "I'm fine."

"You don't look fine."

"I'm *fine*. But, you should all know"—I turn to the girls here—"I know Jordy pretty well. And he acts all sweet, and sincere, and he makes you feel like you're the most important person in the world. But it's an act. One he has *perfected*. Sometimes he almost fools me. But he doesn't mean anything he says. He doesn't care about you, any more than he cares about me. He cares about himself, and what he can get out of any of you, at any given time."

I know the cameras are on, but screw the cameras. If I'm going out, I'm saying my piece. Maybe some people watching will believe me. *Someone's* got to.

The girls gape at me, speechless, and Perrie grabs my arm. "What happened?" she presses.

"Not now," I say. "I'll explain after, but not now. Can you please just go talk to Jordy? I'll be fine. I just . . . want to be alone for a second."

Perrie hesitates, her brow drawn together, but then, finally, she nods and leaves. The camera stays on me for a bit, but when it becomes clear I'm not going to start throwing chairs in the pool or screaming about men and their stupid faces, I'm left in peace. I make a beeline for the wineglasses with the intention of trying to choke one down, sour swamp water or not, only to find a tray of Jell-O shots lined up.

Oh, hell yes. This is much more my speed.

I suck one down, and grimace. There's so much alcohol in these it tastes a little like nail polish remover. But, you know, nail polish remover with a pleasant fruity aftertaste, at least. I do another, and another, until I have a whole collection of empty plastic shot glasses on the table in front of me. I have no idea how many drinks this is, and I don't especially care. I am *calm*, I am *professional*, and I am going to get so shitfaced off Jell-O I won't remember a second of this cursed night.

I grab a couple shots for the road, then, with absolutely zero urge to join the love seat crew without Perrie there, but no one else to talk to, I walk with purpose across the garden and find a spot where the trees and bushes more or less hide me from the eyes of the others while I knock back another shot. When I lower the cup, I catch sight of a camera operator across the garden, his camera fixed right on me.

Turns out the only thing worse than being the rejected

loser no one wants to talk to at the party is being rejected *on camera,* to be streamed to millions.

My instincts take over, and I jump back into the trees. If I can't see the camera, it can't see me, right? I hide in there for what feels like a lifetime, but is probably only a few minutes, picking at the Jell-O in the remaining shot until I work up enough bravery to go back out. I half expect the operator to be waiting for me, so he can film me meekly reemerging from the bushes with an empty shot glass for the kids watching at home, but thankfully he's wandered off by now.

I head closer to the fairy-lit gazebo to check if Jordy has released Perrie yet. To my dismay, I can still make her out in his clutches. Figuratively, sure, but it is *still distressing.* I'm tempted to charge over there and make up an excuse to rescue her from the conversation. The only thing that stops me is the small chance that Perrie might actually be enjoying her talk with Jordy. I mean, I can't relate, but that doesn't mean it's impossible. And if she is, I'll only ruin her night.

I hesitate, not totally sure where to go, and that's when I hear my name murmured. I creep closer to the hedges, and tune in to a conversation between two of the producers I don't know the names of yet.

". . . Gwendolyn will be disappointed, though," the first woman is saying. "I think she saw her as a front-runner. They were together for a while."

"And Isaac will be *pissed* to be the first to lose a girl," says the other.

"Yeah, but he'll have the Canadian still. The really pretty one. Jordy's got his eye on her."

I've heard enough. I wrench myself away, tears pricking at my eyes, and my heart starts thudding against my chest like it's trying to tear its way out so it can't be hurt anymore. So,

Skye is the pretty one that Jordy still has feelings for. I'm the ugly, leftover reject who's being sent home first.

I don't even freaking care that Jordy has chosen Skye over me again, but also I *do* still care, and maybe it's because I wanted my plan to work, and maybe it's because I don't want to be sent home first and have thousands of strangers think I'm unlovable. Or maybe it's just that I'd finally been regaining my self-confidence before this show appeared, and being rejected again rips that confidence away from me and replaces it with generous goddamn helpings of self-doubt and hurt.

Fuck, this *hurts*. He wasn't supposed to be able to hurt me anymore. I wasn't supposed to let him. I don't want to feel this sadness. This *ache*. Aching is too hard to fix. It can't be channeled. You just have to put up with it.

So, instead, I choose anger. Anger can be channeled, and relieved. Anger makes me stronger. Anger builds my defenses, so it doesn't matter if a producer thinks I'm not pretty, or Jordy thinks I'm not worth his time, or the other girls think I'm in the wrong to be mad at Skye. Anger is power, and control.

And I know exactly what I want to do with it.

NINE

Maya

I scan the garden like a hunter until I finally spot Isaac, speaking to Grayson under a glittering tree.

"Isaac," I say, closing in on him.

Grayson backs away to give us space, and Isaac gives me a wary look. "Hi, Maya. What's up?"

"Two things. One, I'm so sorry, but I've ruined your Phuket plans. You have to invest in Skye, but, who knows, she could win Jordy away from the others—she's good at that. You might still go. I hope you take lots of pictures if you do. I'll like them on Instagram, okay?"

He glances around us, and offers a perplexed smile. "What's the second thing?"

"I wanna go on camera. Can I? Is that a thing we can do?"

He takes me by the arm and steers me to a garden bench to sit. "You . . . *can*, technically. But in the interests of maximizing Phuket, I'd like to know what you want to say."

"I'm not gonna get you to Phuket, Isaac."

"Well, let's reserve judgment on that until Jordy's made his announcement. Did something happen?"

The floor is starting to shift like my actual body is somehow zooming in and out. Is this a Jell-O shot thing? Or just a general alcohol thing? "Jordy's actually not a good guy, Isaac. He acts like he is, but he *really* isn't. And I'm not just saying that because he's sending me home. Did you know he cheated on me?"

Isaac shakes his head. "Unless you mean tonight, which doesn't technically count, because you *did* agree to this."

"No, I mean the two months he was seeing Skye while he was still my boyfriend."

Isaac's eyes widen. "Oh." Then, they go even bigger as it seems to click. "*Oh.*"

"Yeah. And I am going to tell everybody. The whole world. They need to *know.* And you can't stop me." I get unsteadily to my feet, then look back at Isaac. "Well, you probably can, I guess. But please *don't.* You're not a feminist if you stop me. Ha. Got you there."

"I'm not going to forbid you," Isaac says. "But can I make a case for *not* doing that, first?"

"I will only ignore it."

"That's your right. Now, I hear you. Seems like Jordy's scum. He deserves to be exposed, sure. But he's attached to the royal family, and they have a lot of power over the media here. I don't know all the details, but I can tell you that conversations happened behind the scenes before Jordy signed on to the show. There's an editing agreement in place."

"What's an editing agreement?" I ask, sitting back down reluctantly.

"Essentially, they would've *absolutely* agreed not to trash Jordy on the show. So, by all means, you can go ham on the confessional, but I'm sorry to tell you ninety percent of what you have to say won't make it into the episode."

"But . . ." I grapple for a reason to doubt him. "But it's good TV."

"Yeah. But they'll get their asses sued. And knowing the

royal family, even if they *did* air it, you'd end up with a defamation lawsuit in front of a bought-off judge. Nah. What they *will* do, Maya, is take what you say, chop it up, and reorder it so you sound like you're a jealous, mean, petty ex-girlfriend out to destroy his life. And that's *great* TV."

I straighten. "Is that a threat?"

He places a hand on my shoulder. "I'm not threatening you; I am *warning* you. At my own risk, honestly, because Gwendolyn would *much* prefer you gave her plenty of villain material. She'd kill me for telling you this at all."

"So, why are you telling me?"

He grins. "Villains don't win shows like this, and I haven't given up on Phuket yet."

Well, whatever Isaac says, he wasn't there to watch Jordy's vibe transition from "it's been way too long" to "I'm being forced to hang out with my homophobic great-uncle while my parents go to the grocery store." I'm going home tomorrow. Without a doubt. And now, apparently, I can't even expose Jordy before I'm kicked off without either being villainized or sued by a probably corrupt monarchy. I can't warn the other girls, except maybe Perrie, because they think I'm a bitch, and maybe I was a bitch, but *so were they*. Not that it matters who was right anymore, anyway. All that matters is who gets to write the public narrative.

And, once again, that someone is not going to be me.

There's no way to win this. I've been checkmated on night one.

"So, what do I do now?" I ask Isaac.

He gets up and pulls me to my feet with him. "You're in a ball gown, at a mansion, with unlimited alcohol, and some really awesome girls to hang out with. How about you wash your face, grab a drink, and make the most of the night while you can?"

I run a fist under my eyes and nod.

He's right. I'm going down either way, and I'm not going down in a blaze of fire. So, a haze of vodka will have to do.

After a trip to the bathroom to clean up, I make a beeline for Perrie, who's sitting alone. Not too far from her, Kim and Francesca are having what seems to be a very serious conversation, the camera crew hovering right beside them.

"Hey," Perrie says. "I was looking for you. Where've you been?"

"Bonding with my producer. I found Jell-O shots. Do you wanna do some Jell-O shots?"

Perrie raises her eyebrows as I pull her up. "How many Jell-O shots have *you* had, exactly?"

"Shots, shots, shots, shots!" I chant, which is a close enough answer in itself.

Even better, they've refilled the whole tray and cleared the evidence of my shame. The flavor is lime now, too, just to mix things up, you know, keeping shit fresh, keeping us motivated to drink. And drink, and drink, so they can film us falling over and yelling about drama and other stuff, but I won't do that, because I am *smart* and I am *onto them* and I will not be coerced. They will not take me down with Jell-O shots. Not tonight! Not any night!

Perrie tries one, and widens her eyes at me. "Oh, damn, these are *good.*"

"Yes. They're very, very good. And wine is awful. Jell-O, good. Old grapes, bad."

"Wine," Perrie explains after another shot, "is one of those things that tastes different if you beat your taste buds into submission with it over and over again."

"But why? Why go through that torture when you can just do Jell-O shots?"

"Because Jell-O shots aren't always appropriate, I guess. Like, what if you're eating a meal with the royal family?"

"Jell-O shots at the table. Jell-O shots for the queen!" I slam my empty glass down for emphasis, and Perrie holds hers up in a cheers. I pick up another, because pacing is for chumps and I am a chaos gremlin. "Did you like seeing Jordy?"

"It was okay, I guess. He's sort of a stranger these days, though. Plus, he did all that stuff to you, which is kind of hard to push past."

"Thank you for *believing* me!" I say, banging my forehead against her shoulder.

"Is that not normal?"

"No," I say to the floor, leaving my head where it was. "It is not normal. I'm *anguished.*"

"Anguished, huh?"

"Also, I don't think Jordy wants me here at all. I heard the producers say I'm getting sent home tomorrow."

Perrie pulls me upright so she can look at me in horror. "*What?* Oh no!"

Before I can tell her my tale of woe, Skye wanders in. *Fuck.* Not *Skye.* I freaking *hate* Skye. The *wooooorst.*

"I heard there were shots," she says awkwardly.

"There are no shots," I say.

"Maya, she can see the shots," Perrie says.

I shuffle sideways to stand in front of the table and spread my arms out. "Nope."

"Oh, good, you've decided to be mature about things." Skye scowls at me as she approaches.

I stay in front of the table. "I didn't mean I'd be mature to *you.* And no, I'm not immature, *you're* immature. I'm just real."

"Let me get to the shots," Skye says.

"What shots?"

"Oh my god." She looks to Perrie, who shrugs. "Okay, we're doing this."

"What shots? What shots? Wha— *You aren't allowed to touch me, this is a workplace.*"

Skye wraps her arms around me and moves me to the side so she can get to the table. "Help!" I yell. "HELP!"

"Maya, shh," Perrie urges. But it's too late. The cameras have found us. They have found us, and they are running in to record everything and . . . oh, wait, they're gonna record everything. That's *good*. Ha.

"*Ow*," I moan, rubbing my arm for the camera. "She attacked me."

"Oh, come on, I barely touched you," Skye says, shaking her head as she collects some shots.

"She just came for me out of nowhere," I tell the operator, who's still filming me. "Like a jaguar in the night!"

"Somehow, you will recover," Skye says over her shoulder as she pushes past us. "I have unwavering faith in you."

"*Shut up*," I call after her. "Just . . . shut up, okay?"

The camera operator ducks her head around the side to look at me. "What happened just now, Maya? Why were you screaming? Use names."

"Probably better not," Perrie whispers, but she doesn't understand. I need the world to know the truth about *something*, at least, and if I can't tell the truth about Jordy, I can tell the truth about this. There will be justice.

"There I was," I say, "standing at the table, when *Skye Kaplan* burst in like a . . . like a jaguar!"

"You're sticking with that descriptor, then?" Perrie asks, and the operator shushes her with her hands.

"And she demanded access to the shots! Before I could react, *bam*, she pounced on me like a . . ."

"Jaguar?" the camera operator offers.

"No, like a bitch."

"*Okay*," Perrie says, steering me by the shoulders. "They get the gist, I think. I wanna show you something outside."

When we get outside, there is nothing. She has nothing to show me.

The betrayal grows and grows.

"You cut me off for nothing." I scowl. "I was telling them all about Skye!"

"You'll thank me for it tomorrow, I promise."

Nearby, Jordy is chatting with the love seat girls—who are now all holding shots—while the rest of the camera crew hovers nearby. As soon as he sees me, something changes for the worse. For the way, way worse. I feel like I'm staring into the barrel of a sniper.

Crapcrapcrapcrap—

"Maya!" he calls. "Could I grab you for a minute?"

"Don't make me go," I whisper to Perrie.

"Just say no."

"He's coming this way."

"*Just say no.*"

"I can't just say no, the royal family will chop off my head."

"*What?*"

"Hi, Jordy," I say as he gets within earshot. "What's up?"

"Walk with me."

The camera operator follows us as Jordy leads me to the bushes. Oh, this isn't ominous at all.

"I actually wanted to touch base," he says. "I've been speaking with some of the girls tonight, and they had some concerns."

Yeah, I bet they did. "Oh, really?"

"Yes. They said . . . well, they said you haven't had the nicest things to say about me, honestly. And I was . . . I'll admit, I was surprised to hear that. I thought we'd been getting along really well? I couldn't figure out why you would be saying nasty things about me. I didn't want to believe it, but then when I heard it from more than one girl, I figured it has to be true."

He looks at me.

I look at him.

He circles a hand in the air, and I blink. "Sorry, what was the question?"

Jordy's eyes flash with something unpleasant. So fast the camera probably misses it. Then he goes from furious to patronizing. "I guess I was wondering if you're feeling jealous? It's the only thing I can think of, considering how well we've been getting along."

I suck a deep breath in. *Think of the cameras. Think of the cameras. You will not be beheaded tonight.*

Is that even how royals settle disputes still? I'm not actually sure how they do things in Chalonne. And I can't google it, so, who's to say? "Okay, Jordy."

"No, don't get upset," Jordy says hurriedly.

"I'm not upset."

"Well, but you are," he says, putting a hand on my shoulder. I try to shake him off, but he presses harder. "And I want you to know that I'm not angry. I understand. But you don't have to be jealous, Maya. I don't want this jealousy to come between us like it did last time."

"Oh, is that what came between us?" I snap.

"Yes."

"My overwhelming, irrational jealousy?"

"Yes."

"Uh-huh. Don't worry, Jordy, I'm not jealous. In fact, I will not talk about you for the rest of the night. Perrie and I have better things to do than to talk about you."

"I saw you've clicked with Perrie. She's great, huh?"

"Actually, yes. You have excellent taste." I poke him aggressively in the chest on the word *excellent*. I'm not sure if it's meant as a compliment or not anymore. Everything's confusing.

"Do we have the same taste in girls?" he asks, biting his lip suggestively.

Haaaaaaah, this asshole is pushing it. I am going to ignore the bi dig, because I am too mature for this bullshit. Sometimes. "I am being as honest as I *possibly* can right now. I am completely uninterested in what you do with the other girls, Jordy."

"Is that so?"

"It's what we're all here for, right? 'Fuck Monogamy: The Reality Show'?" I ask.

All of a sudden, Jordy doesn't look so pissed off anymore. He . . . looks like he's enjoying himself. And not in an "I love to watch you suffer" sort of way. "You're giving me sass," he says slowly.

"I am just. Telling. The truth."

He takes a step closer, placing himself right in my space. "Uh-huh," he says, dropping his voice down low. "Well, as it happens, I've missed you telling it like it is."

The camera lens zooms in. I glance at it, distracted, and that, plus being kinda sorta drunk, I guess, makes me realize way too late that Jordy is leaning in to kiss me. I jump back just in time, and he misses. He widens his eyes, shocked and indignant.

"No?" he asks, glancing at the camera. I know what he must be thinking, but he doesn't have to worry. The only way this is making it into the show is if they can cut it in a way that makes me look evil for pulling back. Stress less, Jordy Miller, your ego is safe.

"Sorry," I say. "I'm feeling kind of sick. How about a hug?"

"A hug I can do," he says.

He pulls me in close, blocking my lips from the camera's view with his head, and that's when I whisper, "Honestly? You can try every day for the next seven weeks if you want, but I am *never* going to kiss you again. You are a pathetic asshole, and you will be doing me the biggest favor of my life when I leave tomorrow."

He stiffens as I speak, then we pull apart with identical, false smiles. "Honestly?" he says, in the same way I said it. "I'm glad we had this talk. It's been illuminating."

"That's great," I say, picturing him dying in a fire.

"You have changed," he says, tipping his head to one side and nodding. "And I think that might be a good thing."

It's . . . not *exactly* what I expected him to say. I stand wordlessly, trying to figure out if I misheard him, and he smirks and saunters off. Only moments later, Perrie comes to find me. "Hey," she says. "The producers said we're wrapping up. We can take these *heels* off."

"Oh, thank god, thank Jesus, thank Christ." I sigh, unbuckling my straps where I stand while holding onto Perrie for balance. The grass is cool and soothing under my bare feet.

"See, this is why we need to normalize sneakers as formal wear," Perrie says as I remove the other shoe. "Anyway, what did Jordy say to you?"

"Nothing interesting."

"So, it's a secret?"

"No." I grunt as I straighten. "I mean it was nothing interesting. He just said he heard I've been trash-talking him."

"Oh my god, of course they told him. Great use of the girl code, everyone. What did you say?"

"Not much. I mean, I *was* trash-talking him, so."

Perrie giggles. "Well, yeah, but he doesn't need to know that."

"He is shit, Perrie," I say. "A heaping pile of shit. And the sooner he learns that about himself, the better the world will be."

"Okay, Miss I'm-Gonna-Drink-Half-the-Bar-and-Spill-the-Tea. I think it's bedtime for both of us."

"I wish *you* were my roommate. Can you swap with yucky Skye?"

"I would if I could, sweetie."

By the time we're assisted in undressing and removing the mic-packs, it's approximately holy-shit-it's-*how*-late o'clock. Skye goes to the bathroom to take her makeup off before bed, which gives me a few minutes alone with my iPad.

I send a message to Mom: Wish you where hghn

Rosie: I love you I love you Jordy id a ducking duckface I MEANT FUCK I sdai what I said pgpne

And Olivia: I made a friend and you wkulf love her we are all fgoing to meet up one day and you will love her soooooooooioioik ,much

I'm just stashing my iPad back in my jeans when the door creaks open, and I slam the drawer shut and whirl around.

Skye, who's changed into a baggy old T-shirt and shorts, stares at me. "What?"

"What?" I ask. "Stop *looking* at me. Why are you always *looking* at me?"

"Because you're always *there*," she snaps, climbing the bunk bed. "To my unending disappointment."

"Yeah, well, it's *my* . . . unending disappointment . . . to be stuck with you, too," I shoot back.

Nailed it. Devastating blow. She'll regret verbally sparring with *me* tomorrow.

I turn off the light and climb into bed. For good measure, I add, "You should just be quiet, and stay out of my way."

"I didn't say anything."

"Good. Keep it that way."

"I'm *trying,* but you keep talking to me."

Damn it, she's good.

"Whatever," I say. "Good night." Shit, that was automatic. "Not. Not good night. I hope your night sucks."

"I hope your night's great, because it'll be your last one here. Everyone knows you're going home tomorrow. Jordy basically admitted it."

I blink through the darkness and suck on my lips. "Good," I mutter. "I don't wanna spend a minute around all of you, anyway."

"Good."

"Good."

"Good."

I don't want her to have the last word, but I don't have the energy to keep this going. As quietly as I can, I whisper "good," and she doesn't reply, so, technically, I win.

With that out of the way, I'm finally able to fall asleep.

TEN

Maya

I'm wrenched from unconsciousness into the land of the living by "Get Ready" blasting at around one billion decibels.

Gasping, I shoot up and look around for the source, only to regret it as bowling balls roll from one end of my skull to the other, slamming against the sides. I clutch at my head to hold it steady and yelp in pain.

"Oh, you're up," Skye yells over the music. "Good."

Then, through the haze of agony, I piece together what's happening. Skye's perched on her bunk playing music through a portable speaker. Sunlight is forcing its way around the cracks between the curtains and the wall, and something about the intensity of it, and the heat of the room, tells me this isn't crack-of-dawn sunlight. What we're dealing with is closer to lunchtime sunlight. Which means I'm running just *so* freaking behind schedule, considering filming starts, oh, *immediately after lunch.*

This is fine, great, fine. Great.

Then, the events of last night hit me. Gelatin. So much gelatin. Lime, raspberry, blueberry . . . arguing with the girls, snapping at Jordy, and I'm pretty sure at one point I did an interview about Skye being a wild animal?

Shiiiiit.

I go to reach for my phone before remembering I don't have it. Seriously, how did people survive the nineties? "What's the time?" I mumble through the cloud of pain.

"Oh, you want to know the *time*?" Skye asks, bouncing on the top bunk so the whole bed rocks violently back and forth. She is one thousand fucking percent doing that on purpose.

"Yes," I hiss through my teeth.

"This almost feels like a conversation. But I thought I was supposed to go talk to the others if I want to talk to someone?"

I grit my teeth and close my eyes against the too-bright light. "You're really not going to tell me the time?"

"I would definitely tell you the time, Maya. Definitely. But, you're awful. So." She gives the bed another shake, which I think is taking it a bit too far, and hops to the ground. I open my eyes a crack and see she's already fully dressed in shorts and a flannel shirt. Not a great sign. She catches me looking, and gives me a shit-eating grin. "I sincerely hope you finish nailing your coffin today. You talk in your sleep. Loudly. I'd *really* like to have my own room tonight."

I give her the finger and pull the blanket over my head so I can let my eyes adjust to being open without my head splitting in half. Weren't we supposed to get a wake-up knock hours ago? Did they forget us, or did I just sleep straight through it?

Keeping a hand on my head, and my neck as stiff as possible, I force myself out of bed and into the dress-and-boots combo I had the genius idea of planning yesterday afternoon. I could kiss past-me, if I wasn't so annoyed with her for getting this wasted last night. I am humiliated, and I am sore, and that is about the worst combination I can think of.

Woe is me. Woe is I.

About ten gallons of water and two Advil later, I'm ready

to shuffle into the hallway and find out how late it really is. Perrie's door is open, thank god, and both she and her roommate, Francesca, are still inside. They're both dressed, but neither of them have touched their hair or makeup from the looks of things. Which either means both girls are being weirdly chill about how they'll look on camera today, or it actually isn't as late as I'd worried.

"You look like shit," Francesca greets me without even faking a smile.

I ignore her. "Do you know what time it is?" I ask Perrie. She points to the digital alarm clock she has plugged in on her desk—why didn't I think to bring a relic like that along with me?—and I discover to my great relief it's only ten thirty.

"Awesome," I say, and promptly curl up in a ball in the middle of the carpet, ducking my head to block out the light. Oh, sweet relief.

"You can't sleep in here," Francesca says. "Why's she sleeping on our rug?"

"Have you taken any painkillers, sweetie?" Perrie asks. Her voice is close. She must have kneeled down beside me.

"Yes," I say in a small voice.

"Okay. You'll perk up. We're gonna start getting ready soon. Guess we'll put you down for the second shift in the bathroom?"

I try to reply with a yes, but it comes out as more of a strangled groan of unimaginable suffering.

"Noted."

There's a long silence. Long enough I think maybe I've been left alone in the room, and I realize with fascination I'm so tired I can hear my own eyeballs. Then, Francesca breaks the silence by stage-whispering, "She's not leaving."

I peek up, glare at her, then return to my facedown fetal position.

"I think you might need to let her ride this one out," Perrie says diplomatically.

If I survive this hangover, I am going to make it my life's mission to ensure that girl gets nothing but rainbows and happiness for the rest of her goddamn life.

ELEVEN

Skye

After a rushed lunch of *mas chaux*—a sort of Chalonian sandwich made of processed turkey loaf, ham, and mayonnaise, of all things—we gather at the Kool-Aid lake to start filming. Up close, the lake is even more impressive than it'd looked from the car. It seems to stretch on forever, only ending in the distance where it hits towering, snowcapped mountains.

I'm actually feeling wonderful today. Last night was incredible, if you ignore the drama Maya insisted on starting, which I'm choosing to because I am mature, unlike *some people*. Truly, though, she's been taking the "you stole my man" schtick *a lot* further than I expected her to. I'm just glad Jordy had the good sense to warn me before she had the chance to accuse me of cheating in front of the group. If I'd been caught off guard, who knows how I might have reacted. I might have even believed her. She *does* seem awfully sure of herself.

Regardless, I'm not here for Maya, so I'm not going to give her a second's more thought. I'm here for Jordy, and that's what I'm focusing on today.

Speaking with Jordy last night, and breathing him in, and hearing his voice, and having him brush my hair behind my ear, set off something visceral. It reminds me somewhat of when I first arrived in London and a group of us played a drinking game in the hostel and I got far too drunk on coconut rum, then the smell of coconut started making me dry heave because it reminded me of the time I almost died. Similar, but, I suppose, the positive version? Smelling Jordy last night made my head spin because it reminded me of the time I almost fell in love.

"Today, we're going back to the beginning of the ouroboros," Gwendolyn says. She's wearing another suit, although today's is indigo. It doesn't get especially hot in Chalonne—particularly near the mountains—but it's still summer, and today is in the high seventies. If it weren't for the beads of sweat on her upper lip, I would've wondered if this woman can feel the heat at all.

"An ouroboros doesn't have a beginning," Francesca mutters. She's sprawled on a picnic rug beside me, wearing a sundress and a scowl.

"What's that, Francesca?" Gwendolyn asks.

Francesca straightens and raises her voice without hesitation. "It's infinite. That's the point."

"Yes, but we are living infinity as we speak. Today, we are revisiting where our infinities began."

"That doesn't mean anything," Francesca says. "That literally means nothing. You're making it up."

"The beginning of the ouroboros," Gwendolyn says over her, "in your case, was the day you and Jordy met."

"It's like the universe," Francesca whispers fiercely to me, Kim, and Lauren. "Like time itself. It never had a beginning; it couldn't have."

"The beginning was the big bang," Lauren whispers back.

"But what caused the big bang?" Francesca presses. "If there were particles to collide, there was *something*. So, time existed already."

Lauren and Kim look distinctly green at the thought. In their defense, it's quite early in the day to be pondering the sweeping vastness of the universe against the insignificant speck of our existence, nestled somewhere between never and forever, to be ultimately forgotten in the whisper of time. We've only *just* finished lunch.

"You're recounting how you met," Gwendolyn almost shouts. "We can't wait to hear all your marvelous fables."

"You want us to lie?" Maya asks from her spot a few feet away, where she's lounging on her own blanket with Perrie. Francesca breaks into a sudden coughing fit that sounds suspiciously like laughter.

Gwendolyn looks confused. "What? No. Fables. Like your stories. Your tales."

"I don't think—" Maya starts, but Gwendolyn cuts her off.

"And let's get started!" She claps, and the crew springs into motion.

Immediately, Isaac heads to Maya. "You two are up first," he says, looking between her and me.

He leads us to a tree with a stone bench beneath it. The camera crew is finishing their setup, surrounding the bench with softboxes, reflectors, and microphones.

It looks as though Maya's recovered from her hangover, more or less. She's perky, vibrant, and studying me venomously with renewed vigor. It's quite amazing what some water and food can do for a girl's constitution.

"Okay, Skye, let's film you first," Isaac says. Several crew members rush in to help me sit on the bench—because apparently that's less intuitive than you'd think—and, when I'm perfectly lit and sitting at an angle that twists my back but makes my nose look "*much straighter*" (according to Isaac, anyway), Jordy locks eyes with me and approaches to sit by my side.

"Hey," he whispers. "You look great."

I'm wearing a faded flannel shirt that seemed much nicer two months ago when I packed it, over a cropped cami. I'm fairly sure it was *not* what Gwendolyn had in mind when she asked us to dress "casually gorgeous" today, but that's on her for giving us such a subjective direction, as far as I'm concerned. But still, the compliment makes me relax into a grudging smile.

"Okay," Isaac says, stepping forward. "Jordy, you know the drill. Skye, what we're gonna do is, I'm gonna ask you some questions, and you just answer them by including the question in your answer. So, if I say what's your favorite color, you say, 'My favorite color is blue.' Got it?"

"Got it," I say. "Although, does it matter that my favorite color is peach?"

"Not as much as you'd hope," Isaac says with a sweet smile, before he straightens and steps back behind the camera's line of sight, beside Gwendolyn. "Okay, here we go. So, Skye, when did Jordy and you meet?"

"I met Jordy October twenty-ninth, the year before last."

Isaac starts, then laughs. "But who's counting?"

Jordy bumps his shoulder against mine, giving me a fond smile. I fumble, my cheeks heating. "I'm not . . . it's not like that. It's easy to remember because it was right before Halloween. It was a Halloween party."

"So, you met at a Halloween party? Tell us about that."

I clear my throat. Wait, what if I cough on camera, and they keep it in, and I end up immortalized forever, red-faced and spluttering? *Don't cough, don't cough, don't*—"Jordy had just come to town, and he didn't know an awful lot of people, but he knew a friend of mine. So, during the party, this guy I've never seen before suddenly starts standing with our group, and he's dressed like a celebrity's corpse."

"I was a zombie Nicholas Thibault!" Jordy says indignantly. "Because he was in all those horror movies when he was alive? It was ironic."

"No, trust me, I get the joke, Jordy. It was just *such* poor taste, and he'd *just* passed away. Anyway, I was absolutely not going to speak to him because of the costume, but our mutual friend disappeared, and Jordy was all alone. I felt bad for him, so I let him talk to me—"

"Very generous," Jordy adds.

"You were a *real person's corpse*, Jordy. And I told him I hated his costume, so he found someone with a mad scientist coat, and *paid him* to take it so he could put it over the outfit, then he wiped off all the makeup, and I realized he was actually good-looking. I have a weakness for uniforms, though, so that could've come into play."

Isaac is in silent fits at this. My eyes trail past him and fall on Maya, who's sitting on the grass and watching us. Her face is a storm cloud. I tear my gaze away.

Gwendolyn's smile is strained. "Oh, that's . . . cute! I'm just worried about . . . we want this to spark *positive* discussion. It might be less . . . controversial, if we were to change up the details a little. Like, what if . . . oh! What if you both wore masks? Masks are very romantic."

"Like . . . our costumes had masks?" I ask.

"Yes! Or maybe it was a masquerade party, instead of a Halloween one. Have a play with it, see what you can come up with."

I flounder. What does she mean? How am I supposed to make up a story that didn't happen? I can't think on my feet like this. If we'd had notice, possibly, but now?

Jordy nudges his knee against mine. "I can take this one, if you want," he whispers, and I give him a relieved nod.

He turns to the camera and switches on his charm

offensive. "I met Skye two years ago, at a Halloween party. It was one of those masked parties, where no one really knows who anyone else is. We had a mutual friend, and I was new in town, so he introduced me to Skye, but I had no idea how beautiful she was. So, you can believe me when I say that it was her personality that made me fall for her. And I fell fast." He laughs. "Super-fast. Then, we went out into the yard for some air, and she took her mask off and I got a look at her face, and I was just . . . stunned. Like, awestruck. And I remember thinking to myself, oh my god, I cannot leave this party without kissing this girl. And I didn't."

He says it without even pausing, or stumbling, as though it's what actually happened. In reality, we didn't even kiss that night. He got my number through our friend and texted me a few days later to ask me out. But hearing Jordy talk like this, I almost believe in the masked party. That we kissed in the moonlight, masks hanging by our sides.

Something uneasy pulls at the pit of my stomach. Only for a flash, though.

"Wow, Jordy," I say with a dry laugh. "That lie came almost concerningly easy to you."

Jordy looks as though he considers this a compliment. "I'm used to cameras. When journalists and paparazzi ask me about Sam, or the palace or whatever, I have to make shit up sometimes. To keep everyone safe. I swear, I use my powers for good."

"Hmm." I raise my eyebrows teasingly. "You'd better."

After a few more questions, it's time for me to swap places with Maya.

"How romantic," she says, with a smile as sweet as an arsenic-laced gumdrop. "I especially loved the part where you compromised your morals by making out with a guy you thought was problematic."

I choose not to dignify this with a response, and glide past her to settle on the still-warm patch of grass she left behind.

"Jordy and I met two years and three months ago," Maya says to the camera. "And I *am* counting." Her eyes flicker to me before she goes on. It occurs to me that she seems more consumed with her dislike of me than any apparent fondness for Jordy. "When my softball team played against his sister's. Princess Samantha. He was in the crowd watching her. I rolled my ankle and spent the rest of the game on the bench, and he sat next to me to keep me company. Then every Saturday after that he was always, like . . . *there*. Watching my games instead of his sister's, and making a point to congratulate me after every one, until I realized seeing him was the thing I most looked forward to each weekend. A month after we met, he got up the nerve to ask me out, I guess, and we dated for *nine months*."

She looks at me again, and I stare right back at her pointedly.

"And Jordy, what did you think of Maya?" Isaac asks.

Jordy glances at me, then Maya. I suppose this is fairly awkward for him, gushing about us in front of each other. But it *is* what he signed up for, just as the rest of us signed up to date him alongside five other girls.

"She was special. She had this packed schedule, but she balanced it all, and she seemed to be good at everything she ever tried. I remember thinking, 'No way would a chick like this ever give me a second look.' Then she did, and it was like . . . wow, this girl who has her eyes on the prize, and has no free time, is willing to put me on that list of stuff to do. That must mean I'm worthwhile."

I don't know how to feel about that comment. I wish I weren't listening to this, suddenly. It was one thing to know, on some level, that part of this experience would necessarily involve Jordy discussing his other romances, and, potentially, rekindling some of those romances right in front of me. But knowing it and living it are two very different things.

That, and, I suppose, a part of me had been certain Jordy felt differently about me, in particular, from the way he spoke to me on the phone.

Could that have been an act? Or am I paranoid for assuming he was lying to me, just because he has the audacity to recount a romance that happened before he even met me?

Now that I think about it like that, it's fairly clear I need to get ahold of myself if I don't want to become an irrational, jealous, reality-show stereotype.

Maya listens to Jordy's story with an unimpressed expression, giving him a thin smile. So, even he's not spared from her attitude.

I'm not entirely sure why she's here at all, if I'm honest.

After their interview, Maya heads directly over to me. She has a way of walking that's closer to floating. It's something in the way she carries herself. I stand to meet her, and she cocks her head to one side. "Do you think the people watching at home can do basic math?" she asks.

It takes me a moment to realize what she means. The nine months she referred to must include the period of time when Jordy was in Canada, with me, and Maya was under the delusion he was still her boyfriend. Day two, and she's already lying to the camera in the hopes that people will call me a homewrecker? So much for not bothering me if I don't bother her. "Grow up, Maya," I say, and she pushes past me to go back to Perrie.

"How'd you go?" Francesca asks as I rejoin her, taking the place of Lauren and Kim.

"They made me change my story so it became a masquerade party, for some reason."

"Truth," Francesca says, "is a lot less romantic than *fables.*"

As they work through filming the rest of the interviews, my group fills the endless hours with small talk and champagne. I wouldn't have expected six interviews to take hours, but between retakes, and shuffling around the lighting as the sun moved, and water breaks and food breaks, we move through things about as fast as a sloth sprinting across a major highway.

As the sun drops lower in the sky, I shuffle around to see what Jordy's doing. Perhaps naively, I'd thought I would be spending more time with him than this, at least on filming days.

Right now, he's by the shore, being filmed as he stares wistfully into its depths. The ambient light starts to take on an orange glow, and, suddenly, on what looks to be Gwendolyn's instruction, he unbuttons his shirt and starts walking to the camera with his six-pack bared.

Someone makes a strangled noise behind me, and I turn around in alarm, only to find out it's Maya, who's enacting a pantomime of gagging.

"She's going home tonight, right?" Kim whispers, a little desperately.

The rest of us nod in unison.

Still unbuttoned, Jordy and his abs walk up the hill and straight to the blankets, holding a full glass of champagne. He offers it to me, as the camera crew surrounds us. "Hey," he says. "Wanna go for a walk?"

The first thing I do is look to the other girls. Even if we did sign up for this, there's an air of awkwardness. The girls give me strained smiles that look a little too thrilled to be sincere. With an apologetic smile, I accept the champagne and join Jordy for a romantic walk. Just us and the lake and Gwendolyn and Isaac and the camera crew.

"Skye, something you said last night has been on my mind," Jordy says as we walk.

"Hold on, hold on," Gwendolyn yells. "Hold that thought."

We freeze in place as a makeup artist sprints over and applies what looks like oil over Jordy's bare chest. Gwendolyn looks through the camera and whispers something to the operator.

Jordy looks down and frowns. "Maybe a little bit more on the bottom left," he says, and the artist obliges. "Perfect."

"You're glistening." Gwendolyn beams.

"You look like a model," the operator says.

"You look like a vampire," I say lightly, because I think honesty is important in a budding relationship redo.

"Aww, thanks, Skye. Just be careful if you touch them, it's a bit sticky."

"I will keep that in mind if I'm overcome with the urge to caress your bare stomach. So, uh, you were saying something about last night?"

Walking backward, Gwendolyn mimes sticking her chest out. Jordy copies her. The new pose transforms him from a glistening, oiled-up, shirtless guy to a glistening, oiled-up, shirtless guy who's walking like Tarzan.

"Well," he says. "I get the whole 'traveling Europe' and 'living in London' thing. But why are you going alone? Isn't it kind of dangerous for a chick to be by herself?"

He sounds like my dad did for the past six months. "I'm fine," I say, my tone icy.

"No, I don't mean it like that. I mean it in a feminist way. Like, girls are always talking about how they can't travel alone. I'm just wondering why you didn't bring Chloe or someone, at least for the traveling-around part?"

I shrug, then hold onto the hem of my shirt. "I like being alone, remember? I don't need to worry about what someone else wants to do, or see. I'm not on anyone else's schedule.

This way, I make the plans I want to make, and the only time it gets changed is if I decide to. I recommend it. It's been the best eight weeks of my life."

"You haven't been lonely?"

"I'm surrounded by dozens of outgoing strangers every day. How could I be lonely?"

Jordy lets out a peal of laughter. "Oh, man, that's the most Skye thing I've ever heard."

"What do you mean?"

"Nothing. Just, I always loved that about you. You aren't the 'let's make each other our entire worlds and sew our hearts together' type. You're like, 'Yeah, cool, I like you, I guess, but I don't need you, I'm going to go have fun, woo, bye.'"

I start. "Am I like that?"

"One thousand percent, but it's a good thing. A really, really good thing, trust me. You're fun, you're not intense or clingy, you're . . ." He pauses. "You're the dream girl."

I catch Isaac nodding to the camera, the corners of his eyes crinkling. Not to be cynical, but that *did* sound a little like a cheesy line designed for a trailer pull, and Isaac's reaction confirmed it. Where did the Jordy from the phone go? That's who I came here to meet. Not the guy who walks shirtless along the lake's edge while he thinks up canned pickup lines to use on me and the five other girls here.

"I thought you were looking for someone to be by your side for the future, et cetera," I say. "Now you're telling me you want someone noncommittal?"

"I want to be with someone who has her own life, so I can live mine without guilt. Is that too much to ask?"

Gwendolyn shakes her head at the camera. Somehow, I don't think that line is making it into the episode.

His words remind me of the month he moved away. I lived my life, and he lived his new one.

And when I realized he was ignoring my texts, and then promptly matched his silence? When I retreated into myself, and reinforced my walls, until I could barely remember what it was like to feel anything at all, let alone something approaching love? When I reminded myself in a silent litany that I didn't need him, or anybody, until it felt like truth?

Is that how one becomes a dream girl?

I suppose I'm a natural, then.

"Hey, tell me more about your life," I say quickly, banishing the voice in my head. "I know all the news headlines, but I assume there's more to it than that."

"Right, right. Well, I'm living in Loreux. I'm renting my own place not too far from Mom and Dad. It was important to us to stay near Sam, just in case she needs us for anything."

Reading between the lines, that means he's staying somewhere near the palace. Also known as the most high-end area of the city. Jordy's family is well off, but I didn't realize they were *that* wealthy. I wonder if his parents had a good few years, or if the palace has helped subsidize.

"Are you working?" I ask.

"Yeah, lots. I've got a few pretty active Insta sponsorships. I modelled for *Jaquirisional* the other month, in this really cool celebrity campaign. I have some pretty high-maintenance stocks I need to keep an eye on. It's all happening. Exhausting, though, you know? Like, when do you get a second to yourself?"

"Mm, I can relate," I say. He seems to miss the sarcasm, because he responds by slinging an arm around my shoulders, keeping his abs thoughtfully angled away.

By the time we slowly make our way back to the rest of the girls, golden hour has begun, so Isaac insists on filming some sweeping shots of Jordy and me gazing into each other's eyes with the lake in the background. It takes longer than it probably should've, because I keep snorting with laughter after a few seconds of prolonged, awkward eye contact, and at one point I get Jordy's six-pack oil all over my shirt when he pulls me in for a hug.

Back on the grass, the girls are waiting in one group now, Maya and Perrie included. They've set up in a circle of folded chairs, clutching drinks and huddled under lap blankets to ward against the rapidly cooling air. Almost as one, they look up at Jordy, some of them brightening in hope. My gut squirms at the realization that I basically hogged him, right before the first elimination. I shouldn't feel bad, technically; it's meant to be a competition, right? But I do.

As I give my empty glass to a crew member and receive a full replacement, Jordy holds his hand out to Maya. "Hey," he says. "Wanna go for a quick walk?"

Kim and Francesca look fit to murder.

Maya blinks up at him, then looks back at Perrie. "Oh. Actually, I was right in the middle of a conversation. Maybe you and I can talk later, if you don't run out of time?"

We all gape at her, Jordy included. Isaac included. Gwendolyn—well, actually, no, she seems to be enjoying herself.

So. Maya has decided for unknown reasons to dig her own grave and essentially send herself home tonight, then?

Ding dong, the witch is dead.

TWELVE

Maya

It's almost ten thirty at night by the time we're finally taken back to the mansion, where we're sent inside one of the rooms. It used to be decked out in classy, antique-style décor. Now, it's been transformed into what could only be described as "if a Christmas tree became a room." Lit candles stand on every surface, and red glass decorations fill every spare inch of space. Glittering white fairy lights are strung everywhere and all lit at different intervals so the room itself seems to be moving. Or, to be fair, maybe that's just because I've choked down about four too many wines. I'm not sure if it's a Europe thing, or a reality TV thing, but everyone here is obsessed with the stuff.

Perrie's right about it being an acquired taste, by the way. While yesterday, wine tasted like swamp water, today it has the comparatively scrumptious taste of expired apple juice. It's probably for the best that there are no Jell-O shots available tonight, though, because I discovered around lunchtime that I have a cool new skill. Not to brag, but every time someone mentions Jell-O now, I dry heave. On cue!

Standing in front of a large, unlit fireplace is Grayson, who's scrolling on his phone, oblivious to the world, even as the camera crew, the producers, and Jordy file in.

Suddenly, I get a stab of fear. It's time to film my grand exit. I knew this was coming, obviously, but now that it's here, and we're about to be filmed, I feel like I might throw up. And it's got nothing to do with the wine.

I should never have come on this damn show. All I've achieved is giving Jordy one last opportunity to knock me down a peg or fifty before he continues on playing out his ultimate dream of screwing around five girls at once with no consequences. He sure has upped his cheating game. Talk about trading in a scratch-off for a winning lottery ticket.

Once everyone's in the room, we hang around for what seems like a weirdly long time, even for the snail's pace we've been filming at. It isn't until Gwendolyn clears her throat and says, "So!" in a half yell that Grayson jumps and fumbles with his phone.

"Sorry, sorry!"

Grayson passes his phone to a crew member, checks his reflection in a wall mirror, and aims a high-beam smile our way.

"Welcome," he says, "to *Notte Infinita*."

"The ceremony is the *last part of the night*," Francesca whispers to Kim. "As in, the *end* of the night. If it were actually an infinite night, there wouldn't be an end, so why call the *end part infinite*?"

Her voice is getting screechy with frustration.

"Tonight, Jordy's had a wonderful time getting to reacquaint himself with all of you, and I know you've all enjoyed it just as much as he has. But while some journeys are destined to continue from this moment forth, it's now time for Jordy to decide which of you he wants to keep exploring, and who he's seen enough of."

Did Grayson look at me during that last part? I swear he did.

"Good luck, girls." With that, Grayson abruptly leaves the room, Jordy trailing after him. I look at the other girls, but they seem as confused as me.

"We're going to get some reaction shots, girls," Isaac says. "I just want you to act like you're listening to something very interesting . . . okay, great. Now a little small laughter. Good. Now look a little scared. Not that scared, Kim, there isn't a tornado approaching. More like 'the power's out and there's only five percent battery left on my phone, but I'm expecting an important call' scared. Much better. Now a frown, like you've just seen a puppy being murdered. No, Skye, think *brutally* murdered . . . yes, better!"

After we run through every possible emotion known in the spectrum of human experience, Jordy and Grayson finally walk back in, and it's Jordy's turn to talk at us condescendingly.

"Tonight has been absolutely amazing," he says, all gleaming teeth. "And I've cherished the opportunity to meet every one of you again, and see how you've changed—and how you've stayed the same—since the last time we spoke. For some of you"—he paused for effect—"that's been slightly longer than for others. So, I've had some time to think about everything that happened tonight, and where I'd like the next week to take us."

He definitely looks me in the eye at this. I raise my chin, keep my face blank, and muster every scrap of dignity I still have. After the whole "all of last night" thing, that might not be a lot, but damn it, I'm gonna work with what I've got.

"And tonight I've decided to keep Skye."

For a confused moment I think he means he's keeping *just* Skye. *Plot twist.* Then I realize it's the start of a list. Isaac gestures for Skye to go forward and . . . do something to

Jordy, either hug him or punch him in the stomach, I can't tell which. When Skye gets close enough, Jordy holds out his arms. Ah, so, a hug then. I had a feeling that was probably the case, but I'd hoped for the latter anyway. It's worth keeping a healthy sense of optimism about such things.

She stands over to the side, where the people who didn't alienate half the cast and reject Jordy in front of everyone are going to stand. The cool kids.

"Lauren."

She grabs Francesca's arm excitedly, then joins the hug-to-cool-kids conveyer belt.

"Perrie."

Perrie keeps her face blank, but does give him a nod in acknowledgment. Hug, cool kids. She gives me a sad smile when she turns around, and I mime clapping for her. If one of us has to go home on night one, I'm glad it's me.

"Kim."

Kim lets out a sigh of relief loud enough it turns into a semi-shriek at the end. Hug, cool kids.

"Francesca."

Francesca breaks into a smile, and there's my confirmation. My cheeks are flaming now, and I'm sure it's visible on camera, which makes the whole thing worse. The other girls are *staring* at me, and so is Jordy. He is dragging this out. Revenge for last night, probably. He's won, again. He has no right to win, because he's *incontestably* the asshole here, but he has anyway.

I should've known better. I should've sat in the shame and tried to let him—and what he did—go.

This is what I get for trying to hold my own against him.

"And Maya."

I snap back into focus. Ha, pardon me?

Everyone waits for me to react. I walk forward slowly, kind of expecting a trap, but it never comes. I give Jordy a quick, light hug, before I, too, join the cool kids.

I try to catch Jordy's eye to get some sort of hint or explanation, but he doesn't look at me once. I try to wipe the bewilderment off my face for the cameras.

Jordy clasps his hands before him. "Every single person I've spoken to tonight has grown so much since the last time I saw her. I've grown, too. There wasn't a single girl who didn't impress me with her wit, intelligence, and great attitude today. I want the chance to get to know the new and improved versions of all of you, and the only way I can do that is by seeing you all again next week. So, if you'll all stay, I would be honored to have the chance."

The group is beaming, and Jordy is beaming, and the camera's panning over us. So I beam, too. It's about as natural as fluorescent lighting, but nothing's real, here, so I probably fit right in.

For whatever reason, I'm still in the game.

And I intend to use my second chance for everything it's worth.

THIRTEEN

Skye

I keep to myself as we head back up to the manor. This wrench in the works changes everything. Not only does it mean Maya will be here for another week, it means I'm rusty in my ability to predict what Jordy's going to do. Aka, for all I know, Maya could be here for weeks yet. Sleeping below me. Eating with me. Day in, day out.

I wait until we reach the room and close the door to tell Maya I want to talk to her.

"Well, I don't want to talk to you," she says, but she doesn't have much of a choice, because where is she going to go?

"Too bad. I do," I say, folding my arms and leaning against the bunk bed ladder. "We're going to be stuck together now, you know."

"What, were you hoping I'd get sent home nice and early?" Maya snaps. "Sorry to disappoint you."

Well, yes. But that's not the point anymore. "That's not what I meant."

"Then what did you mean?"

"I *mean* that you've obviously got a problem with me. And I'm proposing you try to get over it."

Maya gapes at me. "Excuse me?"

I throw my hands up. "So, I dated Jordy after you. Who cares? He was always going to meet someone else eventually. And I'm sorry, but holding this grudge for almost two years, and telling people he was your boyfriend at the time, and treating me terribly from minute one is . . . Come on, Maya, it's pathetic. The whole 'jealous ex-girlfriend' thing is such a cliché."

Maya looks horrified, and I brace myself for either defensiveness or an outright counterattack.

"You think I don't like you because I'm jealous of you?" she asks finally.

". . . Yes? Why, is there another reason?"

She doesn't want to share her room? She hates my face? She hates . . . Canadians?

"Uh, *yes*," she says. "How about the obvious one? You dated my *boyfriend* while he was *still* my *boyfriend,* then you *stole him from me.* Ring a bell?"

"Maya, honestly. Do you actually, truly believe that? I'm asking in good faith."

"I don't *believe* it, Skye. It's the truth. And did you actually, truly not have any idea he was with me when he started seeing you?"

I throw up my hands. "I'm not lying. Although, maybe we should talk about that some more. Lauren mentioned you and Jordy might have been under different impressions by accident."

Maya studies me, long and slow. "You know," she says finally, sitting heavily on the edge of her bed with a squeak of springs, "I believe you. I think you didn't know Jordy was taken."

"So, we're not exploring the miscommunication idea?"

"But," she powers through, "you are not off the hook. You keep calling me a liar. You're helping Jordy convince everyone

I'm making up my own worst experience because I'm jealous and petty."

"Well, it's not like you made a good impression on me," I snap. "Why would I have taken your side?"

"It's not my job to start us off on the right foot. I'm the one who was screwed over here."

"But you *just said* you believe I didn't know what you think happened, so, which is it, Maya? Did I screw you over, or am I an unwitting participant?"

We face each other down. Maya's expression changes several times in as many seconds. Checkmate.

"I . . ." she tries, before clearing her throat and speaking in a defeated tone. "I want you to believe me."

"I believe you think you were together," I say. "I don't think you're making it up to make me look bad."

"No, Skye, we *were* together."

"Okay, maybe you were!" I burst out. "But look at it from my perspective. I don't know you. I do know Jordy. He never gave any reason not to trust him." His "fable" today crosses my mind again, and I shove the thought aside. "I wasn't there when Jordy moved away from you. You're asking me to believe, based on your word, that Jordy lied to me, and hid you from me, and vice versa, for two months. I can admit I don't know for sure. I can acknowledge that, maybe, the breakup wasn't as clear as Jordy meant it to be. But if you want me to say I completely trust that Jordy was lying to me for the first part of our relationship, I can't."

"But you don't know for sure," Maya says.

"Of course not. At the moment, it's your word versus Jordy's."

"But if there's even a chance my boyfriend cheated on me with you," she goes on, "are you okay with that?"

"No. I'm not okay with it. I just . . ." I sigh in frustration.

"What if we confronted Jordy together? Maybe it can all be sorted out?"

"He'll just keep lying, Skye. It's what he does."

"And he said it's what *you* do."

We fall into silence. Better than going around in circles, I suppose. It's a riddle with no answer. If Maya's wrong, she owes me an apology. If Maya's right, I owe her one. For Maya to be right, Jordy has to be wrong. And that simply can't be right. Not Jordy. Someone else, maybe, but not Jordy. Not sweet Jordy, who approached *me*. Who started flirting with *me*.

But then I think of the Jordy with oil all over his chest, simpering at the camera. How he smoothly invented a whole new backstory for us without hesitation. The canned lines that were a little too robotic to be romantic.

The way he spoke to me on the phone, using *just* the right words to get me to come. Convincing me I was special, something that hasn't exactly been backed up by his actions today. I kick off from the bed and take slow steps around the carpet, hugging my arms around my chest.

Maya goes on in a steady voice. "*He* wanted to do long distance. We did video chats and phone calls every day. He bought me a ring for Christmas." I shake my head as she continues. "He flew back to visit me in early December. He stayed in the spare room for days. Does that sound like 'broken up' to you?"

I stop pacing and cross to the desk, to lean my hands on it and face the wall. "No."

Maybe I was wrong to think she believes in this version of events. She could be fabricating the whole story to mess with my head, or to drive a wedge between Jordy and me.

But what if she's not?

What if he's actually a very, very talented liar?

"My cousin saw you two at a New Year's Eve party making

out, and she told me. At first, he said it was just a drunken mistake, and begged me not to leave him. I was *this* close to forgiving him. Then he came back a day later and said he couldn't be with someone as possessive as me, and he broke up with me. *He* cheated on me, and *he* broke up with me for not handling it well enough. Next thing I knew, you were all over his profile."

I flinch.

Could it be true? That Jordy said kissing me . . . his *girl-friend* . . . was a drunken mistake? We'd been together for over a month by New Year's. We were still at that giddy, early stage where we spent the day "watching movies," but didn't retain a word because we spent the whole time kissing and gazing at each other, whispering affectionate, sappy nonsense that seemed like earth-shattering truths at the time.

A mistake?

Suddenly, Maya gasps, and springs to her feet. "I can prove it," she says, half to herself. She makes a beeline for the chest of drawers, digs through her clothing, and emerges holding an iPad. Brandishing it in triumph, she dives back onto her bed, while I watch her. After a moment, she glances up at me. "Please don't tell anyone I've got this."

I shrug. "None of my business."

She gives me an impish grin, then busies herself navigating to her message history with Jordy. I realize what she means by proof, and a knot of tension starts to grow in my stomach.

"Here," she says finally, passing it over to me. "Read from here down. You can see the dates."

I can see the dates. Even with Maya's permission, reading this feels like an invasion of privacy. I suppose it's Jordy's privacy I'm invading. But after reading the first few messages, any guilt I have around this evaporates.

There's Jordy saying he loves her on Halloween.

Jordy and Maya exchanging selfies.

Maya and Jordy talking about their days, and how desperately they miss each other.

Jordy and Maya swapping Thanksgiving meal photos. Maya and Jordy making plans to see each other in December. Maya messaging Jordy that she was at the airport.

Early December. When Jordy had ostensibly visited the US for his aunt's birthday. But it doesn't look to me like he stayed with his aunt. It doesn't look as though he went for his aunt at all.

My vision starts closing in from the edges, and my stomach twists. My mouth starts watering in a warning. Whether it's the alcohol, or the news, or both, I'm going to be sick.

"I've got to . . ." I force out, making a break for the door.

I rush down the hall to the bathroom and stop at the sink, gasping.

Jordy cheated on me.

No. He cheated on her. *With* me.

He cheated on *us.*

All of it. The months I gave to him. The parts of myself I cautiously handed over, trusting him with sides of me I rarely show to anyone. The kisses, and the first times, and the knowledge that once we were us, Skye and Jordy, unstoppable and special. It was all. A godforsaken. Lie. A fucking *lie.*

It's me. I'm the villain, here. Oh my god, I stole someone's boyfriend. And then I told her to get over it. I called her a liar, to her face. I told the girls she's a liar. Oh my god, oh my god, oh my god.

How many times have I told friends there are two sides to every story? How many times have I raised a skeptical brow when girls are called names like psycho, or manipulative, or clingy? Only to turn around and do it myself, because why? Because I wanted to believe that I was special. That *my* situation was different. That I was simply defending Jordy and myself against someone who wanted to hurt us. Did Jordy ever even care about me? Was any of it even real? How can I know, if he can lie so easily? He lied to me. He's lying to me right now. He lied to Maya.

I should've known. I should've *known*. There is a reason I don't do second chances, and this is it. People don't grow and become better. If they hurt you once, they will continue to hurt you.

The truth is, Jordy and I didn't part mutually. He left the country, and he ghosted me, and I *knew* that until I heard his voice on the phone, denying my version of reality. Insisting that, outside of a few messages, he never heard from me, despite desperately wanting to. Messages that he *ignored*.

This whole construction of it being the right person, wrong time? I wanted, so desperately, to believe it was true, that I'd bought it. I'd believed that maybe things could be different, because Jordy was different. But of course they couldn't. Things are never different. And this red-hot agony, this feeling of being ripped apart right down the middle? I brought this on myself. I *knew* this was where it would lead, and I refused to listen to my own logic. I knew better than this.

Gasping, I splash water on my face, then drink some from the tap to try to settle my stomach. My throat feels like the Sahara.

Okay. I look at myself in the mirror, panting for breath. *Focus. Game plan.*

The game plan is fairly obvious. I'm going to get the heck out of here. Tomorrow. And if they say I can't leave . . . well, I will threaten to tell the papers *everything,* as soon as filming finishes. They'll have to let me go then. They can fly me to London, and I can video call Chloe, and Dad, and talk about this with people who will understand, not some random girls

I barely knew existed before yesterday. Then I can bury this feeling in some great food, and travel, and I'll . . . I'll go to a club and make out with a person or ten, and I'll forget I ever cared a fraction about Jordy Miller.

When I go back to the room, Maya's already in bed, under the covers. I sit on the edge of her bed, and she props herself up. Her eyes are suspiciously puffy and pink.

"So, now you know for sure," she says.

I nod. We sit in an extended silence, basking in the awkwardness. I know what I need to say, but it's torture to get it out.

"I am so, so sorry," I say finally. "If I'd known, I never would've done it. I know that's no excuse, but—"

"It's actually a pretty good excuse," she says over me. "What were you supposed to do? Figure it out by doing a tarot reading? He played us. It's what he does."

"But I should've noticed. He was messaging you, and going to see you, there must have been signs—"

"You didn't even know him then. Like, barely, anyway. You couldn't have known he was acting weird, because you didn't have anything to compare it to."

"I'm trying to apologize."

"And I'm telling you that you don't need to." She traces her chin with a finger. "Actually, I should apologize to you. Jordy told me you knew everything when he dumped me, but I shouldn't have believed him. That's on me. So, *I'm* sorry for how I acted yesterday."

"You're sorry you didn't believe me?" I echo in disbelief. "Maya. I'm sorry I didn't believe *you.*"

"I'm used to it," she says.

That's even worse.

"I wish I believed you before I saw the messages," I say simply.

"Yeah, me, too. But I get why you didn't. I really do." She frowns down at her blanket, then glances up at me through pale lashes, all traces of the day's mascara long gone. "Are you okay?"

"Me?"

"Yeah, you. I just dropped a bomb on you."

True. Maybe I shouldn't be okay. Maybe I should be sobbing, and mourning the loss of what I suppose I never had. But honestly, it's hard to feel anything but ice-cold resentment. "I'm okay. I've decided I'm leaving in the morning." I give her a humorless smile. "Also, it's probably none of my business, but I hope you've thought it through. Coming here, I mean."

Maya takes an unusually long time to reply. She keeps opening her mouth, then closing it, as though she's talking herself out of saying whatever she's about to say. Then she sighs. "So, what? You just leave? No confrontation, no revenge, nothing?"

"I wasn't exactly planning on gushing during the exit interview, if that's what you're referring to."

"And trust the producers to air you trashing their big romantic lead in episode two? No one wants to watch a show about a cheater finding love. And Isaac told me the royal family wouldn't let them, anyway. They just won't run it."

I shrug. "Then I suppose they don't run it. I can't control what other people do. The only person I'm in charge of is me, and I'm leaving. And if you had any self-respect, so would you." I pause, replaying that last part again in my mind. "I didn't mean that to sound so harsh."

"I agree with you," she says. "You tell people how they should treat you when you accept bad treatment."

"Sure. I suppose that's true."

"I wasn't going to come here, you know," she says carefully.

"But then I thought, he embarrassed me in front of everyone I knew. What if I did the same right back to him?"

I quirk an eyebrow. "What do you mean?"

"I figured if I can get to the very end, I can break his heart, just like he broke mine."

A slow smile creeps across my face. "The long game," I say. So, that answers the question that's been niggling at the back of my mind. She didn't come here to get her heart broken all over again. She came here to make him pay.

Maya smirks at my impressed expression. "So, tonight you've called me pathetic, and accused me of having no self-respect. You wanna take either of those back yet, or . . . ?"

I purse my lips sheepishly. "Maybe I could stand to hold off on the name-calling before I have the full story," I admit.

"Or even altogether. Go all out."

It takes me a second to realize she's only teasing me. Even though I only hated her for two days, I can already tell it's going to be an adjustment to not expect the worst from her.

"So," I say. "You want to make it to the end?"

"That's the plan."

I proceed carefully. "No offense, but . . . you're doing a terrible job."

Maya kicks me through the blanket. "You know, usually when people say 'no offense,' they then go out of their way to insult the other person as gently as they can."

"I don't like games."

"It's not a game, it's, like, a social contract."

"Wonderful, I'll keep it in mind."

"Well if you say it like that, I'm not going to believe you, am I?"

"Good, you're learning. Anyway, Maya, Jordy mentioned you were being quite sweet last night. Before you went on a rampage trashing him to everyone, anyway. I think you might need my help making it to the end."

Maya bristles. "I did date him once, remember. I know him."

"Yes, but I've *analyzed* him."

"How romantic," she says drily.

I link my fingers. "The only risks I take are the ones I can't lose. I'm not going to give my heart to anyone I don't understand inside and out."

"I guess you miscalculated with Jordy," Maya says. "I get it. He's pretty convincing."

My smile is tight and cold. "Trusting Jordy was a mistake. But it's not as big a mistake as he's just made."

"Meaning?"

"Meaning maybe I stay, and we do this together?"

She hesitates. "Oh. Wow. I . . . don't know."

I press on. "Think about it. We could cover each other. Both of us can sing the other's praises to Jordy. It'll be an extra pair of eyes to watch out for sabotage from the producers or the other girls. Then, whichever one he picks gets the honor of crushing him."

"But I want to be the person who crushes him," she protests.

I fight the urge to roll my eyes. "We'll do our best to get you in that spot, then. I don't care which one of us it is. And if we're in it together, that brings our chances to thirty-three-point-three percent, all things being equal."

"Did you just calculate that?"

"It's a third, Maya, take a math class sometime," I say, and she blushes.

"Whatever. And how do I know you won't betray me?"

"Honestly? If I wanted to date that asshole again, I wouldn't need to play dirty. I'd just do it."

Maya considers this. "Fine," she says. "Welcome to team Fuck Up the Fuck Boy."

I stare at her flatly. "We need to work on the name."

"What's wrong with the team name?"

I don't dignify that with a response. Instead, I climb to my feet and stretch. "My head's spinning. I'm going to bed before I pass out. I'll see you tomorrow?"

Maya watches me climb the ladder. "Are you gonna tell him you know?" she asks. "About me?"

Good question. "I don't know yet. It might be fun to watch him squirm. But it seems like the sort of thing that might put him on his guard around us. Let's see how it goes."

Maya's laugh is bitter as I climb under the blankets. "All right. Good night."

"Do you mean it this time?" I grin despite myself.

If I'm reading Maya's tone right, she's smiling, too. "Yeah. This time."

"Good."

"Good."

"Night."

As I close my eyes, my mind tries to conjure up thoughts of grief and betrayal, but I force them away. Then, of all things, my mom's face pops up, and I shut that down, too.

Not tonight.

I'm not ready to process all of this just yet.

One step at a time.

FOURTEEN

Skye

The next morning, I decide I'm ready to process. Or, at the very least, I'm ready to commence the act of processing. For about an hour, I lie staring at the ceiling, my stomach twisting as I replay the beginning of my relationship with Jordy, memory by memory. There was the time he flew home for the week—obviously that was to visit Maya. But what other signs were there? The habit he had of leaving the room when his "mom" called. Was that Maya, too? The way he'd angle his phone away from me when he used it, obviously enough that I'd noticed it more than once. Was he messaging Maya?

Could there have been a third someone else still in the picture while Jordy and I were exclusively dating? There's no way to know.

The realization wraps around my heart like a constrictor, tighter and tighter, until it feels like there isn't a shred of love left in it, and no space for love to worm its way in. I should have known better. I *must* have known something wasn't right with Jordy, because I'd never entirely let him in. But a small part of him must have slipped in through the cracks, because

I can feel him like acid in my veins, burning me from the inside out.

Maya and I need a game plan. If we're going to make Jordy pay for what he did to us, we can't simply play it by ear and hope for the best, like Maya seems to want to. We have to combine what we know about Jordy Miller, for a start.

Speaking of Maya, she's still fast asleep, a pale, freckled arm thrown over her head. I consider poking her awake, but the effectiveness-to-irritating balance isn't ideal. And I suppose I *do* want her as a friend, now that I know she's probably only a nightmare to people she believes actually deserve it. So, I go for option B, the same as yesterday morning: connecting my iPod to the speakers, playing "Cell Block Tango" from *Chicago,* and slowly turning the volume up.

Not long after the chorus, Maya groans. "What the fuck is that?" She plucks at the consonants so they're razor sharp.

"It's our theme song. Good morning."

She responds by putting a pillow over her face. "We don't even have anything on the schedule today, Skye, fuck *off.*"

She might be swearing at me still, but there's significantly less venom in her voice than yesterday. This bodes well for our working relationship. I hop off the bed, land heavily on the ground, then dig through the wardrobe for my bikini.

"We have a lot to talk about," I say to the pillow, which growls at me in response. "But I haven't spent time in the pool yet, so I'm going to do that. If you feel like scheming, I'll see you there." I wait for the chorus to finish playing, then turn off the song and head out, taking my speakers with me.

Maya appears at the pool about ten minutes later during "Material Girl." She's wearing a black one-piece with cutouts on the side and a plunging neckline. It's the sort of suit that draws the eye to every curve on her chest and hips, and I don't *mean* to stare, but I catch myself doing it anyway.

"Do you think it's warm enough to swim?" she asks skeptically.

"In Calgary, this is about as hot as it ever gets, so, yes," I say as I descend the steps.

We're the only ones here. Perrie and Francesca were in the kitchen when I passed, and Lauren and Kim hadn't made it out of their room yet. What will the others think when they notice us out here together?

Maya scrunches her nose and gingerly lowers herself into the water. She squeals and carries on for a few seconds, but eventually submerges up to her neck.

"So," I say, paddling in place, "we need a game plan."

Maya puts on a serious face and swims over so I don't have to shout at her. "Okay."

"Step one. You really messed up at the party."

Maya chokes out a laugh. "Oh, you're not holding back then, okay."

"You realize they'll cast you as the villain now, right? Like, for certain? You can't go on camera saying the lead guy is an asshole and *not* be the villain. It's math."

"Is it?"

"Logic, then. And if you're the villain, it's going to make it impossible for viewers to take your side when you break Jordy's heart. Can you imagine the whole world deciding Jordy's the good guy in your story? I'm assuming that's not what you want, correct?"

Maya lets her head sink up to her nose, her hair floating around her in weightless tendrils, and narrows her eyes before resurfacing. "I see your point. So, what do I do about that?"

I backstroke in a circle around Maya to help me think. "Well, the most obvious choice is to pick someone else to be the villain and manipulate them into looking bad enough that they take your spot."

Maya swings around in the water to stare at me in shock. "Skye!"

I stop midstroke. "But, of course, we'd never do that?" I ask sheepishly.

"I'm here to mess with Jordy, not to ruin the lives of his other victims."

I appreciate her morals, but, counterpoint: without a scapegoat, it's going to be much harder to get the producers to swerve from the established narrative. We'll need to turn Maya into the next best thing to a saint to pull this off. That, or she's going to have to adjust to the idea of me taking down Jordy in her stead.

"Okay, fine, fine. You need to be *super* careful about what you say, then. And you should get on the good side of the other girls so they don't smear you on camera. Otherwise, it doesn't matter how you behave, the audience will decide you must be two-faced if all the other girls hate you."

"Do I show them the proof, then?"

"You can. But if it gets back to Jordy, he might be suspicious that neither of us seems to care when we're around him. He's self-absorbed, but he's not a newborn. And it might give him and the producers warning to prepare a story that makes him look good before it gets out. Something that makes us look like liars."

Maya's face falls, but she nods. "You've thought this through, huh?"

"I prefer to be on the attack rather than the defense. As far as I'm concerned, failing to plan is planning to fail."

"Okay, well, can I count on you to help me there?"

"I'm on it. I'll start your image clean-up today, Captain."

When she smiles, I can't help but smile with her. I didn't realize it was so infectious. In my defense, that's likely because she spent the last forty-eight hours scowling at me.

"Also, we need a backup plan," I say. "Just in case one of us doesn't make it to the end. A delayed-action grenade."

"But figurative, yes?"

"Okay, fine, figurative works, too. But seriously, the more girls we can recruit, the better our chances. I like thirty-three percent, but I like a hundred much more."

Maya makes a face. "That sounds like a good way for us to get caught."

"Well, we won't fill them in on the plan. We'll just . . . open their eyes to the sort of person Jordy is. If we're really lucky, a couple of them might drop out themselves. We just need to nudge it along."

"Uh-huh. And how are we going to do that?"

"Maya, people like Jordy don't cheat on two girls at once and then go on to respect and care for everyone else they ever meet. If anything, they usually get worse, because they start to learn they can get away with it. If a single girl in there doesn't have *any* Jordy red flags, I'll be shocked."

"Perrie dated him before us," Maya says. "And she doesn't have any horror stories. Not that she told me about, anyway. But she already knows about the cheating stuff, obviously, and I bet she'll be even madder about it when I tell her he played both of us. I'm pretty sure she's just here to get more followers, anyway."

"What makes you think that?"

"She told me she's just here to get more followers."

"Ah. Well, that means she'll be able to see him more clearly than the others. That's a good start."

"What about the other girls?"

I think for a second. "Francesca's a mixed bag. She only hooked up with him, so she's not exactly invested. But it was so short that she probably didn't get a chance to see his bad side."

"Maybe we leave her 'til last, then. He might do our job for us if she's around him long enough."

"That's actually very possible. Then, Lauren . . . Lauren seems more interested in meeting the royal family than being with Jordy. Pros: she might be easier to reason with. Cons: she might not care if Jordy's an asshole if she thinks she'll get to wear a crown if she dates him."

"But she won't get to wear a crown."

"Yes, I know, but she . . . you'll see. She's awfully attached to the whole royalty thing. And Kim, I think, actually has real feelings for Jordy still. That might make her harder to talk to, but on the other hand it actually might work in our favor. Love turns to hate quite quickly, in the right circumstances."

"Gotcha. So, Perrie, Kim, Lauren, Francesca?"

"Subject to change."

"Naturally."

Maya holds out her hand for a high-five. I glance at it and raise my eyebrows.

"Come on," she urges. "We're a team now. We need to high-five for morale."

With as big a sigh as I can muster, I lightly tap my palm against hers.

"Close enough."

"We can start today," I say. "Lunch is probably the best time, because we'll all be forced together. I'll start a conversation with you, and we'll just act like everything's normal. The other girls have no reason to dislike you outside of what happened between you and me, so if I don't have an issue, they won't either. Theoretically, at least."

"Won't they ask what's changed?"

"Maybe, maybe not. I'll just say we had a talk and worked things out, if they do."

Maya swims to the side of the pool and leans her back

against it, kicking lazily as she speaks. "Okay, great. Also, I'll be really nice to them. Let's brainstorm some compliments."

"Let's not," I say with pep. "As much as it pains me to discourage you from planning something out . . . if you want us to convince everyone to go along with this like it's normal, you have to act *normally*. Well, not normally, but the version of you I've come to know and tolerate as of last night."

Maya pouts. "No way. All people want is for you to be nice to them."

". . . You've never experienced people despising you before now, have you?"

"No, why?"

A smile touches my lips at the sincere look on her face, and I fight to stay earnest. "Just . . . don't try too hard. That stuff only works if people don't already know how awful you can be if you put your mind to it."

Reluctantly, she acquiesces. "I have a really good feeling about this, you know? Like, we might actually pull this off together."

"Oh, we will," I say darkly. "Jordy doesn't know who he's poked."

At lunchtime, a couple of assistants bring over our meal. It's prison food. I mean that in the literal sense: Kim tells us when she sees the packaging that the catering company is famously contracted by prisons and boarding schools (and— apparently—by reality shows who spent most of their budget on buying plane tickets to fly contestants three feet down the road). Every night they have us fill out an order form for the next day's meals. Today's lunch was a choice between spaghetti in a meatless tomato sauce, and grilled chicken sandwiches. I've figured out quite quickly that the vegetarian options are safer here, because the catering company seems to have a bit of a love affair with gristly meat, which is terrible news for my gag reflex. When I was younger, my mom used to cook chicken thighs and T-bone steaks and insist I finish every bite, even though I was never able to stand the texture of chunks of fat. The squishing sensation between my teeth was enough to make me dry heave, but she'd insist I was just a picky eater and I needed to learn. When she left Dad and me, it was one of the only things I was happy about. No more chicken thighs!

No more Mom, either, if you insist on focusing on the negatives, but I feel it's good to remember the bright side.

Maya sits at the dining table across from me, Perrie at her side. Most of us got the spaghetti, but she has a grilled chicken burger on her plate. Time to commence operation "what do you mean we're enemies?"

"Maya," I say before she can take a bite. "Prove a theory for me. Is that thigh or breast in the sandwich?"

She lifts the top bun, studies the contents, then replaces it. "Thigh. How come?"

"I was just wondering if I should regret the spaghetti."

"Do you regret the spaghetti, Skye?"

"Not even a little bit. I'm feeling great about my life choice now. Thank you."

Perrie, Kim, Lauren, and Francesca are staring at us with open mouths. No one's taken a bite of their meal yet.

I eat a forkful of pasta and stare them all down until they collectively snap out of it and start on their own meals, save for Francesca, who seems too bewildered to react.

There's a long silence. I rack my brain for a way to fill it, but suddenly, words fail. I should have prepared examples.

"How's the pasta?" Maya asks the group.

Francesca double-takes at her plate as though she's startled to see it there. Lauren and Kim stare at Maya like they're convinced she's about to flip the table.

Perrie purses her lips. "It's good. Maybe a little bland? But I have high standards after my dad's sauce."

"Oh, cool," Maya says, before shooting me a look of panic.

I clear my throat. "So. It's wonderful that we're all here still, huh? I didn't expect Jordy to do that. We got so lucky."

Francesca tilts her head to the side and leans forward to look down the table at me. "Did we?"

"Yes, I think so," I say. It's time to change the tactic a little. "And now that we're all going to be here for at least another week, I was thinking it would be great to get to know each other. All of us."

Kim and Francesca still haven't touched their food.

Lauren starts twirling her fork in hers. "Sure, that sounds like a good plan."

"Awesome," Perrie says.

"Why?" Kim asks suspiciously.

"You know," Maya says, pointing a fork at Kim, who eyes it like it's a Class 3 weapon. "I haven't had the chance to tell you this, but your hair is beautiful."

Kim looks gobsmacked. "Why?"

"Maya," I hiss, giving my head a tiny shake. "The thing is, Maya and I think we got off on the wrong foot. And we spoke last night, and worked some things out, and now we want to start fresh."

Maya nods frantically. "Yup. That. You're all so great, I would really, really love to get to know all of you and be friends. I bet you all have the most interesting stories about Jordy."

I make a cutting motion by my neck, and Maya glares at me. Meanwhile, Francesca and Kim glance at each other.

"So, it's an intelligence-gathering mission," Francesca whispers.

"Know thy enemy," Kim whispers back.

"I . . . I can hear you," Maya says, but Francesca holds up a hand to silence her.

"Do we trust her?" Kim asks.

"Not for a second. Act normal."

Maya looks helplessly at me, before Kim and Francesca straighten back up.

"Pasta's great, thanks for asking," Francesca says.

"Lovely day outside," Kim adds.

Maya gives them a tight smile and eats the rest of her sandwich in relative silence. I *did* tell her not to compliment them under any circumstances, but *no.* Why don't people ever believe me when I tell them the best way to make friends is to open up as little as possible and never show signs of weakness?

After we've all stacked our stuff in the dishwasher, Kim, Lauren, and Francesca physically yank me backward to stay behind as Maya and Perrie leave.

"What's going on?" Kim asks.

"What does she have on you?" Francesca asks.

"It is a little strange that she's being so nice, don't you think?" Lauren says.

I shake my head and untangle myself from their grips. "Like I said. We worked things out. She's actually fine, when you get to know her."

The three of them exchange loaded glances.

"So, she *has* got something on you," Francesca says.

"Nope."

"That's exactly what a blackmail victim would say," Francesca says darkly.

"Please," I say. "Can we just lower the drama? I, for one,

want to have a good time as long as I'm here. If I'm happy to be friends with Maya, can't you just trust me?"

The three of them nod with varying levels of enthusiasm. The moment I turn to leave the room, however, Francesca whispers to Kim again. "Wait until she falls asleep, then we interrogate Maya by candlelight."

"Don't even think about it," I say without turning around.

Nobody replies.

FIFTEEN

Maya

The morning of our first challenge date with Jordy, Skye wakes me up by blaring "Hit Me with Your Best Shot" through her speakers.

"You know, a gentle nudge would do fine," I grumble thickly. "I also respond to my name."

"I'm getting you in the right headspace," she says from the top bunk. "I had an idea."

I massage my closed eyes with my fingertips. Why do filming days have to start so *early*? "Shoot."

"I figured out how we can turn you into a hero without hurting anyone."

"Physically *or* psychologically?"

"Neither this time!"

I flip onto my back. "You have my attention."

"Okay, so. I can't swim very well."

"Oh, you must be thrilled about today's activity, then." Yesterday, Isaac swung past our room in the morning to give us a heads-up about today's challenge for episode two. We're all heading to the lake to learn how to kayak, and then we'll race to win a whole night alone with Jordy. Worst first-place medal I've ever heard of, personally, but the others seemed pumped about the prize when we all discussed it over breakfast. Different strokes for different folks.

"Yeah. I especially love the part where life jackets aren't 'sexy' so we have to leave them under the seats," Skye says drily. "Then I thought, it's a good thing we're getting paid to risk our lives. *Then* I remembered, we're not getting paid, because love's worthless."

"Oh, you saw the slideshow, too," I chirp. "Great read. I'm hoping for a sequel."

"Sure. Anyway, Jordy knows I can't swim. If we wait for everyone to be distracted, I could throw my oar overboard and drift out to the middle of the lake."

"Skye, I want to get away from Jordy as much as you do, but that seems a little dramatic."

"*No.*" She bangs the wall lightly. "So you can rescue me on camera. Obviously, our plan to get the girls on your side isn't working out so well, so I thought it might be time to focus on rehabilitating your image on the show. They're not going to let Jordy pick their villain as the winner, so it's fairly important we make sure you're not the villain. At least, not anymore. Yes?"

I hoist myself out of bed and peek over the bars of the top bunk at Skye, who's sprawled on top of her made bed, casually tossing a stress ball and catching it.

"But you can't swim," I say.

"As we've established; glad you're listening this time."

"So, your idea is to place your life in imminent danger just so I can stage a dramatic rescue, to help us more effectively get revenge on our ex-boyfriend?"

"Yes."

I stare at her until she catches the ball and holds it. She shoots me a nonchalant sideways glance.

"Well," I say perkily, "I think it's a great idea."

"That's the spirit."

"If you trust me not to let you drown."

She starts tossing the ball again. "Hmm. But what would be your incentive to kill me?"

"There aren't any obvious ones. I mean, I could be playing the long game, and this was part of my plan all along."

"Ha. You being able to plan. That *would* be a plot twist."

"Hey, nice one, fuck you."

Skye tries and fails to hide a smirk. "Also, I'm just going for a leisurely sail without a paddle. I'm not cliff-diving. That's where I draw the line."

"Have you ever kayaked before?" I ask.

"Well, no. But how hard can it be?" She playfully lobs the ball in my direction, and I lunge to the side to dodge it with a squeal.

It turns out that Skye is right. Kayaking isn't too difficult. It probably doesn't hurt that the lake is mostly still, with only a few gentle waves bobbing the kayaks up and down. Even Skye, whose eyes widened a little too much as Isaac helped her into her own kayak, seems to have chilled out again now we've been taught by Lauren and Kim's producer, Wai, how to go forward and backward and to turn. Although, Skye never looks especially bothered by anything, so that might just be, you know, her face.

Once all six of us are tethered to the pier, Grayson and Jordy walk to the edge to stare down at us. I instinctively turn to Skye, to check in on her, I guess. It's her first time seeing Jordy since she found out who he really is. Her face is pretty blank, but the corner of her mouth noticeably twitches into a small sneer as she catches sight of Jordy. It disappears as quickly as it comes, and she swallows, hard. Like she's trying to force down her emotions or something.

I look back to Jordy to find him staring right at me, and something flashes in his eyes. It feels like a message I'm supposed to be able to read, but I, for one, am stumped. Why did he decide to keep me? He obviously isn't that interested in me. He even said so to the producers last week. So why am I sitting in this kayak at all?

Does he realize I'm messing with him? Is he messing with me right back?

That fucker.

"I forgot I get motion sickness," Perrie whispers next to me.

Jordy vanishes from my mind, and I flip around. "Oh no. Are you okay?"

"Mm. Debatable."

"We should ask if they have any pills."

"It's too late. They won't kick in in time. I'll be fine."

Damn it, she's right. It's too late. Gwendolyn claps to bring our attention back to the crew. "Okay, ladies, time to get started."

We know the drill. Smiles plastered on, eyes on Grayson and Jordy.

While Grayson is in his suit as always, Jordy is dressed in such a clichéd, preppy sailing outfit there has to be a level of self-aware irony somewhere. In a light blue button-down with the sleeves rolled up, white shorts, and a white Balenciaga baseball cap he wears backward, he looks like he's stepped out of some sort of sailing-themed photoshoot.

Jordy Miller, a knockoff royal who talks like a knockoff Brit and dresses like a knockoff Hamptons douchebag.

Be still, my beating heart.

"Did you pick that outfit out yourself, Jordy?" I ask, as Francesca and Kim give me furious side-eyes.

He forces a tight smile. "No, Maya, I did not."

"Oh. I won't bully you about it, then," I say sweetly.

"*Much* appreciated."

Grayson, as usual, goes first. "Welcome, ladies, to beautiful Lake Loreux, where the glacier-fed water is clean enough to drink, and cold enough to give you a heck of a shock, as I'm sure you've all noticed by now."

I trail my fingers in the water to test it, and shudder. I make a mental note not to fall in.

Skye dips her own fingers in and grimaces at me.

"Today's challenge is simple. See that buoy in the distance? Your goal is to kayak up to it, around it, and back. This will be a race, so the first person to tap the pier again will be crowned our winner. That person will be heading off with Jordy to a penthouse suite in Loreux to spend the night . . . reacquainting themselves with each other."

Oh *gag* me.

"Are you all ready to go?" Grayson asks.

"Yes!" we chorus.

"Beautiful," Gwendolyn chimes in. "Now, just one more time for me, with a little more oomf?"

We do it seven more times.

Then we're being untethered, and suddenly, my heart starts pounding. Scoring a whole night alone with Jordy would give me the sort of advantage I could only dream of. I could make him remember what we had together, I'm sure of it. And there's a chance I could win this race. Maybe. The other girls might be driven by love, but I'm driven by pure rage, and rage brings adrenaline, and adrenaline brings *gold medals.* It's why there are no calm celebrities. The ones who are only look that way because they're really good actors, as angry celebrities often are.

"Get ready," Jordy calls.

Oh, I'm ready all right. I am going to pretend the water is Jordy's face, and my oar is an oar.

"Get set."

"You've got this," Skye whispers. I grip my oar harder.

"And . . . go!"

I paddle furiously, steering around Kim and Lauren as quickly as I can. I picture myself on the softball field, pushing my body as far and as fast as it can go. My breathing comes fast and heavy, and my arms burn as I paddle faster, faster, *faster,* experimenting with the angles of the paddle until I find the right way to strike the water to propel myself along. *Thwack. Thwack. Thwack.* Right into Jordy's face, harder, and faster, and *harder.* This imagination exercise was a *great* idea.

The hum of an engine grows louder as a speedboat holding one of the camera operators follows us. The boat churns up waves in its wake, and my kayak bounces over them roughly, icy cold droplets hitting my face as I go, but I've got tunnel vision. I'm going to win. I'm going to spend the night with Jordy. I'll be able to undo all the damage I did last week.

I hit the buoy first, letting out a breathless cry of victory as I do. Navigating around it isn't too bad, either, and suddenly I'm on the second lap, heading back to the pier, and I can see what has been happening behind me.

Skye and Kim are neck and neck a few feet back, followed by Lauren, then Francesca. Somewhere farther behind them still is Perrie.

Something out of the corner of my eye makes me turn back around. Kim is gaining on me, the nose of her kayak starting to draw even with mine. *No.* I need to secure this romantic night alone with my worst enemy at all costs. I try to push myself even faster, but I'm already operating at max speed, and my arms are starting to feel all leaden and tingly. So, as hard as I try to hold my lead, I watch helplessly as the distance between the fronts of our kayaks grows shorter and shorter, and Kim touches the pier with a victory cry two seconds before I do.

Skye pulls in beside me a heartbeat later, panting so hard her breath is hoarse. "So close," she forces out. "You did great."

"Not great enough," I gasp.

Kim, who's been helped onto the pier, hugs Jordy for the cameras. "I just thought about spending the night with you," she says to him. "And it's like I doubled in speed."

Jordy grimaces. "Wow, Kim, that's . . . so sweet. Wow. Yeah."

The others are pulling into the pier now, and I look around to find Perrie, only to spot her fifty feet out, hunched over, gripping her oar with one hand and her head with the other.

One of the camera operators has zeroed in to film her. "Hey!" I call to the crew as my kayak is yanked over to be tied back to the pier. "Don't just film her. She needs help. Hey!"

My shouting catches Wai's attention, and once she spots Perrie, she jumps into her kayak to go rescue her.

"Can you untie me?" I ask the crew member who's tethering me to the pier with a thick rope. "I wanna make sure she's okay."

"She's fine," he says. "Wai's got her."

Perrie doesn't lift her head from her hands as Wai ties their kayaks together and tows her back in. I let the crew help-slash-unglamorously-hoist me onto the pier, and watch from the edge of it as Perrie's brought in.

"I'm fine," she insists between rounded breaths once she's back on dry wood. "I'm just . . . really nauseous . . ."

"Come on, let's sit down," I say. The other girls, who've been cheering for Kim to the camera as instructed, look over to us as one. I guess someone noticed Perrie's face. I realize too late that the producers have been filming an "everyone be a good sport and congratulate Kim, because even though you're all fighting viciously for the same unworthy man, sister-hood isn't dead" scene without me. Great. I bet they'll be *sure* to mention in a voiceover that I wasn't there because I was with a friend, and not because I was bitter at the close loss. For sure. Definitely.

I am so screwed. Skye's plan had better work.

We make a beeline for the grassy area near the shore and plonk down. A minute later, Isaac brings a bottle of water over to us, and Perrie sips it pathetically.

"I'm humiliated," she moans when her breathing finally evens out. "I didn't even get five seconds in before I thought I was gonna be sick, and that freaking camera guy was filming me. I thought I was gonna throw up on *camera.*"

"They're *assholes,*" I hiss. "I didn't even see you pull over! I'm so sorry. I would've helped you."

She shakes her head. "You were focused on the race."

No. I was focused on slapping Jordy's imaginary face with my oar. "I'm still sorry."

"Nothing you could've done anyway."

By the pier, Gwendolyn is saying something to the group of girls. From the few words I can make out, they're getting ready to do promo shots for the episode.

"Tell them you don't want to get back in the water," I say quickly. "You and I can pose on the pier together or some-thing."

In the end, they let Perrie pose on the pier—because, I guess, it doesn't do them any favors to take promo pics where one of their girls looks like she's about to hurl everywhere—but they insist on putting me back in the water.

When I get back in the boat, I try to catch Skye's eye, but she doesn't notice me. If she's planning on going ahead with the whole rescuing thing, now's the time for it. But I'm starting to wonder if it's such a good idea after all. The crew responsible for our safety barely noticed Perrie needed help before. We might need something more dramatic.

One by one, they tie the girls to the pier so the camera crew can take photos of each girl in the kayak with Jordy in the corniest poses possible: facing each other, or spooning, holding the oars together.

"Flirtier!" Gwendolyn yells at Lauren. "Jordy's just saved you from a burning building! You and Jordy are office rivals, and your passionate hate has morphed into passionate yearning! You've just found out he's a secret billionaire! *Seduce him, Lauren, do you want his riches or not?*"

After Lauren is released from what seems to be the tenth circle of hell, Francesca takes her place. While Jordy and Francesca touch each other's cheeks in the kayak, whispering and giggling to each other like newlyweds on a honeymoon, I paddle over to Skye.

"I think I might hate him, you know?" she says mildly as she watches Jordy pull Francesca into a bear hug for a photo.

"Yeah, his whole 'nice guy' act starts to feel a lot more insidious when you know his other side, huh?"

"That's putting it lightly."

I grab onto her kayak to pull myself even closer, and lower my voice. "So. You still wanna do this?"

"Definitely. I think now is the perfect time, too."

"Yeah, same. Just, I was wondering if it'll be enough?"

Skye gives me a wooden look. "What is it with you and changing plans last minute?"

"I just want to make sure it gets into the episode."

She squeezes my upper arm, and I glance at her hand. It's the first time she's touched me since last week when she moved me away from the shots. Are we touching-friends already? "Maya," she says, oblivious to my surprise. "It'll get in. It'll be big enough. Just do it exactly like we planned, okay?"

"Okay."

"*Promise?* No changes?"

"I promise," I say.

She drops her hand, and I quickly paddle back to the pier, pretending I'm interested in watching the photoshoot, but keeping an eye on her.

In full stealth-mode, Skye gives herself a strong push backward and lets her oar slip under the shockingly blue water. The wind does the rest, grabbing her kayak and gently pulling her out. I watch her in my peripherals, trying to time it so she's far enough out that the "rescue" is big enough, but not so far that she's in any danger. Exactly like she told me to. *See, Skye? I can totally follow instructions.*

That just about does it. Okay. Time to raise the alarm and go after her. Just as I turn to check that the cameras are nearby, my kayak is tugged roughly forward.

"Oops, sorry." Wai giggles. I watch in horror as she deftly ties my kayak to the pier. "Your turn in a sec, Maya."

"No, hold on—"

"You've got a minute, I'm just gonna untie Francesca, okay?"

"But—" But she's already sprinting down the pier. I turn frantically back to Skye, who's starting to look, um . . . small. "Can you untie this?" I ask Perrie, who's sitting on the edge of the pier, with a touch of panic.

She examines it, then grimaces. "What the hell even is this knot? How did she do that?"

"I've got to get loose now."

"Why?" she asks. "Are you okay?"

"No, I—" I glance back at Skye again. She's small, but not so small I can't catch her if I leave *now*. Any longer, and I'll need to get a producer to rescue her. And if I point Skye out to Perrie, she might raise the alarm before I can, and our whole plan will be shot. So, with my brain buzzing in a panic, I do the stupidest thing I could do.

I steel myself, draw my knees up, then topple into the water and begin to swim.

Sorry, Skye. Sometimes we need to improvise.

Well.

I *did* want dramatic.

SIXTEEN

Maya

About a minute into the swim, I realize just how bad an idea this is. The water is freaking *cold*. I am going to freeze and sink to the bottom of the lake in a human-shaped ice cube, and Jordy is going to get a disgustingly romanticized TV special about the exquisite grief of watching an ex-girlfriend die right in front of him.

Potentially two ex-girlfriends, if I don't reach Skye soon.

Skye watches me with amused exasperation, one eyebrow quirked, as I gradually inch closer and closer. "Do you need help?" she calls.

"*You* need help," I pant.

She looks around her with her lower lip stuck out. "I'm actually doing pretty well. It's a lovely day for it."

Gee, I'm glad *one* of us has the energy to make jokes right now. This would be a lot easier if the kayak weren't drifting almost as fast as I can swim. With a burst of effort, I launch into a freestyle stroke with my head down. Hell yeah, *now* I'm moving. I swim for about thirty seconds at full speed before I peek up to check my progress. I'd fully expected to have reached the kayak by now, but to my frustration, I'm still about twenty feet out. "Stop *moving*," I groan between gasps.

"Sorry," Skye says drily. "I'll try harder."

Gradually, I manage to close in on the kayak. By the time I slap a hand on the plastic side, my vision is starting to close in on the edges.

Skye props her chin on laced fingers. "My hero."

"You know, a little less sarcasm and a little more gratitude wouldn't go astray here," I get out.

The corner of Skye's mouth twitches. "I'll work on that, but first, just quickly, what was your plan here? Given that, yet again, you're strayed from the one we agreed on?"

I pause. "What?"

"Are you going to pull me back to shore?"

Water is streaming from my hair into my eyes, so I slick it back off my forehead, agitated. "If you jump in, I can swim us back."

She bursts out laughing. "That's not happening."

"It's fine, I promise. I've got you."

"Can you touch the bottom?"

"Well, no, but—"

"Maya, listen to me closely. I would not join you in there if you offered me a million dollars and Jordy's head on a platter."

"Okay." I rest my forearms gently on the bow of her kayak. The weight tilts the kayak a little, and she looks over at the water in alarm. "So, now what?"

"Great question." Her brow furrows as her gaze trails over my head. "Oh. Apparently we're saved. Magnificent."

I look over my shoulder. Two boats are speeding our way, one carrying Isaac, Gwendolyn, and the camera crew (who are currently filming us, so, at least that part worked out), and the other carrying Jordy. Gwendolyn must have told him to pose, because he's standing with his legs planted apart, holding onto the windshield to steady himself with one hand, and shielding his eyes from the sun with the other as he stares out to us. It's too far away to tell, but I can only assume he's wearing a dramatically concerned expression.

Also, his shirt's unbuttoned again.

Gwendolyn pulls out a megaphone. "Maya! Get back in the water!"

"I'm already in the water," I say to Skye. "Does she have us mixed up?"

"I think she means let go of the kayak," Skye supplies helpfully.

"Let go of the kayak!" Gwendolyn clarifies, her muddied, metallic voice booming across the water.

I do as I'm told, and Skye begins to float away from me again.

"Hold on, Maya!" Jordy bellows at the tops of his lungs. "Just hold on!"

"I'm literally fine," I mutter, bobbing in the water. Behind me, I can hear Skye's cackles over the roar of the approaching speedboats. I assume they'll remove those from the final cut.

"Just try! To stay! Afloat! I've got you!"

Gwendolyn is gesturing frantically at me. I realize a little too late she wants me to feign drowning. I have just enough time to get in a weak splash and drop my chin below the surface when Jordy's boat reaches me. He leans over the side and stretches his hand out, his face the picture of concern and—impressively—even the tiniest hint of fear. I can almost believe it myself.

"Are you okay?" he asks.

"I'm fi—"

"*Are you okay?*"

I scowl and take his hand. "*Yes,* Jesus."

With a grunt, Jordy yanks me easily out of the water and onto the boat, where he pulls me into a hug so rough I choke on my own gasp. Over his shoulder, I have full view of the lake, along with Skye, who is growing small again as she drifts. I feel like we should probably follow up on that. You know, given Skye is the one who actually, in real life, not in a man-ufactured way, is at risk of drowning, here. "Hey, Skye's—"

"You're safe now," Jordy says over me.

"Yes, thank you. That was . . ." I search for a compliment that I can force out without it coming across as sarcastic. "Very chivalrous of you."

"Good job, Maya," Isaac calls from his boat, giving me a thumbs-up as their boat circles us.

"That was great," says Gwendolyn. "Can we just get that rescue one more time at a different angle? A little more grace-ful this time? Think *sex*, like the front cover of an old-school romance novel." She frames an imaginary picture with her hands. "The rugged, handsome hero pulls the breathless maiden from the clutches of death and then ravages her. Met-aphorically."

"Sexy drowning!" Jordy says as Gwendolyn beams and nods. "I love it."

Isaac's smile has gotten mighty tight.

"Oh." I blink. "Um."

"Jump on back in, there, Maya," Jordy says. "Don't worry. I'll be right here." He shoots me a dazzling smile, then gives me a little shove toward the edge of the boat.

"Maybe we should go collect Skye first?" I try. "We can get the shot later—"

Gwendolyn shakes her head impatiently. "No, right now, nice and quick. Come on."

Okay, clearly the more I protest, the longer we're going to leave Skye stranded. Just as I'm about to jump in the water, Jordy gives me another little shove, and I fall in with a shriek. I emerge like a drowned rat, gasping, and Jordy winces down at me. "Sorry!" he says. "I was trying to steady you!"

If there wasn't a camera around I'd pull the prick into the fucking water with me. Instead, I let Jordy pull me back up again, making sure to look as fear-ridden yet inexplicably sexy as possible, to avoid the need for another retake. Luckily, they let us off with just the two takes at saving my life, and a couple of minutes later we're off, racing after Skye. To my relief, Skye is totally safe when we finally reach her, if *kind of* unimpressed.

"What happened?" Jordy laughs as we pull to a stop.

Skye looks at me as she replies to him. "I thought I'd check out the other end of the lake."

"And how was it?"

"Water's always bluer on the other side." She tears her eyes from me, then surveys the boat warily. "How am I supposed to get in?"

Jordy stretches his hand out, and Skye can barely hide her look of disdain at the idea of touching him. I start to rise to help, but Gwendolyn motions for me to sit back down and get out of the shot.

If Jordy drowns my co-conspirator I'm going to actually kill him.

Luckily, the transfer goes smoothly. Jordy lifts Skye into the boat, and, apparently, does it sexily enough on the first attempt that they don't need to reshoot. Life is so simple for beautiful people.

"We're going to have to cut the photoshoots with these two," Isaac says to Jordy. "We're out of time now."

"Got it." Jordy slips back into the front seat beside the driver, as Gwendolyn and Isaac's boat speeds off ahead of us. Skye and I sit behind Jordy, ignored, apparently, now we aren't in immediate danger of drowning. Or, more accurately, now we aren't doing anything interesting for the cameras. Now that the adrenaline rush is wearing off, I suddenly notice how quickly the temperature has dropped with evening approaching. I curl into myself to brace against what's going to be a super freaking uncomfortable trip back to shore. My shoulders are already shaking from the cold.

Skye glances at me, then frowns. "Do you have a towel, or a blanket or something?" she asks. "She's freezing."

The driver shakes his head. Jordy turns around, frowning. "I can take my shirt off?" he asks.

So he can show off his chiseled back, too, and get a shot of him acting chivalrous? I think the fuck not. I shake my head sweetly. "For the sake of the show, you should leave it on," I say. "You can't be naked the *whole* first two episodes, or the people at home will be immune to it by next week."

"Good thinking," Jordy says, before promptly turning around and forgetting all about us again.

Skye sighs and sends a pointed glower to the back of Jordy's head, then wraps her arm around my shoulder and pulls me into her. So, we *are* touching-friends now, then.

Now that I'm tucked into her chest, the sting of the wind is dulled, and suddenly all I'm aware of is the heady scent of perfume on her neck. And the pressure of her arm. And the steady rhythm of her breathing as she rests her head against the top of mine.

"He's missing a golden promo shot opportunity," Skye whispers, just loudly enough for me to hear her over the roar of the engine. "It should be him sitting here."

I grin up at her, then look around to check on the camera operator. He's filming our boat dutifully, and he gives me a little wave when he notices me looking. I raise a hand in return.

"I would place any bet that this isn't getting into the final cut," Skye says. "Can you picture it? Sweeping music, a voiceover insisting that he's devoted, and romantic—no, truly, everyone, we promise, it's not what it looks like."

"Then the camera pans to him sitting in the front of the boat, pretending we don't exist."

"The voiceover cuts to a clip of him shoving you in the water."

"Oh, you saw that?"

"I did see that. I think our ex-boyfriend might be a psychopath, you know."

"That's what I've been *trying* to *tell* you!"

When we finally make it back to the pier, the other girls are already gone, whisked away to the mansion to get ready for the next *Notte Infinita*.

"You won't have time for a shower, Maya," Isaac says apologetically. "Just . . . scoop your hair up, get dressed, and I'll run to the hotel with Jordy and find you one of his coats to wear. We'll spin a thing about him rescuing you and taking you both straight here."

"Thanks," I say wryly, and he wiggles his eyebrows at me. He, at least, seems thrilled with the "rescue" plotline we've given them.

Pity it made the wrong person look like a hero.

Back at the house, Skye and I hurriedly change into the dresses we laid out for tonight—Skye's, a shocking-pink two-piece that exposes a tanned strip of stomach, and mine an off-the-shoulder with puffy sleeves in a shade of soft violet. Then we pack the rest of our suitcases—just in case Jordy decides to kick one of us off right after dramatically saving our lives—and run downstairs, where everyone else is hanging out at the bottom of the staircase.

". . . photoshoot was actually really fun," Francesca is saying to the girls. "I think I'm actually starting to like him, a little? Is that too soon? He said he thinks I could be a model, which is ridiculous, obviously, but it gave me—"

"Oh my god, Skye!" Lauren says as she sees us. "Are you okay?"

The girls swarm in as we join them.

"We told the producers you were drifting," Kim says. She's standing with her own packed suitcase, ready to be whisked off with Jordy straight after we finish shooting tonight. "But you were so far out by then! They made us go inside before they even got to you."

"I can't believe you swam after her," Francesca says to me, and Lauren and Kim turn, wide-eyed and earnest.

"Yeah, that was wild," Kim says.

"It was *brave*," Lauren adds.

"It was *dangerous*," Perrie says, frowning at me.

I shrug at the ground, uncomfortable with all the praise. Maybe if I'd earned it, sure. If they knew how un-accidental the whole thing was, they might be a little less impressed with me. "My kayak was tied up, and she was drifting, and I couldn't get the producers' attention, so I figured if I quickly went after her I could reach her."

Perrie's eyebrow quirks at what she knows to be a lie, but, bless her, she doesn't sell me out to the others.

Lauren places a hand on my shoulder. "That," she says, "says a lot about you."

The others nod in a chorus, while Skye valiantly suppresses laughter.

Well, let's look on the bright side. Earned or not, this is the first time they've looked at me like maybe they wouldn't enjoy my immediate, unexpected death. So, maybe we didn't manage to rehabilitate my image for the camera. Is it possible that, completely by accident, we've managed to rehabilitate my image with the other girls?

"Well, I suppose I owe you my life now," Skye says as we head into the filming room.

"Sweet. I love having people owe me." I grin. "I might abuse this."

"I wouldn't expect any less."

In the room, Isaac is waiting, as promised, with an enormous brown overcoat. "Jordy didn't have one that looked right," he says, "so I borrowed this from the camera crew."

I put it on. It drowns me.

Gwendolyn peeks her head out the door to check on us, and presses a hand over her heart when she sees me. "You look so pathetic," she says, sighing. "Like a little drowned puppy. Oh, Isaac, it's *perfect*."

As soon as she leaves, I go to yank the jacket off, but Skye and Isaac wrestle me back into it and convince me to head inside.

"Well," Jordy says, once Grayson has finished his regular generic spiel for the cameras. "Today was . . . eventful. But I hope you all enjoyed yourselves as much as I did. Today, I had the opportunity to see even more sides to all of you, and I have to say I'm getting more impressed by the day. But, sadly, if I'm going to get to know some of you even better, I need to figure out who I think is just a really awesome chick, and who I think might be the one who was right there all along. So, with that being said . . . tonight I've decided to keep Lauren."

Lauren beams, hugs Jordy, and joins Kim, who's standing beside Jordy already. Naturally, winning the night alone with him has given her a free pass through tonight's culling.

"Perrie."

"Maya."

I can't suppress a grin of my own, hearing my name. Jordy gives my back a condescending pat as we hug, like I'm a baby he's trying to burp. "So glad you're okay," he stage-whispers, and I fight the urge to squeeze the air out of him until he chokes.

"And Skye."

My stomach swoops with relief as Skye embraces Jordy and joins the rest of us. She locks eyes with me as she does, and we share a secret smile. It's only when Jordy stops speaking that I realize the significance of the "and."

I turn to Francesca, who's staring at Jordy with a look that can only really be described as betrayal.

"Francesca, it's been so amazing getting to know you better," Jordy says, and I remember Francesca's excited babbling about Jordy earlier. How he'd complimented her, and, by the sounds of it, charmed the heck out of her. Now, he's choosing to cut her loose, right as she was feeling comfortable around him.

Gee. I wonder what *that* feels like.

Francesca wipes the look of pain off her face for the cameras, and nods with a forced smile.

Grayson takes over at this point. "Time to say your goodbyes," he says with a look of pity that somehow seems like a smile as well.

Francesca walks numbly over to us. "I . . . didn't see *this* coming after today," she says under her breath, her lips barely moving. "I'll, uh . . . wow. Well. It was so great to get to know all of you."

"You, too!"

"We'll see you soon."

"When this is over, we'll all catch up again, okay?"

And, with the cameras following her, she walks, alone, out of the room.

"And then there were five," Skye whispers into my ear. The heat of her breath makes my neck prickle.

Personally, I'm shocked to not be the first one sent home.

Especially when I missed the chance to talk to Jordy alone today.

But here I am.

And between Skye and me, our chances of revenge have just gone up to 40 percent.

Now those are odds we can work with.

SEVENTEEN

Skye

Kim returns from her night with Jordy apparently brimming with the urge to share every detail. And given that, like the rest of us, she can't analyze the details with friends and family—and Francesca has suddenly departed—that leaves us as the unwilling audience.

"We stayed up until practically sunrise," she gushes, spinning on her barstool by the kitchen island counters. Lauren is sitting on the counter next to her, and Maya, Perrie, and I are at the dining table clutching mugs of coffee and tea. "Talking and . . . other stuff . . . Oh, and we called my parents, and Vivaan, because he said he missed them, but *really* I know he knew I missed them. Isn't that the most thoughtful thing you've ever heard? And they brought us a cheese plate, and he has an Xbox in his room so we played that for a while. He said he's never met a girl he could game with before."

Maya snorts into her coffee, and Kim swings around, annoyed. "*What,* Maya?"

"Oh, nothing," she says. "Just, Jordy and I used to play Xbox all the time."

Kim's expression cools even further. "Well, congratulations."

Maya and her inexplicable inability to self-censor are absolutely going to make winning this far more difficult than it needs to be. At this rate, she's going to have erased all the ground she gained with the kayak ploy by lunch. "I don't think she meant it like that," I jump in. "I think she just meant it sounds a little like a . . . line."

"It wasn't a line." Kim's voice is icy. "You weren't there."

"Don't you think it's a bit weird to make up something like that, though?" Maya asks. I nudge her foot with mine under the table, but it's too late.

Kim smacks a hand on the counter. "Maybe he just forgot, Maya, you were together, like, a billion years ago."

"I doubt it," Maya mumbles.

"You're such a bitch when you get jealous, Maya, you know that?" Kim asks.

"What game did you play?" Lauren asks loudly before Maya can dig her hole any deeper.

As Kim goes on, I lean in to whisper to Maya and Perrie. "He used to play Xbox with me, too." I shoot Maya a loaded look. *Here. I'm validating you. You're not imagining things. But for the love of all that is holy, let it go.*

". . . then he said he was especially hoping I'd come on the show," Kim says. I notice a slight raise in Lauren's eyebrows at this. I'm quite sure mine do the same. *That* line sounds familiar. "I mean, we only broke up because he had to move, so it's not like we ever left things on bad terms . . ."

Perrie shares Lauren's "excuse me?" expression. Maya looks as though she's about to overflow with the urge to say something. I catch her eye, and shake my head.

Be. Smart.

Unfortunately, Kim catches me giving Maya this obviously loaded look. "Yeah, okay," she says, hopping off the stool. "Got it. Don't talk about Jordy with you guys."

"Oh, Kim, that's not it," Maya says, but Kim is already flouncing out of the room.

"Why did it have to be Francesca?" Kim mutters as she leaves, just loudly enough for me to make out.

Lauren shoots the table a chiding look. "You could've at least pretended to be interested," she says. "I know it's weird, but all we've got is each other, and it could be you wanting to talk about a date next week."

"Sure," Perrie says slowly, "but, correct me if I'm wrong, did all of that sound familiar to anyone else?"

"*Yes,* for fuck's sake, yes," Maya bursts out, throwing her arms up.

"Let it out, Maya." I grin. I'm not sure if I want to tell her off or burst into laughter and hug her. Not that that's new, when it comes to Maya.

Lauren gives a single-shoulder shrug and sets about washing her mug. "I don't know. Is it really that shocking that we all had similar experiences dating the same guy? Of course there are going to be overlaps. It's not a conspiracy."

"You don't think it's gross for him to use the same lines on all of us?" Maya presses, because she simply can't help herself, apparently. Well, at least she's sticking to the "convert Lauren and Perrie" plan. "Especially the ones that are basically lies?"

"Flirting is lying," Lauren says, putting the mug in the cupboard with a clang. "You try being honest the next time you meet a guy, go on. Tell him he's about a five out of ten, and that you're willing to kiss him even though his chin's so big you can barely navigate around it. Tell him his laugh is cute enough to make you look past the fact that he doesn't know how to joke without quoting *The Simpsons.* See how far your honesty gets you."

"It worked for Mr. Darcy," Perrie says.

"No, Perrie, it got Mr. Darcy's butt rejected," Lauren says. "And in any case, even if you do believe it, time and place. We want to be supporting each other, not tearing each other down, right? That *includes* not making one of our own feel crappy after having a nice time with Jordy, okay? If you want to be part of the royal family, it's all about etiquette. Social graces, girls."

She says it calmly and in a pleasant enough tone, but even Maya looks a little chastened by it. I think I might need to take notes.

"Has anyone told you you'd make an amazing elementary school teacher, Lauren?" I ask lazily. "You've really got the whole 'sweet guilt trip' thing down to a T."

"Actually," Lauren says, brightening and raising her chin in a dignified way, "I'm studying to become a kindergarten teacher."

"Well," I say, getting to my feet and shooting Maya another look, "you've picked a good path. Consider this extra-credit training. If you can make these kids behave, you'll be able to handle anything."

Maya sticks her tongue out at me, and I blow her a kiss as I head out to finish my coffee by the pool.

I have just enough time to catch the perplexed look on her face before I close the door behind me.

The next Tuesday, I spend the better part of the afternoon getting ready with the bathroom all to myself. An unprecedented luxury. This episode, we're doing things a little differently. Instead of a group challenge, each of us is spending some time alone with Jordy, re-creating our first dates, spread out over the whole week.

Unfortunately, my one-on-one date with the bathroom is rudely interrupted by Maya bursting in on me without knocking as I'm applying a sweep of brown eyeshadow.

"So, Lauren just got back," she says, hoisting herself to sit on the counter. "And guess what she and Jordy did."

"Hi, come on in, please join me."

"A helicopter ride over all the royal buildings in the state!"

I slam my hand on the counter, makeup brush and all. "So the helicopter *does* exist!"

"What?"

"What?"

"Never mind. She and Jordy were *fifteen*. Who's going to believe two fifteen-year-olds chartered a helicopter on their first date?"

I go back to my eye makeup. "Why didn't I think to lie? I dated a future fake-royal and all I got was a chocolate fondue date."

"At least you get chocolate. We went for a hike. A *hike*. Do you think it's too late to tell Isaac we went Jet Skiing?"

"When's your date?"

"Tomorrow."

"Yeah, I think it might be a little late for them to source Jet Skis now."

Maya sighs dramatically and kicks the cabinet. "This is such bullshit."

I put down the brush and sort through the clutter in my makeup bag in search of a lipstick.

"Hold on," Maya says, leaning forward. I look up and she squints at me. "You missed a spot. Can I . . ."

"Oh, yeah, sure."

I close my eyes and a second later there's a gentle pressure on the corner of my eyelid as she rubs her thumb over it.

"I think you at least have enough time to tell them you

forgot to mention a picnic at the end of the hike," I say as she works. "If you're spending the day walking around with Jordy, the least you deserve is some good food at the end of it."

"You're a genius, hell yeah I'm doing that." She pulls back, and my skin feels cold in her sudden absence. "Perfect. As you were."

"So, I was thinking," I say, turning back to the mirror. "We've got the girls mostly on our side now. It's time to help them see what Jordy's like."

"Got it. Any thoughts on how?"

"That's what we need to brainstorm," I say. "So far, we've tried pointing out his hypocrisy, but I think we need to get them to come up with their own Jordy horror stories. I think Lauren and Kim are in denial a little."

"Gee, you think?"

"But if they think about their own experiences more critically, something might click."

Maya nods briskly. "Roger. Can do."

"Can do what? We haven't figured out the plan yet."

"What's there to figure out? We'll find a way to make them share Jordy stories. I understand the assignment."

"But how? The *how* is generally the hardest part."

"Eh. I'll figure it out." She starts to walk to the door.

"*How?*" I repeat.

"I'll *figure it out*. The only thing I want to help you plan right now is an outfit. Come on."

With that, she vanishes, leaving me to sigh in frustration and follow after her.

"Honestly, they all look great," Maya says as I pull on option three, a cropped, boxy T-shirt. "I don't think you have the ability to look bad in anything. It's like a superpower."

"Hardly," I say, but I can't help but smile as I look at myself in the mirror.

Maya stands beside me and examines my reflection in the mirror. "Stay with the crop."

"Yeah?"

"Totally. Jordy will appreciate the strip of skin."

"Did he tell you that once?" I ask absently, tugging on the bottom of the crop while I survey myself in the wardrobe mirror.

"No, but I love when girls have a little skin showing there, so I have to assume Jordy does, too. He's an asshat, but he has good taste."

My ears prick up at that. Does she mean she loves it aesthetically, or she finds it attractive? Before I can ask, she plows on. "Are you nervous? I don't even wanna *think* about how I'm gonna get through three hours alone with that . . . that chunk of *swamp scum.*"

"Burn."

"But seriously, are you good?"

"Maya," I say, folding my arms. "I am more than good. It's Jordy who should be nervous."

She nods, and bounces on her heels. "You've got this," she says.

"I've got this," I echo. And smile.

It's a strained smile, though.

The production team has arranged a small mountain of dessert on a wooden table, in a forest clearing approximately a hundred meters from the mansion. They've included the chocolate fondue as promised—although they've improved it somewhat by including marshmallows, pretzels, and sliced bananas along with the strawberries. It's no helicopter ride over the lake at sunset, but, in a marvelous stroke of good luck, according to Isaac, apparently the chocolate itself is something to be excited about. Lucky me.

"We got it in Switzerland," he'd said when we arrived, like that was supposed to mean something especially impressive. When I hadn't reacted as excitedly as he'd hoped, he'd tutted. "Swiss chocolate is made with milk from Happy Cows. Something something, the grass they eat is watered by glaciers. It's fucking fancy, okay? You're welcome."

The surrounding trees have been draped with strings of twinkling fairy lights, which I'm sure will look picturesque when the sun has set enough to show them off. As the crew sets up the cameras and lighting, Jordy saunters over to stand beside me. I clench my teeth as soon as he comes close, and fight the urge to get as far away from him as I can.

"I wish we lied and told them we had fried chicken on our first date," he says. "I'd kill for some right now."

"Didn't you already lie to get that helicopter ride?" I ask mildly. "Don't be greedy."

"No, Lauren lied. I just didn't correct her."

"Which is basically lying."

"You're actually wrong about that," Jordy says without skipping a beat. "If you look up the dictionary definition, you won't see a word about staying silent. You can't just lump one term in with another because you think they're equally morally wrong, now, can you, Skye?"

"Seems to me like you're using semantics to get away with something you know is immoral."

"You told me once you liked my moral flexibility."

"If you're referring to the time we skipped bio to make out in the bathroom—"

"One of my favorite memories."

"As far as crimes against humanity go, that particular piece of flexibility was victimless."

"Speaking of flexibility, do you think they ever repaired that tap we broke that day?" I glare at him, and he tugs on my jacket. "Don't tell me you've gone all Goody Two-Shoes on me, Skye. That's no fun at all."

I pull away. "You're irritating me."

"And you're cute when you're irritated."

It's fascinating. Before Maya's reveal, it hadn't occurred to me how . . . smug, I suppose, Jordy is. But now I'm aware, it's all I can see, to the extent where I'm baffled I never noticed earlier. I suppose when you trust someone not to hurt you, red flags look heart-shaped.

To think I'd fancied myself careful then. *God*, I was barely scraping the surface of how careful I actually need to be.

The team keeps us waiting for what feels like an eternity, until twilight eases into dusk and the trees begin to glitter noticeably. Then, finally, we're allowed to sit. Sit, but not eat.

"Just chat for a while," Isaac says. "We won't be able to pick you up clearly if you have a mouthful of food, and chewing sounds terrible on film."

Great. So, I'm starving, and we have all this Happy Cow chocolate sitting in front of us teasingly, and we can't even eat it? They might as well have just gotten us chocolate made from regular old morose cows.

Jordy, at least, doesn't seem surprised by this. "You look beautiful tonight, Skye," he says, shaking his head as he talks like he can't quite believe it. "You've always been beautiful, though. I used to look at you and think, huh, that girl is beautiful the way a sunset's beautiful. You just can't look away."

"Oh. How poetic. Thank you, Jordy."

He looks awfully pleased with himself.

After we finish not eating dinner, Isaac and Wai set me up

on a garden swing hanging from a nearby tree, and film some talking-head lines.

"How did you feel when you saw the setup?" Isaac asks.

I make sure to include the question in my answer so it can be used as a voiceover. "When I saw the setup, I was blown away. It was *just* like our first date, except more magical. The chocolate fondue, the fairy lights . . . Jordy . . . it was perfect."

Isaac winks at me. "You're getting good at this," he says.

"Practice."

We take a break after this to plan the next shots and review the footage they've got. I stay on the swing, and Jordy lowers himself beside me. He leans forward and gently tugs on the length of my hair. "I'm so glad you decided to grow this out," he says. "It's so . . . feminine now."

My fingers trail unconsciously to it. "I've been meaning to cut it again," I lie.

"You should consider keeping it."

I blink, and shift in place. "I don't remember you having a problem with it short?"

"Not when we were kids. But you're . . . a woman now, right?" He laughs at himself. "Did that come out corny?"

Corny isn't the word I'd use, no. "I see."

"I just mean it's nice to . . . use what you've got. Like, look at her."

He's pointing to Perrie's producer, Violet, who's showing Isaac something on her iPad.

"What about her?"

I can't keep the edge entirely out of my voice.

"She's wearing jeans and a T-shirt. To her *workplace*. And I bet you anything you like that if she misses out on a promotion she'll bring up unfairness, blame the bosses, et cetera."

The way he words it is savvy. Jordy's too careful to spell

out what he really means while he's being recorded. But the implication simmering beneath his words is palpable.

He's not careful enough to keep those sorts of comments to himself altogether while he's being recorded by a team of Violet's coworkers, of course. Maybe he's forgotten?

No, that's unlikely. Not Jordy.

He simply doesn't care if she finds out what he said about her.

"I just think you need to take responsibility for your own role in how your life goes," Jordy goes on, oblivious to my discomfort. "If you don't respect yourself, you can't expect others to."

"You think if I cut my hair short I'm not respecting myself?" I ask before I can help it.

Jordy looks horrified, like he can't *imagine* how I leapt to a conclusion like that. "No! Not you. I was talking about that female producer."

"Well, I disagree with your thoughts on her," I say coolly. "I think she looks great, and I'd wear jeans if my job let me, too."

"All right. Let me know how that goes for you, Skye," he says with an eyebrow raise and a grin. As though this is an adorable inside joke we now have. "But in the meantime, just know that I appreciate you as you are. You're sweet. You're funny—you're probably one of the only *actually* funny girls I know. And you're classy. There's a reason you're still here and someone like Francesca isn't, put it that way. Don't undervalue that about yourself, okay?"

Then, he excuses himself for a bathroom break, leaving me to stare after him.

Jordy's opinion means less than nothing to me, so there's absolutely no point in getting upset. The indignant anger that's prickling at my fingertips isn't useful. I have a goal, and I'm not going to fall on my sword over *this*.

Still.

"Isaac," I call. As he approaches the swing, I dig my heels into the dirt to stop it in its tracks.

"Hey," he says, beaming. "You're doing great. He looks like he's actually connecting with you."

"Wonderful . . . Hey, Isaac? Can you get me an electric shaver?"

His eyebrows fly together. "Why do you need—"

"Can you do it?"

"I mean, sure. We've got at least one in hair and makeup."

"Tonight?"

"Skye, what—" He pauses, then sighs. "Tell me no one's gonna get hurt. Don't do anything reckless."

"No one's getting hurt. Who do you think I am?" I press a hand over my chest in mock offense. "Although I can't make any promises about the reckless thing."

EIGHTEEN

Maya

When Skye returns from her date with Jordy, she's armed with scissors and an electric razor.

"Hey, you. Did you wash his blood off of those already?" I ask from the bed as she kicks her shoes off so viciously they bounce off the wall.

"Will you help me?" she asks, swinging around.

I sit up. "With what?"

She just beckons me out of the room, and, with a groan, I drag myself up and follow her to the bathroom.

In front of the mirror, she starts sectioning her hair. Just as I click onto what's about to happen, she grabs a fistful of long brown hair and hacks it off with the scissors.

"Oh, okay, cool, this is what we're doing." I try to keep the surprise out of my voice, but it only half works.

"Yes, we are. If you could help me with the back, that'd be great."

"Sure. But, um . . . you okay there, bud?"

"Fantastic."

"Great, great . . . it's just, usually when people cut all their hair off without notice—"

"It's fine, I've done it before. This has actually been the

first time I've worn it long. I'm bored with it, don't read into things."

"Bored, huh?" I say skeptically, watching another chunk of hair drop to the floor. "Usually I'd suggest trying out a new Netflix show or something, but, no, this works, too."

"Can you get this piece?" she asks, swiveling so her back's to me. She's holding one last chunk of hair, twice as long as the surrounding bits.

"I . . . are you sure?"

She huffs. "No, Maya, I'm going to walk around with one piece of long hair in the middle of my back. I'm committed now, aren't I?"

So, I take the lock from her, our hands brushing in the changeover. Turns out her hair's just about as soft as it looks. I turn it over, trying to figure out the best way to hack it, and it catches the light with a flash of reddish gold.

"Just chop it," Skye says. "We'll tidy it after. Just . . ." She makes a slicing motion in midair.

I do, the scissors scraping at the hair as I cut through the thickness of it. My stomach swoops as the hair falls to the floor. Done.

What a normal way to spend a Wednesday night.

The rest of the haircut is quick work. Me working at the back, her taking care of the front, we tidy up the ends of the hair until she has a pretty damn impressive pixie cut going on, complete with a deep side part. As a finishing flourish, she shaves down one of the sides, leaving a soft, downy area behind. It's the kind of hairstyle I'd never, ever, in a million years even dream of trying out, but she does it like it's nothing, and looks fucking incredible while she's at it.

Can't relate.

"I think this is the first time I've ever seen you do something spontaneous," I say, kicking my foot out so a lock of hair falls off the sock and to the ground. "Unless you were always planning on changing your look in week three. Long-term game plan?"

She catches my eye in the mirror. "No. It just felt right, so I did it. You of all people get that, surely?"

"No, I get that. Fair." But there's something about her expression. A sort of mixture of defiance and sadness that makes me want to press things just a bit harder. "Do you wanna talk about why it felt right all of a sudden?"

She shrugs, then turns to me. "I do, but . . . don't take this the wrong way, but not to you. Not to anyone in the house. I just wish my friend Chloe was here."

Well, I can do something about that, can't I?

"Come on," I say. "What's the point of smuggling in an iPad if you're not gonna use it?"

Ten minutes later, Skye's hanging by the closed door, standing guard while I fish my iPad out. "Why didn't I think to bring my own?" she grumbles.

"Now who's got foresight?" I tease.

She stays silent.

"Say it. Say I have foresight."

"What's that saying about broken clocks being right twice a day?"

"I'm not a broken clock, Skye, I'm a genius. And I also happen to be the only person who knows the passcode to this thing."

"Okay, okay, you're a genius who's got foresight."

I log in to the iPad and hand it over.

"Occasionally," she adds under her breath, and I shoot her a *look*.

We climb onto the bottom bunk and she logs in to one of her accounts. Suddenly, I realize I should be giving her some space, but I don't really have anything else to do so I settle for standing in front of the wardrobe and staring at our clothes awkwardly.

Wow, there sure are . . . clothes in here.

"She's around!" Skye says excitedly, drawing her legs up to her chest to chat. Her whole vibe has changed, like she's lit up from within. She looks like the weight of the world has vanished from her back. Now she finally has someone she can talk to.

The smile that came over me when I first looked at her fades, and this realization sort of tugs in a sad way at my stomach. I'm not sure why, though, because it's hard-core ridiculous, right? To be upset she doesn't want to talk to me more than her oldest friend? I mean, for god's sake, we barely know each other. Hell, a week ago we couldn't stand each other.

I guess it's just that I'm starting to like her a whole lot, and it hadn't occurred to me that feeling might not be mutual. Which is something I need to get over fast, because how pathetic is that, moping around because you like someone more than they like you? *Get a grip, Maya.*

"Do you mind if I message my dad, too?" she asks.

"Oh my god, no, of course. I wish I'd thought to let you use it earlier."

"You know," she says in an absentminded way, "you could use this to win over Kim and Lauren. They'll be much more susceptible to influence if they're your biggest fans."

"True. But I'm not sure I'm ready to risk losing my iPad."

"Well, what do you want more? To chat with your friends, or to take Jordy down?"

I don't reply. A few more minutes pass, and Skye lets out a gasp of horror.

"What happened?" I ask, straightening. "Is everything okay?"

"I googled us. I'm sorry, I had to see."

"Oh." I climb onto the bed next to her to look at the screen. "Yeah. I've been trying not to look, actually. It's just been annoying me."

She has the screen open to a forum. The topic is whether or not Skye seems stuck up in episode two, which aired tonight. Most of the commenters are furiously standing up for Skye against the original poster, but, still. The way this random person could be so wrong, yet so loud about it? Trash.

"Don't read that," I scold, pressing back to take us to the main page.

Out of curiosity, I scan the topics on the page.

Team Skye!!!

Team Kim <3

Anyone else noticed . . .

Mayas such a bitch wtf

Jordy's too good for all of them

Are they all drunk?

TOO MUCH GIRL HATE ON HERE!!!!!!!

Obsessed with Jordy's accent

My stomach sinks when I see my name. I mean, I knew it wouldn't be good, otherwise we wouldn't be trying so hard to make me likable now. But there's a reason I've been avoiding googling any mention of the show on pain of death.

I've already had a lifetime's worth of random people thinking I suck before even meeting me, and I don't need any
more of that shit.

Someone has to stand up for Skye. And someone has to
stand up for me, for once. So, if no one else is going to be that
someone, screw it, I'll do it myself.

I take the iPad from her and click onto the login page.

"What are you doing? You can't post anything, you'll get
caught."

"It's my burner account. They won't trace it back to me."

I start a new topic:

> The truth about Jordy.

"Maya, be careful. Think it over," Skye urges.

"It's fine. I know what I'm doing."

> I know Jordy in person, and in real life he's not like he
> seems on the show. He cheated on Maya Bailey, then
> spread horrible rumors about her. He's patronizing, and
> rude, and says awful things about women. He's a slut-
> shamer, too. And his accent isn't real. He grew up in
> the US.

"Maya!" she gasps as I press enter. "You'd better be certain there's nothing on your burner that can trace this back
to you!"

"I'm *sure*, Skye, chill out."

Skye is silent for a long time. Then, finally, she gives a
reluctant smile. "I hope it goes viral."

"That's the spirit."

"You know what?" she says suddenly. "I need a walk. I have
too much angry energy right now."

She rolls off the bed, then turns back to me with raised eyebrows. "Aren't you coming?" she asks.

"Oh." I hadn't realized I was invited. "Cool. Let me just grab a jacket."

Once I've finished expertly styling my pajamas with a puffer jacket and slippers, Skye takes me into the forest, where she filmed her first-date re-creation with Jordy earlier. She looks hopefully at a picnic bench, then sighs. "They didn't let us eat any of the chocolate. I thought maybe they'd left it behind."

"I guess it became the producers' dessert."

"They didn't even feed me! I should sue."

"Oh, shit. I bet we can find something in the kitchen for you?"

"That is simply not the point."

She flops down into a garden swing with flower wreaths snaking around the arms. I sit beside her, and she shuffles over to make room for me. It's a tight fit, but we make it work.

"So," I say. "Any advice for my date?"

Skye kicks us off the ground and we swing gently. "Yes, in fact. Act like you couldn't care less about him." I laugh, but she doesn't join in. "I'm serious."

"I'm not following."

She sighs. "You said you two met when you were at softball, right? And he used to come to see *your* games? Show up wherever *you* were?"

I think of Jordy coming to talk to me when I rolled my ankle. Cheering me on from the sidelines with his friends. Asking me on that hike after weeks of me assuming we were just friends.

"Yeah," I say finally. "I guess so."

"That's Jordy's thing. He wants what he can't have, trust

me. I know him. Think about your first night here. You said he wasn't interested, right?"

"Right."

"Because you were trying to win him over, right?"

I blink, nodding reluctantly.

"Then when you didn't want anything to do with him, magically he didn't want to send you home anymore?"

Suddenly, things are making a whole lot more sense. "Wow."

"Exactly. I told you, I understand him. So, I'm not saying to be absolutely awful to him. But if you want to get to the end, make sure he's pursuing you the whole time. Don't let him think he's won."

I kick my legs out in front of us and huff. "I feel like we're setting feminism back by a few decades right now."

"No, we are weaponizing Jordy's fetish for outdated gender roles to beat him at his own game. Personally, I'm perfectly comfortable."

I think on this. "How is it possible we both survived Jordy without serious issues?"

"Well, for me, I suppose it's because I had serious issues before I met Jordy. Also are you quite sure you haven't been left with issues? The last time I checked, you dropped literally everything in your life to come on reality TV to bring him down."

"Hey!"

"I am just stating a fact, Maya, don't shoot the messenger."

The moonlight catches on her newly shortened hair as we swing. I stare at it for a few moments. Silver now, instead of gold. "What sort of issues?" I ask.

"Hmm?"

"You said you had issues before Jordy."

"Oh." She laughs airily. "It was mostly a joke. I suppose I just mean I'm pretty careful about who I let in."

"How come?" I ask.

"I assume it's related to the fact that my mom left the family when I was a kid and I haven't heard from her since."

"Oh. I didn't realize."

"Oddly enough, I don't regularly bring it up in conversation. When people ask how you're doing, they don't want you to say, 'Fine, thanks, but I'd be better if I knew for a fact whether or not my mom's watching the show. You know, because that would mean she's interested in seeing what sort of person I've grown into.'"

I catch the ground with the bottom of my shoe as we swing past. "So, I guess, when Jordy suddenly came back into your life after leaving it, it must have been weird."

"Weird how?"

"Like, it totally would've brought up a bunch of your mom stuff for you, right? Like, oh, here's this person I thought was gone forever, but now they're back, and they're interested in knowing the person I am now, yadda yadda."

Skye stares at me with wide eyes until I drop my head, cheeks flushing. "Um . . . or not. I guess I'm putting words in your mouth. I just assumed . . . whatever." I fumble for a subject change. "My parents are divorced, too, actually. But my dad's still around. Kind of. He lives in Missouri, but he's good at phone calls and flying me out for visits. I can't imagine what it would feel like if he'd disappeared."

Skye nods, her expression serious. "That's still hard, though."

"It is. But he always says he left Mom, not my sister and me. Even though he could've probably left Mom and stayed in Connecticut. He's better than a lot of deadbeat dads, so I give him a pass. At least I know he loves me." I wince when I replay my words. "Sorry."

"No, I know what you meant. But it's funny, right? Mothers are put on this pedestal. There's this stereotype that if a parent hurts their kids, or doesn't love them, it's got to be a dad, because *moms* are supposed to do anything for their kids. There's nothing stronger than a mother's love, and all that. But mine was never that into me. It's the sort of love that's *supposed* to be guaranteed, but . . ." She trails off, but I hear the unsaid implication.

"That's not your fault," I say.

"I know it's not. I was seven. She just wasn't capable of that, and there's nothing anyone can do about it." She clenches and unclenches her jaw, the muscles working furiously. "At least I have Dad, and he loves me enough for both of them."

"That's good," I say. "Still hurts though, huh?"

"Yeah. It still hurts." Skye bites her lip, her brow creasing. "You know, maybe you were onto something before. About my mom. When you told me about the cheating—that night—I kept thinking about her. I suppose I hadn't considered why that was."

"Oh." Thank god, I didn't put my foot in it after all. "Well, it makes sense, right?"

"It'd make a lot of things make more sense. Even why I came here in the first place, really. It's not me. I don't do second chances. You always end up regretting them. Case in point."

The contrast between the cool night air and the warmth radiating from Skye makes me lean into her unconsciously, then consciously. It feels as though the whole world is right here in our little bubble. Even though the night stretches out into endless blackness, and it could contain anything, none of it can reach us.

"So. We share an ex," she says lightly.

"Wait, we do?"

"But I don't know anything about your other exes. If you even have any?"

Somewhere nearby, a cicada starts chirping. It somehow makes the air feel even colder.

"Jordy's the only real boyfriend I've ever had," I say. "I've had things with people before, but they never really went beyond . . . things."

"People?" Skye asks, and I give her a funny look.

"Yeah, like, people. You want names? Chris from biology flirted with me for a while. I had a sort of thing with my cousin's friend, Isabelle, but it didn't get serious. And I used to make out with a guy in my study group called Nico, but I think it was more stress relief than anything."

I study her face, to see if there's a reaction when I mention Isabelle. It's one of those weird things about being out. I'm out to everyone I want to be out to, but that doesn't mean that, magically, everyone I meet ever again can just *tell*. Coming out didn't plaster BISEXUAL across my forehead like we're in a game of Celebrity. And I'm yet to pick up the habit of introducing myself to people as "Maya the bisexual," even though it'd probably simplify things. So, it's more of a "wait for it to come up in conversation" sort of deal most of the time.

Luckily, Skye doesn't seem even a little concerned to hear a girl's name thrown in there. "How about you?" I ask.

"Well," she says, kicking off to pick up our swinging speed, "I *can* get feelings for people. I just don't let myself. Jordy's the only person who almost . . . but if anything he proved me right. People leave." My stomach twists at the faltering in her voice. "I dated a girl once, and she fell for someone else. Then there was another girl I really liked, and she led me on for a while before she vanished. After Jordy, there was a guy on the debate team with me who was kind of cool, but he wanted to commit faster than I did, and apparently it was everything or nothing with him."

"No names," I observe.

"Nah. They're all dead to me now."

"Ruthless."

"Necessary. But, I suppose we have something else in common. I'm fairly equal opportunity when it comes to who I briefly care about before they inevitably let me down."

I wouldn't let you down, I want to say. I'm nowhere near brave enough, though.

She sucks in a breath, and the shaky sound of it explodes into the silence.

I want her to kiss me, I realize all at once. I want her to kiss me because she's beautiful, and because the air is crisp and it smells like chocolate. I want her to kiss me because we're the only two people that exist right now, and that fact is pulling me to her like a magnet.

Her lips have parted. Fallen open, really. She's scanning me, and for a moment, I think it's actually going to happen. She's going to lean forward and change everything.

But then she doesn't. And the magical feeling evaporates, and it's like it wasn't there to begin with.

"It's late," she says, hopping off the swing. She holds her hand out to help me up, and walks me back to the mansion.

In the bedroom, I watch her carefully, looking for a sign that I didn't imagine that magnetized sort of feeling. I get nothing, though.

Pushing the thought to the back of my mind, I climb onto my bed. I stuffed my iPad beneath my pillow to hide it when we left, and I pull it out and open it to my post.

It's exploded with comments. Dozens and dozens of comments, with dozens and dozens of likes each already.

Someone's jealous hahahaha

You know it's slander, coming online to make up lies
about people?

This is pathetic. Jordy would never cheat on anyone.
If you're gonna invent stuff, at least make it
believable. He's kind, caring, and smart. Probably
all the things you wish you could be.

YOU CAN TRY TO CONVINCE PEOPLE OF THAT
BUT WE KNOW THE TRUTH, WE KNOW
JORDY!!!!!!!

Didn't he go to a British school? That's what I read.
It's normal to have an accent at an international
school, not everything is about America. American
accents aren't the default!

I didn't know much about Jordy, because I'm not
a fan of the royals. My friend saw this post and
got upset, though, and it's inspired me to learn
more about him, and all the wonderful things he
does for humanity. I've decided I'm going to do
a feature on him for my online magazine so more
people can learn about how great he is. Thank
you, anonymous hater, you've made a new Jordy
Miller fan out of me!

I see red.

"Has anyone commented on your post?" Skye asks, obviously noticing the light.

"Um, not really. Nothing interesting."

"Oh. Damn. Maybe the forum's not very popular."

"Yeah. Maybe." I take a deep breath, and try to shove the fury down. To distract myself, I go into my messages. There's a new one from Mom, telling me she's made everyone at work watch both episodes, and they all think I'm stunning and out of Jordy's league. Oh, and they're *so* impressed I'm going to be a doctor one day. A message from Rosie that I read while Skye was on her date, asking me how long I've been a secret Olympic-level kayaker without telling her. And one from earlier today, Olivia telling me she was going to watch the next episode with some friends later on in her evening, which probably means she hasn't started it yet.

By the time I reply to everyone—and message Rosie, who happens to be around, for a bit—I'm sure Skye must be fast asleep. Still, after I creep to the drawer to tuck the iPad away and return to bed, I whisper, "Night, Skye."

Her response is instant and hushed. "Good night, Maya."

NINETEEN

Maya

The next evening, I wait by the driveway with two cameras in my face and Isaac and Gwendolyn hovering nearby, dressed for the hike in yoga pants and sneakers, replaying Skye's instructions from the night before. Don't act interested, huh? If that's all I have to do, I've got this win in the bag.

Then, I think of Skye the night before in general. How easy it was to talk to her. How her hair looked in the moonlight.

How, for a split second, I thought maybe she was going to kiss me. Talk about reading into shit too much. Like, two girls can tell each other they like girls without immediately making out, right? Obviously.

I'm just glad I didn't lean in or anything horrendously humiliating like that. Luckily for me, Skye will never need to know the thought that crossed my mind last night.

And while I was falling asleep.

And the moment I woke up this morning.

When Jordy gets out of the car, he takes one look at me and screws up his face. "You're wearing *that*?" he asks.

"Uh, yeah?" I say, stepping back with a confused look. "And you're wearing . . . that?"

"That" being a pristine pair of Nike high-tops, jeans, and

a Dolce & Gabbana button-down with the sleeves rolled up. I know it's Dolce & Gabbana, because he's carefully chosen one with the brand name repeated along the piping. I'm surprised he's wearing a shirt at all—I would've thought a hike was the perfect excuse to bring the abs out to smile for the cameras.

Okay, Jordy's a bit vacant, but even he knows not to wear a dress shirt on a workout.

"Hey," Isaac says to Jordy. "How about you get back in the car and we reshoot that?" Then he whispers something in Jordy's ear, like *that's* not going to make me suspicious, and Jordy smacks a hand to his forehead before jumping back in the car and climbing back out.

"Hey, Maya," he says, pulling me into a hug. "You look great. What a perfect hiking outfit!"

"Uh, thank you, Jordy. I'm so excited for the hike I definitely still believe we're going on."

"Did you tell her?" Gwendolyn whispers furiously to Isaac. He shakes his head, then leans in to me.

"Hey, so, obviously you're not going on a hike," he says.

"Wait, I'm *not*?"

"Yes, perfect, that. Can you maintain that surprise? For the cameras? We spent a lot of money on this scene."

"Maybe. First, just tell me this: Are you taking me to a room full of puppies?"

Isaac hesitates, and for a second I'm hopeful. "No. We're not doing that."

I sigh so loudly it scrapes at my throat. "Maybe a future episode idea?"

"Maybe a season two idea."

"But that won't benefit me at all," I protest as he shoves me into the car next to Jordy.

I play with my jacket zipper as we drive through the hills,

heading god-knows-where. All I know is, we aren't heading to puppies, and if we aren't heading to puppies I'd rather we weren't heading anywhere at all.

"I hope you've stretched," Jordy says, shattering the silence after a lifetime.

I side-eye him. "I know we aren't going for a hike, Jordy."

"I know you know. I said what I said."

He gives me a smug, teasing smile. I refuse to take the bait, and stare out the windows instead.

Trees.

Roads.

Houses.

Businesses.

"Okay, fine, where are we going?" I snap.

"I can't tell you," he sings, and I clench my fists.

"Tell me right now or I'll make sure your family suffers for generations."

"How will you do that?"

"I don't know," I say, folding my arms. "But I'll think of something."

"You know," he drawls. "I believe you would, too."

"So, what is it?"

"You'll just have to make me suffer," Jordy sighs. "Guess I'm a sucker for pain."

Oh, I'll give him pain, all right.

Finally, after driving through the outer suburbs of Loreux and all the way into the city center, we roll into the lot of a public park. If all this buildup is so we can go for a walk through a random park, I'm pushing Jordy into the first pond we pass.

We get out of the car, and I furrow my brow as I hear music in the distance. And people. A lot of them. Over the smell of plants and nearby sprinklers, I can make out the faint scent of sunscreen and fried food carried on the wind.

"Why?" I ask Jordy as he reaches my side.

Gwendolyn, Isaac, and Grayson—who I guess was traveling with them—get out of their own car and head right over. "Okay, you two, stand over here," Isaac says, steering us to an enormous linden tree.

While we wait, Grayson films a quick segment for the camera. I make out the words "surprise" and "doesn't know." I raise an eyebrow at Jordy, who gives a cocky shrug.

Finally, Grayson and the cameras reach us.

"So," Grayson says, turning to me with a megawatt smile. "Maya. I'm sure you're wondering why you're here."

"Flatter walking terrain?" I say sweetly, and Grayson laughs way too loudly.

"Ha, *no*. Now, your first date with Jordy was a while ago, so I'm not sure if you remember this, but Jordy remembers every moment, and he told us about a detail you left out."

Oh yeah? Like a helicopter?

Jordy takes my hand. "When we got to the top of the hill, we listened to some music."

I do remember that, actually. I played him my favorite song, "Tears in Grayscale" by the Motherload. Then Jordy made me listen to five Two Seater songs, because that band was *deep* and their songs were *layered* and *metaphorical* and obviously way more entertaining to anyone with taste than the Motherload. I mean, he didn't spell out the last bit, but he didn't have to. I'll never forget that, because it was the moment I started feeling uncomfortable sharing my music with other people, in case they thought my taste sucked.

Aww, who said Jordy and I didn't have a special first date?

"That day, you showed me your favorite band," he says.

"Well, today, we're going to listen to them again. Only, a little louder this time."

"Wait—" I say.

"Yeah."

"But they broke up last year!" I screech. I know I'm supposed to stick to the "distant" plan, but screw the plan, this is the Motherload! And it's not like Skye expected me to stick to that plan anyway. God, I wish she were here. I'd go to a concert with her over Jordy "my band is better than this" Miller any day. She's going to freak when she hears this. I feel even worse about her fondue now, but—

"No, they didn't," Jordy says. "They're on their second world tour. And it just so happens that today, they're in Chalonne. And we have backstage tickets!"

I feel my smile dropping, and I plaster it back on desperately for the cameras. "Wait, who are we seeing?"

Jordy takes my other hand as I realize what he's about to say. "Two Seater!"

Getting this smile to stay on my face is like wrestling a lion into submission. "Wow. My favorite band, Two Seater. Wow."

"Your face right now is all the thanks I could ask for," Jordy says.

"Why would I thank you? Didn't the producers organize this?"

Off-camera, Isaac nods emphatically.

"But I remembered your favorite band," Jordy points out. *Well* . . .

"I'm ecstatically . . . ecstatic," I say. Realizing it wasn't super convincing, I give a little jump. There. They'll be able to cobble that into actual excitement with movie magic, right?

He throws an arm around my shoulder and gestures toward the park. "Let's go, then! Come on!"

Gwendolyn beckons Jordy, and he lets go of me. "Here,

you just need a little powder," she says, and the makeup artist, Kelly, runs over.

While they degrease Jordy, Isaac pulls me aside to record some talking-head stuff to the cameras for voiceovers. I don't call Jordy a self-absorbed narcissist, I don't admit I couldn't name a single Two Seater song, and I don't even bring up the Motherload. Frankly, I'm killing it at the whole "image rehab" thing.

We make our way toward the concert down a dirt path, following the sound of the crowd and bass. I recognize the music as we get closer; it's sort of country-meets-rock, heavy on the guitar, lots of songs about drinking after a breakup and driving down abandoned roads at dawn, yadda yadda.

Around a path, the thick foliage and trees fall away, and suddenly we can see the stage. It's an enormous black and blue half dome with endless, grassy space in front of it, where thousands upon thousands of people are standing and screaming, fenced in by metal barriers. The smell of stale beer drowns out the sunscreen now, but I can still smell the fried food. I scan around until I spot a food stall selling something called *dhunplirs*. I know I've just had dinner, but the smell is making me want second dinner something fierce. Maybe they'll let me find out what the heck a *dhunplir* is on camera?

A couple of camera crew members head to the crowd to take some shots of the concert itself, while the rest of us head backstage. I can't tell how far into the concert we are, but it seems a bit weird that we didn't get to catch the beginning of the set.

Gwendolyn drops us off side-stage. Here, standing in the dark, we have a prime view of the stage. Even *with* my mic-pack, it's loud enough that the camera isn't gonna be able to pick us up, so I don't have to make small talk with Jordy, at least.

He cranes his neck to get a better view of the performers. His face is lit up purple and yellow from the stage, and his smile is just about big enough to pull a muscle. At least one of us is having fun. Eventually, he remembers I'm there and we're being recorded, apparently, because he wraps me into a hug and sways me from side to side to the music while I cringe.

As the song ends, he lets go of me. "They're even better in person," he shouts.

"So deep," I shout back. "Their stuff is really layered and, like, metaphorical, don't you think?"

"Yes! *Yes,* I do think!"

"Wow, you have such good taste, Jordy."

"Of course I do. I fell for you, didn't I?"

I wince, and turn to him with what I hope is a look of flattered adoration. "Mm!"

"Also, get ready. I have one more surprise for you."

I give him a questioning look, then I realize the lead singer of Two Seater, Someone Someone No-Idea-What-His-Name-Is, is still talking to the crowd. Oh, god, Jordy's given him a sappy message to give to me, hasn't he?

". . . we actually have some special guests here, tonight. Which ladies in the crowd can say they've ever wanted to date a prince?"

The crowd loses its mind.

Gwendolyn wrote this script for him, for *sure.*

"Well, one lucky girl has come pretty darn close."

Isaac taps me on the shoulder, and gives me what looks like a folded blue sheet. I shake it out, and see orange and green stripes, and a white triangle. It's the Chalonian flag.

"She's dating Jordy Miller, who you might recognize as the *mighty* handsome younger brother of Princess Saman-tha."

Jordy takes the flag and drapes it around my back like a cape. "Hold onto it, like this."

"Jordy, wha—"

"Give it up for our temporary backup dancer, Maya Bailey!"

Jordy shoves me, and I shriek and grab a nearby pole. "No. No!"

"Go on, it's your moment."

"I don't want a moment. I never asked for a single moment!"

"I believe in you! Face that stage fright head on!"

"*No!*"

"And out—"

"Jordy!"

"You—"

"Please, please, please don't—"

"Go!"

Gwendolyn helpfully pries my fingers from the pole and Jordy shoves me once again. Somebody Who-the-Hell walks to the side of the stage and holds his hand out, *winking* at me. "Care to join me, Maya?" he asks.

No, I absolutely do *not* fucking care to join him. The question here is, do I have any way out of this that won't result in me being the bad-guy buzzkill?

No. No, I do not.

About as enthusiastically as a royal headed to the guillotine, I take Somebody McWhat's-His-Face's hand and follow him onto the stage as the crowd roars. I squint out over the crowd, my heart hammering so hard I might pass out live onstage. Up here, the lights are blinding, burning white and fluorescent into my eyeballs. It's also approximately a thousand degrees, so, good thing I'm dressed for exertion, I guess.

It's also really great that I'm currently onstage in a pony-tail and sports bra. Yeah. Really love this turn of events for me.

Somebody Never-Heard-of-Him goes back to the microphone. "Why don't you hold out that flag, Maya? Show the crowd what you've got there."

I hold it out, and the roar shakes the stage.

A guitar riff rings out, and, suddenly, the next song is underway. I glance side-stage in a panic and take a step toward it, but Isaac, Jordy, and Gwendolyn all frantically gesture at me to dance. At least, I think that's what's happening. Jordy's waving his fists around in front of his face, Gwendolyn's doing what I think is the Macarena, and Isaac's shimmying from side to side.

Okay. Right. Okay. Except, little flaw in this plan, I can't dance for shit. Granted, I'm no worse than Jordy, from the looks of things, but I'm the one in the middle of the stage.

I step from side to side, waving the flag weakly and wishing something would fall on me and put me into a well-earned coma. Where's the phantom of the rock concert when you need him? Next, I sort of box step, because I remember that from middle school dance class. Then, I do a spin, because I'm running out of ideas, and I *think* the crowd gets louder? Although that might be them laughing at me, it's hard to tell.

No, it's *definitely* getting louder. Like, panic levels of loud. Is there a fire? I look around, only to find Jordy, which is objectively worse.

He waves at the crowd for a while, walking across the stage right in front of the band while he mouths the lyrics. Meanwhile, I bop along in the background, sort of stepping in time to the music and waving the Chalonian flag in front of me to distract everyone.

Stage smoke starts shooting up at us from the sides as Jordy circles back and holds his hand out. I hand him the flag, and he bursts out laughing, then hands it to Isaac backstage, before turning back to me.

Oh, right, he wants to dance together.

I take his hand and he spins me around before pulling me into his chest. We rock from side to side, bouncing to the music, until, grudgingly, I smile. It *is* fun to be up here, actually. Like we can't get it wrong, no matter what we do. Jordy breaks into a grin as soon as he sees it. "That's better," he shouts, and even this close to him I basically have to lip-read to understand him. "Have some *fun*, Maya!"

"Fuck you, Jordy, I'm never forgiving you for this!"

"Fuck you more, I know you're enjoying it. Just give in."

Steering us to the front of the stage, Jordy throws his hands up and jumps, and, screw it, I copy him, and the crowd copies us, jumping in time like we're mass puppet masters. Then, he pulls my hands around his neck and starts slow dancing with me. Given the song is, from what I can make out, about either setting fire to an attic or letting go of childhood trauma, it seems a *bit* inappropriate, but, you know, it's better than the macarena, so I'll take it.

Finally, the song comes to an end, and Jordy and I pull apart and face the crowd. My heart's stopped racing now. With all these lights, I can barely make individual people out. Without the faces, it's like it's not real. I'm not really onstage in front of thousands of people.

Then I put my hands above my head, and those thousands of people scream for me, and it's real again. But instead of terror, I feel victory.

I've danced the way I was told to dance. I played my part. And they love me for it.

Fake or not, as long as I keep dancing with Jordy, the hate disappears. The scorn, the laughter, all of it. They've never heard the lies about me I'm so used to people believing.

And, god, even if it's totally immoral and wrong, it feels good to give in to that and be loved. Just for a minute.

Even if it's not real.

TWENTY

Maya

"Are you actually serious?" Skye cries. "Lauren gets a helicopter ride, you star in your own concert, and I get *chocolate dip*? That I don't even get to *eat*?"

"They did make me jump around with a flag and slow dance with Jordy," I remind her. "I was basically a dancing monkey."

"Still. At least it'll give you a memory," Skye says. "I'll forget last night by next week."

We're sitting against the wall on my bed, sharing a jumbo bag of potato chips and listening to her dad's ancient playlist on her speaker.

"True," I say. "I'll need it to get me through next year."

"You always talk about college like it's a death sentence. Nobody's forcing you to go, you know."

She says it so offhandedly, like dropping out of college is the most normal, run-of-the-mill, no-consequence thing someone could do. "Uh, they kind of are? The job market, for one."

"There are jobs that don't require degrees. And you can go to college in a year or two if you realize there's something you do want to do. Next excuse?"

I frown. "My mom spent the last, like, decade working her ass off so I could have a future."

"You've already got a future. I promise you, people without med degrees exist. They're out there, as we speak, living their futures. Don't be a snob, Maya!"

"Yeah, but . . . but now Jordy knows I'm going to college next year, and I just know he's waiting for me to drop out so he can judge me for it. I want to prove him wrong."

"That's possibly the worst reason I've ever heard to spend the next decade studying to enter a grueling career field devoting your life to others. Honestly, if you said you were just doing it for the paycheck, I'd be quite a bit less concerned."

A decade of study. I wince, hearing that. I mean, obviously I *know* it's a decade. But I try not to think of it in numbers like that. In fact, I try not to think about it too much, period. If I pretend it's happening to someone else, I barely panic at all.

"Don't they say the best revenge is being happy?"

"I don't know about 'they,' but it's not what my mom says."

"Well, who says you need to decide now? Why don't you take a year to open yourself to new ideas? You might still go to college. And if you don't, all the better; your mom's years of work can buy her a year-long travel vacation. And who cares what Jordy thinks? I mean, *really*?"

I stuff a handful of chips in my mouth. "Is that what you did? Take a year off to decide?"

"Maya, chew, good god. Yes, actually. I worked extremely hard in school, and if I go to college, I imagine I'll work extremely hard there, too. I wanted to give myself a year to do as little work as I possibly can, and then I'll commit to the next step when I feel more ready to."

I put another chip in my mouth and go out of my way to loudly crunch it for several seconds before I swallow and reply, mouth empty this time. "You know? This is the first time I've seen you not-plan something."

"Oh, I'm still planning. I'm planning to return to London, and stay in the pre-planned apartment I already have a lease for, for a pre-planned period of time. I plan to apply for wait-ressing or bartender work, and once I have enough money, I'll plan multiple weekend trips. Then, I plan on planning the next steps, about six months in."

"Okay, so what I'm hearing is, you're planning to plan your life out at a pre-planned time. Yeah, that sounds more like you. Where are you *planning* on visiting?"

She stretches out, letting her socked feet hang over the edge of the bed. "I haven't had a chance to see the Mediterra-nean yet. I'd like to see Greece and Spain, and definitely Italy. I met a girl while I was backpacking who raved about Genoa. Apparently, if you go, you should skip the restaurants and just buy from the food stores in the alleys. She said they have butchers with the most incredible meat you've ever tried, ge-lato on every corner, fresh fruit stalls every few feet, and—oh, she said the focaccia there is indescribable. She said it's like a chewy, fluffy bread that gets covered in oil and lard, and it's nothing like what they call focaccia in other countries."

Suddenly, the chips taste like goddamn trash. "Well, now I want to try it, and I can't. That's *teasing*."

"The town is built by the sea, on hillsides. When you look up, all you can see are brightly colored houses, layered like arena seating."

"Oh my god." I go limp, and close my eyes. "I want to go. *So* bad."

"Huh."

"What?"

"Nothing. It just seems like we might have found some-thing you'd rather do than med school."

I think about being on that stage today. Of the lights, and the heat, and the feeling of endless power. The Maya that was up there would agree with Skye. She'd jump on a plane and see things, and do whatever felt right to her in the moment, regardless of how it made her look. She wouldn't base her decisions around avoiding the world's judgment.

The memory of the concert blends into the music blaring from Skye's speaker, and a tingling, contented sort of happiness washes over me. So, when she touches my hand, it takes a beat to realize she has, because it fits so perfectly into that warm buzzing.

But then that beat passes, and my brain snaps into attention.

I glance up at her, and she's looking at me with an intense half smile, and the energy shifts, like the molecules in the air we're breathing have disrupted their holding pattern. My heart catches on to what's about to come a second before I do, and it starts pounding so hard I'm surprised the ground doesn't vibrate along with it.

So, I wasn't imagining things last night?

Time slows.

"I want to kiss you," Skye says, matter-of-factly. Casual, not earth-shattering.

Funny. Those words shatter time and space for me.

"So, kiss me," I force out.

And she does. Her hand, still on top of mine, presses down, anchoring me into place. As our lips meet, I melt. Into her, into myself, into nothing. I kiss her back, and that energy builds up, thrumming from my throat to my fingertips until I feel like a dying star. Like I'm about to shatter into a thousand shards of light.

It's been so long, I'd forgotten this, all of it. The frenzied serenity of a first kiss. Perfect, frozen stillness slamming against frantic energy.

Being ignited.

She climbs onto her knees and leans an arm against the wall to steady herself, and she becomes an eclipse, blocking out the ceiling light until it haloes around her.

She kisses me over, and over, until I'm not sure where I end and begin anymore. Amongst the mush, a thought finally breaks through, and I manage to put it to words during a break in the kisses.

"Hey. Um. Why are we kissing?"

She falls back on her knees and chokes. "Did you just ask me that?"

"I just, I mean . . ." I sit up straighter and run my hands over my hair to smooth it. "Um . . ."

"Does this mean something?" She smiles.

"I guess. But not because I need it to mean something. I just . . . want to know."

"Well." She teases the word out on her tongue as she flops back down beside me. "Honestly? I've just been wanting to kiss you. That's all."

I think this over, and something warm and excited blooms in my stomach. No-strings-attached kissing, huh? It feels carefree and adventurous. It feels like being on that stage, unlimited and breathless. Overnight, I've gone from Maya, angry and rejected and vengeful, to Maya, lovable and confident.

I think I like this new version of me.

And if this version of me is someone Skye wants to kiss, then all the better. Full steam ahead.

"Awesome," I say.

"Yeah?" she asks.

"Quick question, though."

"By all means."

"Did you plan this?"

Skye lets her head fall back against the wall and giggles, before pushing a piece of hair from my face. "I did not."

"Well, welcome to winging it. Twice in two days, that's got to be a personal record! How does it feel?"

She drops her hand and gives a one-shoulder shrug. "You know what? It feels pretty good."

I look at her hand, which she's let fall to the bed between us, and then I take it in mine.

She doesn't pull away.

TWENTY-ONE

Skye

I'll admit, until Maya wakes the next day, I regret the kiss. Well, to be more precise, I regret the many, many kisses. Not because they were bad, to be clear. Actually, as far as kisses go, they were up there with some of the best I've ever had. But if I gave Maya the wrong impression with them, I'll be furious with myself. Yes, she said she was on the same page as me last night, but somehow the idea that this could be uncomplicated seems too good to be true.

For a while, I toss around the idea of waking her to press her about this and ease my anxiety—with the most unromantic song I can find on the playlist, to set the vibe: "Another One Bites the Dust." In the end, I decide to let her sleep, and go downstairs to join the other girls.

When Maya finally deigns to join us—at *eleven*—she's acting completely normal. She doesn't ignore me, anyway—which is, if TV dramas are anything to go by, a promising sign. She simply makes herself some muesli, shoots me a friendly smile without a hint of awkwardness, and joins us hanging out in the living room, taking the spare seat beside Lauren on the couch.

The tension pours out of my muscles as I realize she truly

doesn't seem to mind what I said last night. Maybe she understands, as I do, that pursuing anything between us would only lead to heartbreak. It doesn't matter how many scenarios I envision for us, they all end much the same way. No matter what, in a few weeks, we'll be living on different continents. Even when I return from London eventually, we'll still be in different countries. Why on earth would either of us choose to emotionally invest in something that can't possibly work out?

I learned my lesson perfectly well the first time around, thank you very much.

Perrie is out with Jordy today, filming the last of the first-date re-creations before tonight's *Notte Infinita*. Because this week's episode doesn't involve a challenge, Jordy gets to hand select the person unlucky enough to win a night alone with him at the event. Kim, who's already in full hair and makeup hours in advance, seems quite confident that the unlucky winner will be her.

"Jordy told me on our date he wants to spend another night alone with me," she tells us for the forty-third time today as she paints her nails. "So, it's perfect, really. Usually you don't get any notice, but because I know it's coming, I get to make sure everything's as it should be."

"And by *everything*, you mean you?" Lauren asks.

"Duh. I've got moisturizer and perfume on every inch of me."

"A proven formula," Maya says drily, because she simply can't help herself, apparently.

Kim, to her credit, doesn't take the bait. She simply raises her recently shaped brows and starts on the next coat of berry polish.

Maya catches my eye and frowns. I'm sure I know what she's thinking. Kim seems to adore Jordy more than ever. If she wins this thing, he'll get his public happy ending, without a doubt.

There has to be something we can do to open her eyes. The problem is, I'm running out of ideas.

Unfortunately, even though Maya and I conduct a whispered brainstorming session while getting ready, we can't come up with any useful plan to bring Kim over to the dark side. *Useful* is the key word here, because Maya, to her credit, throws herself into strategizing with gusto, but I simply cannot co-sign "set Kim up with a camera operator," "write Kim a fake, mean letter from Jordy," or "conduct a séance and ask the spirits for help." We end up circling back to the original plan, which we're no closer to "figuring out," despite Maya's quiet confidence that we will.

When Perrie returns, Maya and I have given up altogether, and are watching a rom-com. We're both dressed and ready to go. Perrie's hair and makeup held up well during the skating session thanks to half a can of setting spray, so all she has to do is kick off her sneakers and change into a dress before she sprints back to speak to Maya and me, stilettos in hand. Upstairs, Lauren and Kim are putting on their finishing touches—which seems incredible on Kim's part, given she seemed as put together as humanly possible six hours ago.

So, when Perrie tells Maya and me all about her date—ice-skating in a rented-out rink in Loreux while receiving pointers from the Chalonian Olympic coach—we get the rare uncensored version she wouldn't dare to say in front of the other two. Mostly Kim.

"I think he picked ice-skating for our first date so he could show off the first time around," she says, sticking a protective gel pad onto the widest part of her shoe. "And he was *definitely* showing off this time. He spent more time doing spins in the middle of the rink than he did actually talking to me."

"Did he take his shirt off?" Maya asks.

I snort. "Maya, it's freezing in there."

"I asked what I asked."

"He did, actually," Perrie admits.

Maya turns to me smugly.

"He's not a bad kisser these days," Perrie continues. "He's improved since ninth grade."

Maya gasps and whirls to tap Perrie's shoulder with the back of her hand. "You *kissed* him?"

"I was curious! Plus, Violet told me if I did, they'd make my part of the episode longer." She shrugs with a wicked grin. "Gotta get that screen time."

"Wonderful," I say. "Use him up."

"Just make sure to throw him away," Maya sings.

"Please. After what he did to you two, no amount of screen time in the world would make me commit to him."

"And this is one of the reasons I love you," Maya says.

Perrie pauses. "Actually, that's a lie. I'd do it, if only because winning this would be *great* publicity. But a couple of months, max, then I'm donion rings."

Maya and I force smiles, but I don't think either of us is particularly convincing. That wouldn't exactly be terrible for Jordy's image. If anything, watching him get dumped by the love of his life a couple of months after committing to her would only make him *more* appealing. We'll need to give this some thought, and see if we can come up with a way to gradually make Perrie reconsider accepting him, if she does get to the end—

"If you want maximum publicity, you should reject his ass on TV," Maya says. "*That's* a way to make headlines."

Or we could just jump in with the first thing that pops into our heads, thank you, Maya.

Perrie shakes her head emphatically. "Yeah, headlines about what a stone-cold bitch I am. No, thank you. Anyway, can we put on a better movie, please? Rom-coms make me gag."

A clanging noise in the kitchen alerts us that Kim and Lauren are finished. Moments later, they burst into the living room armed with flutes and bottles of champagne.

"We're pre-gaming," Kim says, setting up the glasses on the coffee table. "Join us?"

"That'll work, too," Perrie says, turning off the TV with the remote.

Kim and I take the couch, Lauren spreads out on the love seat, and Perrie lowers herself into one of the armchairs. Maya hesitates at the edges of the group, lost in thought. "What if we played a drinking game?" she asks.

"Like beer pong?" Lauren asks.

"No," Kim says with a long-suffering look. "Not with champagne. How about Kings?"

"Spin the Bottle?" I ask innocently, just to see Maya's face, and Perrie kicks me.

Maya, to my delight, turns a lovely shade of maroon. "*No*," she says, giving me a pointed look. "I've invented one, actually."

I chuckle. "When?"

"Just now." Maya fills her glass. "The game is Jordy-themed Never Have I Ever." She looks around to make sure we're suitably intrigued before continuing. "The rules are simple. When it's your turn, you say 'Man, did Jordy ever,' and finish it with something Jordy did in your relationship. Like, man, did Jordy ever kiss me on the first date. That kind of thing. If you had the same experience, drink. If no one drinks, you get a point. The first person to five points wins."

I think Maya might be a genius.

"What do they win?" Kim asks.

"I don't know, bragging rights, I guess," Maya says. "Knowing deep inside they're Jordy's special snowflake?"

"I'm in," Kim says.

Perrie and Lauren agree, so we all fill our glasses while Maya sets up a scorecard on a notepad she finds in the kitchen.

I volunteer to kick us off. "Never—I mean, man, did Jordy ever . . . tell me he's never felt like he could be vulnerable around someone before me."

Perrie, Maya, Lauren, and Kim all drink, and then everyone but Kim giggles uncomfortably.

Oh my god, Maya figured it out.

She's a genius, a beautiful, evil genius.

Kim looks defensive already. "Man, did Jordy ever . . . buy me a pair of white gold stud earrings for my nineteenth birthday and give them to me the day before because he couldn't wait to see my face."

Maya raises her eyebrows halfway to the ceiling and puts a dash next to Kim's name. "Conveniently specific," she mutters, and Perrie starts laughing hysterically until she falls onto her back and kicks her legs in the air like a stranded turtle. It's her turn next, so we wait for her to collect herself.

"Um . . . boy did Jordy ever tell me I was the first girl to ever meet his parents," she chokes out, breathless.

Well, she *was* his first girlfriend. But, amazingly, Maya and Lauren both drink. "Oh *shit*!" Perrie says, and she takes a drink of her own for good measure. "That's messed up. I promise, I met Alan and Phoebe."

Maya, next. "Boy, did Jordy ever tell me I was beautiful 'the same way a sunset's beautiful.'"

I finish the last part of that sentence along with her. Everyone but Perrie drinks. Apparently, he invented that line on Lauren and never looked back. We start to glance at each other and smile. Kim stays unamused, though. "So? It's a nice thing to tell someone," she says. "And he probably meant it for all of us. You *are* all beautiful the way a sunset's beautiful."

"Kim!" Lauren cries, tackling her in a bear hug. "You are a gosh darn ray of sunshine." She breaks from the hug and picks up her own glass. "Boy, did Jordy ever . . . take me to a lake and make me shout at the water because he wanted me to know 'what it feels like to be alive.'"

Kim and I drink. Mine was a hill, but close enough.

"Specific, and yet." Maya grins.

We're back to me. Wonderful. I decide to take a chance on a gut feeling. "Boy, did Jordy ever call me to ask me to come on the show himself, and to tell me he didn't want to be on the show if I wasn't on it."

There's a shocked silence. Well, most people look shocked. Maya looks at me like she wants to kiss me again. I quirk an eyebrow at her, and she tucks a lock of hair behind her ear and ducks her head.

Then, everyone takes a drink. And, one by one, they start laughing. Even Kim apparently sees the funny side now, squeezing her eyes shut and grinning into her glass.

"Did he con us to come on the show?" Lauren asks, shaking her head.

"No," I say with a serious face. "I'm sure he truly believed, in the moment he was talking to each of us, that we were the most important girl in the world to him. He's just easily distracted."

Maya hums. "I don't think you're giving him enough credit," she says. "I think he knows exactly what he's doing. He just forgot to account for the fact that he was locking us all up in a house together."

"Well, I'm telling the cameras about this," Lauren says. "He can't get away with that. He's playing dirty."

"He's not playing at all," Maya says. "He's not even in the game. It's a guaranteed win for him."

Kim, who's stopped smiling, scans the room, then narrows her eyes. "Boy, did Jordy ever . . . tell me I'm the only girl here who's not vapid."

I double-take. That one's brave, even for Jordy. But, predictably, Perrie and Lauren both drink, and Kim gasps in shock.

"I can't believe he said I'm vapid!" she cries.

"Oh, but it's okay when he says it about the rest of us?" Maya teases. Kim finishes her drink in response, and pours another.

"You know," Kim says, "he used to say all sorts of shit about all of you. And his other exes. I can't remember names, but he said one was a psycho, one was boring, a couple were shit in bed, one was way too clingy . . ."

"Oh, the boring comment was about Perrie," Lauren says with a hiccup. "I remember that."

"*What?*" Perrie yelps. "That projecting, judgmental, motherfucking—"

"He said Lauren was clingy," Maya says. "I remember, because it made me paranoid that *I'd* be clingy."

"I wasn't clingy." Lauren sniffs. "I just had a routine where I texted good morning to him every day. I wanted him to start his days off right."

"He trashed Maya to me," I say, to nobody's surprise. "He waited awhile, but he did it."

"He said some stuff to Francesca, too," Kim says, rolling forward onto her knees and slamming her hands against the table. "I just remembered! She said I was the only one he didn't have anything bad to say about."

We all stare at her, until she wilts. "Francesca just said that to spare my feelings, didn't she?"

"Probably."

"Totally."

"Sorry, babe."

"You're amazing, though."

"We," Maya says firmly, "are all amazing. The common denominator I see is Jordy, and his total lack of taste."

I catch her eye and smile.

It really is too bad we're going to live so far apart soon.

Much too bad.

By the time the producers come to collect us for the *Notte Infinita*, we've all drunk enough that we're falling over each other as we stand.

"Wait, wait, wait," I say, grabbing onto Maya as she lurches to the side steering around the love seat. "Um. I have to grab something from my room. Really, really fast, I'll be incredibly fast."

"You'd better be," Isaac says to my back as I retreat.

I hold onto Maya's arm a little too long, and run my fingers down it as I let go, causing her to look at me sharply. *Follow me,* I mouth.

I'm only in the bedroom for ten seconds or so before Maya peeks in, her cheeks flushed as though she ran upstairs. "Whatcha doin'?"

"I just wanted a minute away from the girls." I grin.

She closes the door behind her and rushes to me. "Was the game a good idea?"

"It was an *inspired* idea."

"Kim might have even come around," she says as I snake my hands around her waist and pull her in. "*Kim!*"

"We're closer than we've been yet," I say, before closing the gap between us.

She kisses me fiercely, running her fingers through my hair. It still feels odd to have it this short again—I feel a phantom tug as her fingers travel down the nape of my neck. We stumble backward until she's pressing me against the wall, where she holds me and kisses down my jaw and onto my neck.

"We can't stay," I say. "Someone will come after us in a second."

"Let them. They can film it without us."

"Come *on.*" I giggle, prying her off my neck. She kisses me one more time on the lips before we run back downstairs, trying to calm our breathing and look as casual and innocent as we possibly can.

They're waiting for us in the *Notte Infinita* room as we enter, all the girls and producers and crew. *Sorry,* I mouth as we take our places. Isaac gives me an exasperated look, and Jordy double-takes when he sees me. It's only then that I remember he hasn't had the pleasure of witnessing my new haircut yet. I fluff up the top and give him an innocent shrug. It's impossible to tell from his face whether he's amused or irritated, and I can't find it in myself to care either way.

Maya is swaying rather concerningly, and I tune out during Grayson's and Jordy's speeches as I keep an eye on her. Note to self: drinking every time Jordy screws around with a nearby woman is an awfully efficient way to give oneself alcohol poisoning.

I don't pay attention until Jordy announces he's decided who he's going to spend the night with. *That* causes me to straighten extremely quickly. In all the fun, I'd forgotten one of us might draw that card tonight.

"I had so much fun with all of you this week," he says, "and it's brought up so many memories. Some I'd forgotten, some I've refused to let go of. But one date in particular made me realize there's one girl I'd love to spend some more time with tonight. And that girl is . . . Perrie."

Something inside me collapses with relief as Perrie totters up, keeping her composure impressively. Well, with any luck, she won't remember much of tonight, and will be in bed nice and early.

Before I can worry there's a chance I might leave tonight, Jordy continues. "Skye." I take a deep breath, focus, and cross the floor unsteadily on my heels. I forget to give Jordy a hug at first, so I have to double back while Maya breaks into giggles across the room.

"Kim." Kim gives Jordy a strange look as she approaches him, and the hug she gives him is far more detached than normal. It's difficult to say if she's cold because of the game, or because he chose Perrie over her. More than likely, it's a combination of both.

"Lauren." Lauren gives Jordy a pleasant smile, hugs him, and joins us.

Jordy pauses, and I realize a beat too late Maya isn't up here with us. My heart leaps into my throat, and I seem to sober up in an instant. He can't be letting her go, can he? Surely not? But she . . . she did what I told her to do, right? Was she sufficiently standoffish in her date yesterday? Did something go wrong? Did she tell me everything?

She can't be leaving.

We catch each other's eyes, and hers widen slightly in a panic.

"And Maya," Jordy says finally, and I'm so relieved I feel light-headed. Maya hugs him, then takes her place next to me. I brush my finger against hers as casually as I can, to let her know I'm happy she's here. We're still in the game.

She draws in a sudden, quiet breath.

"So, ladies," Grayson says. "At least one more week together."

One more week. The same chances as last time.

Jordy truly doesn't like sending people home, does he?

TWENTY-TWO

Maya

On the morning of the episode-four group challenge, Skye wakes me up by playing "Hit Me with Your Best Shot," and it's literally impossible to start your day with a song like that and not be pumped and ready to go to battle.

Unfortunately, that mood quickly deflates when we find Kim crying at the breakfast table, flanked by Perrie and Lauren.

"Hey, what's the matter?" I ask, as Skye and I sit across the table from her.

Kim sniffles and rubs a fist under her eyes as she stares at the table. "My best friend was in a car crash last night."

"Oh my god, Vivaan? Is he all right?" Skye asks.

"Apparently he's fine. But *because* he's all right, the producers won't let me call him. They only let me send him a message through them."

"It's so messed up," Perrie says, shaking her head.

"I'm sure he understands," Lauren says, rubbing Kim's back.

"How would you feel?" Kim asks thinly. "If it was your best friend who was hurt, and you weren't allowed to talk to him in case you leak some *bloody* information? It's fucked!"

Skye looks sideways at me, and I know she's thinking the same thing as me. "Kim," I say. "Can I talk to you upstairs for a second, please?"

When I fish my iPad out from its hiding place, Kim starts crying again.

"Thank you, thank you," she chants as she logs in to her profile.

"It's nothing. I can't believe they won't let you talk to him. That's so messed up."

I leave her alone for a while with the door shut while I fix my hair in the bathroom. When I return, she's still crying, but the grief is now mixed with total panic and distress.

"He's in the hospital," she says once I close the door. "The *hospital.* He broke an arm and some ribs. One of our other friends was driving, but she wasn't hurt, thank god."

"God," I breathe. "What are you gonna do?"

She grips my iPad so tightly her knuckles go pale. "I don't . . . I mean . . . I'm not leaving, if that's what you're suggesting," she says sharply.

"I wasn't."

"Good. Because I'm here for the long haul." She scowls at me, then her face softens. "I just want to call him."

"Feel free. I'll keep an eye on the hallway to make sure no producers barge in."

She nods, gives me a shaky smile, and returns to the iPad while I go to stand guard. Skye joins me after a few minutes, and we sit on the floor together against one of the walls. "How is she?" she asks, and I update her.

"All this for Jordy Miller," she whispers. "I'd be so furious if I were Kim."

"I'm sure she'll get there soon."

Skye nods, then brightens. "So, did the iPad trick work as well as I predicted?"

"I didn't do it as a trick," I say. "It was just the right thing to do."

"Yeah. I know." She sighs. "You know, there's a good chance you'll lose it now. You'd better send a last message to everyone, just in case. So they don't wonder why you disappeared."

"Oh. Right. Good idea."

"All my ideas are good. When are you going to realize that?"

I give her a weak smile in response. We sit in silence for a while, then she fluffs the bottom of my hair, which I've curled and brushed out. "I like this," she says. "Very princess-y."

Things with Skye are . . . interesting. Right now, we seem to be mostly platonic, except for when we're making out in a distinctly un-platonic sort of way. Don't get me wrong, I'm enjoying every second of it. But I can't help wondering how normal this is. Like, more than once over the last few days I've disappeared into our room alone to google things like "friends with benefits but she touches my hair" and "hookup vs relationship." From what I've read, we don't really act like we're just hooking up. But Skye said she wants it to be casual, and I'm totally fine with casual, especially when we're trying to focus on our takedown mission.

It's just that, sometimes, she confuses me.

"I'm prepared today," I say, touching my hair where her fingers just were with a self-conscious smile.

"I can see that. Let's cross our fingers for a win." Skye leans in and lowers her voice. "So . . . can we talk about something?"

Us? Is she going to ask me about us? "Of course."

"I was intending to take this to the grave, but I'm feeling really guilty about something, and I need your advice."

So . . . not us? "What's up?"

"I know we said we wouldn't do anything to the other girls . . ."

I narrow my eyes. "Yes, we *did* say that, Skye."

She drops her voice to such a small whisper I can barely hear her. "I know, but Kim's been worrying me. She's coming around, but not quickly enough, and we've only got two eliminations left before the finale. So, yesterday, I told her to make sure she really lets Jordy know how much she likes him."

"Skye!"

"I maintain it was the right thing to do if we want to increase our chances of destroying him. But that was before this. She's having a bad enough day as it is, and I'm not a *monster*."

I will kill her later, when we have more time. "You need to tell her you were baiting her."

"I'm also not that saintly. Can we try for a happy medium?"

"Ugh. Fine, let me handle it."

"Hey, Maya? I'm done," Kim calls out, and I head back into the bedroom to retrieve the iPad.

"How'd it go?" I ask Kim as I type out my "I may vanish soon" messages to Mom, Olivia, and Rosie.

"I . . . I don't know. I don't really want to talk right now, if that's okay."

"Yeah. Yeah, of course." I pause. "But, um, if you're feeling awful . . . Don't feel like you need to put on a romantic show for Jordy or anything, okay? If he's the guy for you, he'll understand. You want a boyfriend who'll support you if you need it, not one who wants you to be, like, his perfect woman even if you're going through something like this. Right?"

Kim, to my relief, actually seems to give this some thought. "Yeah. Right. Thanks, Maya. And thanks for the iPad."

Outside, she gives Skye a small, emotionless smile, and then pushes ahead of us to go and meet the producers. Behind her back, Skye gives my hand a squeeze, then lets go of me as we follow.

A few hours later, we're standing outside the palace in literal ball gowns.

One of the things I did not know about Chalonne before this week is that their royal family only sort of moved on from the Victorian era when it comes to their formal wear. Like, hard-core. Meeting with the prime minister? Put on a three-hundred-pound ball gown. Fancy dinner? Put on a three-hundred-pound ball gown. Charity event? Three-hundred-pound ball gown.

If I thought the dress I wore on the first night was fancy, it was a goddamn sack compared to these babies. We're all wearing crinolines under our dresses, which are rustling, flowery, lacy works of art, stretching out at least two or three feet away from our bodies on all sides. Mine is in a soft sea green, and Skye's is a beautiful rich maroon that looks kind of perfect with her chocolatey brown hair.

Lauren, who's dressed in a baby pink gown that reminds me of a strawberry cake, is pacing back and forth along our group while the producers prepare and talk to some of the palace staff. "Remember to curtsy if you meet anyone more senior than you," she says. "And if you're in doubt, better safe than sorry. I'd rather embarrass myself in front of staff than accidentally offend a lord or lady."

"Got it." Perrie nods, scratching at the glittery sleeves of her pale blue gown.

"If they offer you tea, hold it with your *thumb* and *index* finger. Don't grip it like a caveman."

"There goes my plan," Skye mutters.

"And *don't* ask anyone for autographs," Lauren says. "They're not allowed to give them."

"It actually wouldn't occur to me to get the queen's autograph," I say.

"You don't think we'll see the queen, do you?" Lauren yelps, looking between us. When she gets no response, she takes several deep breaths, and threads her fingers together. "Okay, if we meet the queen, do not *talk*. Not unless you have to. You'll mess it up— Oh no, there are too many rules, it'll all go wrong!"

Luckily for us, we do not meet the queen. In fact, we don't meet any member of the royal family. We don't even really enter the palace. Instead, we take some photos and footage from the front of it to make it look like we're about to go on a grand tour, then we're led around the side to a conference room, where we enter from outside.

"Jordy!" Lauren cries when she sees him, running up to wrap her arms around him. "Thank you *so* much for bringing us here. You're the best ex-boyfriend *ever*. Seriously."

Jordy delicately extracts himself from her grasp. "My pleasure, Lauren. Seeing you all this happy is all the thanks I need."

"Well, *we* organized it," Isaac mutters to himself, quietly enough that I only just overhear. "But, sure, yay, Jordy."

"Do we get a tour of the palace after this?" Lauren asks hopefully as we take our seats at a long mahogany dining table.

Our guide, a woman named Dominique, one of *many* low-ranking staff members at the palace, gives her a horrified look. "*Nie, nie,*" she says in Chalonian, before adding a thickly accented, "zey do not allow theengs such as thees in ze palace. *Nie, nie, nie.*"

Lauren looks crestfallen.

Grayson, who's dressed like he's off to a costume party as a fairy-tale prince, complete with a feathered hat, explains today's challenge to the camera.

"Today, the girls will be learning all about royal etiquette, as well as the history of the Chalonian royal family. It will be *crucial*, as Jordy's partner, that the winner understand how to properly conduct herself in the presence of royalty, and, of course, the ins and outs of the country she will have extremely close ties to before long. The girl who demonstrates the most thorough knowledge of Chalonian royalty will win a whole night alone with Jordy."

I swear Lauren cracks her knuckles under the table.

Jordy, sitting at the head of the table wearing a much more reserved navy dress shirt (Prada), jacket (Gucci), and neck scarf (unspecified, but probably obnoxiously expensive), suppresses a smile.

First up, Dominique drags Jordy to his feet to use him as a prop. To my delight, she seems to be showing him the respect he deserves: absolutely none, he's not fucking royalty.

"Now, if you were to come into zis room and you see Jordy standing here, you will not need to bee-have any differently," Dominique says, "as 'e 'as no rank."

Skye looks as though all her dreams have come true at once. I can relate.

"But, for now, we are going to pretend Jordy eez heez sister, Princess Samantha."

Jordy visibly cringes at this. I hope they got that on camera.

"Now, to curtsy to 'er, you will do as so." Dominique demonstrates a light curtsy, dipping her head a little and only bending a couple of inches. "And you will address 'er as 'Va Fillefrein.'" Now, come. Practice."

One by one, we stand in front of Jordy, and curtsy to him.

"Did I nail that, or what?" Perrie asks after she finishes hers.

Jordy's grin is genuine. "It's like you were raised in the palace."

"Ha. I'm telling my dad that when I see him next. He'll think that's the funniest thing he's ever heard."

Jordy actually seems charmed. Which, duh, who *wouldn't* be charmed by Perrie? But it does make me freak out a little. Maybe Skye's theory that Jordy doesn't want a girl that's especially nice to him is off base.

Still. I told her I'd follow the plan. And she'll literally kill me if I stray from it one more time.

Hi, Sam, I mouth when I reach him. His smile is a little bit too wide to be natural. It's a silent-screaming sort of smile.

Well, I don't think I've won myself any brownie points, plan or not. But it *is* funny to torture him, so.

When Kim curtsies, she holds eye contact with him for a super long time. After they get the shot, she asks him to talk in an urgent whisper. "Later," he whispers back.

"Please?" she says. "I really, *really* need someone to talk to."

"We can't now."

Dejected, Kim returns to the table and avoids the rest of our eyes.

Once we're done, Dominique has us repeat the process as though Jordy is now Queen Aimée, with a much deeper curtsy, and the words "Va Ferrefreiner."

It takes about half an agonizing hour to learn all the possible curtsy combinations, at which point we're seated back at the table and provided, to Lauren's delight, tea. To Lauren's even greater delight, she'd been right about how to hold the cup, and Dominique has her demonstrate her technique to the rest of us.

After this, while we all elegantly sip our tea—which I dump four sugars into, to Lauren's great *un*-delight—we're treated to a long, boring lecture on the history of the royal family. By the end of it, I kind of wish I were back in the frigid lake swimming after a rogue kayak. At least that was a little exciting.

"And now, ze quiz," Dominique says. Everyone in the room gives her a forced smile, except for Lauren, who looks genuinely thrilled, and Kim, who hasn't really smiled all day.

"What was ze given name of ze grandmuzzer of ze queen of Chalonne?"

I'm just about to open my mouth when Lauren spits out, "Alma!"

"Correct."

And so it continues on. Every question, Lauren leaps in before the rest of us can even get a shot.

"Switzerland!"

"1937!"

"Red and purple!"

"Horse liver!"

By the time Grayson announces Lauren as the clear winner, I'm tired, bored senseless, and ready to get out of this princess ball gown, because it weighs about five tons.

"Next week," Skye says, squeezing my arm as Jordy throws his arms around Lauren in an embrace.

Yeah, well. We'll see.

At the rate I'm going, I'm not sure if my luck's ever going to turn around.

Unfortunately for me, things are about to get worse.

Back at the manor, we find out that Gwendolyn has decided it would be a great idea to keep us in our ball gowns and cram us into the *Notte Infinita* room while we're each six feet wide. Jordy and Kim aren't here yet, and Gwendolyn is talking to the camera crew about something, and it is *way* too freaking hot in here, so, after a minute or two of patiently waiting, I dash into the hall for some fresh-ish air. I'll go inside when Jordy and Kim get back, I figure.

That's when I hear a hushed argument. It sounds like a private conversation I shouldn't overhear, so, naturally, I'm overcome by curiosity and I inch down the hall to stand by a closed door.

I make out Kim's voice. ". . . all day. I *needed* you. I came on this show *for you*, and you couldn't even spare me *thirty seconds* to talk to me? He was your *friend*, Jordy."

Jordy replies, "I didn't know that happened! I'm not a mind reader, Kim."

"Gee, I look like I've been crying half the day, and I specifically tell you I need to talk to you. What could I possibly need right now?"

"I'm sorry, in case you didn't notice, we were in the middle of filming a time-sensitive episode! You could've asked me to talk after we wrapped filming instead of storming off in a mood."

"You know what, Jordy? I deserve a boyfriend who will notice I'm upset, and who will *fight* to make sure he can speak to me and support me if I need him. I deserve a boyfriend who will chase me if I storm off after a day of him being a wanker!"

Oh, shit. Yup, I've definitely heard enough. As quietly as I can, I sneak back down the hall to hover by the *Notte Infinita* room door. A minute or two later, Jordy bursts out of the room and storms down the hall.

"You handled that *great*," I say lightly. "Wonderful humaning, Jordy."

He glares at me, red-faced and wordless, then disappears inside. A few seconds later, he reappears with Gwendolyn and Isaac, and they make a beeline for Kim without acknowledging me.

The remaining girls decide to join me in the hall at that point, which is probably wise. Even without corsets, we're at risk of passing out in there.

"Do you think Kim's going home?" Perrie asks.

We shrug.

After ten minutes of wondering, Isaac leaves the room, makes eye contact with me, and beckons.

"Oh, no," Skye says, touching my arm in sympathy as I leave.

Oh, yes. I have a bad feeling I know exactly where this is going. Once again, Skye called it.

"So," Isaac says cheerfully, walking ahead of me upstairs. I get the feeling I'm supposed to follow him. "*Kim* has spent the day freaking out because her friend is in the hospital. And now Gwendolyn knows how Kim found out her friend is in the hospital."

Goddamn it.

"*You* should've told her," I say. "She has a right to know."

"She didn't need to know, because her friend is *fine,* and now she's feeling worried and helpless and guilty. She shouldn't have been put in that position. And she wouldn't have been, if *someone* didn't smuggle a contraband iPad into the mansion!"

We stop in front of my room, and Isaac tips his head toward the door.

"You want the iPad?" I sigh.

"Of course I want it! You shouldn't even have it. I just spent a solid five minutes talking Gwendolyn out of fining you for it, too, so. You're welcome."

Without much choice, I dig it out of my drawer, power it off, and hand it over to Isaac with a sulky expression. "Thank you. For talking Gwendolyn out of it."

"Anything else in there I should know about?"

"Nothing I'm telling any of the girls about now, that's for sure," I joke.

Isaac doesn't laugh, though, so I roll my eyes. "*No.*"

By the time I get dropped back off in the *Notte Infinita* room, Kim is back with Skye and Perrie. She catches my eye and mouths, *Sorry.* She looks genuinely remorseful, so I wave a hand. *Don't worry about it.*

If anything, I feel like I might owe her an apology. Because I am *pretty* sure that fight I just overheard between her and Jordy might be kind of sort of my fault. I *did* tell Kim he should be supporting her, after all.

"Today was so much fun," Jordy says. "The past few weeks, we've spent a lot of time exploring our past. It's been wonderful to have the opportunity to show you all a piece of my present, and explore what will be, for one of you, our future."

Yeah, sure thing, Jordy. I'm starting to doubt if Queen Aimée actually knows he exists.

"But, tonight, for one of you . . . that future doesn't belong to you. So, tonight I've decided to keep Perrie."

"Skye."

"And Maya."

As it sinks in what that means, I freeze beside Kim. Did I just unintentionally get her kicked off the show?

Kim's face twists with pain and betrayal, and her eyes fill with tears. That's when my guilt turns into anger. Is Jordy for fucking real? He's going to send her home today? After the day she's had?

It takes everything, literally *every ounce of self-control I have* to hug him instead of slapping him.

Then, I notice the looks on the faces of the other girls as I join them. There's not a relieved smile in the room. Only disbelieving, disgusted looks.

He didn't *have* to send anyone home tonight at all. There's no rule about that. Even if he didn't want Kim to win, he could've held off.

He could've. But he chose not to. And, if the looks on Perrie's and Lauren's faces are anything to go by—not to mention the barely disguised looks of contempt from some of the crew—he just did more damage to his image with the girls in ten seconds than Skye and I have managed in five weeks.

I guess I was right the first time, months ago, when Rosie talked me into coming on the show.

Jordy's his own gasoline. Maybe all I needed to do was light a match.

And there're two weeks left for him to go up in flames.

TWENTY-THREE

Maya

I'm having a lovely dream about the leaves on the ground transforming into five-dollar bills when the sound of a gentle breeze is interrupted by the opening notes of "Rock the Casbah."

"The challenge is *tomorrow, Skye,*" I shout over the music without opening my eyes. I am going *straight* the hell back to sleep the second she turns the music off, and then I'm going to hunt her down in a few hours to yell at her some more.

"Isaac's here to see you."

"Tell him to come back at a decent hour."

"It's ten thirty, Maya, you're the indecent one, come on."

"At least turn the *music off,*" I growl as I finally open my eyes. Skye's sitting crisscross-applesauce on the floor, holding the speakers above her head and looking really damn pleased with herself.

"I will when you get up. Up, up, up!"

I throw a pillow at her face and hit a bull's-eye. She grabs it and leaps on top of me, one knee on each side, and holds the pillow up while I shriek and beg for forgiveness with my arms over my head. I only bring them back down when she drops the pillow, and she takes the opportunity to kiss me quickly on the forehead before rolling off me.

Five minutes later, I trudge downstairs after Skye, dressed but not happy about it.

Isaac's in the kitchen alone with a glass of water. "Finally," he says when we enter.

"She wasn't up yet," Skye says, throwing some bread in the toaster.

"Oh, I'm sorry," Isaac says. "You didn't have to wake her up. It's not that important."

"Yes, I did," Skye says, and I stick my tongue out at her. Just because she's a morning person doesn't mean she has to drag everyone else down with her.

"Skye said you wanted to see me?" I ask.

"Yeah, I have a message from your mom. She called to ask us to tell you she loves you."

Skye glances up at this, a funny look on her face.

I roll my eyes back into my head. "You came all the way over here for *that*?"

"I was already here. She called us two days ago."

"Jesus," I say, but I'm smiling.

"Well, I think it's sweet," says Skye, retrieving the toast. "Peanut butter?" she asks me, but she's already unscrewing the lid by the time I nod. She knows damn well I want peanut butter.

"I get it, Maya," Isaac agrees. "My parents call me about fifty times a day. Usually because they need help with the computer, but still."

"I guess she wanted to check in, since she's used to hearing from me every day," I say lightly, taking the plate of toast Skye passes to me.

"Mm, funny that. She wasn't supposed to be hearing from

you *at all,* so you won't get any guilt from me," Isaac says. "Anyway, you girls excited about tomorrow?"

"Thrilled," I say.

"Hope you're not afraid of heights," he says. "Tomorrow you're scaling a cliffside."

"The fuck I am," Skye says calmly, spreading a thin layer of margarine on her toast.

"You are if you want the getaway date."

I pause with a glass of juice halfway to my lips. "Go on?"

"You'll have harnesses, don't worry. And it's not as bad as I made it sound. We had our crew test it, and half of them didn't even bother with harnesses. The contestant who gets to the top the fastest wins the night away with Jordy. And trust me, if there's ever an overnight you want to win with Jordy, it's this one."

"Wait. What, exactly, does our ability to rock climb have to do with how well we'd work with Jordy?" I ask.

Isaac shrugs. "I dunno. Something about how outdoorsy he is, I think?"

Skye blinks. "I once saw him go home and change his jeans halfway through the day because he noticed he had a patch of dirt on them."

"One time," I jump in, "he set up a tent in his backyard for us to have a fake-camping date, and he dragged me back inside at two a.m. because he thought he heard a wolf. In his backyard. In *Hartford.*"

"Could it have been a coyote?" Skye asks.

"It was the neighbor's dog, Skye. But sure, maybe he's had a personality transplant since we knew him," I say, turning to Isaac. "It's not like we've spent much time with him. He could be our generation's Bear Grylls for all I know. Defeating German shepherds with wild abandon."

"Well, win yourself this challenge," Isaac says, moving to leave, "and you'll have a chance to find out."

Skye and I look at each other, and somehow, I know she's coming up with a plan already.

It takes us a good chunk of the afternoon to figure out which cliff we're going to be scaling tomorrow. It's about a fifteen-minute walk away, surrounded by forest. It also has a flag at the top of it, a candy wrapper on the ground near the edge, and a car parked fifty feet away with what definitely looks like climbing gear in the back seat.

"I'm not climbing that," Skye says as I pick up the wrapper with a tut. "No way."

"No?" I ask, following her gaze up. "I don't think it looks so bad."

She shakes her head vigorously. "I don't like heights. I hate them. No way."

It's maybe thirty feet high at most; like, *truly* not that bad. Skye must have an actual phobia. I bump my shoulder against hers. "I thought you were Little Miss Adventure, running around Europe with a backpack for the last couple months?" I ask. "You can't swim, you hate heights . . ."

"I like hiking, and I like new places. That doesn't mean I'm going to jump out of a plane anytime soon."

"I bet I could convince you to jump out of a plane."

"I assure you, it's not possible."

"I'd hold your hand," I tease.

"You can try it for the next fifty years and you won't wear me down."

"You're on," I say, before I realize the implication of that. I look away, blushing, then walk closer to the cliff face to inspect it. "But as for tomorrow, just tell them you feel sick."

"What, and have Jordy kick me out?" she asks. "I don't think so."

"Jordy is *not* gonna kick you out," I say. "If anything, I'm the one at risk."

He's *constantly* calling me up last at the *Notte Infinitas,* and that can't be a coincidence. And if he's already kissed Perrie, but not me or Skye, I don't love our chances. If I win this challenge, though, maybe I can turn it around.

A whole night with Jordy—the last night before we film the finale episode next week—is a game changer. It'll not only guarantee that I make it to the finale, but it'll give me the time I need to convince him.

If I can mentally figure out a route, will that give me the advantage I need tomorrow? I'm not exactly a seasoned rock climber—in that I've never climbed anything more complicated than a backyard tree—but are any of us?

"Do you think I can convince Jordy to stand up for me if I do back out?" Skye asks.

"Yeah, I bet if you do the whole damsel thing, you've got a good shot," I say, stepping back. "He'll love the chance to look all masculine and protective, especially if he can get half-naked during it. But if worse comes to worst, I'll yell at them for you if they try to force you."

"Thank you, because I really can't do it."

"Skye," I say. "You have my word. They're forcing you up that cliff over my dead body."

Breathing out and shaking her shoulders, Skye steels herself and pulls out the notepad and pen she insisted on bringing. Squinting at the cliff, she taps the pen against her chin. "Okay. Where do you think you should start?"

I study the rocks, drawing a mental path, and then slap one of the flatter ones on the bottom left. "Here."

Nodding, she begins to draw.

By nighttime, I'm actually feeling pretty confident about tomorrow. The climb *looked* simple enough, and I've had plenty of time to psych myself up for it. And with Skye's diagram—which I spent half the afternoon memorizing with her help—I won't even have to think. I'll just have to climb. Theoretically, anyway, but, like Skye always says, her ideas are always good. All things considered, I'm pretty sure I've got this in the bag.

That is, until Perrie, Skye, and I are gathered on the back porch—Skye and Perrie with wine, me with a Pepsi—and Perrie leans in to tell us a secret.

"So," she says, "apparently tomorrow's challenge is rock climbing. I'm pretty sure they want me with Jordy tomorrow night. Why else would they do rock climbing?"

I choke on my drink. "Uh . . . what's rock climbing got to do with you?"

Perrie looks surprised. "I love it. I go bouldering a couple of times a month. It's fun, it's great for building up your lats, which are *super* hard to target, and you get the best photos at the top with the view behind you. I'm surprised I haven't mentioned it before."

"Nope," I say faintly. "Guess it never came up."

"I literally work at a climbing gym."

"I thought you were a receptionist," I say.

"Yeah, I am. At a climbing gym."

Now that I think about it, I did notice the amount of mountaintop shots on Perrie's Instagram when I checked it out before losing my iPad (I'd been curious to see if her follower count had grown from the show, and was happy to see a healthy boost from what she'd told me). It hadn't clicked that she could be climbing her way up, though. I figured she just walked—or dragged—her way up, complaining the whole way, before smiling for the camera. You know, like a normal person.

Skye slumps into her chair, dejected. There goes our shot at me getting the night with Jordy. I'm just going to have to try hard to get some one-on-one time with him tomorrow.

And there's only one week left until the finale.

I'm gonna have to make it a hell of a five-minute chat.

"Hey," Perrie says, grabbing the camera from the bench beside her. "Could you guys get a photo of me? Maybe under the porch lamp, there? Ooh, then a group selfie?"

Skye jumps to her feet. "Yes, and get that tree in the background," she says, using her thumbs to map out a camera lens angle.

I get up to help and focus on clearing my mind. There's no point freaking out about tomorrow.

I'll get my moment with Jordy. I'll make sure of it.

It's impossible to sleep, because I'm freaking out about tomorrow, *I am freaking out about tomorrow!* Which is a problem, because if I don't get enough sleep, there's no *way* I can pull a physical challenge off in the morning. But, of course, panicking about not sleeping is only making me more awake, and the more awake I am, the more possible problems my brain thinks up to worry about.

What if I fall on camera because it's harder than it looks?

What if they chose this challenge because Perrie's the obvious front-runner—Perrie, who has made it *super* clear she has no intention of rejecting Jordy on camera no matter how she feels about him?

What if I forget Skye's path? Or, worse, what if the path doesn't work in practice?

Finally, I realize I have to go back to the cliff. If I can just spend ten minutes or so examining it, I might give myself some sort of advantage over Perrie. It's unlikely, but possible, right? Is it ridiculous? Yes. Is it dangerous to wander off into the woods in the middle of the night? Also yes. Am I going to do it?

Yeah. It's happening.

I climb out of bed as quietly as I can, and grab the notepad, along with some clothes and shoes. I check on Skye, who's breathing in the soft, steady way she does when she's fully out, and then dash to the bathroom to get changed.

Twenty minutes later, I'm standing at the cliff's base inspecting the rocks. The moon's almost full tonight, and there are no clouds in sight, which is helping a whole lot.

Now that I'm looking at the cliff again, I can see it's not vertical; not even close. If anything, it's an extremely steep, rocky hill. Well, that's different. A hill, I can do. Now I get what Isaac meant about it being possible to climb without a harness. To test it out, I step up a few rocks, making sure to choose the ones Skye and I identified earlier today. It's easy enough.

I can go as high as I feel safe, I realize, and get a feel for how to scale it. Then I can head back down. Even doing a fraction of the route will confirm I have a chance at winning tomorrow. I just won't go too far.

I take a step, then another. The icy night wind whips at me, but not strongly enough to throw me off course. The rocks are sturdy under my hands and shoes, and I don't have to stretch too far with each step. My calves are burning in a nice "oh, hey, you're actually doing some exercise" way, and not a "dear god we weren't made for this" way, which is a good sign, I think.

It's not *horrible*, or even all that bad.

That is, until one rock is a little too far for me to easily step on. I reach out until I get a good grip on a rock farther up and use it to lug myself up to the next rock. It's only when I reach it that I realize the next rock is farther away still. There's no *way* I can reach that.

I can't check the notepad without letting go of the rocks—which I have just about zero intention of doing—but I'm *sure* I'm on the right route. It just must have looked more doable from the ground. Neither Skye nor I have any bouldering experience, after all.

This is exactly why I came here. At least I can solve this problem calmly, without a ticking clock. If I'd realized this tomorrow, I'd have been *really* screwed.

I look back down at the place I stood a few seconds before. Getting up here was one thing, but getting back down? It looks like, to put it mildly, a hell of a jump. One I am not anywhere near athletic enough to even try.

So, I can't go up or down. That's fine. I'll go sideways. I feel around to the right with my hand, then my foot. And to the left with my hand, then my foot. And I find absolutely squat. There's a rock that looks like it could probably hold my weight, but it's a full jump away, and there is no way I'm leapfrogging my way around these rocks without a harness.

So. To recap. I've gotten myself trapped twenty feet off the ground, on a cliff face, in the middle of the night, in the middle of the woods. With no phone on me. And no one who knows where I am.

Okay.

Cool.

Now I let myself panic.

TWENTY-FOUR

Maya

"Maya?"

My heart leaps in my chest at the sound. The voice is distant, but unmistakable. "Skye?" I call back. "I'm here."

"Are you okay?"

"Uhh. I'm sort of stuck," I say, looking over my shoulder. Oh Jesus, she looks, uh, *very* small. "I can't reach the next step."

Any comfort I felt on seeing her fades when I make out the "oh shit" expression on her face. It's not exactly what you want your rescuer to look like in this sort of situation. "Can you come back down the way you went?" she calls.

I shake my head.

"Okay. Don't panic. I'm going to get help," she says. Her tone of voice is approximately as comforting as her expression. If she wants me to not panic, she's not doing the *best* job at calming me down.

"Don't let them bring cameras," I say. "And hurry, please?"

"I will." She doesn't move, though. "Are you safe where you are?"

"I've been here for about five minutes now, so, I guess," I say. "I'm in an awkward pose, though. I'm just gonna . . ." I step to the side so I can untwist my hips, and the rock shifts beneath me. I let out a cry of alarm and lurch sideways to return to my original foothold. Nope, nope, nope.

"Maya! Stay there, stay there. I'm coming up. No, actually, I'm going to the top and coming down, it'll be easier to reach you. Give me a minute."

I gasp over the pounding of my heart. "Sure. Take your time."

About a century or so later, she appears at the top of the ledge. "Are you okay?" she asks.

"Oh, sure, I'm great. Having a freaking blast."

She scales down the first few steps in a matter of seconds. When she turns down to check on me, her jaw is clenched in determination, and her brow is furrowed in fear. "Be careful," I say.

She draws a shaky breath and lowers herself again. And again. I watch her descent, taking note of which rocks hold steady under her. She isn't far above me now. There's a ledge coming up. If she reaches it, she could help me get to it, and we can go up from there.

"Aim for the left a little," I say. "See the ledge?"

She looks down, and then sucks in air through her teeth with a hiss. "This is too high," she says, turning back to the black sky. The wind catches her hair, and her shoulders tense.

"You're doing great," I say. "You've got this."

"No. Maya—"

Something in her voice sets my instincts on high alert. She's drawing closer to the cliffside, gripping the rock with white knuckles as her legs buckle at the knees.

"Skye," I say urgently. "Breathe. You're okay. You don't have to move. Just breathe."

Her shoulders rise and fall as she takes several deep breaths, then several more. Faster, and faster, in a pattern that sounds dangerously like hyperventilation. "I can't. I can't."

She sways where she stands, and she ducks her head forward, squeezing her eyes shut. The unsteadiness of her stance sets off something primal in my spine. I don't decide to move. One moment I'm standing on my precarious perch, the next I've launched to the side, easily clearing the gap I was too scared to attempt before. As Skye gasps for air, adrenaline propels me up. Hand over hand, rock by rock, until suddenly I'm drawing up beside her.

"Hey, I've got you," I say, wrapping my arm behind her to pull her firmly in against the rocks. "We're going back up. Okay?"

"I can't. I can't."

I'm pretty sure pushing her will only make her panic, so, I stand in silence, my arm still locked around her. It's much sturdier here than where I got myself stranded. The rocks jut out farther, so we can stand comfortably. If we need to hang here for another fifteen minutes while Skye rides this wave, that's what we'll do.

After a while, Skye shrugs her shoulders roughly. "Get off me," she snaps, and I tear my arm back like she's stung me. "I need air. I need space."

There's only so much I can do to give her space, given the circumstances and all. In the end, I sort of shuffle to the left, and this apparently does the trick, because another thirty seconds later she looks up with focused eyes. "Okay," she says in a thin voice.

"Okay. Do you think you can climb back up?"

She nods wordlessly and starts moving. I follow after her, making sure to take her tested rocks to be safe, because as it turns out, I do *not* have a natural talent at rock climbing, and

I'm not taking any more risks. When she reaches the top, she turns around to pull me over the edge, and holy shit I have never appreciated how wonderful solid land is. Suddenly, I get the dramatic movie scenes where people kiss the ground. I mean, I'm not going to do it, because gross, but the vibes are there.

"Thank you." I breathe, following after her as she starts to storm back to the mansion. "Although, I guess I *wasn't* stuck in the end. But I don't know if I could've pushed through it without that extra motiva—"

Skye whirls around, and I stop in my tracks at the look on her face. She is firmly past storm clouds. This is lightning and thunder territory. "That was *idiotic*, Maya. What the hell did you think you were doing?"

I start, taken aback. "I was *trying* to get a leg up on the competition. If tomorrow's a speed run, I figured learning the route would be smart."

"*Smart?* You thought sneaking off in the middle of the night to climb a cliff without telling anyone where you were was *smart?*"

"It's more of a hill, and I wasn't going to climb it if it looked dangerous."

"You were alone. *It was going to be dangerous.*"

"It was a risk I was willing to take."

Skye's mouth drops open, and she brings her hands up in front of her as she speaks for emphasis. "Maya, nothing is worth risking yourself over, okay? Jesus! Screw the getaway, and screw Jordy. You could've been hurt, and for *what?*"

"But I wasn't. And now I think I can win this tomorrow, I really do—"

"*Who cares?*" Skye shouts, throwing her arms up.

I raise my own voice as outrage bubbles up in my chest. "I

thought we did? Isn't that what we've been working toward? Why are we here, otherwise?"

"There's a *line*, Maya. And if you don't know where yours is, you need to rethink your priorities."

"Look, if you don't want this as badly as I do, that's fine. I swear, I didn't mean to get you involved in this. I'm sorry. I didn't think anyone would notice I was gone."

"Thank god I did," Skye snaps.

"What are you mad at me for? You *chose* to come after me, and to climb down. And thank you for that, but you didn't have to."

"Why am I mad?" she repeats incredulously. "I woke up in the middle of the night and your bed was empty. I looked around the whole mansion and couldn't find you anywhere, then I remembered the cliff. I thought, no, there's no way she would've done something like that, but I went to check anyway, just in case, and what do I find? You're halfway down, standing on crumbling rocks, and you almost fell right in front of me. I thought I was about to watch you *die*, Maya."

I shake my head. "You're *mad at me* because I almost got hurt?"

She runs a hand over her mouth, shaking her own head right back at me. Then, out of nowhere, she steps forward and pulls me into a tight embrace. We press together so tightly I can feel her heart thudding against her ribs. Can smell the faint remnants of her perfume from the day. Could press my lips against her neck if I turn my head a fraction to the right.

No sooner has the final thought crossed my mind than she takes my chin between her fingers and kisses me, fierce and deep. Usually, she kisses me in a gentle and lazy way, full of feather touches and soft hair and velvet skin. Tonight, there's fire underneath it. She digs her fingernails into the flesh of my neck, and grasps my waist, and scrapes her teeth along my lip.

Then, all at once, she tears away. Her fingers flutter against her lips, and her eyes are fixed on me so intensely I wonder if she's aware of her hands at all. "Figure out where your line is," she says. "Okay?"

"Okay," I say. "I'm sorry. I didn't mean to put you in danger."

She just shakes her head.

The walk back to the mansion is almost totally silent. My mind scrambles to process that kiss, to assign meaning where there was none. There was something different about it, wasn't there? Or do I just want there to have been?

Do I want there to have been?

The thought surprises me, but as soon as it pops up, I shove it back where it came from. Making a sappy romance out of this would only complicate everything. I can't afford complications.

I know where my lines are. And as long as she's clear on hers, we won't have a problem.

TWENTY-FIVE

Skye

"It's a piece of cake," Perrie assures me after I'm fitted out in climbing gear. "I promise, they couldn't have chosen an easier route."

"It could be a staircase and I still wouldn't climb it at that height," I say.

Not again, anyway. Once was more than enough. My heart is pounding just looking at the drop.

Well, partly because of the drop, partly because being here brings me back to last night. How terrified I felt when I couldn't find Maya. The adrenaline surge when I realized she was stuck. The dizzying, overwhelming relief when I pulled her back over the edge.

It was the adrenaline, I'm quite sure. That's why our kiss felt so . . . significant. It felt different because it was a kiss spurred on by hormones and cortisol, followed closely by an explosion of chemicals when we connected. Entirely biological. For example, right now, looking at Maya—who's speaking to Jordy over near the base—I can appreciate how beautiful she is. I would *like* to kiss her, because kissing her is lovely, but I don't feel like the world will stop turning if I don't have my arms around her, like I did last night.

So, therefore, the significance of that particular kiss was clearly an exception, and I don't have to worry about a thing.

Jordy finishes talking with Maya, then heads over to speak to Gwendolyn while Maya gives me a subtle nod.

"Chicken," Perrie teases when she realizes what's happening, but it's good-natured.

I would tell her about my cliff-climbing escapades last night to defend my honor, but I feel like Maya would prefer last night to be kept between us, so I just shrug. "They already made me get in a kayak. I've hit my upper limit, sorry."

Suddenly, Jordy makes a beeline for me, flanked by Gwendolyn and a camera operator. "Looking sexy, girls," he says, gesturing to our harnesses.

"Thank you, I picked it out especially for you," I deadpan. "You like bondage, right, Jordy?"

Jordy chuckles nervously and looks toward Gwendolyn. "Cut that out," he whispers, and she nods and makes a note in her iPad. "Hey, can we talk for a second?" he asks.

What he means is, can we go off together and talk on camera where it's quieter. I nod, and we walk into the trees, then wait several minutes for the camera crew to find a spot with good lighting.

"So," Jordy says, when we're finally ready to have this conversation. "Maya tells me you're scared of heights."

Gwendolyn's mouthing something to me behind the cameras that I can't quite make out. "Yes," I say, trying not to let her distract me.

"Why didn't you tell me when we got here?" Jordy asks, taking my hand.

Gwendolyn's waving her arms above her head now. Then she pounds a fist against her chest. Gorilla? *Oh.* "I was afraid?" I say, and Gwendolyn nods vigorously.

"Of what?" Jordy asks.

". . . heights?" I say, and Gwendolyn throws her hands up in disgust. Then, it clicks. "And, that if you knew I'm afraid . . . of heights . . . you might not want to be with me because of all the . . . outdoor stuff you like to do. Involving heights."

There we go. Now Gwendolyn's happy with me. "Like helicopter rides," I add.

"Skye," Jordy says seriously. The camera zeroes in on him. "I never want you to be uncomfortable, or *ever* feel like you're being made to do something you don't want to do. Consent is *so* important in the MeToo era."

Gwendolyn gives him a thumbs-up.

"Thank you, Jordy," I say. Suddenly, it occurs to me that I can manipulate this discussion in a way that'll increase my chances of making it to the finale. "So, I can sit this one out? You won't be mad?"

Jordy cups my cheek. "Of course not."

I place my hand over his and stare into his eyes, so they *have* to keep it in the episode. "I should've realized you wouldn't send me home over something this trivial." Then I take my hand away, so they can't just cut that particular piece of dialogue out without losing the moment of physical touch. "Thank you so much for being so understanding. I was silly to be scared."

There. It's not entirely foolproof—Jordy did send Kim home during a personal crisis last week. The only difference is, as far as I know, Kim didn't mention her friend at any point during filming, so Jordy's image didn't take a hit. Even if she did, I doubt it would make it into the episode. If I gave them good enough television just now, though, maybe Gwendolyn will pressure Jordy into letting me stay. If only to give the episode more of a story arc.

"Skye," Gwendolyn says, "hang around. We'll just get a talking-head shot."

They turn the camera on me now, and I run through the lines I know they want to hear for the voiceover. *When I got here, I knew I couldn't do this challenge. I've been terrified of heights since I was a kid, when I fell off a jungle gym and broke my arm. I was so afraid to tell Jordy . . .*

"Were you mad at Maya, for telling Jordy about your fear?" Gwendolyn asks. "Do you think she was trying to sabotage you with Jordy?"

I fight to keep from glaring at Gwendolyn. "I was grateful to Maya for telling Jordy," I say. "She was trying to encourage me to tell him myself, because she knew he'd understand. She's so good at reading people."

Gwendolyn looks rather disappointed.

As the girls get ready at the base of the cliff for the time trial, I make myself comfortable with a glass of wine—available to me because I'm not doing any dangerous activities I could sue them over if it goes wrong—and watch the show with Isaac and Violet.

Lauren's up first. My stomach plunges in empathy as she stumbles over the first few rocks, but she gets the knack of it quickly. In fact, she's doing very well, scaling at a high speed with a determined look on her face. I'm just thinking she might give the others a run for their money when she slips with a scream. The harness catches her, of course, and she hangs there pitifully for several seconds while she collects herself. The producers call out to check on her, but she waves them off and gets a grip on the cliff again. She races to the top, and grabs the flag, but I can see on her face she knows she's lost. Dejectedly, she heads down the nearby walking trail back to the base, but finds a spot by herself to stand and watch the other girls.

Maya's next, and I resist the urge to cheer her on. It's possibly not the best look to vocally root for her to beat the other two, after all. She lunges upward at lightning speed, even faster than Lauren. I suppose our pre-planning, combined with last night's venture, helped more than I could've hoped for. She seems to know exactly where she's going to put her feet next. She reaches the point she got trapped on last night, and my shoulders tense up, but, safely attached to the harness, she doesn't hesitate to jump sideways to the next rock.

I'm glad she didn't attempt that last night.

With a victory cry, she grabs the flag a full fifteen seconds faster than Lauren's time. I clap enthusiastically as the producers undo her. She practically skips her way down the walking trail, and makes a beeline for me.

"Worth it," she whispers right into my ear.

"Do you want me to kill you?" I whisper back, and she snorts.

It's Perrie's shot next, and straightaway, I can see the difference in comfort levels. She's obviously done this a million times before.

"Is it bad that I'm rooting for my friend to lose?" Maya asks.

"Eyes on the prize," I say.

"I guess."

This time, it's not possible to call it. Even without the practice, Perrie seems to be going just as fast as Maya did. Up, up, up, barely pausing to check the stability of each rock before trusting it with her body weight.

"Come on," I whisper under my breath, and Maya takes my hand and squeezes it until I lose feeling.

Perrie snatches up the flag at the top and bends over, out of breath, and we dutifully clap for her.

When Perrie returns to the base, she, Maya, and Lauren

line up in front of Grayson with the cliff in the background, and wait an eternity for the cameras to set up. Finally, just as I feel as though I'm about to die from the suspense, Grayson speaks.

"And the winner of today's challenge, by a margin of only one-point-five seconds . . . our dark horse, Maya! Congratulations!"

Lauren and Perrie clap for Maya. I raise my hands to join in, then I lower them as the implications of Maya's hard-earned win dawn on me fully.

So. Maya and Jordy will be alone together in a spa resort all night?

That's wonderful.

I'm so very happy for her. For us.

Jordy sends Lauren home at the *Notte Infinita*.

She wilts when she realizes he's not calling her up, and he gives her a prepackaged speech about how much it's meant to him to have her on the show. I can't help but feel they kept her around for the palace challenge, then sent her home at the first opportunity, but I keep it to myself.

Our odds have shot up to 66 percent. We're more likely to win than not now, all things being equal.

Which, to be fair, they never are.

Afterward, I crawl onto the bed and watch quietly as Maya fusses around packing for an overnight trip. "I should bring my bikini, right?" she asks. "Is that the sort of thing you do in a spa?"

"There aren't any weight restrictions on luggage, right?" I ask. "You *are* driving."

"Right, duh. I'll just take . . . everything."

"Everything?" I ask.

"Not *everything*, obviously, just . . . everything I could possibly see myself needing."

She turns in a circle in the middle of the room, putting her hand over her mouth in distress.

"Are you okay?" I ask.

"Yeah. Yeah, I am," she says. "Just a little freaked out about spending this long with Jordy, I guess. I wanted it so badly I forgot it'd mean I'm stuck with him. I hope we get our own rooms."

Oh. I hadn't even thought of that. I frown at the floor as Maya shoves the last few things in her bag.

"Okay. I'm pretty sure I'm ready," she announces, and I snap my head up and force a smile.

"Have fun!"

"I won't," she chirps back. Then, she studies my face, her eyes flickering from my eyes to my lips. Her expression is serious.

"Skye?" she asks.

"Yes?"

"I know we're just hooking up—"

"Yes, definitely," I say over her.

"—right. Well, sounds like I know the answer then, but I wanna cover my bases. Would it be weird if I kiss Jordy tonight? Or anything?"

As soon as the question leaves her lips, I'm hit with an irrational rage. Why should Jordy get to kiss her when he's done nothing but hurt us? Why can't he choose her as the winner next week without needing to rub his tongue all over hers tonight? Can't he just pick her based on her personality? Her humor? How much fun she is?

But it doesn't work like that, and I know it. Especially when Perrie's already kissed him.

"Not at all," I say. "You do whatever you need to do to win this. It's not weird."

"Okay." She picks up her suitcase, then hesitates. "It's just, I could make an excuse if it's weird. I could say I have a cold sore or something."

"I said it's not weird, Maya," I snap. Where did that come from? I didn't give my voice permission to come out like that. "I promise," I add, much more pleasantly.

"Okay. Great. I'll . . . see you tomorrow then, I guess?"

"See you tomorrow."

With that, she's gone, and I'm left alone in my room.

Finally, a night to myself. That's what I've wanted from the start, right? Some alone time?

I crawl onto my bed, and stare at the ceiling for a while. Then, I climb down the ladder, flop onto Maya's bed, and roll onto my side. It's easier to be down here until I go to sleep, so I don't have to climb up and down every time I leave the room.

The pillow smells like her.

I breathe in, until the lump in my throat finally loosens.

I don't mean to fall asleep on her bed.

But . . .

TWENTY-SIX

Maya

The best thing about a couple's massage is the blessed break in conversation.

It's not as relaxing as I would like—it's kinda hard to chill out when you've got a camera panning back and forth along the length of your body, several producers staring at you silently, and your nemesis lying on a bed a few feet over from you—but I do my best.

Until Jordy ruins it by making conversation. Like he ruins *everything*.

"How are you enjoying things at the house?" he asks. "Hopefully there's not too much stress to knead out of your back."

My masseuse digs his elbow into a sensitive spot at that moment, like he's trying to make a point. I wince through it. "It's been great," I say. "Kind of like a monthlong sleepover party. Movies, the pool, wine. Endless, endless wine. Perrie and Skye are bigger on the whole 'wine' thing than I am, though."

"Not a fan?" Jordy laughs.

"Not a fan. Skye says she wasn't, either, before her trip, but she kind of got used to it. She says Europeans are huge drinkers. Especially in the UK."

"Yeah, I'd agree with that."

I try to relax into the massage again, but I can feel the cameras staring at me on one side, and Jordy staring at me on the other. *Fine.* "How about you?" I ask. "We're getting close to the end now. Has it been what you hoped?"

"Yeah, it is, actually. You know, things have been different for me since . . . Samantha. You might think it's all good stuff, being famous. Sponsorships, all the clothes and skincare you could ever want. Electronics, cars, all given to you at the snap of a finger. People excited to see you wherever you go. Hearing all day every day how you've changed strangers' lives, and all that. But girls throw themselves at you, you know?"

There's a long pause. "Oh, was that last part supposed to be bad?"

"It is bad, Maya! I mean, obviously I've always had attention from girls, but it's gotten hard to tell when I'm being used. It's been a breath of fresh air, hanging out with you all. I mean, you all liked me *before* I was named one of *Opulent Condition*'s Top Fifty Sexiest Men. That means a lot. You know, that I can be pretty sure none of you are gold diggers, or chasing fame, or whatever."

"Wow, Jordy, that's beautiful."

"Thank you, yeah. I thought so."

"You should make sure you tell that to Skye. She'll be *super* touched to hear it."

I think I do a pretty great job of disguising my sarcasm. But the snort Jordy gives me tells me he doesn't miss it. I guess he *does* know me.

After the massage, we're given half an hour to get dressed and, in my case, touch up my makeup, before we're led to dinner in the spa courtyard. Although the area is set up for multiple guests, the place has obviously been rented out for us, as the only table that's been set is the one overlooking the gardens, with a single lit candle in its middle.

We sit, scan the menus, and place our orders.

"No offense to the catering at the manor," I say to Jordy once they take our menus, "but I am *dying* to get some food that isn't group dining. Skye would die if she were here."

Jordy gives me a searching look, then leans an elbow on the table. "You bring up Skye an awful lot," he says. "Have you noticed?"

"Oh. Not really. I think I mention the other girls pretty evenly."

"Nah, you've definitely mentioned Skye about a dozen times tonight." He gives me an infuriatingly knowing smile. "Are you trying to test my reaction?"

I give my head a quick shake. "Huh?"

"You know. Bring her up to see if I act any different?" When I continue looking bewildered, he gives me a patronizing hand pat. "It's okay if you're feeling jealous or insecure about Skye. There's history there, and you're only human."

"Oh."

"Look. Maya. I'm not the same person I was back when I dated Skye, and neither are the two of you. We've all grown."

"Thank god for that," I say sweetly.

"Ha, yeah. You know, this morning, the producers were annoyed at me when I asked them to let Skye sit out of the challenge. It made the competition smaller, you see?"

I glance at Isaac, Wai, and Violet. They're watching, expressionless. It seems kind of weird for Jordy to talk about them when they're a few feet away from us, but sure.

"Right," I say, not totally sure where this is going. Does he want an apology?

"I did it anyway," he goes on. "But only because you asked me to. Only for you."

The bullshit artist returns. "For me?" I ask, channeling old-school Disney princess energy.

"Yes. Haven't you noticed, Maya? Is it really possible you haven't noticed?"

"Noticed what?" I play along.

He takes my hands across the table. "How you've captured me."

Oh, fucking gag me with a wet rag. "Did you write that line, or did you have help?"

"Bit of both."

I squeeze his hands back. "I'm not jealous of Skye," I say. "But Skye and I did get off to a bad start because of you."

Jordy prickles and pulls his hands free. "Maya, you can't still be blaming your outburst on me."

"I'm not blaming anything on you, I promise. But I do have a serious question. Please, just one? It's been driving me crazy for weeks. I think I need to know the answer before . . . anything else."

Jordy nods warily. "Uh, sure, go on, then."

"How come you told me Skye knew about us?" I ask.

He glances at the cameras, blink-and-you'll-miss-it quick. "I didn't."

"Jordy! You *definitely* did."

He looks at the cameras again, wary. Then, the tension melts off his face. I wonder if he's remembering the contract clause. It doesn't matter what I make him say on camera. None of it's going to end up on television.

"No. You asked if Skye knew about *you*, and I said yes."

He gives me a wicked smile. "She did know about you. Your existence, anyway. You were in my old profile pictures."

"That is not what I meant, and you know it."

"Then maybe you"—he gently pokes me in the center of my chest—"need to pick your words more carefully in the future."

"I accused her of dating you when she knew we were still together," I say testily. I'm choosing my words carefully *this* time. "It took us two days to figure it out. *She* thought you two were broken up, and *I* thought she knew we weren't. It was *very* confusing." I break into a smile to put him at ease, and he returns it.

"It *sounds* confusing," he agrees. "Sorry about that."

"But we're friends now," I say.

"I'm glad to hear you figured things out. I thought you two might hit it off, actually. It was my idea to have you bunk together."

I almost choke on my glass of table water. "*Was* it? Thank you. That's really thoughtful."

The fucking prick.

At that moment, the waiters bring our food over, and it's time to get some classy shots of us eating our classy meal and pretending to be in love.

Saved by the bell.

After we finish acting smitten with each other over pork chops and steamed broccoli, it's time for another outfit change, this time into our swimsuits so we can be plonked in one of the hot tubs. It's warm, thank Christ, but since we can't keep our mic-packs on in the water, they have to keep the bubbles off so the boom mics can eavesdrop on our conversation.

The producers are all standing in a row in front of the spa, staring and waiting for us to do something interesting.

"Well, this is awkward," I say to Jordy under my breath.

Gwendolyn is gesturing at Jordy. It's nonsense to me, but obviously they have some kind of sign language figured out, because he leans in to whisper in my ear. "If we make out," he says, "they'll leave us alone soon. They just want some good footage."

A tingle of horror goes down my spine. "You sound pretty confident about that. Not your first rodeo?"

"Not your business." His eyes glint.

Fine. *Fine.* I knew this moment would come sooner or later, and here we are.

Here he is.

Leaning in.

Leaning in to kiss me.

With his lips.

I move back a few inches, but he has his eyes closed, so he doesn't notice. Collision is impending. There are cameras everywhere.

So, I take a deep breath like I'm about to go underwater, and I let his lips meet mine.

And god, it feels like I'm sixteen again. He tastes just like he used to. I can remember how totally head over heels I was about him. How, the first time he kissed me, he was holding my hand, and he squeezed it tighter and tighter without realizing because he was so nervous.

He's not nervous now.

He used to kiss me in the yard, while we watched the sun go down. Then he would tell me he'd never felt like this about anyone in his life.

He used to kiss me during movies, until we'd both burst into giggles and promise each other we were going to pay attention to the screen, only to be lost in each other within seconds.

He used to kiss me on the forehead whenever Mom came to pick me up from his house, gently, like he was afraid he might never see me again.

He used to kiss Skye while messaging me, telling me how much he missed me, and how excited he was to see me again.

Skye.

Her lips are so much nicer than his. Softer. When she kisses me, it feels like the stars are falling out of the atmosphere, and landing around us in a spray of glitter and dust.

It's nothing like this.

This is just two mouths meeting in the middle.

I pull away, and pretend to blush when I "notice" the cameras. Everyone laughs, and, finally, they agree to pack up and leave us.

Pros: no more performative kissing.

Cons: it's time to be alone with Jordy for real. And I don't think I can be held accountable for what happens when I get him alone.

The suite they've booked for us is a two-bedroom one, thank god. Once we've changed into comfortable clothes, I turn the heater on and grab a beer and a hard seltzer from the generously stocked bar fridge we've been told to go nuts on. A part of me wonders if Isaac got the seltzer in there because he's heard me complaining about wine. Who says he's never done anything for me?

I hand the beer to Jordy, then settle in on the sofa.

"So," I say, cracking open my can. "This is the first time we've talked without an audience over the last five weeks."

"It is indeed."

"Spill," I say.

Jordy gives me a confused smile. "Spill about what?"

"What's it really like, to have a sister who's dating royalty? The unscripted version?"

He laughs, then takes a swig of beer. "Oh, man. Time to do this, is it?"

"Yeah, time to do this."

He tosses his head from side to side. "It hasn't affected me as much as you'd think. I reckon I got the long end of the stick. It's weird to have the paparazzi stalking you wherever you go, but, you get used to it. At least, I have. And I'm loving all the charity work. I think I was made for that, you know? It suits me."

I fight to keep a straight face. "Totally."

"It's been an adjustment for Sam. She's had to uproot her whole life, you know? But the royal family is pretty chilled out here, nothing like in England or whatever. They ride bikes into town on Saturdays and pick out their own truffles at the farmer's market. Really down-to-earth stuff like that."

"Might as well be working class."

"Almost! We don't see them that often. I mean, Sam comes to visit us a bit still, but it's not like we're going for dinners at the palace every Friday night." He grins. "Don't tell Lauren."

"I can't tell Lauren, you sent her home."

"Oh yeah. Anyway, in some ways, my life's changed more than Sam's has. The media really loves me, and I'm not locked up in a palace half the week, so I get dragged to a lot more events and stuff. Which is great, like I said earlier, because of sponsorships and the like, but it's made dating a bit tricky."

"Mm. So, bit of a drought?"

"Drought of decent, classy women, flood of gold-digging bitches."

"Never change, Jordy."

He pauses, lost in thought, like he's deciding whether he wants to spill his guts to me. Then, he must figure it's safe, because he leans in. "I was so excited about the show, though. Because it's the first time it's been about *me*, you know?"

Hmm, gotta say, I do not know. "Elaborate?"

"Ever since Sam met Florian, it's been our whole lives. Yeah, I'm famous, and beloved and rich, but at what cost?"

". . . You still haven't made the cost clear."

"I'm not Jordy Miller. I'm Jordy Miller, Samantha's brother. We live here because of Samantha. I have to be careful what I say or do in public in case it affects her standing with the royals. My parents are obsessed with her, the public is *obsessed* with her, it feels like I talk about her all day every day."

It takes everything I've got not to "champagne problems" him. "That sounds . . . tough."

"It's not that I don't want good things for her," Jordy says, before swilling his beer. "I just don't want those good things to come at a cost to me."

"Sure . . ."

"My life was already good, you know? I was born good-looking and rich. Everything was easier before I became nobility."

"You're not nobility."

"Close enough. Like, before this, I never had any issues with girls. Ever. I mean, obviously, look at what we're doing right now. But . . . okay, how's this? I met a girl last year."

I don't think I've ever met a guy who gets around the way Jordy does. "Was that before or after Francesca?" I ask.

"Before."

"Ah. Go on."

"I won't go into too much detail about her, because I don't want to upset you."

"Very thoughtful."

"I loved her, though." When he says it, his voice goes funny. I don't think I've ever heard Jordy Miller sound like that.

"What happened?" I ask. "I won't be upset. You might as well tell me the full story. I promise, I'll keep my raging jealousy in check, just for you."

Jordy gives me a lopsided grin. "Okay, well . . . the whole thing happened crazy fast, like, I'd barely met her before I was mad about her. I thought she felt the same about me, but it didn't take me long to realize she was a lot more into my sister than me."

"Oh, was she queer, too?"

Jordy gives me a sharp look. "I mean Samantha's *status.*"

"Right, sorry."

"Anyway, she's with another guy now. They seem very happy together."

"And now you're on here, dating everyone you've ever met," I finish for him.

"Something like that, cheeky git," he says, elbowing me.

I study him. He kind of looks like his puppy's just died. "Are you still in love with her?" I ask.

"Maya, don't start this."

"I'm not starting anything! It's a genuine, empathetic question, Jordy. Have you ever heard of that? Empathy?"

"Terrible condition, I'm yet to be struck by it. And no, I'm not still in love with her. I've re-met someone else."

"Have you, now?" I ask with a laugh.

"Yes, and I'm contractually obligated to not tell you who, so don't try to get it out of me."

"Wouldn't dream of it," I say. "But, um . . . I'm sorry that happened. It really sucks, getting your heart broken."

He glances at me, then back to the ceiling. "Like I did to you," he says casually.

I pull the throw blanket around my shoulders to cover a chill. "Yeah."

We sit in the silence until it weighs a little too heavy. Then, to my surprise, Jordy cracks first.

"I'm sorry," he says, shuffling on the couch to face me. His voice is serious suddenly. "I was just a stupid little shit who thought I could take whatever I wanted if it was available to me. It wasn't cool."

I look at him in surprise. Of all the things I'd expected to come out of his mouth, "I'm sorry" wasn't one of them. Even though he'd *basically* admitted it at dinner—by not correcting me when I said it—it's different to hear him come out and acknowledge that he cheated on me.

After all this time, hearing him insist over and over and over again that he hadn't done anything wrong, hearing him admit it is . . . strange.

The thing is, I'd actually figured that he'd convinced himself he hadn't done anything wrong. You know how you can twist conversations in your mind until you remember them going another way? I could've sworn that was what Jordy had done to himself. Rewritten one of our conversations in his mind until it became a breakup, so he could convince himself he was actually the good guy in the situation.

But he hadn't convinced himself of anything. He's known the whole time that he cheated on me. The whole fucking time.

And he told everyone I was lying about it anyway.

"What?" he whispers gently as I stare at him, a smile teasing the corner of his mouth.

I blink myself back into focus. "Thank you for apologizing," I say.

I am going to get to the end of this show. And I am going to crush him.

He brushes a strand of hair from my eyes. "I should've done it earlier," he murmurs.

Yes.

Too late.

I lean into his hand, and he runs his fingertips around to the back of my head and pulls me in. As our lips meet, I ignore their size, and the taste of his mouth.

It's Skye, I tell myself.

She pulls me to my feet and leads me to her bedroom, where we tumble onto her mattress. I crawl on top of her, my knees on either side of her body. Closing my eyes, I lean down and kiss my way down her neck, scraping my tongue lightly along her skin until she groans in the back of her throat. She snakes her hands up underneath my shirt, and I ignore the sudden roughness of her fingers, going back to kiss her full on the mouth instead. I kiss her again and again, harder each time. I can't get enough of her. She pulls me down farther, grinding her hips against me.

"Maya," she pants, and suddenly, she's Jordy again. My name doesn't belong on his lips, so I kiss it off them, long and deep.

Then I extract myself delicately, and climb off the bed.

He lets out a cry of protest. "Where are you going?" he asks between heavy breaths.

I saunter to the doorway then stand in it, leaning against the frame. "As long as I'm one of many, I'm leaving it there," I say silkily. "I'm pretty set on monogamy, these days."

He huffs at me in a mixture of humor and frustration. "You aren't really gonna leave me—" he says. He doesn't get any further, though, before I shut the door and head to my own room to sleep.

TWENTY-SEVEN

Skye

When Maya arrives back at the mansion, I'm right there to greet her. She practically launches into my arms, and I spin her around in a hug by the steps.

"Wish we got that on camera," Isaac muses, before saying goodbye to us.

"So," I say, taking pains to sound casual as she wheels her suitcase to our room. "How did it go? Any success?"

"Honestly," she says, "maybe. Solid maybe."

"Really?"

"Yeah. Like, you know Jordy, it's hard to tell what the truth is and when he's just bullshitting his way through life, but I definitely felt like I left him wanting more. I did everything I could."

"You weren't too nice to him?"

"Landed on a happy medium between hate and love."

"Did you kiss him?"

"A bit."

"Oh." I try to ignore the sensation that washes over me at this. It's quite difficult to ignore it, however, because it's the distinct sensation of being crushed beneath a falling elephant. "Good. That should've helped."

"Depends how strong my powers of seduction are," Maya says.

"Very." The word escapes my mouth before I have the chance to grant it permission.

"Really?"

"I wouldn't worry."

Maya gives me a curious look, but I just wiggle my eyebrows at her.

"Soooooo," she says, closing the door gently.

My heart skips a beat, which my heart simply does not do. My heart is usually extraordinarily calm and rational, especially when it comes to actions as simple as closing a door. "So," I say. It comes out fractured, and I clear my throat.

Maya leans against the door, then kicks off from it and claps once. "It's just the three of us now. I think we should talk strategy."

Oh. I'd thought . . . she was going to say something else. "Strategy."

"Yeah. Like, I'm pretty sure I'm not gonna get picked for the final night alone with Jordy next week no matter what, because I *just* saw him. But we should think of some things for you to do and say if you get through, because, honestly, it's about fifty-fifty between you and Perrie, and having that last night with him will go a long way, considering you haven't really had that big long date with him yet. Hey, how's this? I'm planning! Are you proud of me?"

My smile is so tight I can almost hear it creak with the effort. "Mm!"

Maya, totally oblivious to my discomfort, plows on and starts pacing. "And, also, I was thinking we should pre-plan what we say when we reject Jordy next week. We could probably come up with the same speech, I guess, because it's not like both of us will get a shot to use it, right? I was thinking something along the lines of 'Actually, Jordy, I want to ask *you* a question. Why would I *ever* want to be with a slimy, lying, misogynistic, cheating asshole who's only here to make headlines that have nothing to do with his sister?' Good, huh? Because, by the way, he basically said that to me last night. Like, what a fucking narcissist, right?"

"One week to go, then it's over for good," I say, watching her carefully. Has it occurred to her that, if one of us *does* win, there's a chance that we'll be separated from that moment onward? And after the finale, we'll be flying to different continents?

"I know," she crows. "I am *so! Ready!* For this to be over!"

Apparently not. Color me shocked at the shortsightedness.

"But I'm also freaked out, you know?" she says, swinging around to face me. "Like, there is a *solid* chance of Perrie winning this thing. Then what? It'll all just be for nothing?"

"I don't know," I say. "I want to see him suffer, too, but I wouldn't say all of this was for nothing. I've actually enjoyed it here, funnily enough."

Maya surveys me fondly. "That's really nice," she says.

"And," I say, swinging my legs where I sit on the edge of the bed, "look at the positives. If Perrie wins, we'll have a whole week to hang out together, alone, in a hotel. No cameras, no other contestants . . ."

Maya slowly steps over to me. "I wouldn't hate that part, I guess," she says.

"There, that's the attitude."

"But I'd much rather hang with you for a week after *crushing him*."

I shuffle on the bed to put some extra distance between us. "Right."

"Actually, now I'm thinking about it, the stuff he said about Sam last night is useful. We can really build it into the speech! Like, if we said something like 'If it weren't for your sister, the world wouldn't care you existed'—oh, man, talk about *cutting*."

Had she even thought of me last night, while she was planning her speech and kissing Jordy? While I lay on her bed suspended in her absence, breathing in the memory of her on the sheets?

"Oh, and he mentioned a girl," Maya continues. "We should include her. Like, 'Oh, you're surprised she didn't stay when she found out who you are? Who would?' What do you think?"

"I . . . think whatever you come up with will be great," I say.

It's not quite what I want to say. I *want* to say, "Actually, Maya, it's becoming harder and harder for me to care about hurting Jordy, because that moment marks the end of our time together, and, as it turns out, I want it to never come." I want to say, "A not-so-small part of me would vastly prefer Perrie to win, because it'd give us one more week of pretending we don't have to say goodbye." I want to say, "Last night, I didn't feel victorious that you won the shot we needed to help you win over Jordy. I was wishing you were lying beside me."

But I simply can't. I can't, because I'm too afraid of what she'll say in response.

That she'll smile, and say, "Oh, Skye, you're great, but I thought you didn't want anything serious?" Or, even worse, "Skye, I really like you. But the hatred I feel for Jordy is so much bigger, so much more encompassing, than any feelings I have toward you."

The opposite of love isn't hate. Not by a long shot. Hate and love are cousins. Possibly even siblings. So many ballads are sung about the power of love. Not nearly enough time is devoted to the passionate fulfilment only a perfectly matched enemy can bring.

And maybe I'm simply not enough to compete with Jordy.

"Are you okay?" Maya asks, suddenly faltering. She looks concerned, and gentle, and I want to trust her and speak, but the words don't come. Instead, I force out the words that will.

"Yeah, I'm just tired. I think I'll take a nap by the pool for a while, but, uh, let me know how the speech goes, okay?"

"Okay," she says. I don't like the look I've put on her face, but for the life of me, I can't gather the strength to say the words that might ease it.

So I leave.

That night, Maya follows me upstairs to bed at only 10 p.m. Most nights when we don't have filming the next morning, she wakes me up sneaking onto the top bunk hours after I fall asleep. What, I wonder, is different about tonight?

"Didn't get much sleep last night, huh?" I ask lightly as I rub in my moisturizer.

"Nope," Maya says, bouncing onto her bed. "I think it was just weird sleeping alone. It was, like, *too* quiet, if that makes any sense?"

This catches my attention. "You didn't sleep with Jordy?" I ask. "I mean, in his bed?"

"Nope. I ditched early."

Those might be the sweetest words I've ever heard.

"Ooh. After that rejection, you might win after all."

"Knock on wood for me." Maya grins.

Maya waits for me to climb into my own bed before turning off the light. Once I'm plunged into darkness, I throw my arm over my head and try to sleep. This proves difficult, though, when I realize Maya is wide awake.

The bed groans and creaks as she tosses from side to side. I stare at the ceiling, and wonder if I could possibly be brave enough to say some of the things I want to say. The things that have been swirling in my head all day.

Instead of speaking, I let my hand fall over the side of the bed and dangle in midair. I hold it there for second after breathless second, unsure if Maya can even see it. Unsure if her eyes are open. But then, she touches my fingertips with hers.

The contact of our skin sends lightning bolts down my arm, and my nervous system explodes with the energy. My fingers trail down her palm and engulf her hand, gently at first, then squeezing, firmer and firmer until it becomes a pull. She follows my tug to a sitting position, then lets go of my hand, climbs the ladder, and straddles me as I cup her face. There's just enough light streaming through the gaps in the blinds, from the moon and the porch lights, that I can make out her features.

I tug on the blanket, and she joins me beneath it. With the blanket draping over her shoulders like a cape, she lowers her head to kiss me, but I hold her there for a moment.

"I hated last night," I whisper, locking eyes with her, my expression serious.

"Really?" Maya asks, her expression unreadable.

Something shifts. I couldn't say what, or why, exactly, but something does. Whether it's chemical, or spiritual, or something else entirely. The spark of bravery I couldn't ignite earlier today is back. And with a word, it becomes a fireball.

"I've changed my mind," I say.

"About what—" Maya asks, then I pull her the rest of the way down and kiss her.

Her hands find their way beneath my shirt, her long nails dragging lightly against my skin, leaving an invisible tattoo to mark where she's been. She pulls me in with a sort of desperation, pressing us together until it almost hurts.

I kiss her with a ferocity, tasting her tongue, biting the

cushion of her lip. She's shivering above me, even though it's a thousand degrees beneath this blanket with our body heat and our sweat and our breaths coming hotter and faster and more urgent by the second.

I've never wanted anything like I want her. Nothing could be enough. I could touch every inch of her, taste every surface, and I'd need to start it all over again. An unexpected noise escapes my throat, and she clasps a hand over my mouth. "Someone could hear us," she whispers, which makes me feel like I might pass out from wanting.

She releases me, and replaces her hand with her mouth, and I change angles so I can press harder against her. Then her hand slides between us, and I think my brain short-circuits for a second.

"Can I?" she asks, and I respond by taking her hand and guiding it down, and nothing matters but this.

Nothing.

Afterward, while we lie awkwardly layered on a bed that was *not* designed for two, Maya plays with a longer strand of my hair between her fingertips. "Changed your mind, huh?" she whispers.

"Yes."

"You gonna elaborate, there, Skye?"

Oh. I'd been hopeful that the last half hour would've been self-explanatory. "Sure. I . . . Hmm."

"Hmm?"

"Sorry, it's difficult."

"No, take your time."

"I—I mean, you—and . . . when I . . ."

"This isn't casual, is it?" Maya asks for me, and I breathe out a whoosh of air.

"No. I don't think it is."

"Oh." She thinks on this for a while, too long, and I feel a rush of panic. She's going to say—I don't even know what I'm afraid she'll say. Something that will break me somewhere she never would've been able to touch if I'd simply kept her at bay. Why couldn't I keep her at bay?

"Awesome," she says finally, and I have to replay her word in my mind to understand it properly.

"Yeah?"

"Yeah. Hey, Skye?"

"Yes?"

"Why does your voice sound like that? Is this a bad thing?"

I burrow into her neck, like I can hide from the world there. "It's not a bad thing. It's just a little bit earth-shatteringly terrifying."

"What is?" she asks, her cheek pressing against my hair. "You mean, because the world will find out? Are you worried about hate, or homophobia, or . . . ?"

"No. No, I want the world to know, if anything. I'd tell them today if I could. It's just that I'm not used to this."

"Because I'm a girl?"

"*No.* Because you're you. I don't . . . *do* this. I don't let things get this far. I didn't even mean to this time. You're just different, and I don't know how to navigate that, and I'm scared of what it might mean."

When I peek up at her, she's staring at me with an intense, searching expression. "What could it mean?"

My heart rate speeds up uncomfortably at this. "I don't know."

She considers this, and drops her hand to run a finger down the back of my neck, sending me into a full-body shiver. "Do you trust me?"

How to answer a question like that? "More than I want to. More than I usually trust people."

"But not totally?"

"Well . . . I wouldn't say it like that."

"What would you say?"

"I would say that we're in an extremely strange situation, and things are complicated. And we don't have a clue what's going to happen in the finale, or when we have to say goodbye, or what life is going to look like after that. I suppose I'm in an in-between place. I don't want us to be nothing, because you're not nothing. You're a lot. You're a surprisingly large fraction of everything."

"But?"

"*But,* I don't know how to begin defining us."

"Can I kick us off? We're Maya and Skye. We fit together like we were made that way on purpose. How's that for a definition?"

"It's not a definition at all, it's more of a description."

"How is that different?"

"*Besides,*" I press on, "I just don't feel comfortable defining us until we have all the variables. Everything's too vague right now."

"I care about you. You care about me. What else do you need to know?"

"A lot."

Maya pauses. "Okay. Is this your way of saying you don't want things to ever be official?"

"No. It's my way of saying I have very, very strong feelings for you, and I'd like to discuss what we are once we know who's going to be where, and when, and what the fallout of the finale is. That's it. Don't read into it, please?"

Maya's laugh comes out as more of a snuffle against my

head. "Fine. So, we hold off on the definitions for a week, until you have all the variables? Does that mean we can still see each other?"

"Of course."

"Does it mean we can still talk about our feelings?"

"I have no issue with that."

"Then it's great by me. No one's anyone's girlfriend, for now. We are just us. Hanging out, being awesome, planning Jordy's downfall. Hot girl shit."

I snort against her neck, and she shrieks with laughter, squirming in place.

"I can't wait until we never have to talk about Jordy again," I say.

"Ha," Maya says. "A life without Jordy. Sounds like paradise. I can't even imagine it."

Yes. Well.

That's exactly what I'm a little afraid of.

TWENTY-EIGHT

Maya

The morning of finale-eve, Skye wakes me up with "The Final Countdown," and for once I don't even mind it. Especially because the moment I open my eyes she crawls into bed with me and wraps me in a bear hug, kissing my head until I'm properly awake.

Even though it's ungodly early, it's already time to get ready. Casual clothes first, so we can film Grayson drawing the lottery to see which lucky girl gets to spend the last day with Jordy before he picks the winner. Obviously, it's a lottery in about the same way that I'm a bookcase. They know damn well who's spending the day with Jordy. But we pretend, anyway, because that's just what we do around here.

"Hey, Maya?" Skye says, settling in next to me. "Can I talk about something awkward?"

"Some of my favorite conversations are awkward ones."

"That's a blatant lie. Anyway. I'm just going to dive in."

"By all means."

She takes a long time to say the next part. I guess she's psyching herself up. When she finally speaks, it's uncertain. "I don't want you to kiss Jordy anymore."

"Done," I say without hesitating.

She smiles hesitantly. "Wow, that was easy."

"Skye, I don't care about Jordy. Not like that. Only you."

"I'm still fine with whatever happens today," she says quickly. "If you get chosen for today's date, I really, honestly don't mind if you do other stuff. Hold his hand, pretend to flirt with him, whatever you need to do to win this. It won't affect us."

"Deal. Although I'm pretty sure I'm not getting picked today. I *just* spent the night with Jordy last week."

"Well, if it's me, I won't kiss him, either."

I trace a finger over her lips. "Good," I murmur, before I do what Jordy can't.

In the end, to my complete unsurprise, the winner of the last day with Jordy is Perrie.

"Finally," she says to us as she gets up to follow Grayson to the car. "I was worried the only extended episode time I'd get would be the first-date re-creations."

As for me, my emotions are sort of all over the place about this. I'm happy for Perrie, but also nervous that she gets the last word in before Jordy makes his final choice tomorrow. I'm frustrated that it isn't Skye out with him, because at least if she wins the show, I know Jordy will still get what he deserves, even if it doesn't come from me. But at the same time, a secret part of me is relieved Skye isn't going to spend the day flirting with Jordy. Instead, she'll be here, with me, alone in the manor.

Totally alone.

So, naturally, the very first thing we do with our alone time is grab our swimsuits and head straight to the pool.

In the water, it's almost impossible not to grab her and kiss her. Apparently, she feels the same.

"I absolutely can't wait to tell everyone about us," she says, breaking the kiss finally.

"You think we'll able to be together once we finish filming?" I ask. "Even if one of us wins?"

"I thought we said we'd revisit that once we saw the fall-out?"

"No." I smile. "I mean *physically* together. Like, do you think they'll let the winner stay in the hotel with the other two?"

"I suppose it's hard to say. It *does* seem like it would be a weird choice to force either of us to stay in a suite with Jordy if we said no to him, right?"

"Right," I agree. "So, I guess, either way . . . we won't have to hide us anymore, tomorrow."

Skye claps, then, all at once, the smile falls from her face and she paddles in place, pensive. "Tomorrow it's real, huh?" she asks. "No more scheming. Just you, and me, and a healthy . . . real . . . thing."

"You almost sound bummed out," I say, only half joking.

"I'm not. I just . . ." She swallows. "I just didn't expect all of this, okay? I thought it was easy to choose not to fall for someone. But it's not. It's not something you can control. You don't jump. You get pushed."

"You make it sound so violent," I say.

"They don't call it *gently cascading* for someone. You don't *gracefully descend* for someone. You fall. Head over heels, right? And either someone catches you, or they don't, and you don't have any control over how badly bruised you are at the bottom of it."

I study her, my eyebrows furrowed. She drops into the water so it's covering her nose and watches me warily.

"Skye," I say finally. "I'm not going to hurt you."

She resurfaces. "Neither of us knows that for sure."

"Well . . ." I shrug. "You don't know for sure your car won't crash when you get into it. You don't know there won't be a tsunami when you go to the beach."

"Almost fifty percent of marriages end in divorce!"

"I heard that's not true anymore."

"Well, even if it's close. I promise you, if fifty percent of car trips ended in a crash, I'd be walking everywhere for the rest of my life."

"So that was your plan?" I ask. "Just go through life without ever being in love with anyone, so you never get hurt?"

"I didn't want it to be, but . . ." Her voice catches on the "but."

"And now?"

She shakes her head and cups a hand over her mouth to hide it. "A part of me wonders if it's not smarter to . . . panic, and back out of this, and go back to what I was doing before. I was happy alone. And it's safer, you know?"

It sounds like the sort of thing that should hurt me to hear, but somehow it doesn't. She doesn't say those words like someone who wants to be left alone. She says them like someone who's standing at the edge of everything, but needs someone to hold her hand as she crosses the threshold.

So I take her hand in mine and pull her toward me. "You can. But do you want to?"

She shoves wet tendrils of hair off her face and groans to the heavens. Then, silently, she shakes her head, defeated.

"I'm not planning on breaking your heart," I say, stroking her hand with my thumb.

She stares at our hands for a little bit too long, lost in thought.

"Also," I say, pulling her in even closer, "there's one phrase about being in love you forgot."

She crosses her arms over her chest. "What?"

"You can be swept off your feet," I say, wrapping my arms around her middle and hoisting her up as she lets out a gasp of surprise. "No bruising required."

She looks down at me incredulously, then breaks into a grin. "You're so *corny!*" she says, kicking in the water.

I walk her backward, spinning us around slowly, as she grips onto my shoulders. "Excuse you, I'm romantic!"

"So I'm finding out."

I lower her down until she bobs in the water, then meet her lips with mine. When I finally pull away, we tread water, facing each other, our legs touching under the water.

"I trust you," she whispers.

"Tomorrow night, then."

"Tomorrow night."

TWENTY-NINE

Maya

On the day of the finale, they separate us.

We're taken to what I've dubbed the Loser Hotel—the hotel on the edge of town where they're imprisoning us until the live show next week. By us, I mean whichever two of us don't end up with Jordy. The winner and Jordy are set to live out their week in a totally different hotel. I assume they're keeping us as separate as possible so the losers don't break into Jordy's room and steal his skin or whatever.

Anyway, it means all Skye and I get is a hurried "goodbye and good luck" before we're taken into separate rooms to be dressed and made up one last time.

I'm feeling pumped and ready as I sit in one of the rooms getting hair and makeup done. I put it down to the fact that this morning's song was "Eye of the Tiger." It's not possible to hear "Eye of the Tiger" and not end up buzzing. That's just science.

Once my hair and makeup are finally done, the styling team helps me step into my dress, which is, I'm pretty sure, actually a wedding dress. It's a floor-length, mermaid-cut dress with beading down the whole bodice and chains of pearls draping over my shoulders and upper arms.

Seriously, am I getting married today? Is that the plot twist?

"You look gorgeous," Saskia, who's moving between our rooms to check on our progress, says, before kneeling down to pick at a loose thread. "Now, we 'ave you in a pair of beautiful heels, but they are a *little* taller than you are used to. You will be fine, just walk slowly, *sa?*"

"Uh . . . *nie*," I say when I see the monstrosities. The heels on these things are about three feet tall. "Can I try on a . . . safer pair?"

"No, you will be fine, walk slow," Saskia says again, patting me on the arm before leaving.

They leave me in the room alone for about half an hour with a magazine once I'm finally ready. They're staggering each of our final scenes with Jordy, so there's no way to tell whether we're about to win or lose.

The magazine's about six months old, unfortunately, so there's no mention of the show or how we're all doing. Jordy's mentioned once, in a celebrity gossip section. It's a photo of him with an unfamiliar blond girl, walking down a street in Loreux at night. I wonder if this is the girl he mentioned. The one who actually managed to break his heart.

"Maya," Isaac says, hovering in the doorway. "You ready?"

Oh, I'm ready.

Whatever happens now. I'm ready for it.

THIRTY

Skye

They leave me in my hotel room dressed in a glittery, figure-hugging black gown for what feels like an eternity and a half before they finally collect me and bring me to a sun-dappled glade to wait for Jordy. While I wait, I think of Maya.

I used to think that the biology of all of this made it matter less. As though I could keep it just physical with Maya, because that's all it was, and I could simply decide to keep my emotions out of it. But whatever it is that links me to her . . . chemicals, or hormones, or pheromones. The thing is, those pheromones chose her. My body chose her to be my home. It recognizes her as mine.

As for my emotions? My independent, don't-need-anyone *feelings*? I think they're woven into those chemicals. Inseparable. She feels like my safe place. She feels like finding a missing part of my soul that was floating around in space until it finally burst into my orbit, and I latched on to it. I latched on to her.

And that's scary. It's so terrifying it makes my fingertips burn and my neck prickle, and I feel like running, but I don't know where to, because I don't know what from. The thing that's scaring me lives inside of me.

I'm scared, because I think I've let Maya in, and I never meant to. But now she's here. And she can hurt me from the inside in a way that no amount of hardening my shell can prevent.

And the scariest part of all is, maybe I don't even want to prevent it. Maybe I want her in here. Because with her taking up space in my heart, I feel more hopeful that love could exist than I've felt in a long, long time.

Finally, Jordy's car pulls up, and he steps out, dressed in a gray-blue suit. He spends a frustratingly long time speaking with Grayson on camera near the car before he finally, *finally* makes his way over to me. With this scenery, and the still warmth of the day, it would be a romantic, idyllic moment. Were it not for the cameras, and the boom mics, and the crowd, that is.

And the suitor.

Jordy meets my eyes and relaxes into that familiar, intimate smile, and for a moment I think I must have won. I return his smile, and the wind catches my hair as I mentally rehearse the devastating rejection speech Maya and I prepared over rosé and Pepsi earlier this week.

"Skye," he says. "From the first day we met, I knew you were going to be the girl that changed my life. You taught me what love could be—and leaving you behind that day we moved to England was one of the worst days of my life."

Then something changes in his manner, and as I understand what it means I'm hit with an unexpected jolt of relief—both that I don't need to do anything too confrontational on camera now, and that this might mean Maya gets the moment she's been dreaming of.

But then that very thought sends an aftershock of trepidation in relief's wake, because if it's not me, then it's fifty-fifty.

I want Maya to win this. She wants it so, so badly.

Jordy takes my hands in his, and for a moment it feels as though we're standing at a wedding altar. The sort of image that, two years ago, might have made my heart give the tiniest flutter. Now, it merely arouses my gag reflex.

"As true as that was for me when I was seventeen, though . . . Neither of us are the same people as we were then. You've grown into a special, beautiful, intelligent woman. A woman that any man—well, any person—would be lucky to have. But that person is not me."

Here's the moment where I'm supposed to appear devastated. I manage a double-blink, which I feel is surely adequate for drama purposes.

Jordy waits, and I realize a beat too late I'm expected to respond, here. I shrug. "Oh these things . . . happen," I produce.

"It really has been such a wonderful experience exploring what might have been with you."

Another pause. I'm not quite sure how to respond to that, so, in a panic, I look toward the sky and blink a few more times, to appear as though I'm holding in emotions too overwhelming to keep my neck straight for.

"We'll always have Canada," he says, and I get the distinct feeling he was told to say that.

"And we'll always have . . . Chalonne," I try.

Jordy laughs. "Yes. Yes, we will. I hope we'll stay in touch this time, though. I look forward to watching you achieve things beyond your wildest dreams."

"And I have no doubt I'll see you around." I smile sweetly. "It's quite hard to miss you."

"Cut," Gwendolyn calls, and she heads over to Isaac and Grayson to discuss something.

"I really am sorry, Skye," Jordy says.

I wave a hand. "Honestly, it's perfectly fine. But can I please know who you're picking?"

"You'll find out soon," he says. I'm disappointed, but not surprised. "Anyway. I'll see you next week?"

"Sure. Have a good week."

"You know? I think I will."

I replay his words mentally, trying to glean a clue from them as he leaves with one camera following him. Only seconds later, I'm wrenched from my thoughts as Grayson approaches with a camera.

"Reaction shot, Skye," Gwendolyn calls, hurrying after him. "Look sadder."

I oblige as best as I can. Gwendolyn seems skeptical, but honestly, I'm out of energy for this. I'm ready for it to all be over. I'm ready to see what comes next.

"How are you feeling, Skye?" Grayson asks, placing a hand on my shoulder. This feels a little dramatic to me, but I suppose I don't run a television show for a reason.

"I promised myself I wouldn't cry," I say, because I'm not sure I can say I'm sad with a straight face. "And I didn't cry."

Grayson squeezes. "You handled it with the dignity and grace the country has come to love about you. I'm so sorry. All the best."

And in a flurry, it's over. Time for me to be spirited to my hotel, and Jordy to his. Will he be alone? With Perrie? Or have they trapped a victorious Maya in that hotel with him for a whole week, despite her rejection speech?

I hope against hope that they haven't. That, successful or

not, she's waiting for me in the hotel room when I get back. That I can run up and kiss her without checking to see who's around. No more secrets, no more games, no more separation.

At last.

THIRTY-ONE

Maya

They take me straight from the Loser Hotel all the way back to the lake by the manor. It seems like a hell of a waste of time to me, all this back and forth, but Isaac just shrugs and points out that the makeup artist needed to be at the Loser Hotel, which I *guess* makes sense.

It's as I feared. These heels are bad enough on solid ground, let alone on the grass. I hesitate as I get out of the car, because there are multiple cameras on me.

"It's okay," Isaac says softly, reading my mind. "Just take it slow."

"If I trip, are you going to put it in all the episode promos?" I ask, only half joking.

"No. And I can actually promise you that, for once. The finale is all about romance. If anything goes wrong, we'll just edit it out."

Something in his words sparks something at the back of my mind. Something uneasy.

As I walk to my spot near the shore, I try to figure out if I have any clues to work with. They left me in the room for about an hour. Was that because they were busy filming the winner? Or were they preparing in general? It's just impossible to know.

Is Jordy about to come and tell me I've won, or to reject me once again, but this time on television?

Grayson and I film a quick exchange where he asks me if I'm nervous, and I say yes, and he says good luck, yadda yadda, then Isaac's words come back to me. They want this to be romantic. They'll edit out anything that's not.

Up to and including my rejection of Jordy?

My heart gives a heavy *thud* of panic. Would that happen? Would they listen to my carefully prepared speech, then yell cut, and tell us to shoot it again from the top, this time with Jordy rejecting me? They could. There's still two other girls he could pick instead if things go wrong with me. If he picks Skye, and she does what I do, they'll just reshoot her, too, and he'll move on to Perrie. Even if they've already shot her rejection scene, that's not a problem for them. They'd only have to reshoot her scene, as the winner this time, and, presto, history rewritten for a romantic finale. She'd play along for the platform boost, of course. She'd never admit she wasn't actually picked. They'd still have their romantic finale.

Oh my god. The plan isn't going to work.

After all this. Even if I win, I'll lose.

And then Jordy will get away with everything, looking better than he ever did before. Just like he always does.

His car rolls up, and the cameras get ready to film him. He locks eyes with me, and breaks into a smile. With every step he takes toward me, my stomach sinks lower and lower.

Then, suddenly, I remember.

The live show is next week.

They can't edit me on a live show.

It's the only chance we have.

"Maya," Jordy says as he reaches me. "Hi."

"Hi," I say. And as soon as I see the expression on his face, I know for sure.

I've won.

THIRTY-TWO

Skye

At the hotel where I'm expected to spend the next week, I'm shown to my room by the production assistants, given the number of the on-call counselor the team has hired for the week, and told to wait for my producer.

It's a sweet little boutique hotel on the outskirts of Loreux, and the two losers have the whole top floor to ourselves. Well, along with a dedicated room for the producers to swap between themselves when they take their shift babysitting us.

As I unpack, it occurs to me that maybe I shouldn't get too comfortable. If it was Maya who won, maybe there won't be a live finale after all. Maybe she'll be coming here to me any moment now, and we'll be done for good.

No, I decide. That makes no sense. Even after Maya rejects Jordy, they'll still have the live show. I suppose they'll just separate Maya and Jordy. Will that mean she'll be coming here with us? Or will they give her a new room near the winner's suite, which is located in a hotel across town?

I hope it's the former. I hope, I hope, I hope. The thought of spending the next week with Maya and Perrie—with Maya and me finally able to be ourselves—leaves me somewhat giddy.

There's a knock on my door. Isaac, I expect. But when I answer it, it's Wai.

"Hey, how you doing in here?" she asks cheerfully.

I look past her down the empty hall. "Great. Is Isaac not coming?"

"Isaac's been held up," Wai says, and at that moment I know. We won. Jordy chose Maya. And Isaac's with them now trying to sort through the rubble of the grenade Maya just threw into the finale.

That's my girl.

"So, Maya won, then," I say.

Wai hesitates, then says slowly, "Yes, she did."

When I don't detonate, she relaxes.

"How did that . . . go?" I ask.

"Fine. She and Jordy are staying across town, but you'll get to see both of them next week to hear all about it."

My stomach sinks. I suppose it was too much to hope that I could have her for the next week. I try to keep my voice casual. "Is there . . . much to hear?"

Wai looks skeptical. "I'm not sure you want to hear the details, Skye. I know today's been hard."

"I'm actually okay. I do want to hear the details. I really, really—it'd make me feel better."

Wai studies me for a long moment, then shrugs. "As far as I know, it was lovely. I'm sure they'll be happy together. I know you and Maya are close. You know, it's nice that you're supporting your friend, even if I'm sure it's not the outcome you wanted."

Even if . . . Oh, because she thinks I wish I won.

But then, does she simply not know? Is it possible that

word about the rejection hasn't reached her? Or is she pretending everything is fine so Perrie and I look appropriately surprised for the cameras during the live event?

It's got to be the latter. That's frustrating, but expected.

After Wai leaves me, I head down the hall to find Perrie's door open. She's still wearing her finale outfit, a floor-length gown of bright purple silk, and appears roughly as unruffled as I feel.

"It's not like I had feelings for him," she says, wandering over to the window in a swish of silk. "I'd have to be stupid to let him in after what he did to you and Maya."

"That's probably why you came this far," I say, examining the minibar, which we have full access to. "Other than the fact that you're amazing, naturally."

"Naturally."

"That guy's got a sixth sense for which girls aren't all that into him. I don't know if he likes a challenge, or the idea of low commitment, or what, but it's there."

"Lucky me," Perrie says ruefully. "If I'd known I could get all that winning-contestant publicity by being a bit more of a bitch, I would've brought it. I can do a verbal takedown like you've never seen."

I select a tiny bottle of white wine and pour it between two glasses. It's about three sips each. "I think we struck a happy medium, personally. We still get plenty of screen time, but we don't have to date Jordy."

I hand her a glass, and she clinks it against mine. "I just wish we were allowed into the pool," she says wistfully, looking down at the grounds.

"We could sneak out," I say. "Ooh, we could have a night swim."

"Nah. I don't wanna risk it getting out that we lost. I'm still hoping to capitalize on the follows from people who think I might have won."

"Okay, well . . . let's give Wai a shopping list made entirely of sugar, and we'll have a sleepover watching horror movies until we pass out."

"That sounds like a *great* idea," Perrie says. "But swap out horror for action."

"Action? Really?"

"Mmm. If there's not a single CGI explosion, it's a waste of time if you ask me."

"Okay, if you've got recs—"

"Oh, I've got recs."

We're interrupted by a knock at the door. Perrie opens it to find Wai.

"Hey, Skye," she says. "Can I grab you for a sec?"

She takes me into the hallway, where she drops her voice to a whisper. "Isaac called. He wanted me to give you a message from Maya."

Here it comes. The victory flag.

"She . . . It's vague, I'm sorry, maybe it'll make sense to you. She says she's sorry for what she did, but she had to do it. She said she'll explain more when she sees you next week."

I stare at Wai, uncomprehending, as my brain breaks the words down and rearranges them in an effort to understand.

She's sorry for what she did?

What did she do?

What—

"Where is Maya right now?" I ask.

"Settling in with Jordy."

"So . . . Wait, she said yes, then? She's with Jordy?"

Wai is the one who's confused now. "Uh . . . Yeah? Why wouldn't she be?"

My voice comes out hollow. "Never mind. Um. Thank you."

I walk back into the bedroom in a daze. Perrie watches me in confusion as I sit down heavily on the edge of the bed and stare at the floor.

She's sorry.

She had to.

She had to say yes to Jordy?

Why? What could possibly have caused that?

Did something change?

Was Maya being honest with me?

Why would she accept him? Why? She hates him. Doesn't she?

Doesn't she?

My breathing starts speeding up, and I clasp a hand over my mouth to stifle it, but it's no use. My hand is trembling, and so are my lips, and my shoulders, and the colors are fading from the room.

Perrie sits beside me. "Hey, Skye, you okay? What did Wai say?"

I gasp for air. "She . . . she said M-Maya and Jordy . . . are in . . . their hotel. I thought sh-she was going to . . . reject him . . . but they're to . . . gether."

She left me.

She left me so she could go and be with Jordy.

She left me, just like everybody always does.

I knew she would. I knew it, but for once, just once, I'd wanted to believe something could be different. That maybe she would be different.

I'm so stupid. I'm so appallingly naive. I knew, and I ignored it, and I could've done something to stop this, to be better, so she wouldn't change her mind. But I'd let my guard down. I'd let her in. I'd trusted.

Perrie rubs her palm flat over my back. "Oh, Skye, honey. I didn't realize your feelings were this strong. I'm so sorry he picked Maya."

I can't hold it in. I can't. I can't

With a gasp, and a sob, I let my defenses collapse. The tears flow freely, hot and stinging on my cheeks.

I let Perrie catch them. This girl I barely know, in the grand scheme of things. I don't do this, I never do this, but I do it.

And she holds me.

In a sea of grief, she forms a buoy. So I don't have to swim for a second. Just for a second.

And it feels so good to rest.

To trust.

Just this once.

THIRTY-THREE

Maya

There's only one bed.

There's only one bed, and I have to share it with *fucking* Jordy.

The fourth morning in the getaway sex suite I'm now trapped in for the next week, I don't have the luxury of being woken up by a top-volume eighties bop. Instead, I wake to a growing sense of dread as my instincts realize something's wrong.

I open my eyes a crack, find Jordy staring at me, and scramble backward with a shout.

"You look so innocent when you sleep." He smiles.

"*Fuck,* Jordy," I screech. "People don't do that!"

"I wasn't watching you for long," he says. "Like, five minutes."

"You were watching me sleep for *five minutes*?"

He holds up his hands. "Maybe it wasn't that long! Like . . . three or four?"

Ha. That settles it, I'm not going to survive the rest of the week. I do not have the willpower to put up with this level of bullshit. "What time is it?" I groan. The sunlight streaming into the room, lighting up the already airy and bright white-and-cream palette, is giving off late-morning vibes.

"Eleven."

Great. That means only an hour or so to kill before they bring up room service for our lunch. Lunch is fast becoming my favorite time of the day apart from dinner, because it occupies my mouth. And if my mouth is occupied, I don't have to worry about Jordy leaning in to kiss me. Which he does an unbelievable amount of times per day for someone who's batting at a 100 percent strikeout rate.

Speaking of which, he's doing it again. Shuffling closer, bedroom eyes and coquettish smile equipped. He hasn't even brushed his teeth yet, and he thinks this will win me over? Good grief.

I give him a tight smile in return, and lean back at the same rate he leans in, until he ducks his head and sniffle-laughs. "Good morning to you, too." He smirks. I'm pretty sure he's enjoying it, actually. The challenge. He thinks it's great fun.

That, or he doesn't want to let me know he's confused as shit as to why I'm suddenly not keen on the physical side of things. But I kind of think it's the former.

I rub my finger across his cheek—one of many token gestures I give to keep him from demanding we call this whole thing off—and roll out of bed. "I'm just gonna get dressed and see Isaac real quick," I say, grabbing the outfit I laid out last night and dashing toward the bathroom. The one place in our tiny little suite I get any privacy.

"Again?" Jordy asks, letting his head fall back into the pillow. "Should I be worried?"

"About Isaac?" I call, tugging my shirt over my head in the bathroom. "He has a boyfriend."

"Oh. Wait, he's gay?"

"Jordy, we worked with these people for *seven weeks*. Do you not listen to a word they say?"

"Hey! I listened whenever they said important stuff."

"You mean stuff about you?"

"Exactly."

I yank on my jeans and do a jumping dance to get them on. "It's just . . . girl stuff, okay?"

"Oh! You're on your period?"

I hesitate. ". . . Yes."

Jordy looks much more cheerful when I reemerge from the bathroom. "That explains a lot." He grins. Because I regularly got a kissing aversion when I was on my period the last time we dated? "You could've just told me. I'm an adult."

I throw my hand to the side. "You caught me. I'm shy about that stuff."

"You don't have to be shy with me. Gross shit and all."

I smile tightly. "I actually don't consider periods gross, but good to know, *thank you.*"

"And if you're worried about it getting messy if we . . . you know, *do stuff,* don't. We'll just put a towel down, babe. That's why we have cleaners. It's their problem, not ours."

"Oh, thanks. Thanks. But, um. I don't . . . like, cramps, and . . . you know?"

He graces me with an understanding nod. "I do. But there's plenty of stuff we can do that you don't need to take your pants off for, too. I'm flexible."

Somehow, I refrain from launching at him with my fingernails bared. "Oh, I'm sure you are. I'll keep it in mind."

I'm almost out the door when he calls out, "I thought we'd try a documentary this afternoon, maybe? Mix things up a bit?"

"Uh, sure, whatever," I say rapidly. "Nothing else to do."

I dash out the door before he can say anything else, then jump up and down, shaking my hands like I can get the *ick* factor out if I wriggle hard enough. Jesus Christ. If the universe thinks it's necessary to punish me in advance for what I'm about to do to Jordy to balance the scales, it's doing a damn good job by trapping me in a hotel suite with him.

Isaac's room is at the end of the floor. It's a relatively small, boutique hotel, and Bushman and Siegal Productions have rented out the whole top floor for us to—well, they say "unwind." I'd say "endure imprisonment while keeping the identity of the winner under wraps," but poe-tay-toe, poe-tah-toe.

Isaac's already rolling his eyes when he answers the door. His curly hair, usually in a ponytail, is loose around his shoulders, and he's swapped out his on-the-job jeans for hanging-around-the-hotel sweatpants. "No, she hasn't left a message for you," he says, stepping aside to let me in. "No, you can't call her."

"Are you *sure* she got my message?" I ask, even though I've asked every day since we got here. I figure it can't hurt to be thorough.

"Maya, Wai said she gave her the message. What do you think's going on here, Wai's *lying* to me? She's playing with your sanity for her own amusement?"

I flop into the chair of his single-seater dining table and lay my head on the table. "I don't know. Maybe she just . . . meant to do it and forgot?"

Isaac gives me a *look,* and I transition from a sigh into a sulk. If Skye got my message and isn't replying, what does that mean? That she doesn't understand it? Or misinterpreted it? That she's annoyed with me for dragging things out? That she thinks it's such an obvious no-big-deal she doesn't think a reply is needed?

The not-knowing is driving me almost as crazy as my standing sentence with Jordy.

"Could I at least send her another one?" I ask, again, like it's not the eighth time I'm asking in half as many days.

Instead of answering that question negatively yet again—we're not *supposed* to talk to the other contestants right now—Isaac pulls out his phone. "I'm heading to the store this afternoon. Do you need anything?"

"Can I come?"

Isaac ignores that. "Gonna put you down as a 'no.'"

"Could you put me down as a Flamin' Hot Cheetos?"

He grins now. "I'll see what I can do. You know if Jordy needs anything?"

"I dunno. Who cares? Maybe a salmon steak to fuel his in-room workouts?"

His endless, *endless* in-room workouts.

"Feisty," Isaac says. "Sounds like the honeymoon suite is going well."

I force a smile. "I'm not sure how many couples would enjoy being trapped together like this."

Isaac turns on the kettle. "Want a coffee?"

"Please."

"And as for your last comment, maybe I'm different, but I would've killed to have seven straight days in bed with Teddy when we first got together," he says lightly, clattering around the mugs. "All our food brought to us, no responsibilities, no people interrupting us? Yes, please."

I try to picture being stuck here for seven days with Skye instead of Jordy. How we might kill the endless hours.

Yup, suddenly I'm getting his point.

"Can I ask you a very rude question?" Isaac asks.

I lift my head and snap back into focus. *That's* a promising preface. "Hmm? I guess."

"Why would a couple of self-respecting girls like you and Skye stick by the guy who cheated on both of you?"

I choke. "Wow."

"You know what?" he goes on. "I have reviewed a *lot* of footage over these past seven weeks. A *lot*. And I am not convinced either of you even like that boy. So, what gives? Tell me your dirty secret."

"Dirty secret?" I squeak.

"Yes. What are you really here for? You're hoping to score a gig as a reality show host? Sponsorship deals? Commercials?"

"No."

". . . *Dancing with the Stars*?"

I fold my arms. "No, Isaac."

"You're a raging masochist, then?"

"It is that hard to believe I just . . . really like Jordy?"

Isaac stares at me.

I hold his gaze.

"You said that like you were sucking on a lemon, Maya," Isaac says, and I groan.

"It's . . . complicated."

He gives me an understanding smile, then gets to his feet and starts wandering around the room, looking at the ceiling like he's lost in thought. "Look, I'm not assuming anything. But . . . if there were another reason you wanted to stick around for, someone who *wasn't* Jordy . . . I think that would make perfect sense."

I cross one leg over the other. "You caught me."

He pauses. "I did?"

"Yes. The thing is . . . I'm madly in love with you, Isaac."

"Just me, huh?"

"Just you."

"Okay. Okay . . . the only reason I'm bringing it up is, if you were thinking about rejecting Jordy soon because your heart's somewhere else, it'd be in both of our best interests for you to give me a heads-up. So I can talk you through the legal stuff, and so we can figure out if there's a way to do this that doesn't result in me getting fired. You know. Hypothetically."

"Right," I say. "Hypothetically."

"Yes."

I study Isaac, who's still standing in the center of the room. "Isaac, do you think Jordy's a good guy?"

Isaac bursts out laughing and falls back into the couch. "Maya."

"Isaac."

"I have been there on every date, yeah? *Every. Date.* Do you think I like Jordy?"

I break into an interested smile now, and prop my head up on my hand, leaning on the table. "I guess I hadn't thought about that."

"That guy," Isaac says, "does not have a nice word to say about me or *any* of my coworkers. He's sweetness and light to you girls, then trashes you to each other behind your backs. But it's always in a way where he can't be called out for it, you know?"

"Oh, I know."

"If it comes out one day that he's got a history of being a racist homophobe, I am not going to be even a *little* surprised. You can see it in his eyes. Honestly, I kept hoping one of you girls would give him a piece of your mind. But you never did."

I smile grimly. "I tried. You told me I'd be edited into a villain."

He pauses. "That's true. I did, and you would've. But it would've been satisfying to me."

"So satisfying. Imagine if someone could've given him a piece of their mind during a live show. That would've been the best of both worlds."

Isaac nods, half smiling, then my words finally register and he snaps his head up. "Maya!"

"Isaac."

He scans me from head to toe, his expression a sort of mixture between appalled and excited. So, I figure my chances of getting his blessing have got to be about fifty-fifty at this rate. Hell yeah, go team Fuck Up the Fuck Boy!

"I'm gonna need you to leave this with me," he says, and I am a popped balloon. "I need to think."

"I'm not asking for permission."

"Please. You go out there if I say you go out there."

"Isaac!"

"I didn't say you can't. I said I need to *think.*" He pauses, then sighs. "In the meantime . . . you want to talk to Skye that badly?"

It's probably the only thing he could've said that'd distract me from arguing my case. I shoot upright, my heart catching in my throat, and nod desperately.

"Okay. I'll see if I can get ahold of her."

He calls Wai—who's on the current shift at the Loser Hotel—on her cell phone, so she can traipse down the hall and knock on Skye's door. To my relief, Skye agrees to take the call. Isaac announces he's going to the vending machine, and leaves me alone in his room, clutching his cell phone in shaking hands.

"Hi," she says in a cool voice, and I know two things straight up. One, I'm in deep shit with her. Two, I need to fix that *right* the hell now.

"Hi, hi," I burst out. "I've been trying to get ahold of you. I didn't realize I wouldn't be able to explain, or—"

"Or you wouldn't have done it?" she asks.

"I . . . hold on, let me explain."

"Yeah, please do."

"I realized when we got to the finale that they'd just edit everything. They wanted their big, romantic ending, Skye. If I'd rejected Jordy, they would've just had him pick you or Perrie, and if you rejected him, he would've picked Perrie, who *wouldn't have*. Then I realized they couldn't edit the live show, so, when he picked me . . . I just . . . I had to make a call."

"So, you made the call to accept him."

"I thought you'd understand when I explained."

"But you didn't explain. Sorry—you *couldn't* explain."

"Exactly." I hesitate. Her words sound like she gets it, but her tone tells me she absolutely does not. "I know you don't do second chances, I know, but *believe me,* I didn't mean to hurt you. It all happened so fast."

She takes a deep breath. "Okay. I can believe that."

"Thank god. Skye, I swear—"

"But," she cuts in, "when you found out you couldn't talk to me, you must have known I'd be here not knowing what's going on. The things I must have been wondering. And I have had. No one. I've just been sitting here, playing out every worst-case scenario imaginable, for four days, with no support system, because I can't tell anyone about us like we agreed we could, because you're still lying about it. And you decided you were okay with that, as long as it meant you could still get revenge on fucking *Jordy*. And screw how I feel, or how much I have to go through, for you to get that. Because it's not happening fast anymore, Maya. It's happening extremely slowly."

I swallow as her words sink in. Of course she thought the worst. Of course she's been suffering over the last few days. Way, *way* worse than I have been. "I . . . didn't realize it would hurt you this much."

"Okay. Well. I'm hurt."

"Skye, I'm sorry."

"Don't say you're sorry. Say you'll stop it, and you'll be here tonight. Say you'd rather spend the last few days before I go to London with me, instead of with *him*, and we can forget all this. How's that for a second chance?"

"I'm not saying no," I say carefully, because jumping into a decision is what got me in this mess in the first place. "But can we hash this out first? I thought you wanted revenge, too?"

"Oh my god, Maya, screw revenge! Who cares about Jordy? Fuck Jordy! Fuck what that asshole did to us two years ago. Would it really have been so bad to let this all go? You still would've had me."

"Are you saying I don't have you now?"

Her voice is even, but slow. "Are you staying there?"

What choice do I have? If I leave now, Jordy will get away with everything he's done. Not just to me, to all of us. And I'll never get to tell my side of the story. I'll be the evil harpy who hurt poor, innocent Jordy—reviled, while he's worshipped—all over again. Only this time, it won't just be within our town. It'll be in front of the world.

The world will *hate* me, and it will love him more than ever.

Where is the *justice* in that?

That can't be where the story ends. It just can't.

But does that mean it's the end of me and Skye?

"I . . . I don't . . . I don't see what difference a few days makes. I don't understand why you're so mad."

"I just need you to . . . choose . . ." She trails off, and gives a heavy sigh. My chest tightens, and I fumble for something to say, but nothing good comes to mind.

"Just tell me one thing," she says. "Let's say something goes wrong at the live event and you can't reject him there. What will you do?"

I blink, caught off guard. "What will I—I don't know? I'd . . . I don't know. We get a lot of publicity afterward, right? I'm sure there'll be some sort of public interview I could do it in."

She takes a long, long time to reply. "This is never going to end, is it?"

"Yes, it is. There'll be an opportunity at some point. Sooner or later."

"You hope."

"I *know.*"

"And in the meantime I just . . . what?"

"Know that I'm coming back to you."

"Eventually," she says flatly. "At some unspecified time."

"You're talking about something that might not even happen!"

"And you're ignoring the fact that you can't control all the variables, and you don't even have a backup plan in place. You're just gonna keep making calls on the spur of the moment, and expecting me to just go with it. So, how long is too long, Maya? What if you don't get an opportunity in a week?"

"We'd talk about it—"

"What if you're still 'pretending' to date Jordy in a month?"

"Skye. It'll be over by then, I'm sure of it."

"It's meant to be over now," she snaps. "So, let's say worst-case scenario. How long are you willing to keep this up for to get that perfect revenge moment?"

I sigh in frustration. "I don't know, okay? It'll depend. As long as it takes."

"Right."

"I thought you wanted this, too?" I ask.

"I wanted you to have your moment. But I didn't know I was signing up for everything you just said. So, you know what? I don't want to do this anymore. You do whatever you want."

"You don't want to do . . . the Jordy thing, or us?"

Her answer is a whip, right across my chest. "Both. Bye, Maya."

She hangs up on me, and I stare at the phone in my hand.

THIRTY-FOUR

Maya

I spend the rest of the day with Jordy, watching bad movies and trying my best not to cry.

How did things go so wrong so fast? One second I'm planning this with Skye, and we're both on exactly the same page, and the next, *bam*. She's out. Out of the plan, and out of . . . Whatever we are.

What changed in these last few days? Is there something I'm not getting?

Is there a way out of this that leaves Skye and me unscathed, but keeps Jordy . . . super fucking scathed?

I glance at him. He's stretched out next to me on the sofa, feet up and resting by my thighs, so he's taking up three-quarters of the couch. I get the leftovers. I could have more, I guess, if I let him use my lap as a footrest, but I'll pass on that.

"Something's up," Jordy says out of nowhere, not taking his eyes from the TV. "I'm not dumb, Maya."

I go to deny it, but the moment I open my mouth, I'm hit by a tidal wave of grief. It makes my voice catch in my throat, and tears well in my eyes, and my heart starts weighing itself down, beat after heavy beat. I tip my head back to try to keep the tears from spilling over, as a frantic chorus takes place in my mind.

You've lost Skye. Forever. Forever. Forever.

"Is it period stuff?" Jordy asks when I don't reply.

I manage a nod.

"You should check out the room service menu. They have a few chocolate things on there. Sam loves chocolate when she's on hers."

I wipe my thumbs under my eyes and stand up. "I'm actually just gonna lie down for a while."

Jordy nods. "Sounds good. I'm gonna get started on my crunches, then."

He maneuvers onto the floor, but before he starts, just as I'm reaching the bedroom, he clears his throat. "Hey . . . Maya?"

I pause, and turn back.

"We're . . . good, right?"

I force a watery smile. "Don't worry. I'm not upset about you."

He gives me a thumbs-up, and I continue to the bedroom and throw myself facedown on the bed.

Eventually, I fall asleep.

The next day, Jordy and I are mixing it up by watching a TV series while he does bicep curls—which is a massive change from the usual routine of watching a movie while he does crunches—when Isaac knocks on our door instead of the other way around.

"Hey," Isaac says. "Can I borrow Maya for a sec?"

Jordy drops the dumbbell to his side and frowns. "Can't it wait? We're just about to find out the identity of Madame Featherblanket. We've waited four hours for this."

"Great," Isaac says. "You can keep building the tension, then."

"Come on, man," Jordy says, turning on the charm—white-toothed smile, dimples, crinkled eyes. His body language, on the other hand, is a little threatening—shoulders straight, arms folded, chin raised. "Be cool."

Isaac blinks rapidly, then gives him a sweet smile. "It's Charlotte Ciderberry, the best friend's aunt. If you haven't figured that out by now, then god help you, honestly. My five-year-old niece got it by episode three."

"Dude!"

Before Jordy can yell at him—which it looks like he's gearing up to—Isaac grabs my wrist and hauls me out of the room.

"Is it really Charlotte?" I ask as we head down the hall.

"Oh, Maya, sweetie. Of course it is." He lets us into the room, and directs me to sit back at his table, which has a laptop set up on it. "So. You might have figured this out already, but did you know that when Gwendolyn asked Jordy for candidates, he told her you needed to be on?"

I startle. "He . . . did? He told me it was important to him that I come on, but honestly, I assumed he was bullshitting me."

"Mm, don't change your bullshit battery yet. He told Gwendolyn you needed to come on this show because you were totally unhinged, and you'd give us plenty of drama content."

I push my hair out of my face and run my tongue across my teeth. "Ah. Huh."

"Yeah. He told us to put you in with Skye. He didn't give us details, but he *did* say you couldn't stand her. He thought it'd be priceless to see how you'd react."

Something is bubbling and boiling. Churning and rolling and heating up, spilling over. Jordy flew me over here. To go on TV. So the world could laugh at me.

Jordy put me in a bedroom with Skye. Because he knew how that would destroy me.

Because he cheated on me with her, and he *knows* he did.

He fucking *knows* what he did to me.

And he thinks it's *funny.*

And now he's stolen Skye from me, too, all because he's so fucking *fragile* he can't go on a reality show without using the royal family to strong-arm the producers into framing him as the good guy. So I have to sit here, instead of being with the girl who means *everything* to me, just to stop him from getting away with his behavior. Because he knows, he *knows*, that if people saw him as he really is, *bam*. All the sponsorships, the interviews, the freebies, the adoring fans. Gone, in a heartbeat.

Now Skye is hurt and alone, because of him.

And so am I.

"I'm going to fucking eviscerate him," I say to Isaac. "That is happening. Okay? One way or another, I am making it happen."

"I'm not here to stop you," Isaac says. "I'm just here to suggest we go bigger."

In response to my questioning look, he turns on the laptop, and opens it to a movie, then presses play.

It's Jordy, telling Skye she's beautiful the way a sunset's beautiful.

Then saying it to Perrie.

Then Lauren.

Francesca.

Kim.

Jordy's voice, saying something horrible about a woman's outfit, although I can't tell whose. Followed by Skye's voice, telling him she thinks the woman looks great.

Jordy's voice again, implying Francesca is a slut.

Jordy, strolling with Kim, telling her she's the only one of us who seems to have any brains in her head, while the rest of us are "fucking vapid, you know?"

Jordy, telling Perrie that she has "the best tits" in the mansion, and that the best part about them is she doesn't shove them in people's faces like Lauren does.

Jordy, telling Francesca he's never felt so in tune with someone before, and he thinks he's falling for her—as they sit in a kayak, hours before he sends her home.

Jordy, slow dancing with Lauren, telling her not to listen to anything I say about him, because I'm a psycho and I'm not gonna be around much longer anyway.

A montage of Jordy telling several of us we're each "probably the only actually funny girl I know."

Jordy telling all of us we're the person he was really hoping would come.

Jordy murmuring to an unseen person about a "crazy fucking bitch."

Jordy leaning into Isaac to ask him if there's a bedroom he can take the girls to for some "alone time."

All wrapped up with an especially long compilation of Jordy saying the word "slut."

The screen goes black, and I turn to Isaac slowly, gaping. "Isaac . . ."

"Maya."

"This would destroy him."

"It would go a long way, yeah."

"The palace would sue the shoes off your feet."

"Our contract says an awful lot about editing, and not a lot about the live show. I had our lawyer look over it."

"They'd say you took it out of context."

"Then I'd be happy to oblige by publishing the full context of every clip."

"Gwendolyn would fire you."

"Mm. Not if it makes enough headlines, she won't. And this would make the front cover of every magazine in Europe and America. And then some."

I slump backward, stunned.

"Are you out of excuses yet?" he asks.

My brain is buzzing, but one thought breaks through. "I really appreciate all this," I say. "But . . . god, I know it's petty, but I want to be the one to call Jordy out. I don't want to hide behind a video. Even one this . . . damning."

"You'll have your moment still. This will not play until you give me the signal. It's your call when you're done saying your piece. Yeah?"

I shake my head at the laptop, then put a hand over my mouth. "Why?"

Isaac laughs. "Simple answer? My job is to generate drama and viewers."

"Complex answer?"

His smile slips, and he shrugs. "I knew a Jordy once, too."

THIRTY-FIVE

Skye

When we arrive at the studio, we're immediately steered back-stage for hair and makeup. Our clothing is sponsored today, and I'm wearing a short red dress with a plunging neckline and long sleeves.

The color of passion and lust.

The color of the Other Woman.

It's fitting twice over now.

They place me in a room with Perrie, and a makeup artist moves deftly between us, applying foundation and mascara and highlighter with a finish so flawless we look airbrushed.

"How do you feel?" Perrie asks as the artist starts on our hair.

I breathe out in a harsh whoosh of air. "Fine. I suppose. A little nervous. You?"

"I'm . . . actually really excited to go home." When I glance at her, she's beaming into her hands.

"Can you believe we go home after this?" I ask.

"Home doesn't even feel real anymore. I don't regret com-ing here, but I miss my apartment. I miss my cat. I miss . . . being able to hop in the car at one a.m. to grab some fries if I have a craving. You know?"

"I do," I say. "I'm not going home, exactly, but it'll be nice to have that freedom. For things to feel normal again."

Perrie giggles in a dark sort of manner. "Skye. I don't think things are going to be normal again for a long time. Maybe not ever."

She's correct. What even is normal, anymore? Who even is that girl who arrived in Chalonne seven weeks ago? I'm not entirely certain I would recognize her if I ran into her on the street.

"I'm just ready to get my hands on my phone again," Perrie says.

"I bet you're missing everyone."

"I am. *So* much. I've never gone this long without speaking to my little brother." She pauses, thoughtful. "Also, I'm dying to check my follower count."

"Aren't the other girls here tonight? Maybe one of them can tell you what you're up to."

Perrie straightens in her seat so suddenly her neck cracks. "Oh my *god*, you're right."

When I'm ready—a feat that takes far less time than it does for Perrie, since my pixie-length hair only has a couple styling options available these days—I'm fitted with a mic-pack and sent off into the green room.

Where I come face-to-face with Maya.

She's radiant in a shimmery gray-lilac dress, strappy heels, and her hair spilling over her shoulders in thick auburn waves.

Her hair is hiding the freckles I love. I want to brush it off her shoulders to show them to the world. And, once I've done that, I want to kiss them, before I lose the opportunity to ever touch them—her—again.

But of course, that's just a fantasy.

"Skye," she murmurs. "Can we talk?"

I absolutely, truly cannot do this. But I give her a moment. Just one moment. "Is there anything I don't know?"

"No. You know everything."

"Nothing's changed?"

Her eyes widen then narrow, like my words have wounded her. But how can I have wounded her when *she* did this to *us*?

"No," she says finally. "But you're acting like I had a choice."

"Of course you had a choice," I whisper. "And you made it perfectly clear that you will choose revenge over me. Last week, today, tomorrow, indefinitely, whenever. And you're entitled to that."

"I can't just let him go," she says urgently.

I scan her face, then give her a slow, sad smile. "I know."

With that, I walk out of the green room, my heels clacking on the linoleum. I push past people, ignore someone calling after me to see if I'm okay, and burst into the restroom, where I hide inside a toilet cubicle.

I sit on the closed toilet seat while I force myself to breathe steadily.

I am going to get through this, then I am going back to England. I am going to finish what I set out to do. Meet new people. Have new experiences. Look out for me, and only me.

I am not going to date anyone. I am not going to make any friends—at least, not for longer than a night. I'm through with trusting people. Through with taking people at their word, only to have them turn around and prove I'm the lowest checkmark on their priority list. I am my own number one priority, and I'm all I need. My job right now is to look after my heart, because it feels eviscerated. Shredded into a million minuscule pieces, light enough to be caught up in the wind and carried away.

I hope it does get carried away. I don't want it anymore.

I don't want anything that leaves me vulnerable to hurting like this ever again.

THIRTY-SIX

Maya

You know when you have to process something really important, but your brain goes on strike, so all you can hear is the
"error" sound a computer makes when you overload it?

Yeah. That's happening to me right now. I'm the human
equivalent of a blue screen.

I stare after Skye, dumbstruck, trying to figure out if I
should follow her and try to talk this through, or give her
some space. I want the former for myself, but I kind of feel
like it's a dick move to force someone into an emotional,
heartbreaking conversation minutes before they go on live
television, so I'm leaning toward "space." Before I get the
chance to decide, it's decided for me when Isaac swoops in
from fuck-knows-where to run me through the logistics of the
plan one last time.

"So, what's the code?" he asks me, steering me to stand
not-at-all suspiciously against a wall, away from the others.

"'You can take his,'" I repeat dutifully.

"Got it. Also, heads up, Gwendolyn knows."

"Gwendolyn *knows*?"

"I'm not gonna go behind my boss's back, Maya." Isaac
rolls his eyes. "Come on, do you want me jobless?"

"How is it possible Gwendolyn is okay with this?"

"Gwendolyn," Isaac says, "is okay with money. Gwendolyn is okay with ratings. Gwendolyn . . . has a team of very good lawyers on her side—we've done worse, don't ask questions because I'm never telling you—*okay*, you good to go?"

"I . . . guess so," I say, before nodding. "Yes. Let's do this."

"Let's *do this*. Knock him dead." Isaac salutes me for some reason, then shakes his head like he regrets it, and heads out of the green room.

Seconds after he leaves, three familiar faces walk in. Lauren, Kim, and Francesca.

I let out a cry and rush forward to barrel-hug them. "Oh my god, hi! You're here!" I pull away. "You look *great*."

Lauren waves a hand. "Never mind that. Maya. Congratulations. How do you feel?"

"Shocked?" Francesca asks. "Because I'm not gonna lie, I was shocked. You're the plot twist of the century."

She has no idea. "You know," I say, "kind of. But if there's one thing we can say about Jordy, it's that he's . . . unpredictable."

Francesca bursts out laughing. "Yeah, you know what? That is fair. Congratulations, love."

"*Is* it a congratulations?" Kim asks.

I look at her, crestfallen. Seriously? After all this time, *still*?

"Yes," Lauren says gently, shooting me an apologetic look.

"No, I don't mean like that," Kim says. "I mean, like, no offense . . . but I've been watching the episodes, and I've been thinking about everything that happened, and I actually . . . sort of . . . think you're out of his league, Maya."

She says it begrudgingly, arms folded and head cocked, but there's a hint of a smile there.

"He shouldn't have done what he did to you," I say.

"Well, he says it's because he didn't want to keep me from my friends and family with all that going on. But . . ."

"Yeah, nah, fuck him," Francesca says.

"Fuck him," Kim agrees. "But, you know, we're mad happy for you, Maya."

"Yay," Lauren says, raising her fists in a weak party dance.

I smile, but it feels weird and hollow. "How is your friend, Kim?"

"Oh, good, really good. Yeah, we've been hanging out heaps. He's got a cast, but he'll be all right."

"Thank god."

"Yeah. I told him the next time I go on a reality show, he has to wear a bubble-wrap suit the whole time. He thinks I'm joking, but I am dead fucking serious."

I grin. "Hey, have any of you seen Perrie?"

Lauren gestures toward the changing rooms. "She was getting her shoulder straps adjusted last time I saw her."

I give them a quick thanks, and make off toward the changing rooms, just in time to catch Perrie coming out of them.

"Hey," she says. "So, guess who's at four hundred thousand followers already."

"You?"

"Me. And I'm verified. Finally. Those bastards rejected me every month on the month before this." She scoffs, but it's through a smile. Then, she grabs my hand. "Almost time!"

"How are you feeling?" I ask.

"Pumped! I love crowds." She pauses. "Being in front of them, not being in them. There's a difference."

"There *is* a difference."

"Exactly. And I figure this is practice for when I become extremely famous and I'm in front of crowds all the time."

I smile. "Perfect."

She studies my face, and she squints her eyes. "What's wrong?"

"Hmm? Nothing!"

"No, something." She takes my arm and steers me down the hall to an empty dressing room, where she closes the door. "Are you . . . having second thoughts about Jordy? Because if you are, it's not too late. It's never too late, really. You're not marrying the guy." She pauses. "Right?"

I hold up my hand to show off my bare ring finger, and she grins. "Okay, good."

"Why do you ask if I'm having second thoughts?" I ask.

Perrie hops up on the makeup bench, mirror-spotlights behind her. "I don't know. You just look like . . . the way you looked the day I met you."

"How did I look then?"

"Like you'd been dragged along to the last place you'd ever wanna be."

I let myself fall back against the wall. Suddenly, more than anything, I want to talk to someone about all of this. I feel like I've been flying totally blind for the past week, messing things up every step of the way. I'm not good on my own. Somehow, I always mess it up.

I don't want to mess this up.

"Can you keep a secret?"

"I'm actually really good at minding my own business."

"It's a really, really important one. And you only need to keep it for the next hour or so. I hope. Is that okay?"

She gives a single, confident nod. "Hit me with it. I can take it."

I brace myself, then, screw it. "I . . . like Skye."

Perrie gives me the *weirdest* look at this. So weird that my brain immediately rushes to homophobia. But she knows

I'm bi. We've talked about it! She didn't have an issue then! Unless she's someone who pretends to be an ally when it's hypothetical but doesn't want anything to do with it if it's right in front of them. Oh god, why is she looking at me like that?

"*What?*" I spit, at the same time she bursts out, "I know!"

"You know?" I repeat, confused. "Skye told you?"

"No. Once I was looking for you guys and you weren't in your room, and I found you outside making out. So I . . . backed away slowly and never told anyone."

"Including me?"

"Remember how I just said I'm good at minding my own business? I *minded my own business.*"

I pause, then laugh with relief. "Wow. Okay. And you didn't tell Jordy or the producers or anyone? Even though it probably could've gotten us kicked off?"

She looks indignant at the very idea. "What kind of monster would do that?"

"A lot of reality show contestants."

"Mm, but we weren't picked out of a crowd based on how much drama we can stir," she says.

"Well, I kind of was."

"Huh?"

"Apparently Jordy told the producers to make sure I came on because I'd be a great villain."

Perrie gapes. "What! You're kidding."

"I am not kidding."

"Maya, why are you still with this guy? What? Skye is right there. *Right there.*"

I must make a weird face at that, because she raises her eyebrows. "Okay. What else don't I know? Catch me up."

Well, hey. She's going to know about it by the end of the

show anyway. I might as well tell her. Except for Isaac's and Gwendolyn's involvement, of course, just in case that's the sort of thing that might make or break a lawsuit if the royal family does sue.

When I'm done, she sticks out her lower lip and breathes out noisily. "Wow. Well. I can't say he doesn't have it coming."

"Right?" I say.

She nods, then furrows her brow. "But . . . do you think you'll be happy after this?"

"What do you mean?"

"It might not go exactly like you're imagining. What happens if the media takes his side? If people online take his side? Is that gonna crush you? Or do you think once you do this, you'll be able to let go altogether?"

I pause. It's a really good question. One I'm not totally sure I know the answer to.

But something in the pit of my gut doesn't like that thought at all.

"I can't just let him win," I say at last.

"Maya . . . I don't know. You've given him two years of your life now. That guy has been living rent free in your mind this whole time, taking up all that energy. It sounds to me like you've already let him win."

I don't even know how to reply to that, so I don't. I just cross my arms over my chest and stare at the wall behind Perrie.

"You know what'd be a real win, for you? To stop giving him all of this power over you. To give him nothing."

I bristle at this. "Are you just trying to talk me out of hurting Jordy?"

She blows a raspberry. "Screw Jordy. Also, if you actually went through with this, it'd get *so* many eyes on this episode.

Like, that would help me with followers *so* much. But I would rather give you my honest, unbiased opinion. I just want to know if you've thought this through."

I sigh, heavy and long. "I just . . . I don't know what else I can do."

She shrugs, and hops off the counter. "You still have a few minutes to think it over."

With that, she leaves me alone in the dressing room, closing the door gently behind her. I stay leaning against the wall, playing her words over in my head.

Is she right? Has my anger at Jordy been consuming me that much over the last couple of years?

So much that I've found it hard to move on?

So much that I've suffered every time his face came on the TV, or an online article?

So much that I've picked a moment of revenge on him over Skye?

Because this is what Skye meant, right? And is she so off base? If I cared for Skye more than I hated Jordy, wouldn't I have let go of this the second I realized Skye was hurt?

Why hadn't I?

Why *couldn't* I?

Because that would mean that all my pain and hurt would've been for nothing.

Isn't it anyway, though?

I don't want to be bitter and angry. I don't want to be the kind of person who's so caught up in the past that she wastes her present and ruins her future.

I don't want to give Jordy the power to turn me into that person.

But . . . in spite of all that, I still want him to hurt, the way he's made me hurt. The way he's made so many of us hurt.

There's a knock on the door, and an assistant sticks his head around. "There you are," he says. "Ready to go out?" This is it, then. I'm out of thinking time.

Now, the only thing I have left to do is to act.

And I'm not going to waste that. Whether I regret it or not, I can't waste it. Not when I've come this far.

THIRTY-SEVEN

Maya

Onstage, the lights are blinding and hot. Hot enough that I immediately start worrying about my makeup melting off from sweat.

My nerves probably aren't helping that.

On one side of center stage, Grayson is sitting in an armchair. A few feet over are Jordy and me, on a love seat, his arm wrapped in a performative way around my shoulders. Farther along still, they've seated the other five girls on two benches, staggering their heights.

The crowd is laughing at something Kim just said, but I can barely focus on them over the frantic beating of my heart. We're coming toward the end of this part of the show. Closer to my moment.

When the crowd dies down, Grayson turns to Skye, and one of the camera operators swivels toward her to grab her reaction shots. "Skye, out of all the girls, I think it's fair to say you had a particularly easy time winning the hearts of our viewers at home."

The crowd swells into a cheer again. It's been doing that a lot. It's a little exhausting. Also, I feel out of the loop. They keep referencing things that obviously make sense to anyone who's watched all the episodes, and seen all the online talk, but I'm missing several weeks of content here. So, Skye's beloved? As she should be, but still—since when? What else don't I know?

"But privately, there was someone you found it a little hard to win over," Grayson continues. "Can you tell us more about Maya, and how you two went from being the most talked-about rivalry on the show to—apparently—on friendly terms?"

Skye and I glance at each other, and my cheeks go warm. She seems calm as she tears her eyes away from me and turns to Grayson, though. "Maya and I definitely get along, Grayson," she says. "I think sometimes you meet people and it's an instant click, and other times you meet someone and it takes you a little longer to figure each other out. But sometimes those people can end up your closest friends. Me and Maya, we're a good example of how first impressions don't always set the tone for the rest of it."

I don't know whether to smile or burst into tears at this, so, of course, the camera swings to me to get what's probably a very confusing reaction shot as the crowd cheers and claps. I hope I look touched.

"Speaking of rivalries—" Grayson says.

Me and Jordy?

"There was a moment of drama when Maya beat out Perrie during the rock-climbing challenge," he goes on. "Perrie, as an avid rock climber yourself, how did you feel about this devastating loss?"

Perrie doesn't look especially devastated. "I was impressed by how well Maya did, actually. But it was a fair game, and I lost, so, you know. It is what it is."

Skye and I catch each other's eyes at this, and we both grin despite ourselves. Grayson, of course, doesn't miss it. "Is there more to the story here, girls?" he asks.

Well, screw it. While I'm creating drama. "It wasn't a fair game, actually," I admit. "I snuck out the night before and practiced the route. Skye had to rescue me when I got stuck."

The crowd roars with laughter, and a few boos. The girls make a show of being fake-outraged, and Perrie starts giggling so hard she has to gasp for breath.

Grayson slaps his knees. "Maya! I'm surprised you're admitting to this on live television."

Jordy squeezes my shoulder. "Did you wanna spend the night with me that bad?" he asks.

Somehow, I manage not to recoil. "I uh . . . yeah, I wanted to stay on, and I wasn't sure about my chances at that stage, so I did what I had to do."

I swear I can feel Skye's eyes boring into me, but I manage not to look at her.

"Well, not every girl can make it to the end," Grayson says. "Francesca, you were actually the first one to go. Were you expecting this?"

Francesca straightens, and looks right at Jordy. "No, Grayson, honestly, I wasn't. I thought Jordy and I had a really great connection, and we had a lot of fun that day. I guess I was stunned to be sent home at that moment."

Jordy takes his arm away from me, and I wriggle in place to shake the feel of him off my skin as he clasps his hands together. "Frankie, we had a really fun time together. You really are an awesome chick, and I'm so glad we got to re-explore that. But unfortunately, I think in this case, the way I care about you, and the way you cared about me, just didn't match up. I hope we can stay friends."

I would kill to see what version of that episode the public got to see. I have to assume, if Isaac included Jordy whispering to Francesca in the montage he made, that it was footage that didn't make it into the official cut, and the public has no idea how much Jordy was flirting with her on her last day.

Grayson doesn't ask Kim about being eliminated. I can't say I'm super surprised—Jordy probably asked them to keep the question off-limits—but I still would've liked to see her get the chance to shame him for it. She deserves that much.

After a few more questions, the girls are escorted off, and it's just me, Jordy, and Grayson. The cameras close in on us, and the room feels a whole lot smaller suddenly.

I zone out in terror as Grayson asks Jordy about his experience on the show, and Jordy runs through every bland, scripted nothing he possibly can to make himself look good for the cameras. It's time, soon. Any minute now, it's going to be time for me to say what I came here to say.

Somewhere at the back of my mind, I hear Grayson ask his next question. "But you weren't totally sure whether Maya would end up being the one that got away, were you, Jordy? Can you tell us more about that?"

I snap back into the present, as Jordy shuffles away from me an inch or so and takes on a grave expression.

"That's right, Grayson," he says. "I didn't want to go into it too much on the show, because I believe in second chances, but Maya and I . . . we actually had a pretty bad breakup. No one was at fault, but there were a lot of hurt feelings all around. It took me a while to get over her, actually, and it was made even worse by the fact that my family moved not long after. I was mourning the relationship I had with this, you know, this wonderful girl, and I was alone, in a brand-new country. That's the state of mind I was in when I met Skye. And, back then, you know, it was the . . . it felt like a miracle, to meet someone who made me feel like things could be okay again."

The crowd *awws*, and I kind of wish I could squirt water at them. Can't they *see* how scripted this bullshit is?

"But, sometimes when people break up, one person moves on more quickly than the other, and in our case, I was . . . well, let's just say I was so happy, I wasn't as aware as I should've been of how my happiness might hurt Maya. And, look, that part's on me. But, all I knew was, one second I'm happily telling everyone about this wonderful new girl I'd met, and the next, I have people from back home accusing me of cheating on Maya. Which was obviously ridiculous. I don't want to speculate on how that rumor got spread, of course. Breakups can be full of hurt feelings, and he-said, she-said, and twisted words. But, regardless . . . yeah, it was a hard time in my life. I would've thought the people who knew me would *never* believe I would *ever* cheat on somebody. It was pretty hurtful."

This can't be happening.

This *cannot* be happening.

"Anyway, that's all in the past—and I was pretty convinced that it must have been a misunderstanding, you know? But then, we had some drama early on in filming, and, truthfully, it made me question if those rumors were a misunderstanding, or something more targeted than that. That was a horrible moment for me in this experience, because I was left questioning if I'd potentially made a huge mistake with one of the girls I'd invited onto the show."

On the screen behind us—the screen that showed a bunch of the biggest moments from the show earlier—the screen Isaac's supposed to be displaying his Jordy montage on soon—my face appears.

I'm drunk, and it's the first night. "He doesn't care about you, any more than he cares about me," I'm shouting, while the other girls give each other awkward, pitying glances. "He cares about himself!"

It looks like I'm trying to turn them against Jordy. Which I *was*, but with the context missing, even I hate myself.

Then there's a shot of the group of us on the first night. "Could you send Perrie over here?" Jordy asks me, sounding all pleasant and reasonable and gentle.

I look like I'm about to explode. "Sure, Jordy. You could probably have gone to ask her yourself, but I guess you're used to being waited on these days, huh?"

There's the clip of me having a dig at Skye on the first night. The clip of me being rude to Jordy on our walk the next day. And finally, back to the first night, when Jordy pulls me aside.

"They said . . . well, they said you haven't had the nicest things to say about me, honestly." The camera jumps, and it cuts to Jordy again: "I was wondering if you're feeling jealous?" It cuts again, to Jordy frowning. "No, don't get upset."

Another cut. "I don't want this jealousy to come between us like it did last time."

It's finally past-me's turn to talk. "My overwhelming, irrational jealousy?"

"Yes."

"Uh-huh."

Oh my god. It looks like he's just trying to talk some sense into me, and that I'm *agreeing* with him.

My head feels like it's about to explode. Like, to the point where if spontaneous combustion is a real thing, this might be a good time to worry for my own flammability.

The screen goes black. The crowd murmurs in confusion.

Grayson looks grave. "Not the best possible start to a new relationship. But, obviously, something changed. What do you think that was?"

Jordy looks deep in thought. "Well, Grayson, I think something in my gut told me that Maya isn't a cruel person. She's never been. Maya's just . . . a woman who needs some extra security. After we had that talk, I think I realized that. Once I started going above and beyond to make sure Maya never went down that jealousy spiral—you know, checking in on her, giving her some extra attention when she looked like she needed it, reassuring her—I really saw her blossom into the girl I fell in love with the first time around. That's when I realized the problem was me—I hadn't been making sure, at every possible moment, that Maya was getting what she needed from me. Once I changed my own behavior, well . . . here we are."

Jordy Miller. Is a fucking genius.

I'm in awe. One speech, and he's managed to frame me as emotionally abusive, forcing him to cater to my demands all day every day so I don't snap and make his life hell. Everyone in the audience must be thinking the same thing right now.

Poor Jordy. He doesn't know what she's doing to him. He's so sweet, he doesn't even realize how messed up that sounded.

But he realizes. Oh, he fucking realizes.

He knew damn well I'm not actually into him. All week. He just didn't care, because he didn't need me to be.

He just needed to use me to make things about *him*, on a national level. He basically told me that himself. I just didn't listen.

Grayson faces me now. "And Maya, what was your experience on the show?"

It's my cue. The one Isaac and I discussed. And perfectly timed for a rebuttal, too. Was Isaac in on this? How long has he known about Jordy's montage of me?

Did he *make* Jordy's montage of me?

Will my rebuttal be enough? It's enough to discredit him. It proves he cheated on me, and he knows it. Yes, I think it will. Sure, like Perrie said, there will be people who take his side, but . . .

Like Perrie said.

I'm so furious right now. My skin is prickling, and I feel

like I'm seconds from hurling on live TV, and tears are hovering at the backs of my eyes, ready to spill over if I drop my guard against them for a second.

And I didn't even have to be here. I could've been sitting beside Skye, bumping my shoulder against hers and smiling knowingly while Jordy bullshitted about his love for whoever else won.

I did this. I entered this war. I accepted this battle.

And it won't end here. Just like Skye predicted, there will be more battles. If anything, it's just going to grow. His side, her side. Who's lying, who's telling the truth. Every time I scream back at Jordy, someone's going to be there to twist my words. To take his side of the story as gospel.

Nothing's changing. I have been stagnating for two years.

I have been fighting this battle for two years of my fucking *life*.

Enough.

I'm supposed to launch into an attack. To tell my side of the story, from when he moved to Canada, to the cheating, to the character assassination he performed on me. To describe his attitude on the show, the way he told us all the same things, the horrible things he'd say about us behind our backs. To tell them what he did to Francesca, and Kim; that chillingly cold, calm way he has of hurting people without hesitation. To reveal why he wanted me on the show in the first place. Then, I'm supposed to finish with the words *I know this sounds like a he-said, she-said situation. But you don't have to take my word for it. You can take his.*

Instead, I catch Isaac's eye backstage, and shake my head. He's staring at me with wide eyes—trying to figure out my reaction to the clips, I guess—and he gives me a hesitant thumbs-up in acknowledgment.

"Overall, I've found this experience really wonderful," I say. "I've gotten to see an amazingly beautiful country I've never visited before, I've met a whole bunch of great new people, and spent time with Jordy again, of course. But the thing I've loved most about this experience has been falling for someone incredible. Someone who's blown me away with their intelligence, their wit, their . . . confidence, and passion." I force a nervous giggle. "It's been a while," I say to Grayson, and the audience laughs with me. Relieved. I guess I broke the tension for them.

"When I told Jordy before that I wanted to stick around to the end, it was the truth. Except, the thing is, I didn't want to stick around for Jordy. I wanted to stick around for . . . another reason."

Revenge, specifically. But I'm not going to admit *that* on camera.

Jordy stiffens next to me. Something close to panic flashes across his eyes. I guess it's just occurred to him that maybe the producers got me to agree to a montage of him, like his for me. Which, obviously, is basically the truth, but that's not the point right now.

"I got to know a lot of the girls during my time on the show, but especially Skye. And after knowing Skye for long enough, I couldn't help but want to stay on the show so I could spend more time. With her."

Grayson, for the first time, doesn't seem to be performing his shock. "Are you saying what I think you're saying?" he asks.

Jordy is holding perfectly still, staring straight ahead.

"Yes. I didn't plan this, and I didn't expect it to happen this way, but it did."

Grayson leans forward, his eyes sparkling with the drama of it all. "So, why did you accept Jordy?"

This is going to be the hardest part to get right. "I wasn't expecting him to choose me, honestly," I say. "There were so many gorgeous, intelligent, fun girls on the show with me. I was more distracted by the fear that he might pick Skye. Then, he chose me, and I . . . panicked, and there were cameras on me, and I didn't know how to say that I'd fallen for someone else. I should've prepared, but I didn't, and I'm so sorry for that, Jordy. I never wanted to hurt you. But my heart . . . belongs to someone else."

The crowd erupts into boos, and my whole face heats up by several degrees, but I guess I deserve this. It's exactly what I'd known would happen. Jordy's the wounded soul. I'm the villain.

But . . . I'm okay with it.

I feel light. Like I've spent the last two years of my life walking around wearing an enormous, faux-fur coat, all stifling and heavy. And I've finally shucked it off.

Grayson switches his attention to Jordy now. "Jordy, did you have any idea this was the case?"

Jordy wipes a hand over his mouth, then curls in a little, like he's trying to protect himself. "Uh, no, Grayson. I didn't."

It's hard to tell whether it's an act or not. It's been a long time since I've had any idea where the lies begin and end with Jordy, though.

"Did the other girls know?" Grayson asks me.

"I told Perrie about an hour ago, but otherwise, no. Perrie, she actually helped me sort through some of this. I think I was hoping—I loved Jordy once, I hoped maybe I could love him again, I guess? But she talked sense into me and helped me . . . not to go through with something I would've regretted."

The noise the crowd is making is . . . weird. I can't actually tell what they all think, and the lights blazing at me make it impossible for me to make out anyone's faces.

"And does Skye feel the same, Maya?" Grayson asks.

I blink, and try not to let the pain show on my face. "If

she did . . ." I say carefully, "I doubt she'd be okay with me accepting Jordy last week. And I think I deserve that, so."

Jordy's lip curls the slightest bit, but he wipes his face clean as Grayson asks him for a comment.

"I . . . well . . ." He lets out his breath in a heave. "I guess I . . ."

He goes on, but his voice fades away completely for me when a movement side-stage catches my eye.

It's Skye and Isaac. She looks at Isaac, and he tips his head toward us.

Then, she smooths her dress down, and steps onto the set.

THIRTY-EIGHT

Skye

My dad says I was born concerned.

My mom doesn't say a word to me anymore.

I met a guy, and he almost made me believe love was worth the risk. Almost.

I made a single friend, and let her know me as well as I knew her. Then I left her to find adventure by myself.

I made multiple friends, without really trying to. An accident, I suppose.

I met a girl, and she made me believe love was worth the risk.

I regretted that misstep immediately.

So, my Maya, where does that leave us?

She rises and turns as soon as I walk on set. It's just us, eyes locked, motionless.

The crowd doesn't know what to make of us. It cheers, and it boos, and it murmurs under its collective breath. There's quite a lot of hate in that crowd, and that alone inspires awe, because she could've stopped this. The out-of-context clips Jordy just played make her look horrendous—the perfect villain. Everything she isn't.

She can stop this. But she hasn't.

Grayson and Jordy look to me, too, now. They're waiting for my move, but I don't have anything planned. I was simply urged onstage by Isaac, and I came because the moment felt significant. But now that I'm here, at the apex of said moment, all I feel is terror.

Maya takes a hesitant step toward me, wearing an equally hesitant smile. "Hi."

I want to trust that she won't hurt me if I give her another opportunity to. I want to. But how can I?

Other than the knowledge that she's told the world about us, instead of about Jordy.

Other than the fact that she barely looks bothered by the judgment and repulsion radiating off the crowd right now.

Other than the fact that she's looking past Jordy and straight at me, as though nothing else exists.

I suppose that's the thing about high risk, high reward.

You fall for someone. Head over heels. And then you take a leap of faith.

Mine is a smile.

As soon as she sees it, Maya understands. She holds out a hand, and I step forward to take it, and the crowd begins to screech.

Grayson shrugs at a gobsmacked Jordy and approaches us. "Skye, welcome back, welcome back," he bellows until the crowd simmers down. "Now, from the looks of things here, it seems as though Maya's feelings might not be unrequited? This is . . . well, I'll be honest with you, ladies, not the love story everyone thought they were tuning in to hear about tonight."

The crowd buzzes with laughter.

"But in any case," Grayson says, gesturing for quiet. "As I'm still your host, I'm going to need to politely ask you for a little more formality, here. We have a procedure on *Second-Chance Romance,* and, Maya, I expect you to follow it."

Let no one ever accuse Grayson of being slow to adapt to curveballs.

Maya looks confused, but then something must click, because she takes my other hand and we face each other.

"Skye," she says, and I let out a sound that's half groan, half giggle, as I realize what's happening. "Long before we met, I'd already decided I couldn't stand you. Unfortunately for me, it didn't take much time actually knowing you to realize you were pretty difficult to hate. Actually, impossible to hate. You're probably one of the best people I've ever met in my life."

I think I must be approximately the shade of an eggplant right now, but I keep my chin straight as Maya continues.

"I . . . I've made some mistakes along the way. It took me longer than it should've to realize what you meant about . . . those mistakes. But I want to make it clear. You're it, for me. Both of us have our own issues, god knows I have a lot of problems, but those problems . . . they used to seem really big. They were the center of my universe. But the way I feel about you is bigger than those problems. It drowns them out. Because I love you."

My mouth drops open. Maya doesn't pause.

"And the love I feel for you is bigger than hate, or bitterness, or any of those things that have dragged me down for way, way too long now. I'm not asking you to say it back. But I am asking if you'll be my future."

She watches me, and so does Grayson, and Jordy, and the crowd, and the cameras—which, I presume, are broadcasting my stunned face to viewers across continents.

Do I want to be Maya's future?

Do I want her to be mine?

It's not a question. Or, if it was, I answered it a long time ago. I simply wasn't ready to admit it to myself.

I step forward to embrace her, and the crowd's volume surges further still. I've missed the feeling of her against me. The smell of her, and how her body fits mine. The way the top of her head rests neatly beneath my chin.

"I'm sorry," she whispers, her breath tickling my collarbone.

"No, *I'm* sorry. I was overdramatic, and I shouldn't have made you do this."

"You didn't make me. I chose to."

We pull apart, and my breath catches in my throat. "I love you, too, by the way."

"I thought you didn't do love."

"There's a lot of things I thought I didn't do."

Grayson is having a hard time getting the crowd to simmer down. Jordy, meanwhile, is sitting on the couch and glaring at us with a storm-cloud face.

He, I'm quite sure, is planning on murdering us when we get backstage.

I, for one, am eager to see him try. There's six of us, and one of him.

THIRTY-NINE

Maya

Isaac grabs me the second I walk off set and matches my pace, his voice low and urgent. "I swear, I didn't know they were planning that with Jordy. Apparently they've had it lined up for a few days. Jordy was worried you'd tell everyone about the cheating, so he wanted to get his side out first. And Gwendolyn figured showing yours right after would be even better. Get people talking."

"It's okay," I say. "Thanks for clearing that up."

"If I'd known I would've tried to pull it."

"We might need to finish this later," I say as we reach the green room, because Jordy's there waiting, red-faced and furious.

Skye's joined the other girls, who are standing slightly apart from him, looking at him warily. Isaac steps away from me, but only moves a few steps away to stand with Violet. It's obvious both of them are watching us in their peripheries—like everyone else in the room.

"Well," Jordy says. "Everything falls into place, suddenly."

It feels like the spot where I'm meant to say *I'm sorry.* Problem is, I'm one million percent not, so I just wait for more.

He points between me and Skye with a dangerous smile. "Just tell me one thing. When did this start?"

I shrug offhandedly. "Oh, weeks ago."

"Weeks ago," he repeats, with a small laugh. Then, in a flash, he darkens. "Weeks ago. *Weeks ago!* Ha. Wow. *Fuck* me for a fool. Nice to know you were cheating on me the whole time, Maya!"

"Cheating?" I shoot back in disbelief. "*Cheating?* Jordy, we were hanging out *on reality TV.* There was nothing monogamous about that shit! I'm sorry if you had this little fantasy idea where you got to date six adoring women while they all counted the seconds until they got the pleasure of breathing your air for a few hours once a week, but you should've known what this was."

"What? A chance to slut around with everyone you can convince to give you the time of day?"

"'Slut around'? Tell me you did not just say 'slut around,' Jordy."

"You know what I think?" Jordy asks. "I think you were *so* upset when we broke up because you knew I'd seen you for what you are. You are jealous, you are needy, you are manipulative, and, now, I guess, you're a cheater."

"Hey!" Skye snaps, advancing on him. "One, Maya is none of those things, and two, the only cheater in this room is you."

Jordy looks back and forth between us, then at the girls standing behind us, and the various staff pretending not to overhear all of this. Then he shifts into a sneer. "Maya, you and I both know what kind of person you are," he says. "I just have to take comfort in knowing everyone else will realize sooner or later, too."

"Ditto," I say.

"And Skye," he says, ignoring my comment. "I can see she's warped your view of reality. That's what she does. Just know that I don't hold this against you, and if you ever want to reach out and apologize, I'll be glad to hear from you."

Skye bursts out laughing. "Oh, thank you, Jords. I'll be sure to never take you up on that."

Jordy takes a deep breath, then turns to me. "Everyone's going to hate you," he says. "You know that, right? Or do you have no idea what being in the spotlight is like?"

I just shrug.

He nods slowly and gives me a poisonous smile. "Well, at least when that happens, you won't be able to blame me for once. There's no possible way you can twist *this* into anything but your own fault, Maya. Have fun with the consequences of your actions."

Skye takes my hand before the anger can surge up too far. I squeeze it instead, and it releases some of the fury.

Sure, I'd decided to start letting go of my feelings for Jordy. But it doesn't mean I can switch off my emotions like a light-bulb. A dimmer switch, at most.

But I am okay, I think. And I will continue to be okay.

We both will be.

Me and Skye, that is.

As I look around the room, the producers and other staff suddenly become very interested in whatever it was they were doing before. Except for Isaac and Gwendolyn. He's staring after Jordy with an expression that looks an awful lot like disgust. She kind of looks entertained by the whole thing. Bet she wishes she could've filmed that showdown.

The girls close in on us in a circle.

"Are you okay?" Lauren asks.

"Yeah," Skye says, and I nod.

"You two are mental," Kim says.

"Right," Francesca joins in. "Who the heck does that? Respect for you, though. Fuck Jordy."

"Oh yeah," Kim adds hurriedly. "Like, you've lost it, but in the best way possible."

"I can't believe we didn't notice," Lauren says.

"I can't believe you didn't notice, either," Perrie says. "I knew the whole time."

"Yes, you're very observant," I say, rolling my eyes with a grin.

"Wait, you knew?" Skye asks, and Perrie gives a one-shoulder shrug.

"I can't believe that clip they played of you, Maya," Kim says. "Where do they get off? It was *so* out of context."

"I have a bad feeling a lot of the show's gonna be out of context when we watch it at home," Perrie says.

Lauren, Kim, and Francesca nod in unison, and the rest of us groan.

"So, now what?" Kim asks. "Jordy's just gonna be . . . single?"

"Well, I don't want him," I say, and Skye snorts. "Which one of you is gonna snatch him up?"

The girls all purse their lips for a long pause, and then burst out laughing as one.

"I'm good, actually," Kim says, while Perrie makes a gagging motion.

Skye's gone quiet and is staring at the floor, so I excuse us and ask her to come for a quick walk with me. We find a door leading to an outside area, where we huddle near the wall in case someone from the audience recognizes us. For now, though, there's no one in sight. Just us and the frigid night air.

"So," I say. "That . . . was a lot."

"Yeah," she says with a tight smile. She's hugging her arms around herself, though, like she's trying to stop something from spilling out.

"You seem upset?" I say, touching her arm. To my relief, she doesn't pull away, but instead leans into me.

"I don't want to ruin things," she says, and my stomach tumbles.

"Probably better to get it out in the open now you've said that," I say lightly.

"Right. Yeah. It's just . . . that was going to be our last week together, and we missed it. I'm not trying to fight about that, but . . . tonight, they're flying me and the other girls straight home."

Oh. In all of the excitement, I've somehow forgotten this one very obvious detail. Somehow, in my mind, it's become a given that Skye will be there every day when I wake up.

But tomorrow, she won't. She'll be in another country. And I'll . . . I guess I'll be on another *continent.* Assuming they're still planning on flying me home tomorrow, that is. Isaac assured me days ago that would be the case, once I've completed a solo press appearance tomorrow morning. Solo, as in separate from Jordy, thank god.

"Do you see why I didn't want to label us until we knew what the next steps were?" she asks wryly.

"We'll figure it out," I say.

"That's what Jordy said once."

"It's only a seven-hour flight."

"That's what Jordy said."

"You were a kid without a bank account."

"I'm still a kid without much of a bank account."

"I'll get a job."

Skye tips her head to the side and crinkles her eyes at me. "*Maya.*"

"I will, I damn well will. I will visit you, as often as I can, and we can take it day by day. If we want it to work, we'll make it work. We," I say firmly, "are gonna figure it out. Okay?"

"Mm."

"*Okay?*"

"Okay," she says reluctantly.

"No, not like that. Come on. Do you trust me?" I ask.

It takes her a worryingly long time to answer. But, finally, this time she sighs and nods.

"So," I say. "Let's go back inside, get those girls' numbers, and save the freaking out. If we only have an hour left together for the moment, do you want to spend it worrying about something that is *not* going to happen? Or do you want to enjoy it?"

Skye takes my hands and spins me around so I'm facing her, inches from her. Then she backs me into the wall, presses me hard against it, and brings her lips a hair's breadth away from mine. "I guess I want to enjoy it," she breathes into me, before closing the gap between us.

EPILOGUE

Maya

**TWO GIRLS ON CELEBRITY DATING SHOW
FIND LOVE . . . WITH EACH OTHER?**

MAYA TELLS ALL

MAYA AND SKYE: THEIR BEST MOMENTS

PERRIE SPEAKS: "I KNEW ABOUT IT FIRST."

**CAN YOU SPOT THE CLUES? FIVE TIMES
WE SHOULD'VE GUESSED MAYA AND SKYE
WERE A THING**

"There's so many more, too," Olivia says, reading over my shoulder as I scan through my phone. "It's totally exploded."

"You're not kidding," I say.

"Just . . . don't google yourself, okay?" Rosie asks, curling up on the couch beside me. She's home for the weekend, specifically to see me. "I know it's tempting, but a lot of that stuff was bullshit. Especially earlier."

"Oh, I know. I've seen it. I didn't lose my iPad until the fourth week in. Unless it got worse?"

Rosie brightens. "Oh, no, actually the public really liked you by then, I think? Most of the articles were about Jordy."

"Ew," I say, passing the phone back to Olivia.

"No," Olivia says, typing something in. "Not like that. Like this."

PRINCE CHARMING OR PREDATOR: THESE BODY LANGUAGE EXPERTS WEIGH IN ON FIVE COMMON RED FLAGS JORDY MILLER DISPLAYS.

JORDY MILLER: A NARCISSIST? DR. SUSAN BELLE SAYS "PROBABLY."

I TOLD THEM I WOULDN'T DATE JORDY AGAIN FOR A MILLION BUCKS: JORDY'S EX-GIRLFRIENDS (YES, THERE ARE MORE OF THEM!) TELL ALL!

"HE DUMPED ME THE DAY MY BEST FRIEND ALMOST DIED": <u>SECOND-CHANCE ROMANCE</u> CONTESTANT BEHIND-THE-SCENES EXCLUSIVE!

"Oh," I say. "This is much more like it."

"What's Skye like in person?" Olivia asks. "I think even *I* got a crush on her. I can't believe you're actually dating her!"

"She's . . . awesome, obviously." I grin. "It's too late to call her now, she'd be passed out. But I can introduce you to her tomorrow or something, if you come over around lunchtime?

I have a video interview with *Opulent Condition* until eleven, but I'm yours after that."

Rosie nods rapidly, and Olivia actually screeches. Good grief, you'd think I just offered to introduce them to an A-lister. I mean, *I* get the appeal of Skye, obviously, but at the same time she's . . . just Skye. Just my girlfriend. About as much of a celebrity as I am.

Although, maybe I'm kind of a celebrity now, from the look of these Google searches. Maybe scratch that, then.

"Olivia," Mom calls from the kitchen, "are you staying for dinner?"

"Yes, please," she says.

I throw myself backward on the couch. "*Dinner.* Home food. I could die happy."

"Really?" Rosie asks. "Because you don't seem very happy."

"What?" I frown at her. "I'm perfectly happy. What did I say that didn't sound happy?"

"Nothing, specifically," Olivia says slowly. "It's more your face."

"Your vibe," Rosie says, swirling her hands in midair.

"We've known you for a long time," Olivia says.

"Some of us longer than others," Rosie adds.

I shake my head. "What this is, is exhaustion and jetlag."

Rosie and Olivia exchange a glance, and Rosie shakes her head, like she's telling Olivia to drop it.

Weirdos.

"How does it feel?" I ask Skye the next day over video call. Rosie's in her room, and Olivia's coming over soon, but for now, it's just us. "To be set up in your new apartment?"

"'Set up' is a strong phrase." Skye laughs. "I've got a couple of suitcases and a sleeping bag." She gives me a tour of her room with her phone. It's a literal shoebox, but she seems thrilled about it. "When I got here, they actually offered me a bigger room, because one of the other housemates moved out. I was tempted because it has a bed, but it's about twenty pounds more a month, and I'm pretty sure I can get a bed for under thirty-five if I keep checking the buy, swap, and sell pages."

"Street smarts." I smile.

"Guess so. How about you? Good to be home?"

I shuffle on my bed and shrug. "Yeah. Sure. It's nice to be somewhere familiar, I guess."

"You *guess*?" she repeats. "Are you missing me?"

"Of course I'm missing you," I say. "That's probably all it is, embarrassingly enough."

"Don't be embarrassed, I'm flattered. What are you up to tonight?"

"Not a lot. I might watch a movie? Maybe go for a walk. YouTube. You?"

"Not watching clips, I hope?"

I bark a laugh. "God no. No, I'm avoiding the show as much as I can right now. I need a break before I confront *that*."

"Yeah, I hear you. It's all my new housemates wanna talk about, and I'm like, yes, hi, I have not processed any of this, can we talk about the eighteen years' worth of life I lived before that? I know it's less interesting, but . . ."

"*Ugh.* Can you blame them, though?"

"No, I cannot."

"What are you up to tonight?"

"Well, the girls here wanna show me a restaurant they say is the best Greek I'll ever eat, which seems like a stretch to me but I'm excited to try it out. Then we're gonna hit up Oxford Street for some shopping, because I am missing some *essentials,* I'll tell you that. And, I don't know. Maybe a movie? There's also a cocktail bar I've been wanting to try out, but it depends how hard I go at Greek, you know?"

I swallow, and look at her wistfully. "That . . . sounds incredible," I say. My voice comes out hollow.

It's not that I'm sad I can't be there with Skye—even though I am. It's more that I'm sad I can't be there at all. It's just, we've lived through this wild experience together, and she's flown off to keep doing all these exciting things, and I'm here back at square one. Killing time until I go to college.

College.

It's not like I've ever been *psyched* about college or anything. But lately, the thought of going there has made me queasy. I'm pretty sure it's not normal to dread college this much, either—Olivia says she doesn't, anyway. I guess I just got spoiled on the show, and I'm being petty about the fact that I have to go back to real life and Skye doesn't.

Why can't I live like her? Why can't that be *my* life?

"Are you lonely?" I ask her.

"Why does everyone ask me that? I'm surrounded by people. I'm psyched."

"But no one you know," I point out. "None of *your* people."

"True. But I don't have an awful lot of 'my people' I'd want here anyway. You, Dad, and Chloe would be it, and *you're* all busy."

Yeah. It's true. Even though I've just gotten back, Mom's already going on and on about college, and shopping for dorm furniture, and textbooks, and all the things I've spent the last two months trying my best not to think about.

"I wish I weren't," I say suddenly. "All this college stuff. It's endless. Literally *endless.* And I'm feeling like this already. What's it going to be like when I'm actually there?"

"Maya," Skye says gently, "you're not feeling like this

'already.' You've been feeling like this since before I even met you."

I slump back and glance at the wall. On the other side is Rosie. I wonder what she'd say if she could hear Skye.

Shout about how it's two against one, I guess.

"I'd kill to be there with you," I say with a sigh.

Skye stands up and opens her window, and shows me the view. Rows of brown and cream apartments. And above that, a cloudy gray sky.

It's beautiful.

"Well," she says. "Like you said. The flight's only seven hours."

I chuckle, but Skye's face is dead serious when she turns the camera back to selfie mode. "Maya," she says.

"Skye," I say.

"Maya. You've already won."

I go to reply, then I stop myself as her words hit home.

She's right. Perrie was right. Everyone, except for me, was right all along.

I've already won.

Skye

Chloe calls me just as I get off the tube at Heathrow. "Are you sitting down?" she asks me rather dramatically.

"No, I'm in a train station," I yell into my phone, dodging the crowd as I find the stairs.

"Have you seen?"

"Seen what?"

"Oh my god, you don't know. Okay, okay, Perrie Matthesson uploaded this video of Jordy—how do you not know?"

I'm bumped to one side by a hurrying traveler, and I

steady myself with a glare in their direction. "I've been listening to an audiobook on airplane mode for the last hour. I only just turned it off when I got to the airport."

"Ooh, is she there yet?"

"Not yet—wait, what's the video? Should I be concerned?"

"Nope, you're gonna love it. Watch it and message me, okay?"

"Okay?"

I anticipate needing to navigate to Perrie's Instagram page, but there's no need to search. I've received a link from what appears to be everyone I've ever met, including my down-the-hall neighbor, Greg, who I've only met once.

I find a semi-quiet spot against a wall, turn the volume up as high as I can, and open it. The video has an alarming number of views for only being a few hours old, and they're going up like The Flash's pedometer. It only takes me a minute to watch it in its entirety, but when I finish, I gape at my phone.

I message Perrie but, unsurprisingly, I don't get an immediate response from her. So, I message Isaac, and he video calls me.

"Hey hey," he says. The video is almost completely dark, save for the odd flashing red or blue strobe, which is strange considering it's not even midafternoon in the US right now.

"Where are you?" I yell, hoping he can hear me over the noise of the station.

"Um . . ." He turns to a man sitting next to him. "Babe, where are we?" he asks, before turning back to me triumphantly. "The Titty Twister!"

"Great," I say. "Which is?"

"Patong!"

It takes me a second. "Oh, you're in Phuket!"

"Yes, and I am *drunk*! And I know why you're calling!"

"Well, you called me, but yeah."

"It was all me," Isaac says.

"A terrible mistake," his boyfriend says over his shoulder, and Isaac shoves him out of the frame.

"Yes." Isaac laughs. "A terrible, huge mistake. See, I made it for Maya to show on the special, but then she went all grand gesture on you, blah blah, and it went to waste!"

"Right. So how did it end up with Perrie, exactly?"

"Colossal error. She wanted me to send her the photos she took with that camera, and I accidentally went into my files, accidentally found the video, and accidentally uploaded it to the file share, oh no, Skye."

"Oh no," I agree.

"Yeah. And it's even worse that it ended up with Perrie, of all people, because you know how she is with her Instagram. And now it's gone viral and she's getting all these thousands and thousands of new followers."

"That's awful." I gasp, placing a hand over my chest.

"I *know*, right?"

"Are you gonna get in trouble?" I ask.

"Mm, I'm American, and Perrie's American, and it was all one big accident, so . . . probably the fuck not! And I can always just hide here until this all blows over if I want to anyway, because I just got off the phone with Gwendolyn and she's given me a big enough bonus to come back every year till I die. It's publicity you can't buy."

"Sounds like it's all worked out pretty perfectly for everyone involved," I say.

"Mm. Yup! Except Jordy. Yeah. But, I figure, that's okay, because he's a fucking prick and I hope he chokes."

I burst out laughing as Isaac excuses himself to return to clubbing.

Going through my messages, I find one from Kim: Can you believe this bellend???? Can you actually believe it????? Im in shock. Is maya there yet? Can we move our catch up earlier? Im not waiting until next weekend to debrief

Lauren: Hey love I just wanted to check if your okay? Im sure there gonna drag you and maya into this so let me know if I need to fight anyone! Perries followers are going up a lot though which is nice isnt it. Hope your well!!

Francesca: Yoooooo I'm DEAD I am dead and deceased and I think mams right. THERE IS A GOD! Idk maybe I should go to church. Im playing the part where he flirts with me then dumps me on repeat until I die for real

When I finish replying, Perrie finally responds. Hey, sorry, it's been crazy. My phone's going nuts, I have about a thousand dms, and I'm pretty sure every newspaper in the country wants an interview. Heads up, because they'll start contacting you soon if they haven't already! AHHH! P.S. you're welcome. This is what he gets for messing with us.

In the arrivals area of the airport, I notice a couple of people looking at me funny. It doesn't take long for them to pull out their phones and take photos of me in a way that's meant to be subtle, but is actually about as subtle as a flock of flying elephants.

The plane landed a while ago, but it'll be at least ten minutes until the passengers make it through immigration. I distract myself by messaging Dad, putting my earbuds in to drown out the endless announcements and dings blaring through the airport speakers. Look up @perriebellematthesson on Instagram

He replies a minute later. How do I do that? Do I need to download Instagram?

I should've predicted that. I send him a link to the video instead.

A few minutes later he responds. Uh oh! He's doing all those things you said he did. . . . Is that your friend who's put that online? She should be careful with the internet. . . . People might see it. . . . Nothing is private these days Skye. . . .

I think she wanted people to see it dad

Yes well. . . . Is maya there? Tell her I say hi and welcome to London!

Just about. Will do!

A girl sitting in the seat next to me has pulled out her own phone and is watching a clip of Jordy, walking briskly down a street and trying not to look at the camera. She smiles to herself, then navigates to Perrie's page to watch the video. When she's done, she becomes one of the thousands upon thousands of people who followed Perrie today.

Finally, the first few people come through the doors. I wait, eagerly scanning them, until she finally walks through. I shove my phone in my pocket, beaming, and she breaks into a jog until she reaches me and throws her arms around me.

"Hi, hi, hi, hi," she squeals as I swing her around.

"How was the flight?"

"Good, flew by. Ha! Flew by. Hi!" She pulls back and looks me up and down, like it's been years and not weeks. "Oh my god, it's so good to see you. I've missed you too much."

"You, too," I say, before pulling her in for another hug. A prickling on my neck tells me there's more photographing happening, but I barely care.

"Okay, so I have a lot of luggage," she says, gesturing at her two huge suitcases. "But it's a long trip, so sue me. I dare you to pack for Italy *and* the snow in one suitcase. And I've just remembered you already did that months ago, so I'm going to need you to not answer that, and—what?"

She breaks off, studying my face.

I smile sheepishly. "Something happened."

"*What?*"

"Well . . . how do I summarize this best? Isaac sent the video he made for you to take Jordy down to Perrie, she's uploaded it, it's gone viral, everyone is about to find out who Jordy actually is, and it's probably going to be the biggest news story in the country tomorrow."

"Wait, what?" Maya laughs. Then, she seems to process it, because she eases into a slow grin. "Huh."

"Yeah. What do you think?"

"I think," she says, "we can talk more about that in a minute. I just have to do something first. I've been waiting for weeks for this."

"What?" I ask. What could possibly be more important than this?

In response, she cups my face in her hands and kisses me until I forget about the video, too. And Jordy. And the show.

Until nothing exists but Maya.

ACKNOWLEDGMENTS

So many people helped make this book happen. To Sylvan Creekmore, who was so involved in the conception of this idea from its unrecognizable infancy when I brought it up over lunch in 2019 through to now: you're the best ever! To Molly Ker Hawn and the team at Bent: thank you endlessly for all of your attention, support, patience, and forward-thinking. To Eileen Rothschild and Lisa Bonvissuto, thank you so much for being by my side to bring this book to life!

Thank you so much to the team at Wednesday Books for continuing to support me and for bringing my words to the world. Special thanks to Rivka Holler, Alexis Neuville, Dana Aprigliano, Meghan Harrington, Sara Goodman, Katy Robitzski, and NaNá V. Stoelzle!

Thank you to Kerri Resnick for the amazing cover design and Debs Lim for the gorgeous illustration! I sincerely hope people judge this book by its cover, and can only hope the contents deserved the stunning package you both put it in!

To the UK and Commonwealth team at Hachette, with special thanks to my editor, Tig Wallace: thank you, as always, for your exceptional support and belief in my stories. I feel so lucky to have such an amazing team abroad and at home.

To my early readers and those who provided advance praise, Julia Lynn Rubin, Becky Albertalli, Jenn Dugan, Kelly Quindlen, Meryn Lobb, and Anna: thank you so much, for both assisting me when I needed encouragement like never before and helping me get the nuances of American and Canadian phrases and culture.

To the people who deal with me every day (wording intentional), Becky, Claire, Jenn, Cale, Diana, Alexa, Jacob, Paige, Ryan, Steph, Brendan, Sarah, Mum, Dad, and Cameron: you're the best people I've had the pleasure of meeting in this world. Thank you for being a part of mine.

Finally, to the guys reading this book and wondering if Jordy is based on you:

A) Jordy is a fictional character.

B) If you're wondering if Jordy could be based on you, that is a *very* strong sign that you need to reevaluate how you treat people. Please do something about that. Love, me—a girl you once knew.

Turn the page for an excerpt from

THE
Perfect Guy
DOESN'T EXIST

Available March 2024

Chapter One

PAST

I think my pacing is alarming Mack.

She's sitting on my bed with her hands pressed together in a praying pose on her lap and one eyebrow quirked as she watches me go around and around my bedroom. I've been doing it for a while now. It's not that I've backed out of telling her or anything. More that, now the moment is finally here, I can't seem to remember a single word in the English language.

She tucks her hands in the pockets of her oversized Nike hoodie—a men's one she found in her favorite shade of teal last year—then takes one hand straight back out and sweeps her long braids back over her shoulder. She's stressed, I'm stressed, this is *stressful*, and I wish I didn't decide to do it today, but I did. I'm committed now, and I'm going to.

Eventually.

"You could write it down?" she suggests finally, and I give my head a vigorous shake. "No problem," she says, half to herself, as I resume my pacing.

"Okay," I say, stopping in the middle of the room. I'm facing my wardrobe, which means I can only see Mack out of my peripherals, but right now I like it that way. "It's actually not a big deal. I know it's not, because it's you, and I already know it can't go badly."

"Great."

"It's just . . . I need a second to . . ."

"There's no rush."

I know what I want to say. Or, rather, what I should say. It's not a complicated point to get across. I'm bi. It should be easy to spit out. It's only two syllables. And it's Mack, so it's not like I need to explain the concept like I probably will when I tell my parents, which is a huge plus. It's not even one of those facts I think I want to keep to myself forever, like the fact that I'm almost definitely in love with Mack. I *want* people to know I'm bi. I'm ready.

But I can't say the words. For some reason, they feel huge, and intimidating. Like jumping into an ice bath all at once.

So, I decide to wade.

"You know how, last year, everything Alice Kennedy did annoyed me?" I ask.

Mack nods. "I noticed, yeah."

Her eyes are locked on me. I've always been fascinated by the color of her eyes. They're brown—but such a dark, rich shade of it that if you take a few steps back, you can't tell where her pupils end and her irises begin. *They're like spilled ink*, I told her once, staring at her in a sort of stupor. She hated that. I meant it as a compliment, but it probably would've landed better if I'd just stuck to telling her they're beautiful. Which they are.

Back to Alice Kennedy. "She did annoy me, but she also didn't. I didn't hate her at all. I just . . . have you ever thought about someone all the time, and all you wanna do is talk about them?"

"Avery."

"Right. Like Avery." Also known as Mack's summer camp crush from last year. "Um. But I couldn't really talk about Alice the way I wanted to talk about her, because I didn't want you to know the things I thought about her. So, I thought, hey, if I only bring her up to complain about her, no one could think that's weird. And it doesn't really make sense saying it out loud, but it made sense at the time, and it felt safe. Safe-*er*."

Mack won't tear those eyes away from me, so I focus on the wall to get the rest out. "Because I didn't want her, or anyone, to know that I actually thought she was perfect. I mean, god, everything about her was flawless, you know? So I pretended she drove me up the wall whenever I spoke to you about her. Just so you didn't realize."

Mack is giving me a funny look, but she's cautious in her answer. "So I didn't realize . . . you didn't hate Alice?"

"So you didn't realize I had a crush on Alice."

I'm fairly sure Mack suspected what I was getting at before I spelled it out. But she waits until I say the words to react. "Oh my god," she says. "Oh my god, Ivy, you like girls?"

"I do," I say, like it's truly no big deal at all. Like this isn't the most momentous thing I've ever told anyone.

Mack shrieks and jumps to her feet. "No. No, no way, congratulations!" And before I know it, she's wrapped me in a bear hug, and we're jumping on the spot in the middle of my bedroom floor. "This is amazing, this is amazing," she chants, and I'm laughing with her, and I'm utterly weightless.

For one naive second, I even let myself wonder if she'll say something about us. It's not that I expect her to or anything. It's that, for just a second, everything is so perfectly wonderful I can almost believe something like that could happen to me.

But, instead of confessing her undying love for me, she just lets go of me and flops back down on the bed. "Oh, man," she says. "This is huge. I'm so glad you told me this. Oh!"

I rub my upper arms right where she was hugging me a second ago and sit beside her gingerly. "I was worried you might think I'm copying you," I admit, and she blows a raspberry at that.

"Not for a second. Anyway, you like guys, too, right? Or do you?"

"No, I do," I say, and she nods eagerly.

"So, what are you thinking? Pan? Bi? Questioning?"

I grin. "I'm thinking probably bi? If I don't have to lock that answer in permanently."

She shakes her head, and I shuffle back on the bed and relax against the wall. "Nothing's permanent," she tells me.

I clasp a hand to my chest and pretend to be offended. "*Oof.* I hope some things are."

Drawing her knees to her chest, Mack tips her head back and looks sideways at me. "Okay, you're right. Some things are. But only the things you want to be permanent."

Before I say something wildly, recklessly romantic, like *I want you to be permanent,* I take a deep breath and try to clear my head. "Okay. Phew. One down."

"I'm the first person you told?"

"Of course. Who else am I gonna tell?"

"Your parents? They know everything else about your damn life," she says, giggling, and I groan.

"Yeah, no. I'll tell them later, but not today."

Mack folds her arms. "You know they'll make having a queer daughter their whole personalities once you tell them, right?"

"Oh, I know. But there are worse reactions to get from your parents."

"True." She nods thoughtfully, then wiggles in place, like she can't hold her happiness in. "Ah, I can't believe you like girls, too. We have so much to discuss. There's a forum I want to add you to and, oh, there's a book I know you'll love, and—"

"I'm so glad you're not weirded out by this," I interrupt. I don't mean to cut her off, but I'm so tightly wound. Somehow, I'd convinced myself that she would think I was just too scared to do anything alone. Heterosexuality included. It *is* true I'm the kind of person who loves to do things in pairs. For example, I joined the volleyball team when Mack joined it. Also, Mack introduced me to seventies rock, which is now my most-listened-to genre. Plus, after she went to summer camp in sixth grade, in seventh grade I begged my parents to enroll me, too. But just because Mack did all those things first, it doesn't mean I only pretended to enjoy all of it.

And I knew I liked girls way before Mack came out as a lesbian a few months ago. It's only that I wasn't brave enough to say it out loud until I saw Mack do it.

"Not only am I not weirded out by it," Mack assures me, "it's the best news I think I've ever had. Now I'm not alone."

Even though I obviously didn't do this for Mack, I feel like I'm sinking into a cloud hearing her say that.

I'm so glad she feels that way. Because I never want her to be alone.

PRESENT

I have spent endless hours wishing my parents would give me space, but now that they're finally doing it, I have reservations. In my defense, almost three thousand miles is quite a lot more space than I pictured.

"I'm just not sure I'm trustworthy without supervision," I protest, following Mom down the hall as she lugs a plastic wheeled suitcase behind her. "What if I make bad choices?"

"You seemed pretty sure you were trustworthy when we were booking the tickets," Mom grunts, pausing in place as the suitcase tips on its side. I kneel to help her straighten it, then silently curse myself for aiding and abetting child abandonment.

"Yeah, but, Mom, I was, like, fifteen then. I thought I'd be more mature by now, but I'm not. Being sixteen didn't change anything, it just gave me acne!"

That, and I'd been too focused on the many pluses of having the house to myself to consider the fact that I'd be totally alone. Pros: I can stay up late, walk around the house in my underwear, eat as much junk food as I want, and hang out with Henry for hours without anyone asking us to give the TV back. It's a substantial list. In contrast, the cons list only has one point, but now that D day is here, it's starting to feel like one *huge* point.

And that point is, I am going to be solely responsible for keeping myself alive if an emergency happens for five solid days.

These are not the kinds of stakes you take lightly. If I don't keep myself alive, I could *die*.

Mom approaches the doorway and, together, we lift the suitcase over the frame. At the bottom of the driveway, Dad stands examining the inside of the car trunk.

I discovered the other day my parents were planning to drive to the airport, to my great surprise. As far as I'm concerned, only exorbitantly rich people use the long-term parking lot at the airport, and my family is, to the very best of my knowledge, not exorbitantly rich. We're a proud tap-water-drinking, coupon-cutting, "you'll grow into it" sort of family. Always have been. This trip Mom and Dad are taking, a business trip to LA for Mom that Dad's tagging along on, is the bougiest thing I've ever seen them do.

But, still, taking the car to the airport seems like a step too far. They insisted it was for convenience, but I'm pretty sure it's because they don't trust me not to drive it in their absence. Because, apparently, leaving me at home to fend for myself against house fires, and tornadoes, and Jehovah's Witnesses is all well and good, but if I were to *very briefly* borrow their car to visit Henry, suddenly they'd have concerns about my safety.

"You've got the Gleasons right across the road," Mom says as she loads the suitcase into the trunk. "We've left you a fridge full of food, we'll call you every day, you've got our number, you've got the Gleasons' number. . . ."

Oh, joy, the Gleasons. Can't wait to never take them up on that.

"What if there's an earthquake?" I ask before I can stop myself. I *know* bringing it up is just going to panic them, but I can't *not* blurt out anxious thoughts when they pop into my head.

"Get under the desk," Mom says at the same time Dad says, "Stand under a doorframe."

My parents give each other a look that I don't like one bit.

"Standing under doorways isn't recommended anymore," Mom says with great confidence. Personally, I feel like it's misplaced confidence, given that, as far as I know, Mom is not the foremost expert on recommended earthquake procedures any more than Dad is.

"Yes, it is," Dad insists. "Load-bearing ones."

"Ivy's not going to know which doorways are load-bearing, David, she can barely turn on the oven." Mom's confidence is faltering. Great. Now they're either going to call me every hour on the hour to check if there's been an earthquake, or cancel the trip altogether. *What if there's an earthquake,* come on, Ivy, really?

"I can so turn on the oven," I protest with dignity. "It's the grill that confuses me."

"What if she's not in her room when the earthquake hits?" Dad asks. "No desk."

"She'll have to use her common sense and find an equivalent," Mom replies.

"Does that seem wise?" Dad asks.

Ouch. But not unwarranted. I don't have a lot of common sense. In my defense, though, it's one of those skills that's hard to develop when someone else is making your decisions for you all day every day. Ask me how I know.

"We'll take her through the house and point out all the load-bearing doors," Mom says with a brisk nod.

"Do we have time?" Dad asks.

"You're already late," I point out, and Mom looks stricken. "Besides, when do we ever get huge earthquakes? We don't."

"That's true," Dad says.

"Well, Pompeii had never had a devastating volcanic eruption before," Mom reminds us. "The dinosaurs had never had a planet-destroying meteor before. Since when is that an excuse not to be prepared?"

"Look at it this way, Mom," I say as she closes the trunk. "If something that catastrophic hits, my death will be so sudden, all the preparation in the world couldn't have saved me. *You* couldn't have saved me. If it's my time to go, that's just how it'll be."

I realize too late it doesn't come out quite as comforting as I meant it. Mom drops her hands to her sides and takes a deep, slow breath. Now I've done it.

Dad steps around the car and wraps his arms over Mom's shoulders from behind. "Everything is going to be fine," he says in a soothing voice. "We trust Ivy. She's responsible, and smart, and she can keep herself alive for a week."

"She can," Mom repeats, closing her eyes.

"She has plenty of food in the refrigerator."

"Lots in the freezer, too."

"Right. She has contact numbers, she has a support system, and we're only a plane flight away."

"Or a really long drive if there's an apocalypse and you can't get a plane," I add unhelpfully.

Mom, wisely, ignores me.

After one last sweep of the house, it's time for my parents to leave, and I find myself with an inconvenient lump in my throat.

"You're sure you'll be all right by yourself?" Mom asks.

"Do you remember the emergency number?" Dad asks.

I blink. "You mean nine-one-one?"

"Thank god. See, Nadia, she knows the one."

Dad grins, pleased with himself, while Mom shoots him an exasperated look.

"We'll message you when we land," Mom assures me, pulling me in for one last hug. Now that, I can be sure of. With them, it'll be less a matter of a message, and more a matter of waking up to ten messages and two missed calls. But for the first time I can remember, the thought doesn't bother me. At least, not as much as it usually does. "And if you need *anything* and you can't reach us—"

"The Gleasons."

"Honestly, sweetie, I'd call them in an emergency before the police," Dad says. "Much quicker reaction time, and more competent to boot."

Some of them, anyway. I agree when it comes to the three older Gleasons. The youngest, however, leaves much to be desired.

"I had a thought," says Mom. "We should do a quick demonstration of the fire extinguisher."

"Absolutely not; we still have to get through security," Dad says in a conversation-ending sort of tone. "If there's a fire, throw a blanket on it. Or run."

"But try to save the photo albums, if you have time," Mom says anxiously.

"I'll be sure to only save myself if absolutely necessary," I joke, and she looks horrified.

"No, Ivy, that's not what I meant, don't you *da*—"

"There's not going to be any disasters," Dad says over her. "You will be absolutely fine. The week will fly by. You'll hardly notice we're gone."

Finally, *finally,* they climb into the SUV. I'm almost shocked when they do. I think a part of me truly expected them to back out after all. But just like that, they're rolling down the driveway and onto the street, and, with one last honk, they drive off into the sunset.

I stare after them for a second, not sure how I feel.

Then, all at once, it hits me. I can do whatever the hell I want—as long as I can cover up the evidence—for the rest of the week.

This is a freedom I've never known.

My trepidation forgotten, I trot to the pantry, grab an unopened pack of chocolate chip cookies, and start demolishing them while I message Henry to come by whenever he wants. The new episode of *Hot, Magical, and Deadly* is out, and we have a long-standing tradition of watching it together at my house. Plus, we have a presentation to give in class tomorrow, and we're mostly done but we should probably go through it and give it any finishing touches it needs. While I wait for him, I open a new carton of milk and take a swig straight from it, kick off my shoes in the middle of the kitchen, and take my laptop into the living room. Usually there's no point using it out here, because if my parents can see me, they want to be talking to me, even if I tell them I'm trying to work on my latest fanfic or that I'm messaging someone.

What was I worried about? This is *awesome.*

Ten minutes later, there's a knock on the door, and I jump up to answer it, licking crumbs off my fingers. To my delight, Henry Paramar is waiting on the doorstep with a shopping bag full of junk food. One of the many reasons he's my best friend now, and someone else, who isn't worth mentioning the name of, *isn't.*

"Holy shit, your hair," he says as soon as he sees me.

"Is that a good 'holy shit'?" I ask, touching the velvety-soft side of my head. Of course, he's seen photos since I chopped most of my hair off yesterday morning, and he said he loved it, but maybe in person he feels differently. Not that I'd regret it if he does. My new hairstyle, which consists of shaved sides and tousled, longer waves at the top, is much more up my alley.

"Duh," he says as he dumps the bag of junk food on the couch. "I think, in the least-weird way possible, you're hot now."

"Oh my god, thank you! Wait, 'now'?"

Henry cocks his head in a half shrug. "You were pretty before. But I'm pretty sure you're objectively what a lot of people would call 'hot' now. *Really* good call to chop it off."

"I think that's the nicest thing you've ever said to me."

Henry hesitates. I think he might be replaying his words back in his head. "Not that I need to clarify, but I'm obviously not attracted to you."

"Obviously." I think someone would have to pretty much propose to me for me to consider they might be into me like that, so he'd be in the clear even if I didn't know he's AroAce. Still, it's nice to think that someone who's not Henry could potentially find me attractive. I'm not sure if that's ever happened before, and if it has, the person never looped me in. Maybe if this possibly imaginary, possibly real admirer *did* fill me in, I'd be more likely to accuse people of being into me. But as it stands . . .

"Whoa," Henry says, circling the living room, bringing me back to the present. "It already feels emptier without your parents."

He kicks off his sneakers and climbs onto the sofa in his socks. As usual, he's wearing one of his eye-catching outfits. Dad calls them "a phase he'll be embarrassed of one day"; Mom calls them "peacock looks"; I call them "damn, my best friend has taste." There's always something unusual about his outfits, from bright red pants, to floral-shirt-and-shorts combos, to oversized jackets layered on top of shirts layered on top of other shirts. It's the kind of stuff you need to have a really good eye to put together. Henry does. I have the eye to tell it looks great, but not the eye to attempt anything like it myself.

Today, for example, he's wearing a matching sweatshirt-and-sweatpants set covered in patches that range from dark gray to black, broken up by the hem of a white shirt peeking beneath the sweatshirt. That, plus his handsome face, makes him look kind of like a fuckboy, but in the nicest way possible. Like, you wouldn't be surprised to find out he's the rich son of a famous, asshole music producer, and not the middle-class son of a nursery-school teacher and an office worker.

It's not a surprise half the grade's had a crush on him at one point or another since middle school.

"It's nice, right?" I say as I sort through the shopping bag. Potato chips and corn chips on the far end of the coffee table, candy in the center, soda on the end. It's like the superior version of charcuterie. I am nailing this whole host thing.

"You know, at first, I wasn't sure what the weird sound was," Henry says, ripping open a bag of chips. "Then I realized it's the sound of *sweet silence*. No one's asking how our day was, what we're doing, what we're watching, what we're eating, if we need anything, what our deepest fears are. . . ."

I snort. "Don't get too used to it, they're back in five days."

"Eh. See how the flight goes."

"Henry!"

"I'm just saying, a lot of things can go wrong when you're that high up."

I throw a potato chip at his head, and he deftly ducks to dodge it.

"So," I say, dragging the syllable out. "Guess who got left enough money to buy us both pizza tonight?"

Henry lights up. "Garlic bread, too?"

"Duh."

"Scratch everything I just said about your parents. I love them, they're the best, I hope they never change."

As I put in Henry's order on the app—I double-check with him, but, as I figured, I got his order right on the first try—he gathers bowls and glasses from the kitchen. Finally, we're ready to start the new episode, and I'm practically vibrating out of my skin with excitement. This has been the longest week of my life, because last episode, like every episode, ended on a huge cliffhanger.

Hot, Magical, and Deadly follows a group of teenagers from the same modeling agency (catalogue, not high fashion) who accidentally receive elemental powers when a photo shoot held near a portal to a parallel universe goes wrong. For four seasons now, I've watched them grow from awkward, outcast teen models to confident, charming teen superheroes, expertly fighting the silhouette demons that entered our world through the same portal.

Without Weston Razorbrook and the others, the demons would've taken over the world by now, because their plan is sort of ingenious: shapeshifting into, and stealing the identities of, America's biggest influencers. I mean, think about it. If all the influencers in the world simultaneously decided it was cool to jump off a cliff, we'd have barely anyone left. The demons could practically stroll into power after that.

I watch, absentmindedly gnawing on a fingernail, as Henry sets the episode up on the TV. When Henry glances at me, he makes a face. "Chew a bit harder, Ivy. If you put your mind to it, you can eat the whole nail. I believe in you."

"I'm *stressed*, okay? I saw an article today that basically confirmed they're going to get rid of a huge character this season."

"They're not gonna kill someone off in a random episode halfway through the season. If someone dies, it'll be in the finale, and anyway, my money's on Jacques."

"Yeah, you and everyone else," I say. "But if I were one of the writers and I wanted to make an impact, I'd kill someone no one expects, when they don't expect it. *That's* good television."

"Oh yeah, kill off a fan favorite with zero warning or buildup. That's always a famously great choice for ratings moving forward." Still, he folds his arms across his chest as he settles into the couch, his brow settling into a concerned furrow.

Last week's episode ended with Weston Razorbrook tied to a pier during a rising tide after he discovered famous movie reviewer Edmund Marquis was possessed by a silhouette demon. The pier thing was devious, because Weston's air powers can only work if his hands aren't submerged or covered. And for the life of me, I cannot *think* how he's going to get rescued, because he told no one where he was going, and the waves were drowning out his screams.

It was all very distressing. I have been in a state of constant suffering all week.

It wouldn't even be the first time *H-MAD* killed off someone important. Last year, one of the models who had real runway potential was eaten by flying pigs with no warning after they broke through the portal. And I didn't even know pigs are vicious carnivores before that, until Henry looked it up and we found out that real-life pigs actually love a good murder. The wings just made the slaughter easier for the fictional *H-MAD* ones. Anyway, the whole fandom went into meltdown that week, and we can't go through that again, we just can't. Especially not with Weston.

I would almost rather die myself than see Weston drown tonight.

"Whatever happens," Henry says gravely as the theme music begins, "we'll get through it together."

It's a rare moment of seriousness from him. Now I'm even more nervous.

I stuff a fistful of potato chips into my mouth.

The episode starts with Vanessa's storyline, which is just teasing. Vanessa is the girl everyone's convinced is bound to end up with Weston. Everyone being the majority of the fandom, that is. The thing is, I'm is pretty sure the showrunners picked her as the love interest on account of her being a fire element, pretty, and blond, and for no other reason. Now, there is nothing wrong with being any of those things—or even all three of those things at once—but it isn't enough to throw two pretty people together and call it love. There has to be chemistry, and passion, and complementary traits. *Bonding,* for goodness' sake!

I'm also pretty sure the writers of *H-MAD* have never read a romance novel in their lives. Like, take right now. Vanessa is off dealing with the B plot, which is about finding a lost elemental child someone discovered in a boarding school, who may have been present at the fated photo shoot. While Weston is being *actively murdered.* Why isn't she there, desperately hunting for him? God, the opportunities for tropes are endless. They could have Vanessa using Weston's first name in a panic, instead of calling him "Razorbrook." She could almost lose her own life in the process of saving him, causing him to panic and realize his love for her. They could squeeze a solid two or three episodes out of Vanessa caring for Weston in the aftermath of his near death if they really went for it! But no. Yet again, Vanessa is swanning around on the other side of the state, being of no help to anyone important. It's anti-feminist, is what it is.

Finally, the camera cuts to Weston, and we both sit up straighter. Weston's perfect, icy-blue hair (it turned that color as the elemental magic flowed through his veins) is stuck to his face, and his hands are still bound tightly beneath the water. The ocean laps higher and higher, high enough now that he has to lift his chin with each wave. There's not much time.

Suddenly, his eyes narrow. "Wait," he whispers to himself. "Of course."

Of course?! So, there is a solution? He's not dying after all? Of course *what*?

Three loud bangs follow. It takes me a second to realize they're real-life bangs. Someone with the worst timing *ever* is at the door, and I am going to kill them.

"Pause it, pause it, pause it," I screech, and Henry fumbles with the remote. Weston freezes mid-sentence, and I get to my feet with a scowl.

"That's the fastest pizza delivery I've ever seen," Henry says. "Is the oven in your front yard or something?"

I don't think it's the pizza, though.

In fact, I have a sinking feeling I know exactly who's on the other side of that door. And I am not going to like it.

I open it, and find my worst fears confirmed.

SOPHIE GONZALES is a young adult contemporary author. She graduated from the University of Adelaide and lives in Adelaide, Australia, where she can be found ice skating, painting, and practicing the piano. She is also the author of *Perfect on Paper*, *Only Mostly Devastated*, and *The Law of Inertia*, and co-author with Cale Dietrich of *If This Gets Out*.